MERRICK

MERRICK

a novel by

ANNE RICE

Chatto & Windus
LONDON

Published by Chatto & Windus 2000

First published in the United States in 2000
by Alfred A. Knopf, Inc., New York

2 4 6 8 10 9 7 5 3 1

Copyright © Anne O'Brien Rice 2000

Anne O'Brien Rice has asserted her right under the Copyright,
Designs and Patents Act 1988 to be identified as
the author of this work

First published in Great Britain in 2000 by
Chatto & Windus
Random House, 20 Vauxhall Bridge Road,
London SW1V 2SA

Random House Austalia (Pty) Limited
20 Alfred Street, Milsons Point, Sydney,
New South Wales 2061, Australia

Random House New Zealand Limited
18 Poland Road, Glenfield,
Auckland 10, New Zealand

Random House (Pty) Limited
Endulini, 5A Jubilee Road, Parktown 2193, South Africa

The Random House Group Reg. No. 954009

A CIP catalogue record for this book
is available from the British Library

ISBN 0 7011 6718 1

Papers used by Random House UK Limited are natural,
recyclable products made from wood grown in sustainable forests.
The manufacturing processes conform to the environmental
regulations of the country of origin.

Printed and bound in Great Britain by
Clays Ltd, Bungay

FOR

Stan Rice

AND

Christopher Rice

AND

Nancy Rice Diamond

THE TALAMASCA

Investigators of the Paranormal
We watch
And we are always here.

LONDON   AMSTERDAM   ROME

MERRICK

Proem

M Y NAME is David Talbot.

Do any of you remember me as the Superior General of the Talamasca, the Order of psychic detectives whose motto was "We watch and we are always here"?

It has a charm, doesn't it, that motto?

The Talamasca has existed for over a thousand years.

I don't know how the Order began. I don't really know all the secrets of the Order. I do know however that I served it most of my mortal life.

It was in the Talamasca Motherhouse in England that the Vampire Lestat first made himself known to me. He came into my study one winter night and caught me quite unawares.

I learnt very quickly that it was one thing to read and write about the supernatural and quite another to see it with your own eyes.

But that was a long time ago.

I'm in another physical body now.

And that physical body has been transformed by Lestat's powerful vampiric blood.

I'm among the most dangerous of the vampires, and one of the most trusted. Even the wary vampire Armand revealed to me the story of his life. Perhaps you've read the biography of Armand which I released into the world.

When that story ended, Lestat had wakened from a long sleep in New Orleans to listen to some very beautiful and seductive music.

It was music that lulled him back again into unbroken silence as he retreated once more to a convent building to lie upon a dusty marble floor.

There were many vampires then in the city of New Orleans—
vagabonds, rogues, foolish young ones who had come to catch a glimpse
of Lestat in his seeming helplessness. They menaced the mortal popu-
lation. They annoyed the elders among us who wanted invisibility and
the right to hunt in peace.

All those invaders are gone now.

Some were destroyed, others merely frightened. And the elders
who had come to offer some solace to the sleeping Lestat have gone
their separate ways.

As this story begins, only three of us remain in New Orleans. And
we three are the sleeping Lestat, and his two faithful fledglings—Louis
de Pointe du Lac, and I, David Talbot, the author of this tale.

1

"WHY DO YOU ask me to do this thing?"

She sat across the marble table from me, her back to the open doors of the café.

I struck her as a wonder. But my requests had distracted her. She no longer stared at me, so much as she looked into my eyes.

She was tall, and had kept her dark-brown hair loose and long all her life, save for a leather barrette such as she wore now, which held only her forelocks behind her head to flow down her back. She wore gold hoops dangling from her small earlobes, and her soft white summer clothes had a gypsy flare to them, perhaps because of the red scarf tied around the waist of her full cotton skirt.

"And to do such a thing for such a being?" she asked warmly, not angry with me, no, but so moved that she could not conceal it, even with her smooth compelling voice. "To bring up a spirit that may be filled with anger and a desire for vengeance, to do this, you ask me,— for Louis de Pointe du Lac, one who is already beyond life himself?"

"Who else can I ask, Merrick?" I answered. "Who else can do such a thing?" I pronounced her name simply, in the American style, though years ago when we'd first met, she had spelled it Merrique and pronounced it with the slight touch of her old French.

There was a rough sound from the kitchen door, the creak of neglected hinges. A wraith of a waiter in a soiled apron appeared at our side, his feet scratching against the dusty flagstones of the floor.

"Rum," she said. "St. James. Bring a bottle of it."

He murmured something which even with my vampiric hearing I did not bother to catch. And away he shuffled, leaving us alone again in the dimly lighted room, with all its long doors thrown open to the Rue St. Anne.

It was vintage New Orleans, the little establishment. Overhead fans churned lazily, and the floor had not been cleaned in a hundred years.

The twilight was softly fading, the air filled with the fragrances of the Quarter and the sweetness of spring. What a kind miracle it was that she had chosen such a place, and that it was so strangely deserted on such a divine evening as this.

Her gaze was steady but never anything but soft.

"Louis de Pointe du Lac would see a ghost now," she said, musing, "as if his suffering isn't enough."

Not only were her words sympathetic, but also her low and confidential tone. She felt pity for him.

"Oh, yes," she said without allowing me to speak. "I pity him, and I know how badly he wants to see the face of this dead child vampire whom he loved so much." She raised her eyebrows thoughtfully. "You come with names which are all but legend. You come out of secrecy, you come out of a miracle, and you come close, and with a request."

"Do it, then, Merrick, if it doesn't harm you," I said. "I'm not here to bring harm to you. God in Heaven help me. Surely you know as much."

"And what of harm coming to your Louis?" she asked, her words spoken slowly as she pondered. "A ghost can speak dreadful things to those who call it, and this is the ghost of a monster child who died by violence. You ask a potent and terrible thing."

I nodded. All she said was true.

"Louis is a being obsessed," I said. "It's taken years for his obsession to obliterate all reason. Now he thinks of nothing else."

"And what if I do bring her up out of the dead? You think there will be a resolution to the pain of either one?"

"I don't hope for that. I don't know. But anything is preferable to the pain Louis suffers now. Of course I have no right to ask this of you, no right to come to you at all.

"Yet we're all entangled—the Talamasca and Louis and I. And the Vampire Lestat as well. It was from the very bosom of the Talamasca that Louis de Pointe du Lac heard a story of the ghost of Claudia. It was to one of our own, a woman named Jesse Reeves—you'll find her in the archives—that this ghost of Claudia supposedly first appeared."

"Yes, I know the story," said Merrick. "It happened in the Rue

Royale. You sent Jesse Reeves to investigate the vampires. And Jesse Reeves came back with a handful of treasures that were proof enough that a child named Claudia, an immortal child, had once lived in the flat."

"Quite right," I answered. "I was wrong to send Jesse. Jesse was too young. Jesse was never—." It was difficult for me to finish. "Jesse was never quite as clever as you."

"People read it among Lestat's published tales and think it's fancy," she said, musing, thinking, "all that about a diary, a rosary, wasn't it, and an old doll. And we have those things, don't we? They're in the vault in England. We didn't have a Louisiana Motherhouse in those days. You put them in the vault yourself."

"Can you do it?" I asked. "Will you do it? That's more to the point. I have no doubt that you can."

She wasn't ready to answer. But we had made a great beginning here, she and I.

Oh, how I had missed her! This was more tantalizing than I'd ever expected, to be locked once more in conversation with her. And with pleasure I doted upon the changes in her: that her French accent was completely gone now and that she sounded almost British, and that from her long years of study overseas. She'd spent some of those years in England with me.

"You know that Louis saw you," I said gently. "You know that he sent me to ask you. You know that he knew of your powers from the warning he caught from your eyes?"

She didn't respond.

" 'I've seen a true witch,' " he said when he came to me. 'She wasn't afraid of me. She said she'd call up the dead to defend herself if I didn't leave her alone.' "

She nodded, regarding me with great seriousness.

"Yes, all that's the truth," she answered under her breath. "He crossed my path, you might say." She was mulling it over. "But I've seen Louis de Pointe du Lac many a time. I was a child when I first saw him, and now you and I speak of this for the first time."

I was quite amazed. I should have known she would surprise me at once.

I admired her immensely. I couldn't disguise it. I loved the simplicity of her appearance, her white cotton scoop neck blouse with its simple short sleeves and the necklace of black beads around her neck.

Looking into her green eyes, I was suddenly overcome with shame for what I'd done, revealing myself to her. Louis had not forced me to approach her. I had done this of my own accord. But I don't intend to begin this narrative by dwelling on that shame.

Let me say only that we'd been more than simple companions in the Talamasca together. We'd been mentor and pupil, I and she, and almost lovers, once, for a brief while. Such a brief while.

She'd come as a girl to us, a vagrant descendant of the clan of the Mayfairs, out of an African American branch of that family, coming down from white witches she scarcely knew, an octoroon of exceptional beauty, a barefoot child when she wandered into the Motherhouse in Louisiana, when she said, "I've heard of you people, I need you. I can see things. I can speak with the dead."

That had been over twenty years ago, it seemed to me now.

I'd been the Superior General of the Order, settled into the life of a gentlemanly administrator, with all the comforts and drawbacks of routine. A telephone call had wakened me in the night. It had been from my friend and fellow scholar, Aaron Lightner.

"David," he'd said, "you have to come. This is the genuine article. This is a witch of such power I've no words to describe it. David, you must come. . . ."

There was no one in those days whom I respected any more deeply than Aaron Lightner. I've loved three beings in all my years, both as human and vampire. Aaron Lightner was one of them. Another was, and is, the Vampire Lestat. The Vampire Lestat brought me miracles with his love, and broke my mortal life forever. The Vampire Lestat made me immortal and uncommonly strong for it, a nonpareil among the vampires.

As for the third, it was Merrick Mayfair, though Merrick I had tried my damndest to forget.

But we are speaking of Aaron, my old friend Aaron with his wavy white hair, quick gray eyes, and his penchant for southern blue-and-white-striped seersucker suits. We are speaking of her, of the long ago child Merrick, who seemed as exotic as the lush tropical flora and fauna of her home.

"All right, old fellow, I'm coming, but couldn't this have waited till morning?" I remembered my stodginess and Aaron's good-natured laughter.

"David, what's happened to you, old man?" he'd responded. "Don't tell me what you're doing now, David. Let me tell you. You fell asleep while reading some nineteenth-century book on ghosts, something evocative and comforting. Let me guess. The author's Sabine Baring-Gould. You haven't been out of the Motherhouse in six months, have you? Not even for a luncheon in town. Don't deny it, David, you live as if your life's finished."

I had laughed. Aaron spoke with such a gentle voice. It wasn't Sabine Baring-Gould I'd been reading, but it might have been. I think it had been a supernatural tale by Algernon Blackwood. And Aaron had been right about the length of time since I'd stepped outside of our sanctified walls.

"Where's your passion, David? Where's your commitment?" Aaron had pressed. "David, the child's a witch. Do you think I use such words lightly? Forget the family name for a moment and all we know about them. This is something that would astound even our Mayfairs, though she'll never be known to them if I have my say in matters. David, this child can summon spirits. Open your Bible and turn to the Book of Samuel. This is the Witch of Endor. And you're being as cranky as the spirit of Samuel when the witch raised him from his sleep. Get out of bed and cross the Atlantic. I need you here now."

The Witch of Endor. I didn't need to consult my Bible. Every member of the Talamasca knew that story only too well.

King Saul, in fear of the might of the Philistines, goes, before the dreaded battle, to "a woman with a familiar spirit" and asks that she raise Samuel the Prophet from the dead. "Why has thou disquieted me, to bring me up?" demands the ghostly prophet, and in short order he predicts that King Saul and both his sons will join him in death on the following day.

The Witch of Endor. And so I had always thought of Merrick, no matter how close to her I'd become later on. She was Merrick Mayfair, the Witch of Endor. At times I'd addressed her as such in semi-official memos and often in brief notes.

In the beginning, she'd been a tender marvel. I had heeded Aaron's summons, packing, flying to Louisiana, and setting foot for the first time in Oak Haven, the splendid plantation home which had become our refuge outside of New Orleans, on the old River Road.

What a dreamy event it had been. On the plane I had read my Old Testament: King Saul's sons had been slain in battle. Saul had fallen on his sword. Was I superstitious after all? My life I'd given to the Talamasca, but even before I'd begun my apprenticeship I'd seen and commanded spirits on my own. They weren't ghosts, you understand. They were nameless, never corporeal, and wound up for me with the names and rituals of Brazilian Candomble magic, in which I'd plunged so recklessly in my youth.

But I'd let that power grow cold inside me as scholarship and devotion to others claimed me. I had abandoned the mysteries of Brazil for the equally wondrous world of archives, relics, libraries, organization, and tutelage, lulling others into dusty reverence for our methods and our careful ways. The Talamasca was so vast, so old, so loving in its embrace. Even Aaron had no clue as to my old powers, not in those days, though many a mind was open to his psychic sensibility. I would know the girl for what she was.

It had been raining when we reached the Motherhouse, our car plunging into the long avenue of giant oaks that led from the levee road to the immense double doors. How green had been this world even in darkness, with twisted oak branches dipping into the high grass. I think the long gray streaks of Spanish moss touched the roof of the car.

The electric power had gone out that night with the storm, they told me.

"Rather charming," Aaron had said as he greeted me. He'd been white-haired already by then, the consummate older gentleman, eternally good-natured, almost sweet. "Lets you see things as they were in the old days, don't you think?"

Only oil lamps and candles illuminated the large square rooms. I had seen the flicker in the fanlight above the entranceway as we approached. Lanterns swayed in the wind in the deep galleries that wrapped the great square house about on its first and second floors.

Before entering, I had taken my time, rain or no rain, to inspect this marvelous tropical mansion, impressed with its simple pillars. Once there had been sugarcane for miles all around it; out back beyond the flower beds, still vaguely colored in the downpour, were weathered outbuildings where once slaves had lived.

She came down barefoot to meet me, in a lavender dress covered with pink flowers, scarcely the witch at all.

Her eyes couldn't have been more mysterious had she worn the kohl of a Hindu princess to set off the color. One saw the green of the iris, and the dark circle around it, as well as the black pupil within. A marvelous eye, all the more vivid due to her light-tan creamy skin. Her hair had been brushed back from her forehead, and her slender hands merely hung at her sides. How at ease she'd seemed in the first moments.

"David Talbot," she had said to me almost formally. I'd been enchanted by the confidence in her soft voice.

They couldn't break her of the barefoot habit. It had been dreadfully enticing, those bare feet on the wool carpet. She'd grown up in the country, I thought, but no, they said, it was merely in an old tumbledown part of New Orleans where there were no sidewalks anymore and the weather-beaten houses were neglected and the blossoming and poisonous oleander grew as big as trees.

She had lived there with her godmother, Great Nananne, the witch who'd taught her all the things that she knew. Her mother, a powerful seer, known to me then only by the mysterious name of Cold Sandra, had been in love with an explorer. There was no father of memory. She'd never gone to a real school.

"Merrick Mayfair," I'd said warmly. I took her in my arms.

She had been tall for her fourteen years, with beautifully shaped breasts quite natural under her simple cotton shift, and her soft dry hair had been loose down her back. She might have been a Spanish beauty to anyone outside of this bizarre part of the Southland, where the history of the slaves and their free descendants was so full of complex alliances and erotic romance. But any New Orleanean could see African blood in her by the lovely café au lait of her skin.

Sure enough, when I poured the cream into the thick chicory coffee that they gave me, I understood those words.

"All my people are colored," she said, with the French in her voice then. "Those that pass for white leave and go north. That's been happening forever. They don't want Great Nananne to visit. They don't want anyone to know. I could pass for white. But what about the family? What about all that's been handed down? I would never leave Great Nananne. I came here 'cause she told me to come."

She had a temptress's poise as she sat there, small in the great winged chair of oxblood leather, a tiny tantalizing gold chain around her ankle, another with a small diamond-studded cross around her neck.

"See these pictures?" she said invitingly. She had them in a shoe box which rested in her lap. "There's no witchcraft in them. You can look as you please."

She laid them out on the table for me, daguerreotypes—stark clear photographs on glass, each one fitted into a crumbling little case of gutter perche, heavily embossed with rings of flowers or grapevines, many of which could be closed and clasped shut like little books.

"They come from the 1840s," she said, "and they're all our people. One of our own took these pictures. He was known for taking portraits. They loved him. He left some stories—I know where they are. They're all written with beautiful handwriting. They're in a box in the attic of Great Nananne's house."

She had moved to the edge of the chair, her knees poking out from under her skimpy hem. Her hair made a big mass of shadows behind her. Her hairline was clean and her forehead smooth and beautiful. Though the night had been only cool, there was a fire in the fireplace, and the room, with its shelves of books and its random Grecian sculptures, had been fragrant and comfortable, conducive to a spell.

Aaron had been watching her proudly, yet full of concern.

"See, these are all my people from the old days." She might have been laying out a deck of cards. The flash of the shadows was lovely on her oval face and the distinct bones of her cheeks. "You see, they kept together. But as I said, the ones that could pass are long gone. Look what they gave up, just think of it, so much history. See this?"

I studied the small picture, glinting in the light of the oil lamp.

"This is Lucy Nancy Marie Mayfair, she was the daughter of a white man, but we never knew much about him. All along there would be white men. Always white men. What these women did for white men. My mother went to South America with a white man. I went with them. I remember the jungles." Had she hesitated, picking up something from my thoughts, perhaps, or merely my doting face?

I would never forget my own early years of exploration in the Amazon. I suppose I didn't want to forget, though nothing had made me more painfully conscious of my old age than to think of those adventures with gun and camera, lived on the bottom side of the world. I never dreamt then that I would return to uncharted jungles with her.

I had stared again at the old glass daguerreotypes. Not a one among any of these individuals looked anything but rich—top hats and full taffeta skirts against studio backdrops of drapery and lavish plants. Here was a young woman beautiful as Merrick was now, sitting so prim and upright, in a high-backed Gothic chair. How to explain the remarkably clear evidence of African blood in so many of them? It seemed no more in some than an uncommon brightness of the eye against a darkened Caucasian face, yet it was there.

"Here, this is the oldest," she said, "this is Angelique Marybelle Mayfair." A stately woman, dark hair parted in the middle, ornate shawl covering her shoulders and full sleeves. In her fingers she clasped a barely visible pair of spectacles and a folded fan.

"She's the oldest and finest picture that I have. She was a secret witch, that's what they told me. There's secret witches and witches people come to. She was the secret kind, but she was smart. They say she was lovers with a white Mayfair who lived in the Garden District, and he was by blood her own nephew. I come down from her and from him. Oncle Julien, that was his name. He let his colored cousins call him Oncle Julien, instead of Monsieur Julien, the way the other white men might have done."

Aaron had tensed but sought to hide it. Perhaps he could hide it from her, but not from me.

So he's told her nothing of that dangerous Mayfair family. They haven't spoken of it—the dreadful Garden District Mayfairs, a tribe with supernatural powers, whom he had investigated for years. Our files on the Mayfairs went back for centuries. Members of our Order had died at the hands of the Mayfair Witches, as we were wont to call them. But this child mustn't know about them through us, I had realized quite suddenly, at least not until Aaron had made up his mind that such an intervention would serve the good of both parties, and do no harm.

As it was, such a time never came to pass. Merrick's life was complete and separate from that of the white Mayfairs. There is nothing of their story in these pages that I now write.

But on that long ago evening, Aaron and I had sought rather desperately to make our minds blank for the little witch who sat before us.

I don't remember whether or not Merrick had glanced at us before she went on.

"There are Mayfairs living in that Garden District house even now," she had said matter-of-factly, "—white people, who never had much to do with us, except through their lawyers." How worldly her little laugh had sounded—the way people laugh when they speak of lawyers.

"The lawyers would come back of town with the money," she said with a shake of her head. "And some of those lawyers were Mayfairs too. The lawyers sent Angelique Marybelle Mayfair north to a fine school, but she came home again to live and die right here. I would never go to those white people." The remark had been almost off-handed. She went on.

"But Great Nananne talks about Oncle Julien just as if he was living now, and they all said it when I was growing up, that Oncle Julien was a kind man. Seems he knew all his colored relations, and they said that man could kill his enemies or yours with the look in his eye. He was a *houn'gan* if there ever was one. I have more to say about him by and by."

She had glanced quite suddenly at Aaron and I'd seen him glance away from her almost shyly. I wonder if she had seen the future—that the Talamasca File on the Mayfair Witches would swallow Aaron's life, as surely as the Vampire Lestat had swallowed mine.

I wondered what she thought about Aaron's death even now, as we sat at the café table, as I spoke softly to the handsome and well-defended woman whom that little girl had become.

The feeble old waiter brought her the fifth of rum she had requested, the St. James from Martinique, dark. I caught the powerful scent of it as he filled her small, heavy octagonal glass. Memories flooded my mind. Not the beginning with her, but other times.

She drank it just the way I knew she would, in the manner I remembered, as if it were nothing but water. The waiter shuffled back to his hiding place. She lifted the bottle before I could do it for her, and she filled the glass again.

I watched her tongue move along the inside of her lip. I watched her large searching eyes look up again into my face.

"Remember drinking rum with me?" she asked, almost smiling, but not quite. She was far too tense, too alert for that just yet. "You remember," she said. "I'm talking about those brief nights in the jungle. Oh, you are so right when you say that the vampire is a human monster. You're still so very human. I can see it in your expression. I can see it in your gestures. As for your body, it's totally human. There isn't a clue. . . ."

"There are clues," I said, contradicting her. "And as time passes you'll see them. You'll become uneasy, and then fearful and, finally, accustomed. Believe me, I know."

She raised her eyebrows, then accepted this. She took another sip and I imagined how delicious it was for her. I knew that she did not drink every day of her life, and when she did drink she enjoyed it very much.

"So many memories, beautiful Merrick," I whispered. It seemed paramount that I not give in to them, that I concentrate on those memories which most certainly enshrined her innocence and reminded me of a sacred trust.

To the end of Aaron's life, he had been devoted to her, though he seldom spoke of it to me. What had she learnt of the tragic hit-and-run accident that had caught Aaron unawares? I had been already gone out of the Talamasca, out of Aaron's care, and out of life.

And to think we had lived such long mortal lives as scholars, Aaron and I. We should have been past all mishap. Who would have dreamt that our research would ensnare us and turn our destiny so dramatically from the dedication of those long loyal years? But hadn't the same thing happened to another loyal member of the Talamasca, my beloved student Jesse Reeves?

Back then, when Merrick had been the sultry child and I the amazed Superior General, I had not thought my few remaining years held any great surprise.

Why had I not learnt from the story of Jesse? Jesse Reeves had been my student even more surely than Merrick ever became, and the vampires had swallowed Jesse whole and complete.

With great devotion Jesse had sent me one last letter, thick with euphemisms, and of no real value to anyone else, letting me know that she would never see me again. I had not taken Jesse's fate as a caution. I had thought only that for the intense study of the vampire, Jesse Reeves had been too young.

It was all past. Nothing remained of that heartbreak. Nothing remained of those mistakes. My mortal life had been shattered, my soul soaring and then fallen, my vampire life erasing all the small accomplishments and consolations of the man I'd once been. Jesse was among *us* and I knew her secrets, and that she'd always be quite far-away from me.

What mattered now was the ghost that Jesse had only glimpsed during her investigations, and the ghost story that haunted Louis, and the bizarre request which I now made to my beloved Merrick that she call the ghost of Claudia with all her uncommon skill.

2

IN THE STILL CAFÉ, I watched Merrick take another deep drink of the rum. I treasured the interval in which she let her eyes pass slowly over the dusty room.

I let my mind return to that long ago night at Oak Haven, as the rain struck the windowpanes. The air had been warm and heavy with the scent of the oil lamps and the busy fire on the hearth. Spring was upon us but the storm had cooled the air. She'd been speaking of the white family named Mayfair of whom she knew so little, she said.

"None of us with any sense would do that," she continued, "go to those white cousins, expecting anything from any of them on account of a name." She had brushed it all aside. "I'm not going to white people and try to tell them that I'm their own."

Aaron had looked at me, his quick gray eyes concealing even his tenderest emotions, but I knew that he wanted me to respond.

"There's no need, child," I had said. "You are ours now, if you choose to be. We are your own. Why, it's already understood. This is your home forever. Only you can change things, if you wish."

A chill had come over me, of something momentous and meaningful, when I'd spoken those words to her. I had indulged the pleasure. "We'll always take care of you." I had underscored it, and I might have kissed her had she not been so ripe and pretty, with her bare feet on the flowered carpet and her breasts naked beneath her shift.

She had not replied.

"All gentlemen and ladies, it seems," Aaron had said, perusing the daguerreotypes. "And in such excellent condition, these little portraits." He had sighed. "Ah, what a wonder it must have been in the 1840s when they learnt to take these pictures."

"Oh, yes, my great-great uncle wrote all about it," she had said. "I don't know if anyone can read those pages anymore. They were crumbling to bits when Great Nananne first showed them to me. But as I was saying, these are all his pictures. Here, the tintypes, he did those too." She had a woman's weariness in her sigh, as though she'd lived it all. "He died very old, they say, with a house full of pictures, before his white nephews came and actually broke them up—but I'll come to that."

I had been shocked and bruised by such a revelation, unable to excuse it. Broken daguerreotypes. Faces lost forever. She had gone on, lifting the small rectangles of tin, many unframed yet clear, from her cardboard treasure chest.

"I open boxes sometimes from Great Nananne's rooms, and the paper is all little bits and pieces. I think the rats come and they eat the paper. Great Nananne says rats will eat your money and that's why you have to keep it in an iron box. Iron's magical, you know that. The sisters—I mean the nuns—they don't know that. That's why in the Bible you couldn't build with an iron shovel, because iron was mighty and you couldn't put the iron shovel above the bricks of the Lord's temple, not then, and not now."

It seemed a bizarre intelligence, though she had been most technically correct.

She'd let her words wander. "Iron and shovels. It goes way back. The King of Babylon held a shovel in his hand with which he laid the bricks of the temple. And the Masons, now they keep that idea in their Order, and on the one-dollar bill you see that broken pyramid of bricks."

It had amazed me, the ease with which she touched on these complex concepts. What had she known in her life, I wondered. What sort of woman would she prove to be?

I remember that she'd been looking at me, as she'd said those words, gauging my reaction, perhaps, and it had only then become clear to me how much she needed to talk of the things she'd been taught, of the things she thought, of the things she'd heard.

"But why are you so good?" she had asked, searching my face rather politely. "I know with priests and nuns why they're good to us. They come and bring food and clothes to us. But you, why are you good? Why did you let me in and give me a room here? Why do you let me do what I want? All day Saturday I looked at magazines and listened to the radio. Why do you feed me and try to get me to wear shoes?"

"Child," Aaron had interjected. "We're almost as old as the Church of Rome. We're as old as the orders of the sisters and the priests who've visited you. Yes, older, I would say, than almost all."

Still she had looked to me for an explanation.

"We have our beliefs and our traditions," I had said. "It's common to be bad, to be greedy, to be corrupt and self-seeking. It's a rare thing to love. We love."

Again, I had enjoyed our sense of purpose, our commitment—that we were the inviolate Talamasca, that we cared for the outcast, that we harbored the sorcerer and the seer, that we had saved witches from the stake and reached out even to the wandering spirits, yes, even to the shades whom others fear. We had done it for well over a thousand years.

"But these little treasures—your family, your heritage," I'd hastened to explain. "They matter to us because they matter to you. And they will always be yours."

She'd nodded. I had got it right.

"Witchcraft's my calling card, Mr. Talbot," she'd said shrewdly, "but all this comes with me too."

I had enjoyed the fleeting enthusiasm which had illuminated her face.

And now, some twenty years after, what had I done, seeking her out, finding her old house in New Orleans deserted, and spying upon her at Oak Haven, walking the broad upstairs galleries of Oak Haven like an old Penny Dreadful Vampire, looking into her very bedroom until she sat up and spoke my name in the darkness.

I had done her evil, I knew it, and it was exciting, and I needed her, and I was selfish, and I missed her, and it was as plain as that.

It had been only a week ago that I wrote to her.

Alone in the town house in the Rue Royale, I'd written by hand in a style that hadn't changed with my fortunes:

Dear Merrick,

Yes, it was I whom you saw on the porch outside your room. It was not my intention to frighten you but merely to solace myself by looking at you, playing the guardian angel, I must confess, if you will forgive me, as I hovered outside the window for the better part of the night.

I have a request for you, which I make from my soul to yours. I cannot tell you what it is in this letter. I ask that you meet me in some place that is public, where you will feel safe from me, a place that you yourself choose. Answer at this post box, and I'll be prompt in replying. Merrick, forgive me. If you advise the Elders or the Superior General of this contact, they will in all likelihood forbid you to meet with me. Please give me this little while to speak with you before you take such a step.

Yours in the Talamasca forever,

David Talbot.

What audacity and egoism to have written such a note and delivered it into the iron mailbox at the end of the drive in the hours before dawn.

She'd written back, a note rather tantalizing in its details, full of undeserved affection.

I cannot wait to talk with you. Be assured, whatever shocks this meeting will hold in store for me, I seek you inside the mystery—David, whom I have always loved. You were my Father when I needed you, and my friend ever after. And I have glimpsed you since your metamorphosis, perhaps more often than you know.

I know what happened to you. I know of those with whom you live. The Café of the Lion. Rue St. Anne. Do you remember it? Years ago, before we ever went to Central America, we ate a quick lunch there. You were so wary of us setting out for those jungles. Do you remember how you argued? I think I used a witch's charms to persuade you. I always thought you knew. I'll come early each evening for several nights in hopes that you'll be there.

She had signed the note exactly as I had signed my own: "Yours in the Talamasca forever."

I had put myself before my love of her, and my duty to her. I was relieved that the deed was done.

Back then, when she'd been the orphan in the storm, such a thing had been unthinkable. She *was* my duty, this little wanderer who had come so surprisingly, on her own, one evening to knock on our door.

"Our motives are the same as your motives," Aaron had said to her most directly on that long ago night at Oak Haven. He'd reached out and lifted her soft brown hair back from her shoulder, as if he were her elder brother. "We want to preserve knowledge. We want to save history. We want to study and we hope to understand."

He had made another soft sigh, so unlike him.

"Ah, those white cousins, the Garden District Mayfairs, as you called them, and most correctly, yes, we know of them," he had admitted, surprising me, "but we keep our secrets unless prompted by duty to reveal them. What is their long history to you just now? Their lives are interconnected like thorny vines forever circling and recircling the same tree. Your life might have nothing to do with that bitter struggle. What concerns us here now is what we can do for you. I don't speak idle words when I tell you that you may rely upon us forever. You are, as David has said, our own."

She had reflected. It had not been simple for her to accept all of this, she was too used to being alone with Great Nananne—yet something strong had impelled her to trust us before she'd ever come.

"Great Nananne trusts you," she had said, as if I'd asked her. "Great Nananne said that I was to come to you. Great Nananne had one of her many dreams and woke up before daylight and rang her bell for me to come. I was sleeping on the screen porch and I came in and found her standing up in her white flannel gown. She's cold all the time, you know; she always wears flannel, even on the hottest night. She said for me to come sit down and listen to what she had dreamed."

"Tell me about it, child," Aaron had asked. Had they not spoken of this completely before I'd come?

"She dreamed of Mr. Lightner, of you," she'd said, looking to Aaron, "and in the dream you came to her with Oncle Julien, white Oncle Julien from the clan uptown. And the two of you sat by her bed.

"Oncle Julien told her jokes and stories and said he was happy to be in her dream. She said that. Oncle Julien said that I was to go to you, you here, Mr. Lightner, and that Mr. Talbot would come. Oncle Julien spoke French and you yourself were sitting in the cane-backed chair and smiling and nodding to her, and you brought her in a cup of coffee and cream the way she likes it, with half a cup of sugar and one of her favorite silver spoons. In and out of her dreams, Great Nananne has a thousand silver spoons." The dream continued:

"You sat on her bed, finally, on her best quilt beside her, and you took her hand, and she had all her best rings on her hand, which she doesn't wear anymore, you know, and you said in the dream, 'You send me little Merrick,' and you said you'd take care of me, and you told her that she was going to die."

Aaron had not heard this strange recounting, and he'd seemed quite taken, amazed. Lovingly, he'd answered:

"It must have been Oncle Julien who said such a thing in the dream. How could I have known such a secret?"

I'd never forgotten his protest, because it had been very unlike him to commit himself even to ignorance, and to press so hard upon such a point.

"No, no, you told her," the fairy child had said. "You told her the day of the week and the hour of the clock, and it's yet to come." She had looked thoughtfully once more at her pictures. "Don't worry about it. I know when it's going to happen." Her face had been suddenly full of sadness. "I can't keep her forever. *Les mystères* will not wait."

Les mystères. Did she mean the ancestors, the Voodoo gods, or merely the secrets of fate? I'd been unable to penetrate her thoughts to any degree whatsoever.

"St. Peter will be waiting," she'd murmured as the visible sadness had slowly receded behind her veil of calm.

Quite suddenly, she'd flashed her glance on me and murmured something in French. Papa Legba, god of the crossroads in Voodoo, for whom a statue of St. Peter with his keys to Heaven might do quite well.

I had noted that Aaron could not bring himself to question her further on the matter of his role in the dream, the date of Great Nananne's imminent death. He had nodded, however, and once again, with both hands he'd lifted her hair back from her damp neck where a few errant tendrils had clung to her soft creamy skin.

Aaron had regarded her with honest wonder as she had gone on with her tale.

"First thing I knew after that dream, there was an old colored man and a truck ready to take me, and he said, 'You don't need your bag, you just come as you are,' and I climbed up into the truck with him, and he drove me all the way out here, not even talking to me, just listening to some old Blues radio station and smoking cigarettes the whole way. Great Nananne knew it was Oak Haven because Mr. Lightner told her in the dream. . . .

"Great Nananne knew of Oak Haven of the old days, when it was a different kind of house with a different name. Oncle Julien told her lots of other things, but she didn't tell me what they were. She said, 'Go to them, The Talamasca; they'll take care of you, and it will be the way for you and all the things that you can do.' "

It had chilled: *all the things that you can do*. I remember Aaron's sad expression. He had only given a little shake of his head. Don't worry her now, I'd thought a bit crossly, but the child had not been perturbed.

Oncle Julien of Mayfair fame was no stranger to my memory; I had read many chapters on the career of this powerful witch and seer, the one male in his bizarre family to go against the goad of a male spirit and his female witches over many hundreds of years. Oncle Julien—mentor, madman, cocksman, legend, father of witches—and the child had said that she had come down from him.

It had to be powerful magic, but Oncle Julien had been Aaron's field, not mine.

She had watched me carefully as she spoke.

"I'm not used to people believing me," she'd said, "but I am used to making people afraid."

"How so, child?" I had asked. But she had frightened me quite enough with her remarkable poise and the penetration of her gaze. What could she do? Would I ever know? It had been worth pondering on that first evening, for it was not our way to encourage our orphans to give full vent to their dangerous powers; we had been devoutly passive in all such respects.

I had banished my unseemly curiosity and set to memorizing her appearance, as was my custom in those days, by looking very carefully at every aspect of her visage and form.

Her limbs had been beautifully molded; her breasts were already too fetching, and the features of her face were large, all of them—with no unique hint of the African—large her well-shaped mouth, and large her almond eyes and long nose; her neck had been long and uncommonly graceful, and there had been a harmony to her face, even when she had fallen into the deepest thought.

"Keep your secrets of those white Mayfairs," she had said. "Maybe someday we can swap secrets, you and me. They don't even know in these times that we are here. Great Nananne said that Oncle Julien died before she was born. In the dream, he didn't say a word about those white Mayfairs. He said for me to come here." She had gestured to the old glass photographs. "These are my people. If I'd been meant to go to those white Mayfairs, Great Nananne would have seen it long before now." She'd paused, thoughtfully. "Let's us just talk of those old times."

She'd spaced the daguerreotypes lovingly on the mahogany table. She made a neat row, wiping away the crumbly fragments with her hand. And at some moment, I'd noted that all the little figures were upside down from her point of view, and right side up for Aaron and for me.

"There've been white people kin to me that have come down here and tried to destroy records," she said, "You know, tear the page right out of the church register that says their great-grandmother was colored. *Femme de couleur libre*, that's what some old records say in French.

"Imagine tearing up that much history, the page right out of the church register with all those births and deaths and marriages, and not wanting to know. Imagine going into my great-great oncle's house and breaking up those pictures, pictures that ought to be someplace safe for lots of people to see."

She had sighed, rather like a weary woman, gazing down into the worn shoe box and its trophies.

"Now I have these pictures. I have everything, and I'm with you, and they can't find me, and they can't throw all these things away."

She had dipped her hand into the shoe box again and taken out the *cartes de visite*—old photographs on cardboard from the last decades of the old century. I could see the high slanted letters in faded purple on the backs of these latest pictures as she turned them this way and that.

"See, this here is Oncle Vervain," she said. I had looked at the thin, handsome black-haired young man with the dark skin and light eyes like her own. It was rather a romantic portrait. In a finely tailored three-piece suit, he stood with his arm on a Greek column before a painted sky. The picture was in rich sepia. The African blood was plainly present in the man's handsome nose and mouth.

"Now, this is dated 1920." She turned it over once, then back again, and laid it down for us to see. "Oncle Vervain was a Voodoo Doctor," she said, "and I knew him well before he died. I was little, but I'll never forget him. He could dance and spit the rum from between his teeth at the altar, and he had everybody scared, I can tell you."

She took her time, then found what she wanted. Next picture.

"And you see here, this one?" She had laid down another old photograph, this time of an elderly gray-haired man of color in a stately wooden chair. "The Old Man is what they always called him. I don't even know him by any other name. He went back to Haiti to study the magic, and he taught Oncle Vervain all he knew. Sometimes I feel Oncle Vervain is talking to me. Sometimes I feel he's outside our house watching over Great Nananne. I saw the Old Man once in a dream."

I had wanted so badly to ask questions, but this had not been the time.

"See here, this is Pretty Justine," she had said, laying down perhaps the most impressive portrait of all—a studio picture on thick cardboard inside a sepia cardboard frame. "Pretty Justine had everybody afraid of her." The young woman was indeed pretty, her breasts flat in the style of the 1920s, her hair in a bob, her dark skin quite beautiful, her eyes and mouth slightly expressionless, or perhaps evincing a certain pain.

Now came the modern snapshots, thin and curling, the work of common enough hand-held cameras of the present time.

"They were the worst—his sons," she had said as she pointed to the curling black-and-white picture. "They were Pretty Justine's grandchildren, all white and living in New York. They wanted to get their hands on anything that said they were colored and tear it up. Great Nananne knew what they wanted. She didn't fall for their soft manners and the way they took me downtown and bought me pretty clothes. I still have those clothes. Little dresses nobody ever wore and little shoes with clean soles. They didn't leave us an address when they left. See, look at them in the picture. Look how anxious they are. But I did bad things to them."

Aaron had shaken his head, studying the strange tense faces. As the pictures had disquieted me, I had kept my eyes on the womanish child.

"What did you do, Merrick?" I had asked without biting my tongue wisely.

"Oh, you know, read their secrets in their palms and told them bad things they'd always tried to cover up. It wasn't kind to do that, but I did it, just to make them go away. I told them our house was full of spirits. I made the spirits come. No, I didn't make them come. I called them and they came as I asked. Great Nananne thought it was funny. They said, 'Make her stop,' and Great Nananne said, 'What makes you think I can do that?' as if I was some wild creature that she couldn't control."

Again there had come that little sigh.

"Great Nananne's really dying," she said looking up at me, her green eyes never wavering. "She says there is no one now, and I have to keep these things—her books, her clippings. See, look here, at these clippings. The old newspaper is so brittle it's falling apart. Mr. Lightner's going to help me save these things." She glanced at Aaron. "Why are you so afraid for me, Mr. Talbot? Aren't you strong enough? You don't think it's so bad to be colored, do you? You're not from here, you're from away."

Afraid. Was I really feeling it so strongly? She'd spoken with authority, and I'd searched for the truth in it, but come quick to my own defense and perhaps to hers as well.

"Read my heart, child," I said. "I think nothing of the sort about being colored, though maybe there were times when I've thought that it might have been bad luck in a particular case." She'd raised her eyebrows slightly, thoughtfully. I'd continued, anxious, perhaps, but not afraid. "I'm sad because you say you have no one, and I'm glad because I know that you have us."

"That's what Great Nananne says, more or less," she answered. And for the first time, her long full mouth made a true smile.

My mind had drifted, remembering the incomparable dark-skinned women I'd seen in India, though she was a marvel of different tones, the rich mahogany hair and the pale eyes so visible and so meaningful. I'd thought again that to many she must have looked exotic, this barefoot girl in the flowered shift.

Then had come a moment of pure feeling, which had made its indelible and irrational impression. I'd perused the many faces laid out upon the table, and it had seemed they were all gazing at me. It was a marked impression. The little pictures had been alive all along.

It must be the firelight and the oil lamps, I'd thought dreamily, but I'd been unable to shake the feeling; the little people had been laid out to look at Aaron and to look at me. Even their placement seemed deliberate and sly, or wondrously meaningful, I'd conjectured, as I went smoothly from suspicion to a lulled and tranquil feeling that I was in an audience with a host of the dead.

"They do seem to be looking," Aaron had murmured, I remember, though I'm sure I hadn't spoken. The clock had stopped ticking and I'd turned to look at it, uncertain where it was. On the mantle, yes, and its hands had been frozen, and the window-panes had given that muffled rattle that they do when the wind nudges them, and the house had wrapped me securely in its own atmosphere of warmth and secrets, of safety and sanctity, of dreaminess and communal might.

It seemed a long interval had transpired in which none of us had spoken, and Merrick had stared at me, and then at Aaron, her hands idle, her face glistening in the light.

I'd awakened sharply to realize nothing had changed in the room. Had I fallen asleep? Unforgivable rudeness. Aaron had been beside me as before. And the pictures had become once more inert and sorrowful, ceremonial testimony to mortality as surely as if she'd laid out a skull for my perusal from a graveyard fallen to ruin. But the uneasiness I'd experienced then stayed with me long after we'd all gone up to our respective rooms.

Now—after twenty years and many other strange moments—she sat across from me at this café table in the Rue St. Anne, a beauty gazing at a vampire, and we talked over the flickering candle, and the light was too much like the light of that long ago evening at Oak Haven, though tonight the late spring evening was only moist, not wet with a coming storm.

She sipped the rum, rolling it around a bit before she swallowed it. But she didn't fool me. She'd soon start drinking it fast again. She set the glass aside and let her fingers spread wide apart on the soiled marble. Rings. Those were Great Nananne's many rings, beautiful gold filigree with various wondrous stones. She'd worn them even in the jungles, when I'd thought it so unwise. She'd never been prone to fear of any sort.

I thought of her in those hot tropical nights. I thought of her during those steamy hours under the high canopy of green. I thought of the trek through the darkness of the ancient temple. I thought of her climbing ahead of me, in the steam and roar of the waterfall up the gentle slope.

I'd been far too old for it, our great and secret adventure. I thought of precious objects made of jade as green as her eyes.

Her voice brought me out of my selfish reverie:

"Why are you asking me to do this magic?" She put the question to me again. "I sit here and I look at you, David, and with every passing second, I become more aware of what you are and what's happened to you. I put all kinds of pieces together from your open mind—and your mind's as open as it ever was, David, you know that, don't you?"

How resolute was her voice. Yes, the French was utterly gone. Ten years ago it had been gone. But now there was a clipped quality to her words, no matter how soft and low they came.

Her large eyes widened easily with her expressive verbal rhythms.

"You couldn't even be quiet of mind on the porch the other night," she scolded. "You woke me. I heard you, just as if you'd been tapping on the panes. You said, 'Merrick, can you do it? Can you bring up the dead for Louis de Pointe du Lac?' And do you know what I heard underneath it? I heard 'Merrick, I need you. I need to talk to you. Merrick, my destiny is shattered. Merrick, I reach for understanding. Don't turn me aside.' "

I felt an acute pain in my heart.

"It's true what you're saying," I confessed.

She drank another big swallow of the rum, and the heat danced in her cheeks.

"But you want this thing for Louis," she said. "You want it enough to overcome your own scruples and come to my window. Why? You, I understand. Of him, I know other people's stories and just the little I've seen with my own eyes. He's a dashing young man, that one, isn't he?"

I was too confused to answer, too confused to will courtesy to build a temporary bridge of polite lies.

"David, give me your hand, please," she asked suddenly. "I have to touch you. I have to feel this strange skin."

"Oh, darling, if only you could forego that," I murmured.

Her large golden earrings moved against the nest of her black hair and the long line of her beautiful neck. All the promise of the child had been fulfilled in her. Men admired her enormously. I had known that a long time ago.

She reached out to me gracefully. Boldly, hopelessly, I gave her my hand.

I wanted the contact. I wanted the intimacy. I was powerfully stimulated. And treasuring the sensation, I let her fingers linger as she looked into my palm.

"Why read this palm, Merrick?" I asked. "What can it tell you? This body belonged to another man. Do you want to read the map of his broken fate? Can you see there that he was murdered and the body stolen? Can you see there my own selfish invasion of a body that ought to have died?"

"I know the story, David," she answered. "I found it all in Aaron's papers. Body switching. Highly theoretical as regards the official position of the Order. But you were a grand success."

Her fingers sent the thrills up my spine and through the roots of my hair.

"After Aaron's death, I read the whole thing," she said, as she moved her fingertips across the pattern of deeply etched lines. She recited it:

" 'David Talbot is no longer in his body. During an ill-fated experiment with astral projection he was ousted from his own form by a practiced Body Thief and forced to claim the youthful trophy of his opponent, a body stolen from a shattered soul which has, as far as we can know, moved on.' "

I winced at the old familiar Talamasca style.

"I wasn't meant to find those papers," she continued, her eyes still fixed on my palm. "But Aaron died here, in New Orleans, and I had them in my hands before anyone else. They're still in my possession, David; they have never been filed with the Elders and maybe they never will be filed. I don't know."

I was amazed at her audacity, to have held back such secrets from the Order to which she still devoted her life. When had I ever had such independence, except perhaps at the very end?

Her eyes moved quickly back and forth as she examined my palm. She pressed her thumb softly against my flesh. The chills were unbearably enticing. I wanted to take her in my arms, not feed from her, no, not harm her, only kiss her, only sink my fangs a very little, only taste her blood and her secrets, but this was dreadful and I wouldn't let it go on.

I withdrew my outstretched hand.

"What did you see, Merrick?" I asked quickly, swallowing the hunger of body and mind.

"Disasters large and small, my friend, a life line that goes on as long as any, stars of strength, and a brood of offspring."

"Stop it, I don't accept it. The hand's not mine."

"You have no other body now," she countered. "Don't you think the body will conform to its new soul? The palm of a hand changes over time. But I don't want to make you angry. I didn't come here to study you. I didn't come here to stare in cold fascination at a vampire. I've glimpsed vampires. I've even been close to them, in these very streets. I came because you asked me and because I wanted . . . to be with you."

I nodded, overcome and unable for the moment to speak. With quick gestures I pleaded for her silence.

She waited.

Then at last:

"Did you ask permission of the Elders for this meeting?"

She laughed but it wasn't cruel. "Of course I did not."

"Then know this," I said. "It started the same way with me and the Vampire Lestat. I didn't tell the Elders. I didn't let them know how often I saw him, that I brought him into my house, that I conversed with him, traveled with him, taught him how to reclaim his preternatural body when the Body Thief tricked him out of it."

She tried to interrupt me but I would have none of it.

"And do you realize what's happened to me?" I demanded. "I thought I was too clever for Lestat ever to seduce me. I thought I was too wise in old age for the seduction of immortality. I thought I was morally superior, Merrick, and now you see what I am."

"Aren't you going to swear to me that you'll never hurt me?" she asked, her face beautifully flushed. "Aren't you going to assure me that Louis de Pointe du Lac would never bring me harm?"

"Of course I am. But there's a bit of decency left in me, and that decency compels me to remind you that I'm a creature of supernatural appetite."

Again she tried to interject, but I wouldn't allow it.

"My very presence, with all its signals of power, can erode your own tolerance for living, Merrick; it can eat away your faith in a moral order, it can hurt your willingness to die an ordinary death."

"Ah, David," she said, chiding me for my official tone. "Speak plainly. What's in your heart?" She sat up straight in the chair, her eyes looking me up and down. "You look boyish and wise in this young body. Your skin's darkened like mine! Even your features have the stamp of Asia. But you're more David than you ever were!"

I said nothing.

I watched through dazed eyes as she drank more of the rum. The sky darkened behind her, but bright, warm electric lights filled up the outside night. Only the café itself was veiled in dreary shadow, what with its few dusty bulbs behind the bar.

Her cool confidence chilled me. It chilled me that she had so fearlessly touched me, that nothing in my vampire nature repelled her, but then I could well remember how Lestat in all his subdued glory had attracted me. Was she attracted? Had the fatal fascination begun?

She kept her thoughts half concealed as she always had.

I thought of Louis. I thought of his request. He wanted desperately for her to work her magic. But she was right. I needed her. I needed her witness and her understanding.

When I spoke, my words were full of heartbreak and wonder, even to myself.

"It's been magnificent," I said. "And unendurable. I am most truly out of life and can't escape from it. I have no one to whom I can give what I learn."

She didn't argue with me or question me. Her eyes seemed suddenly to be full of sympathy, her mask of composure to be gone. I'd seen such sharp changes in her many times. She concealed her emotions except for such silent and eloquent moments.

"Do you think," she asked, "that if you hadn't taken up life in the young body, that Lestat would have forced you as he did? If you'd still been old—our David, our *blessed David*, aged seventy-four, wasn't it?—do you think if you'd still been our honorable Superior General that Lestat would have brought you over?"

"I don't know," I said shortly, but not without feeling. "I've often asked myself the same question. I honestly don't know. These vampires . . . ah, I mean, we . . . we vampires, we love beauty, we feed on it. Our definition of beauty expands enormously, you can't quite imagine how much. I don't care how loving your soul, you can't know how much we find beautiful that mortals don't find beautiful, but we do propagate by beauty, and this body has beauty which I've used to evil advantage countless times."

She lifted her glass in a small salute. She drank deeply.

"If you'd come up to me with no preamble," she said, "whispering in a crowd as you touched me—I would have known you, known who you were." A shadow fell over her face for a moment, and then her expression became serene. "I love you, old friend," she said.

"You think so, my darling?" I asked. "I have done many things to feed this body; not so very lovely to think about that at all."

She finished the glass, set it down, and, before I could do it for her, she reached for the bottle again.

"Do you want Aaron's papers?" she asked.

I was completely taken aback.

"You mean you're willing to give them to me?"

"David, I'm loyal to the Talamasca. What would I be if it weren't for the Order?" She hesitated, then: "But I'm also deeply loyal to you." For a few seconds she was musing. "You *were* the Order for me, David. Can you imagine what I felt when they told me you were dead?"

I sighed. What could I say in answer?

"Did Aaron tell you how we grieved for you, all those of us who weren't entrusted with a speck of the truth?"

"From my soul, I'm sorry, Merrick. We felt we kept a dangerous secret. What more can I say?"

"You died here in the States, in Miami Beach, that was the story. And they'd flown the remains back to England before they even called to tell me you were gone. You know what I did, David? I made them hold the casket for me. It was sealed shut when I got to London but I made them open it. I made them do it. I screamed and carried on until they gave in to me. Then I sent them out of the room and I stayed alone with that body, David, that body all powdered and prettied up and nestled in its satin. I stayed there for an hour perhaps. They were knocking on the door. Then finally I told them to proceed."

There was no anger in her face, only a faint wondering expression.

"I couldn't let Aaron tell you," I said, "not just then, not when I didn't know whether I'd survive in the new body, not when I didn't understand what life held for me. I couldn't. And then, then it was too late."

She raised her eyebrows and made a little doubting gesture with her head. She sipped the rum.

"I understand," she said.

"Thank God," I answered. "In time, Aaron would have told you about the body switching," I insisted. "I know he would have. The story of my death was never meant for you."

She nodded, holding back the first response that came to her tongue.

"I think you have to file those papers of Aaron's," I said. "You have to file them directly with the Elders and no one else. Forget the Superior General of the moment."

"Stop it, David," she responded. "You know it is much easier to argue with you now that you are in the body of a very young man."

"You never had difficulty arguing with me, Merrick," I retorted. "Don't you think Aaron would have filed the papers, had he lived?"

"Maybe," she said, "and maybe not. Maybe Aaron would have wanted more that you be left to your destiny. Maybe Aaron wanted more that whatever you had become, you'd be left alone."

I wasn't sure what she was saying. The Talamasca was so passive, so reticent, so downright unwilling in interfere in anyone's destiny, I couldn't figure what she meant.

She shrugged, took another sip of rum, and rolled the rim of the glass against her lower lip.

"Maybe it doesn't matter," she said. "I only know that Aaron never filed the pages himself." She went on speaking:

"The night after he was killed I went down to his house on Esplanade Avenue. You know he married a white Mayfair, not a witch by the way, but a resilient and generous woman—Beatrice Mayfair is her name, she's still living—and at her invitation I took the papers marked 'Talamasca.' She didn't even know what they contained.

"She told me Aaron had once given her my name. If anything happened, she was to call me, and so she'd done her duty. Besides, she couldn't read the documents. They were all in Latin, you know, Talamasca old style.

"There were several files, and my name and number were written on the front of each, in Aaron's hand. One file was entirely devoted to you, though only the initial, D, was used throughout. The papers on you, I translated into English. No one's ever seen them. No one," she said with emphasis. "But I know them almost word for word."

It seemed a comfort suddenly to hear her speaking of these things, these secret Talamasca things, which had once been our stock in trade. Yes, a comfort, as if the warm presence of Aaron were actually with us again.

She stopped for another sip of the rum.

"I feel you ought to know these things," she said. "We never kept anything from each other, you and I. Not that I knew of, but then of course my work was in the study of magic, and I did roam far and wide."

"How much did Aaron know?" I asked. I thought my eyes were tearing. I was humiliated. But I wanted her to go on. "I never saw Aaron after the vampiric metamorphosis," I confessed dully. "I couldn't bring myself to do it. Can you guess why?" I felt a sharp increase in mental pain and confusion. My grief for Aaron would never go away, and I'd endured it for years without a word to either of my vampire companions, Louis or Lestat.

"No," she said. "I can't guess why. I can tell you . . . ," and here she hesitated politely so that I might stop her, but I did not. "I can tell you that he was disappointed and forgiving to the end."

I bowed my head. I pressed my forehead into my cold hand.

"By his own account he prayed each day that you would come to him," she explained slowly, "that he'd have a chance for one last conversation with you—about all you'd endured together and what had finally occurred to drive you apart."

I must have winced. I deserved the misery, however, deserved it more than she could know. It had been indecent not to have written to him! Lord God, even Jesse, when she'd vanished out of the Talamasca, had written to me!

Merrick went on speaking. If she read my mind at all, she gave no clue.

"Of course Aaron wrote all about your Faustian Body Switching, as he called it. He described you in the young body and made many references to some investigation of the body, something you'd engaged in together, asserting that the soul had certainly gone on. You experimented, didn't you, you and Aaron, with trying to reach the rightful soul, even at the risk of your own death?"

I nodded, unable to speak, feeling desperate and ashamed.

"As for the wretched Body Thief, the little devil Raglan James who'd started the whole supernatural spectacle, Aaron was convinced his soul was gone into eternity, as he put it, quite utterly beyond reach."

"That's true," I concurred. "The file on him is closed, I'm quite convinced of it, whether it's incomplete or not."

A darkness crept into her sad respectful expression. Some raw feeling had come to the surface, and for the moment she broke off.

"What else did Aaron write?" I asked her.

"He referred to the Talamasca having unofficially helped 'the new David' reclaim his substantial investments and property," she answered. "He felt strongly that no File on David's Second Youth must ever be created or committed to the archives in London or in Rome."

"Why didn't he want the switch to be studied?" I asked. "We had done everything we could for the other souls."

"Aaron wrote that the whole question of switching was too dangerous, too enticing; he was afraid the material would fall into the wrong hands."

"Of course," I answered, "though in the old days we never had such doubts."

"But the file was unfinished," she continued. "Aaron felt certain he would see you again. He thought that at times he could sense your presence in New Orleans. He found himself searching crowds for your new face."

"God forgive me," I whispered. I almost turned away. I bowed my head and shielded my eyes for a long moment. My old friend, my beloved old friend. How could I have abandoned him so coldly? Why does shame and self-loathing become cruelty to the innocent? How is that so often the case?

"Go on, please," I said, recovering. "I want you to tell me all these things."

"Do you want to read them for yourself?"

"Soon," I answered.

She continued, her tongue somewhat loosened by the rum, and her voice more melodic, with just a little of the old New Orleans French accent coming back.

"Aaron had seen the Vampire Lestat in your company once. He described the experience as harrowing, a word that Aaron rather loved but seldom used. He said it was the night he came to identify the old body of David Talbot and to see that it was properly buried. There you were, the young man, and the vampire stood beside you. He'd known you were on intimate terms with one another, you and this creature. He had been afraid for you as much then as ever in his life."

"What more?" I asked.

"Later on," she said, her voice low and respectful, "when you disappeared quite completely, Aaron was certain that you'd been forcibly changed by Lestat. Nothing short of that could explain your sudden break in communication, coupled with the clear intelligence from your banks and agents that you were most definitely still alive. Aaron missed you desperately. His life had been consumed with the problems of the white Mayfairs, the Mayfair Witches. He needed your advice. He wrote many times in many ways that he was certain you never asked for the vampiric blood."

For a long time I couldn't speak to answer her. I didn't weep because I don't. I looked off, eyes roaming the empty café until they saw nothing, except perhaps the blur of the tourists as they crowded the street outside on their way to Jackson Square. I knew perfectly well how to be alone in the midst of a terrible moment, no matter where it actually occurred. I was alone now.

Then I let my mind drift back to him, my friend Aaron, my colleague, my companion. I seized on memories far larger than any one incident. I envisioned him, his genial face and clever gray eyes. I saw him strolling along the brightly lit Ocean Avenue in Miami Beach, looking wonderfully out of place and richly like a splendid ornament to the bizarre scenery, in his three-piece cotton pinstripe suit.

I let the pain have me. Murdered for the secrets of the Mayfair Witches. Murdered by renegade beings in the Talamasca. Of course he had not given up to the Order his report on me. It had been a time of troubles, hadn't it, and he had ultimately been betrayed by the Order; and so my story would, within the fabled archives, remain forever incomplete.

"Was there more?" I asked Merrick finally.

"No. Only the same song with different rhythms. That was all." She took another drink. "He was terribly happy at the end, you know."

"Tell me."

"Beatrice Mayfair, he loved her. He never expected to be happily married, but it had happened. She was a beautiful highly social woman, rather like three or four people rolled into one. He told me he'd never had so much fun in his life as he had with Beatrice, and she wasn't a witch, of course."

"I'm so very glad to hear it," I said, my voice tremulous. "So Aaron became one of them, you might say."

"Yes," she answered. "In all respects."

She shrugged, the empty glass in her hand. Why she waited to take more, I wasn't certain; perhaps to impress me that she wasn't the famous drunk that I knew her to be.

"But I don't know anything about those white Mayfairs," she said finally. "Aaron always kept me away from them. My work for the last few years had been in Voodoo. I've made trips to Haiti. I've written pages. You know I'm one of the few members of the Order who is studying her own psychic power, with a license from the Elders to use the damnable magic, as the Superior General calls it now."

I hadn't known this. It had never even occurred to me that she'd returned to Voodoo, which had cast its generous shadow over her youth. We had never in my time encouraged a witch to practice magic. Only the vampire in me could tolerate such a thought.

"Look," she said, "it doesn't matter that you didn't write to Aaron."

"Oh, doesn't it?" I asked in a sharp whisper. But then I explained: "I simply couldn't write to him. I simply couldn't speak on the phone. As for seeing him, or letting him see me, it was out of the question!" I whispered.

"And it took five years," she said, "for you to finally come to me."

"Oh, right to the point!" I responded. "Five years or more to do it. And had Aaron lived on, who knows what I would have done? But the crucial factor was this: Aaron was old, Merrick. He was old and he might have asked me for the blood. When you're old and you're afraid, when you're weary and you're sick, when you've begun to suspect that your life means nothing . . . Well, that's when you dream of vampiric bargains. That's when you think that somehow the vampiric curse can't be so very dreadful, no, not in exchange for immortality; that's when you think that if only you had the chance, you could become some premier witness to the evolution of the world around you. You cloak your selfish desires in the grandiose."

"And you think I never will think such thoughts?" She raised her eyebrows, her green eyes large and full of light.

"You're young and beautiful," I said, "you were born and bred on courage. Your organs and limbs are as sound as your mind. You've never been defeated, not by anything, and you're in perfect health."

I was trembling all over. I couldn't endure much more of this. I'd dreamt of solace and intimacy, and this was intimacy, but at a terrible price.

How much easier it was to spend hours in the company of Lestat, who never spoke anymore, who lay still in a half sleep, listening to music, having been waked by it and now lulled by it, a vampire who craved nothing more?

How much easier to roam the city in the company of Louis, my weaker and ever charming companion, seeking out victims and perfecting the "little drink" so that we left our prey dazzled and unharmed? How much easier to remain within the sanctuary of the French Quarter town house, reading with a vampire's speed all the volumes of history or art history over which I'd labored so slowly when a mortal man?

Merrick merely looked at me with obvious sympathy, and then she reached out for my hand.

I avoided her touch because I wanted it so much.

"Don't back away from me, old friend," she said.

I was too confused to speak.

"What you want me to know," she said, "is that neither you nor Louis de Pointe du Lac will ever give me the blood, not even if I beg you for it; that it can't be part of any bargain between us."

"Bargain. It would be no bargain!" I whispered.

She took another drink. "And you'll never take my life," she said. "That's what makes it a bargain, I suppose. You won't ever hurt me as you might some other mortal woman who crossed your path."

The question of those who crossed my path was too troubling to me for any good response. For the first time since we had come together, I truly tried to divine her thoughts, but I could read nothing. As a vampire, I had great power in this respect. Louis had almost none. Lestat was the master.

I watched her drink the rum more slowly, and I saw her eyes become glazed with the pleasure of it, and her face soften wonderfully as the rum worked in her veins. Her cheeks were reddening slightly. Her complexion looked perfect.

Chills ran through me again, through my arms and shoulders and up the side of my face.

I had fed before I'd come here, or else the fragrance of her blood would have clouded my judgment even more than the excitement of this intimacy clouded it. I had not taken life, no, it was too simple to feed without doing it, attractive though it was. I prided myself on that. I felt clean for her, though it was becoming increasingly simple for me to "seek the evildoer," as Lestat had once instructed—to find some unwholesome and cruel individual whom I could fancy to be worse than myself.

"Oh, I wept so many tears for you," she said, her voice more heated.

"And then for Aaron, for all of your generation, leaving us suddenly and too soon, one after another." She suddenly hunched her shoulders and leant forward as though she were in pain.

"The young ones in the Talamasca don't know me, David," she said quickly. "And you don't come to me just because Louis de Pointe du Lac asked you to do it. You don't come to me just to raise the child vampire's ghost. You want me, David, you want my witness, David, and I want yours."

"You're right on all counts, Merrick," I confessed. The words spilled from me. "I love you, Merrick, I love you the way I loved Aaron, and the way I love Louis and Lestat."

I saw the flash of acute suffering in her face, as though it were the flash of a light from within.

"Don't be sorry you came to me," she said as I reached out to take hold of her. She caught my hands and held them in her own, her clasp moist and warm. "Don't be sorry. I'm not. Only promise me you won't lose heart and leave me without explanation. Don't break away from me hurriedly. Don't give in to some skewed sense of honor. If you did, my sanity might actually break."

"You mean I mustn't leave you the way I left Aaron," I said thickly. "No, I promise you, my precious darling. I won't do it. It's already much too late for such a thing."

"Then, I love you," she announced in a whisper. "I love you as I always have. No, more than that, I think, because you bring this miracle with you. But what of the spirit that lives within?"

"What spirit?" I asked her.

But she'd already gone deep into her own thoughts. She drank another swallow directly from the bottle.

I couldn't bear the table between us. I stood slowly, lifting her hands until she stood beside me, and then I took her warmly into my arms. I kissed her lips, her old familiar perfume rising to my nostrils, and I kissed her forehead, and then I held her head tightly against my beating heart.

"You hear it?" I whispered. "What spirit could there be except my spirit? My body is changed, and no more."

I was overcome with desire for her, the desire to know her utterly through the blood. Her perfume maddened me. But there wasn't the slightest chance that I'd give in to my desire.

But I kissed her again. And it wasn't chaste.

For several long moments we remained locked together, and I think I covered her hair with small sacred kisses, her perfume crucifying me with memories. I wanted to endow her with protection against all things as sordid as myself.

She backed away from me, finally, as if she had to do it, and she was a little unsteady on her feet.

"Never in all those years did you ever touch me in this way," she said under her breath. "And I wanted you so badly. Do you remember? Do you remember that night in the jungle when I finally got my wish? Do you remember how drunk you were, and how splendid? Oh, it was over way too soon."

"I was a fool, but all such things are past remembering," I whispered. "Now, don't let's spoil what's happened. Come, I've gotten a hotel room for you, and I'll see that you're safely there for the night."

"Why on earth? Oak Haven is exactly where it's always been," she said dreamily. She shook her head to clear her vision. "I'm going home."

"No, you're not. You drank even more rum than I predicted. Look, you drank over half the bottle. And I know you'll drink the rest of the bottle as soon as you get in the car."

She laughed a small scornful laugh. "Still the consummate gentleman," she said. "And the Superior General. You can escort me to my old house here in town. You know perfectly well where it is."

"That neighborhood, even at this hour? Absolutely not. Besides, your friendly old caretaker there is an incompetent idiot. My precious darling, I'm taking you to the hotel."

"Foolish," she said as she half stumbled. "I don't need a caretaker. I'd rather go to my house. You're being a nuisance. You always were."

"You're a witch and a drunk," I said politely. "Here, we'll just cap this bottle." I did it. "And we'll put it in this canvas purse of yours and I'll walk with you to the hotel. Take my arm."

For a small second she looked playful and defiant, but then she made a languid shrug, smiling faintly, and gave up her purse to my insistence and wrapped her arm around mine.

3

WE HAD NO SOONER begun our walk than we gave in to rather frequent and fervent embraces. Merrick's old favorite Chanel perfume enchanted me, carrying me back years again; but the blood scent from her living veins was the strongest goad of all.

My desires were commingled in a torment. By the time we reached the Rue Decateur, scarcely a block and a half from the café, I knew we needed a taxi. And once inside of the car, I gave myself up to kissing Merrick all over her face and her throat, luxuriating in the fragrance of the blood inside her and the heat coming from her breasts.

She herself was rather past the point of return, and pressed me in confidential whispers as to whether or not I could still make love in the manner of an ordinary man. I told her it wouldn't do for me, that she had to remember, drunk or sober, that I was, by nature, a predator and nothing more.

"Nothing more?" she said, stopping this glorified love play to take another deep drink from her bottle of rum. "And what happened in the jungles of Guatemala? Answer me. You haven't forgotten. The tent, the village, you remember. Don't lie to me, David. I know what's inside you. I want to know what you've become."

"Hush, Merrick," I said, but I couldn't restrain myself. I let my teeth touch her flesh with each kiss. "What happened in the jungles of Guatemala," I struggled to say, "was a mortal sin."

I covered her mouth, kissing her and devouring her tongue but not letting my evil teeth harm her. I felt her wipe my brow with a soft cloth, possibly her scarf or a handkerchief, but I pushed it away.

"Don't do that," I told her. I feared that a few beads of blood sweat might have appeared. She went back to kissing me and whispering her words of Come Hither against my skin.

I was miserable. I wanted her. I knew that even the smallest drink of her blood would prove too risky for me utterly; I'd feel I possessed her after that, and she, in spite of all her seeming innocence on the matter, might well find herself my slave.

Elder vampires had warned me on just about every aspect of what could happen to me. And Armand and Lestat had both been adamant that the "little drink" must not be conceived of as harmless. I was furious suddenly.

I reached to the back of her head and ripped the leather barrette out of her thick brown hair, letting the barrette and its cross-pin fall carelessly, and I ran my fingers deep against her scalp and kissed her lips again. Her eyes were closed.

I was immensely relieved when we reached the spacious entrance of the Windsor Court Hotel. She took another drink of her rum before the doorman helped her out of the cab, and in the manner of most experienced drinkers seemed sober on her feet when in fact she was not sober at all.

Having obtained the suite for her earlier, I took her directly to it, unlocked the door, and set her down on the bed.

The suite was quite fine, perhaps the finest in town, with its tasteful traditional furnishings and muted lights. And I had ordered bountiful vases of flowers for her.

It was nothing, however, that a member of the Talamasca wouldn't expect. We were never known for economy with our traveling members. And all my many memories of her encircled me like vapor, and wouldn't let me loose.

She appeared to notice nothing. She drank the rest of the rum without ceremony and settled back against the pillows, her bright green eyes closing almost at once.

For a long time I merely looked at her. She appeared to have been tossed on the thick velvet counterpane and its nest of cushions, her white cotton clothes thin and friable, her long slender ankles and leather-sandaled feet rather Biblical, her face with its high cheekbones and soft jawline exquisite in sleep.

I could not be sorry that I had made this friendship. I could not. But I reiterated my vow: David Talbot, you will not harm this creature. Somehow Merrick will be better for all this; somehow knowledge will enhance Merrick; somehow Merrick's soul will triumph no matter how badly Louis and I fail.

Then, seeing further to the suite—that the flowers ordered had indeed been properly set out on the coffee table before the parlor sofa, on the desk, on her dressing table; that the bath held abundant cosmetics for her comfort; that a great thick terry cloth robe and slippers were in their proper place in the closet; and that a full bar of small bottles awaited her, along with a fifth of her rum which I had provided—I kissed her, left a set of keys on the night table, and went out.

A brief stop at the concierge's desk, with the requisite offering, assured she'd be undisturbed for as long as she wished to stay at the hotel and that she might have anything that she liked.

I then made up my mind to walk to our flat in the Rue Royale.

However, before I left the beautifully lighted and somewhat busy lobby of the hotel a faint dizziness surprised me and I was assaulted by the peculiar sensation that everyone in the place was taking notice of me, and that their notice was not kind.

I stopped immediately, fishing in my pocket as though I were a man about to step aside for a cigarette, and glanced about.

There was nothing unusual about the lobby or about the crowd. Nevertheless, as I went outside the sensation overcame me again—that those in the driveway were looking at me, that they had penetrated my mortal disguise, which was by no means easy, and that they knew what I was and what evil things I might be about.

Again, I checked. Nothing of the sort was happening. Indeed, the bell boys gave me rather cordial smiles when our eyes met.

On I went towards the Rue Royale.

Once more, the sensation occurred. In fact, it seemed to me that not only were people everywhere taking notice of me, but that they had come to the doors and windows of the shops and restaurants especially for the purpose; and the dizziness which I seldom, if ever, felt as a vampire increased.

I was most uncomfortable. I wondered if this was the result of intimacy with a mortal being, because I'd never felt so exposed before. In fact, due to my bronze skin I could move about the mortal world with total impunity. All my supernatural attributes were veiled by the dark complexion, and my eyes, though too bright, were black.

Nevertheless, it seemed people stared at me surreptitiously all along the route which I took towards home.

Finally, when I was about three blocks from the flat I shared with Louis and Lestat, I stopped and leant against a black iron lamppost, much as I had seen Lestat do in the old nights when he still moved about. Scanning the passersby I was reassured again.

But then something startled me so that I began to tremble violently in spite of myself. There stood Merrick in a shop door with her arms folded. She looked quite steadily and reprovingly at me, and then disappeared.

Of course it wasn't really Merrick at all, but the solidity of the apparition was horrifying.

A shadow moved behind me. I turned awkwardly. There again went Merrick, clothed in white, casting her long dark glance at me, and the figure appeared to melt into the shadows of a shop door.

I was dumbfounded. It was witchcraft obviously, but how could it assault the senses of a vampire? And I was not only a vampire, I was David Talbot who had been a Candomble priest in his youth. Now, as a vampire, I have seen ghosts and spirits and I knew the spirits and the tricks they could play, and I knew a great deal about Merrick, but never had I witnessed or experienced a spell just like this.

In a cab which crossed the Rue Royale, there was Merrick once again, looking up at me from the open window, her hair loosened as I had left it. And when I turned around, quite certain she was behind me, I saw her unmistakable figure on a balcony above.

The posture of the figure was sinister. I was trembling. I disliked this. I felt a fool.

I kept my eyes on the figure. In fact nothing could have moved me. The figure faded and was gone. All around me the Quarter suddenly seemed quite desolate, though in fact there were tourists everywhere in great numbers, and I could hear the music from the Rue Bourbon. Never had I seen so many flowerpots spilling their blooms over the iron lace railings. Never had so many pretty vines climbed the weathered facades and the old stuccoed walls.

Intrigued and slightly angry, I went into the Rue Ste. Anne to see the café in which we'd met, and as I suspected it was full to overflowing with diners and drinkers, and the wraith of a waiter seemed overwhelmed.

There sat Merrick in the very middle of it, full white skirt flaring, stiff, as though she'd been cut from cardboard; then of course the apparition melted, as the others had done.

But the point was the café was now crowded, as it should have been when we'd been there! How had she kept people away during our meeting? And what was she doing now?

I turned around. The sky above was blue, as the southern sky is so often in the evening, sprinkled with faint stars. There was gay conversation and happy laughter all about. This was the reality of things, a mellow spring night in New Orleans, when the flagstone sidewalks seem soft to the step of your foot, and the sounds sweet to your ears.

Yet there again came the sensation that everyone nearby was watching me. The couple crossing at the corner made a point of it. And then I saw Merrick quite some distance down the street, and this time the expression on her face was distinctly unpleasant, as though she were enjoying my discomfort.

I drew in my breath as the apparition melted away.

"How could she be doing this, that's the question!" I muttered aloud. "And why is she doing it?"

I walked fast, heading for the town house, not certain as to whether I would go into it, with this manner of curse all around me, but as I approached our carriageway—a large arched gate fitted into a frame of brickwork—I then saw the most frightening image of all.

Behind the bars of the gate stood the child Merrick of many years ago, in her same skimpy lavender shift, her head slightly to the side as she nodded to confidences whispered in her ear by an elderly woman whom I knew for a certainty to be her long-dead grandmother Great Nananne.

Great Nananne's thin mouth was smiling faintly and she nodded as she spoke.

At once the presence of Great Nananne deluged me with memories and remembered sensations. I was terrified, then angry. I was all but disoriented, and had to pull myself up.

"Don't you vanish, don't you go!" I cried out, darting towards the gate, but the figures melted as if my eyes had lost focus, as if my vision had been flawed.

I was past all patience. There were lights in our home above, and there came the enchanting sound of harpsichord music, Mozart, if I was not mistaken, no doubt from Lestat's small disc player beside his four-poster bed. This meant he had graced us with a visit this evening, though all he would do would be to lie on his bed and listen to recordings till shortly before dawn.

I wanted desperately to go up, to be in our home, to let the music soothe my nerves, to see Lestat and see to him, and to find Louis and tell him all that had occurred.

Nothing would do, however, except that I go back to the hotel at once. I could not enter our flat while under this "spell," and must stop it at the source.

I hurried to the Rue Decateur, found a cab, and vowed to look at nothing and no one until I had faced Merrick herself. I was becoming more and more cross.

Deep in my thoughts, I found myself mumbling protective charms, calling upon the spirits to protect me rather than to injure me, but I had little faith in these old formulae. What I did believe in were the powers of Merrick, which I'd long ago witnessed and would never forget.

Hurrying up the stairs to Merrick's suite, I put my key into the lock of her door.

As soon as I stepped into the parlor, I saw the flicker of candlelight and smelled another very pleasant smell which I had connected with Merrick in years past. It was the scent of Florida water, redolent of fresh cut oranges—a scent loved by the Voodoo goddess Ezili, and by the Candomble goddess of a similar name.

As for the candle, I saw it atop a handsome bombe chest just opposite the door.

It was a votive light, sunk deep and safe inside a water glass, and behind it, looking down upon it, was a fine plaster statue of St. Peter with his golden keys to Heaven, a figure about a foot and a half in height. The complexion of the statue was dark, and it had pale amber glass eyes.

It was clothed in a soft green tunic etched with gold, and a cloak of purple on which the gold was fancier still. He held not only the proverbial keys to the Kingdom of Heaven, but also, in the right hand, a large book.

I was shocked all over. The hair came up on the back of my neck.

Of course I knew it was not only St. Peter, this statue, it was Papa Legba in Voodoo, the god of the crossroads, the god who must unlock the spiritual realms if you are to obtain anything with your magic.

Before you begin a spell, a prayer, or a sacrifice you honor Papa Legba first. And whoever had made this statue realized these things.

How else explain the deliberately darkened complexion of the saint who appeared now to be a man of color, or the mysterious book?

He had his complement in Candomble, whom I had so often saluted. This was the orisha, or god, by the name of Exu. And any Candomble temple would have begun its ceremonies by first saluting him.

As I stared at the statue and the candle, the very scents of those Brazilian temples with their hard-packed dirt floors came back to me. I heard the drums. I smelled the cooked foods laid out in offerings. Indeed, I let the sensations come.

There came back other memories, memories of Merrick, as well.

"Papa Legba," I whispered aloud. I'm certain that I bowed my head ever so slightly and felt a rush of blood to my face. "Exu," I whispered. "Don't be offended by anything that I do here."

I uttered a small prayer, more formulaic in the Portuguese that I had long ago learnt, asking that whatever realm he had just opened, he not deny me entrance, as my respect was as strong as that of Merrick.

The statue of course remained motionless, its pale glass eyes staring quite directly into mine, but I had seldom beheld something which seemed so animate in a sly and unexplainable way.

"I'm going slightly mad," I thought. But then I had come to Merrick to work magic, had I not? And I knew Merrick, didn't I? But then, I had never expected these tricks!

I beheld in my mind the temple in Brazil once more, where I had trained for months learning the proper leaves for offering, learning the myths of the gods, learning finally, after months and months of struggle, to dance clockwise with the others, saluting each deity with our gestures and dance steps, until a frenzy was reached, until I myself felt the deity enter into me, possess me . . . and then there was the waking after, remembering nothing, being told I had been mightily possessed, the sublime exhaustion.

Of course . . . What had I thought we were doing here if not inviting those old powers? And Merrick knew my old strengths and weaknesses if anybody did. I could scarcely tear my gaze off the face of the statue of St. Peter. But I finally managed it.

I backed away as anyone might do when leaving a shrine, and darted silently into the bedroom.

Again, I breathed in the bright citrus fragrance of the Florida water, and also the scent of rum.

Where was her favorite perfume, the Chanel No. 22? Had she ceased to wear it? The Florida water was very strong.

Merrick lay asleep on the bed.

She looked as if she'd never moved. It struck me now and only now how much her white blouse and skirt resembled the classic dress of the Candomble women. All she needed was a turban for her head to make the image complete.

The new bottle of rum was open on the table beside her, and about a third of it consumed. Nothing else had changed that I could ascertain. The scent was powerful, which meant she might have sprayed it through her teeth into the air, an offering to the god.

In sleep she looked perfect, as people often do when they relax utterly; she seemed the girl of herself. And it struck me that were she to be made a vampire, she would have this flawless countenance.

I was filled with fear and abhorrence. I was filled also—for the first time in these many years—with the full realization that I, and I without the help of anyone else, could grant this magic, the transformation into a vampire, to her, or to any human. For the first time, I understood its monstrous temptation.

Of course nothing of this sort would befall Merrick. Merrick was my child. Merrick was my . . . daughter.

"Merrick, wake up!" I said sharply. I touched her shoulder. "You're going to explain these visions to me. Wake up!"

No response. She appeared to be dead drunk.

"Merrick, wake up!" I said again, very crossly. And this time I lifted her shoulders with both hands, but her head tumbled back. The scent of the Chanel perfume rose from her. Ah, that was precisely what I so loved.

I became painfully conscious of her breasts, quite visible in the scoop neck of her cotton blouse. Down into the pillows I let her fall.

"Why did you do these things?" I demanded of the inert body of the beautiful woman lying on the bed. "What did you mean with all this? Do you think I'm to be frightened away?"

But it was useless. She wasn't pretending. She was out cold. I could divine no dreams or subterranean thoughts in her. And quickly examining the little hotel wet bar, I saw that she'd drunk a couple of little bottles of gin.

"Typical Merrick," I said with faint anger.

It had always been her way to drink to excess at specific times. She'd work very hard at her studies or in the field for months on end, and then announce that she was "going to the Moon," as she called it, at which time she would lay in liquor and drink for several nights and days. Her favorite drinks were those with sweetness and flavor— sugercane rum, apricot brandy, Grand Marnier, ad infinitum.

She was introspective when drunk, did a lot of singing and writing and dancing about during such periods, and demanded to be left alone. If no one crossed her, she was all right. But an argument could produce hysterics, nausea, disorientation, an attempt to regain sobriety desperately, and finally, guilt. But this rarely happened. Usually, she just drank for a week, unmolested. Then she'd wake one morning, order breakfast with strong coffee, and within a matter of hours return to work, not to repeat her little vacation for perhaps another six to nine months.

But even on social occasions if she drank, she drank to get drunk. She'd swill her rum or sweet liquor in fancy mixed drinks. She had no desire for drink in moderation. If we had a great dinner at the Motherhouse, and we did have many, she either abstained or continued drinking on her own until she passed out. Wine made her impatient.

Well, she was passed out now. And even if I did succeed in waking her, there might be a pitched battle.

I went again to look at St. Peter, or Papa Legba, in the makeshift Voodoo shrine. I had to eliminate my fear of this little entity or graven image or whatever I perceived to be there.

Ah, I was stunned as I considered the statue for a second time. My pocket handkerchief was spread out beneath the statue and the candle, and beside it lay my own old-fashioned fountain pen! I hadn't even seen them before.

"Merrick!" I swore furiously.

And hadn't she wiped my forehead in the car? I glared at the handkerchief. Sure enough there were tiny smears of blood—the sweat from my forehead! And she had it for her spell.

"Ah, not merely satisfied with an article of my clothing, my handkerchief, but you had to take the fluids from my skin."

Marching back into the bedroom, I made another very ungentlemanly attempt to rouse her from her torpor, ready for a brawl, but it was no good. I laid her back down tenderly, brushing her hair with my fingers, and observed, in spite of my anger, how truly pretty she was.

Her creamy tan skin was beautifully molded over her cheekbones and her eyelashes were so long that they made distinct tiny shadows on her face. Her lips were dark, without rouge. I took off her plain leather sandals and laid them beside the bed, but this was just another excuse to touch her, not something generous.

Then, backing away from the bed, with a glance through the door to the shrine in the parlor, I looked about for her purse, her large canvas bag.

It had been flung on a chair and it gaped open, revealing, as I had hoped, a bulging envelope with Aaron's unmistakable writing on the outside.

Well, she'd stolen my handkerchief and my pen, hadn't she? She'd retrieved my blood, my very blood, which must never fall into the hands of the Talamasca, hadn't she? Oh, it wasn't for the Order, no. She stole it for herself and her charms, but she stole it, didn't she? And I'd been kissing her all the while like a schoolboy.

So I had every right to inspect this envelope in her purse. Besides, she had asked me if I wanted these papers. So I would take them. It was her intention to give them to me, was it not?

At once I snatched up the envelope, opened it, confirmed that it was all Aaron's papers concerning me and my adventures, and resolved to take it with me. As for the rest of the contents of Merrick's bag, it contained her own journal, which I had no right to read, and which would most likely be written in impossible French code, a handgun with a pearl handle, a wallet full of money, an expensive cigar labeled Montecristo, and a thin small bottle of the Florida water cologne.

The cigar gave me pause. Certainly it was not for her. It was for that little Papa Legba, that cigar. She had brought with her the statue, the Florida water, and the cigar. She had come prepared for some sort of conjuring. Ah, it infuriated me, but what right had I to preach against it?

I went back into the parlor, and, avoiding the eyes of the statue and its seeming expression, snatched up my fountain pen from the makeshift altar. I located the hotel stationery in the middle drawer of a fancy French desk, sat down, and wrote a note:

All right, my dear, I'm impressed. You've learnt even more tricks since last we met. But you must explain the reasons for this spell. I've taken the pages written by Aaron. I've retrieved my handkerchief and fountain pen as well. Stay in the hotel as long as you like.

David.

It was short, but I did not feel particularly effusive after this little misadventure. Also, I had the unpleasant sensation that Papa Legba was glaring at me from the violated shrine. In a fit of pique, I added a postscript.

"It was Aaron who gave me this pen!" Enough said.

Now, with considerable apprehension, I went back to the altar.

I spoke rapidly in Portuguese first, and then in Latin, once again greeting the spirit in the statue, the opener of the spiritual realm. Open my understanding, I prayed, and take no offense at what I do, for I want only knowledge, and mean no disrespect. Be assured of my understanding of your power. Be assured that I am a sincere soul.

I dug deep into my memory now for sensation as well as fact. I told the spirit in the statue that I was dedicated to the orisha, or god, called Oxalá, lord of creation. I explained that I had been faithful in my own way always to that deity, though I had not done all the little things that others had prescribed to be done. Nevertheless, I loved this god, I loved his stories, and his personality, I loved all I could know of him.

A bad feeling crept over me. How could a blood drinker be faithful to the lord of creation? Was not every act of blood drinking a sin against Oxalá? I pondered this. But I didn't retreat. My emotions belonged to Oxalá, just as they had many many decades ago in Rio de Janeiro. Oxalá was mine, and I was his.

"Protect us in what we mean to do," I whispered.

Then, before I could lose heart, I snuffed out the candle, lifted the statue, and, retrieving the handkerchief, set the statue back with care. I said, "Goodbye Papa Legba" to the statue and prepared to leave the suite.

I found myself quite motionless, my back to the altar, facing the door to the corridor outside. I couldn't move. Or rather it seemed I shouldn't move.

Very slowly, my mind became rather empty. Focused upon my physical senses, if anything, I turned and looked towards the bedroom doorway through which I'd only just come.

It was the old woman, of course, the wizened little Great Nananne, with her fingers on the doorjamb, staring at me, and her thin lipless mouth working as if she were whispering to herself or to someone unseen, her head tilted just a little to one side.

I sucked in my breath and stared at her. She showed no signs of weakening, this wee apparition, this tiny old woman who regarded me rather directly in spite of moving lips. She was clothed in a faintly flowered nightgown of flannel that was stained all over with coffee, perhaps, or long-faded blood. Indeed, I became intensely conscious that her image was becoming all the more solid and detailed.

Her feet were bare and her toenails the color of yellowed bone. Her gray hair was now quite visible and distinct, as if a light were being brightened upon her, and I saw the veins moving up the sides of her head, and the veins on the back of the one hand which dangled at her side. Only very old people looked as she looked. And of course this woman looked exactly as she had when I'd seen her ghost in the carriageway earlier this evening, and exactly as she had on the day of her death. Indeed, I remembered the nightgown. I remembered the stains upon it. I remembered that on her dying body it had been stained but fresh and clean.

I broke into a true sweat as I stared at her, and I could not move a muscle, except to speak.

"You think I'll harm her?" I whispered.

The figure did not change. The little mouth continued to work, but I could hear only a faint dry rustling noise, as from an old woman telling her rosary in church.

"You think I mean to do something wrong?" I said.

The figure was gone. It was gone past tense. I was talking to no one.

I turned on my heel and glared at the statue of the saint. It seemed to be material and nothing more. I seriously considered smashing it, but my mind was full of confusion as to my intentions and their implications, when quite suddenly there came a deafening knock on the hallway door.

Well, it seemed to be deafening. I suspect it was ordinary. I was violently startled. Regardless I opened the door and said crossly:

"What in hell do you want?"

To my astonishment and his astonishment also, I was addressing one of the ordinary and innocent attendants who worked in the hotel.

"Nothing, Sir, excuse me," he said in his slow southern manner, "just this for the lady." He lifted a small plain white envelope and I took it out of his hand.

"Oh, wait, please," I said, as I fumbled to retrieve a ten-dollar bill from my pocket. I had put several in my suit just for this purpose and gave one over to him, with which he seemed pleased.

I shut the door. The envelope contained the two-piece leather hair barrette which I had taken off Merrick so carelessly in the cab. There was an oval of leather, and then a long pin covered with leather with which she gathered and fixed her hair in place.

I was trembling all over. This was too dreadful.

How in the hell had this come to be here? It seemed quite impossible that the cabby had retrieved it. But then how was I to know? At the time, I'd been aware that I ought to pick it up and pocket it, but I'd fancied myself to be under duress.

I went to the altar, laid the barrette in front of Papa Legba, avoiding his eyes as I did so, and I went straight out of the suite, down the stairs and out of the lobby, and out of the hotel.

This time, I vowed to observe nothing, to look for nothing, and I went directly to our home.

If there were spirits along the way, I did not see them, keeping my eyes on the ground, moving as swiftly as I could safely move without causing a stir among mortals, and going directly through the carriage-way, back to the courtyard, and then up the iron steps into the flat.

4

THE FLAT WAS DARK, which I hadn't expected, and I did not find Louis in either the front parlor or the back, or in his room. As for Lestat, the door of his room was closed, and the harpsichord music, very rapid and very beautiful, seemed to emanate from the very walls, as is so often the case with modern compact disc recordings.

I lighted all the lamps in the front parlor and settled on the couch, with Aaron's pages in hand. I told myself I had important business.

It was no good thinking about Merrick and her charms and her spirits, and no good at all dwelling upon the old woman with her unintelligible whispers and her small wrinkled face.

As for my thoughts on my orisha, Oxalá, they were grim. The long ago years I had spent in Rio were ones of severe dedication. I had believed in Candomble insofar as I, David Talbot, could believe in anything. I had given myself over to the religion insofar as I could be abandoned to anything. And I had become Oxalá's follower and worshiper. I had been possessed by him many a time with little or no memory of the trance, and I had scrupulously followed his rules.

But all that had been a detour in my life, an intermezzo. I was, after all, a British scholar, before and after. And once I had entered the Talamasca, the power of Oxalá or any orisha over me had been broken forever. Nevertheless, I felt confusion and guilt now. I had come to Merrick to discuss magic, imagining that I could control what happened! And the very first night had been chastening, indeed.

However, I had to get my mind clear. Indeed, I owed it to Aaron, my old friend, to pull myself together at once and look at his papers. Everything else could wait, I told myself.

However, I couldn't get the old woman out of my head. I longed for Louis to come. I wanted to discuss these matters. It was important that Louis understand things about Merrick, but where Louis might be at this hour, I had no idea.

The harpsichord music was something of a comfort, as Mozart always is, with his merriment, no matter what the composition, but nevertheless, I felt restless and unsafe in these warm rooms where I was accustomed to spend many hours in comfort alone or with Louis or Louis and Lestat.

I determined to shrug it off.

Indeed, it was absolutely the best time to read Aaron's pages.

I took off my jacket, seated myself at the large writing desk which faced into the room quite conveniently (as none of us liked to work with our back to the room), and opened the envelope and drew out the pages that I meant to read.

There wasn't very much at all, and a quick perusal indicated that Merrick had given me a complete picture of Aaron's thoughts at the end. Nevertheless, I owed it to Aaron to read these writings, word by word.

It took me only a few moments to forget everything about me, as I found myself hearing Aaron's familiar voice in English in spite of the fact that all he'd written was in Latin. It was as if he were there, reviewing it all with me, or reading me his report so that I might comment before he sent it on to the Elders.

Aaron described how he had come to meet me in Florida, where he had found the aged body of his friend David Talbot dead and in need of proper burial, while the soul of David was firmly ensconced in the body of an anonymous young man.

The young man was Anglo-Indian in background, six feet four in height, had wavy dark-brown hair, bronze skin, and extremely large sympathetic dark-brown eyes. The young man was in excellent health and physical condition. The young man had very acute hearing and a good sense of balance. The young man seemed devoid of any spirit whatsoever save that of David Talbot.

Aaron went on to describe our days together in Miami, during which time I had frequently projected my spirit out of the host body, only to recapture the body perfectly with no unseen resistance from any known or unknown realm.

Finally, after a month or so of such experiments, I'd been convinced that I could remain in the youthful body and I had set about gathering what information I could about the soul which had previously reigned within it.

Those particulars I will not relate here insofar as they have to do with persons in no way connected with this narrative. It is sufficient to say that Aaron and I were satisfied that the soul which had once governed my new body was gone beyond reprieve. Hospital records pertaining to the last months of that soul's life on earth made it more than clear that "the mind" of the individual had been destroyed by psychological disasters and the bizarre chemistry of certain drugs which the man had ingested, though there had been no damage to the cells of the brain.

I, David Talbot, in full possession of the body, sensed no damage to the brain.

Aaron had been very full in his descriptions of things, explaining how clumsy I'd been with my new height for the first few days, and how he had watched this "strange body" gradually "become" his old friend David, as I took to sitting in chairs with my legs crossed, or to folding my arms across my chest, or to hunching over my writing or reading materials in familiar fashion.

Aaron remarked that the improved vision of the new eyes had been a great blessing to David Talbot, as David had suffered poor vision in his last years. Ah, that was so true, and I hadn't even thought of it. And now of course, I saw as a vampire and could not even remember those key gradations of mortal vision in my brief Faustian youth.

Aaron then laid down his feelings that the full report on this incident must not be placed in the Files of the Talamasca, which were open to all.

"It is plain to see from David's transformation," he wrote in so many words, "that body switching is entirely possible when one is dealing with skilled individuals, and what arouses my horror is not David's present occupation of this splendid young body, but the manner in which the body was stolen from its original owner by that one whom we shall call the Body Thief, for sinister purposes of the thief's own."

Aaron went on to explain that he would endeavor to put these pages directly into the hands of the Elders of the Talamasca.

But for tragic reasons, obviously, this had never been done.

There came a final series of paragraphs comprising about three pages, handwritten a little more formally than what had gone before.

David's Disappearance was written at the top. Lestat was referred to merely as TVL. And this time, Aaron's phrasing reflected considerably more caution and some sadness.

He described how I had vanished on the island of Barbados, without leaving any message for anyone, abandoning my suitcases, typewriter, books, and pages, which he, Aaron, had gone to retrieve.

How dreadful that must have been for Aaron, picking up the trash of my life, with no word of apology from me.

"Were I not so busy with the matters of the Mayfair Witches," he wrote, "perhaps this disappearance would never have occurred. I might have been more attentive to D. during his time of transition. I might have held him more firmly in my affections and thereby earned more surely his complete trust. As it is, I can only surmise what has become of him, and I fear that he has met with spiritual catastrophe quite against his will.

"Undoubtedly he will contact me. I know him too well to think otherwise. He will come to me. He will—whatever his state of mind, and I cannot possibly imagine it—come to me to give me some solace, if nothing else."

It hurt me so deeply to read this that I stopped and put the pages aside. For a moment, I was aware only of my own failing, my own terrible failing, my own cruel failing.

But there were two more pages, and I had to read them. Finally I picked them up and read Aaron's last notes.

I wish that I could appeal to the Elders directly for help. I wish that after my many years in the Talamasca I had complete faith in our Order, and complete faith that the authority of the Elders is for the best. However, our Order, insofar as I know, is made up of fallible mortal men and women. And I cannot appeal to anyone without placing in his or her hands knowledge which I do not want to share.

The Talamasca in recent months has had its internal troubles aplenty. And until the whole question of the identity of the Elders, and the certainty of communication with them, has been resolved, this report must remain in my hands.

Meanwhile nothing can shake my faith in D., or my belief in his basic goodness. Whatever corruption we might have suffered in the Talamasca never tainted David's ethics, or those of many like him, and though I cannot yet confide in them, I do take comfort from the fact that David may appear to them if not to me.

Indeed, my faith in David is so great that sometimes my mind plays tricks on me, and I think I see him though I soon realize I am wrong. I search crowds for him in the evening. I have gone back to Miami to look for him. I have sent out my call to him telepathically. And I have no doubt that one night very soon, David will respond, if only to say farewell.

The pain I felt was crushing. Moments passed in which I did nothing but allow myself to feel the immensity of the injustice done to Aaron.

At last, I forced myself to move my limbs.

I folded up the pages properly, put them back into the envelope, and sat quiet again for a long time, my elbows on the desk, my head bowed.

The harpsichord music had stopped some time ago, and much as I'd loved it, it did interfere with my thoughts somewhat, so I treasured the quiet.

I was as bitterly sad as I have ever been. I was as without hope as I have ever been. The mortality of Aaron seemed as real to me as his life had ever seemed. And indeed both seemed miraculous in the extreme.

As for the Talamasca, I knew it would heal its wounds by itself. I had no real fear for it, though Aaron had been right to be suspicious of things with the Elders until questions of their identity and authority had been resolved.

When I had left the Order, the question of the identity of the Elders had been hotly debated. And incidents pertaining to secrets had caused corruption and betrayal. Aaron's murder had become part of it. The famous Body Thief who seduced Lestat had been one of our own.

Who were the Elders? Were they themselves corrupt? I hardly thought so. The Talamasca was ancient, and authoritarian, and it moved slowly on eternal matters, rather on a Vatican clock. But it was all quite closed to me now. Human beings had to go on cleansing and reforming the Talamasca, as they had already begun to do. I could do nothing to help in such an endeavor.

But to the best of my knowledge, internal difficulties had been solved. How precisely, and by whom, I did not know and really didn't want to know.

I knew only that those I loved, including Merrick, seemed at peace within the Order, though it did seem to me that Merrick, and those upon whom I'd spied now and then in other places, had a more "realistic" view of the Order and its problems than I had ever had.

And of course, what I'd done in speaking to Merrick, that had to remain secret between Merrick and me.

But how was I to have a secret with a witch who'd cast a spell on me with such promptness, effectiveness, and abandon? It made me cross again to think of it. I wish I'd taken the statue of St. Peter with me. That would have served her right.

But what had been Merrick's purpose in the whole affair—to warn me of her power, to impress upon me the realization that Louis and I, as earthbound creatures, were hardly immune to her, or that our plan was indeed a dangerous plan?

I felt sleepy suddenly. As I've already mentioned, I'd fed before I ever met with Merrick, and I had no need of blood. But I had a great desire for it, kindled by the physical touch of Merrick, and very much caught up with wordless fantasies of her, and now I felt drowsy from the struggle, drowsy from my grief for Aaron, who had gone to the grave with no words of comfort at all from me.

I was about to lie down on the couch, when I heard a very pleasant sound which I at once recognized, though I hadn't heard it at close range for years. It was the sound of a canary, singing, and making a little bit of a metallic ruckus in a cage. I heard the motion of the wings, the creak of the little trapeze or swing or whatever you call it, the creak of the cage on its hinge.

And there came the harpsichord music again, very rapid, indeed far more rapid than any human could possibly desire. It was rippling and mad, and full of magic, this music, as though a preternatural being had set upon the keys.

I realized at once that Lestat was not in the flat, and had never been, and these sounds—this music and the gentle commotion of the birds—were not coming from his closed room.

Nevertheless, I had to make a check.

Lestat, being as powerful as he is, can mask his presence almost completely, and I, being his fledgling, can pick up nothing from his mind.

I rose to my feet, heavily, sleepily, amazed at my exhaustion, and made my way down the passage to his room. I knocked respectfully, waited a decent interval, and then opened his door.

All was as it should be. There stood the giant plantation-style four-poster of tropical mahogany with its dusty canopy of rose garlands and the drapery of dark-red velvet, the color which Lestat prefers above all else. Dust overlay the bedside table and the nearby desk and the books in the bookshelf. And there was no machine for making music in sight.

I turned, meaning to go back to the parlor, to write down all of this in my diary, if I could find it, but I felt so heavy and so drowsy and it seemed a better idea to sleep. Then there was the matter of the music and the birds. Something about the birds struck me. What was it? Something Jesse Reeves had written in her report of being haunted decades ago in the ruin of this very house. Little birds.

"Then it's begun?" I whispered. I felt so weak, so deliciously weak, actually. I wondered if Lestat would mind so very terribly if I were to lie down for a little while on his bed? He might yet come this evening. We never knew, did we? It wasn't very proper to do such a thing. And drowsy as I was, I was moving my right hand rapidly with the music. I knew this sonata by Mozart, it was lovely, it was the first one that the boy genius had ever written, and how excellent it was. No wonder the birds were so happy, it must have been a kindred sound to them, but it was important that this music not speed on so precipitously, no matter how clever the performer, no matter how clever the child.

I made my way out of the room as if I were moving through water, and went in search of my own room where I had my own bed, quite comfortable, and then it seemed imperative that I seek my coffin, my hiding place, because I could not remain conscious until dawn.

"Ah, yes, it's vital that I go," I said aloud, but I couldn't hear my words on account of the thunder of the tripping music, and I realized, with great distress, that I had entered the back parlor of the flat, the one which looked out upon the courtyard, and I had settled there on the couch.

Louis was with me. Louis was helping me to a seat on the couch, as a matter of fact. Louis was asking me what was wrong.

I looked up, and it seemed to me that he was a vision of male perfection, dressed in a snow white silk shirt and a finely cut black velvet jacket, his curly black hair very properly and beautifully combed back over his ears and curling above his collar in the most lively and fetching style. I loved looking at him, rather as I loved looking at Merrick.

It struck me how different were his green eyes from hers. His eyes were darker. There was no distinct circle of blackness around the irises and, indeed, the pupils did not stand out so clearly. Nevertheless, they were beautiful eyes.

The flat went absolutely quiet.

For a moment I could say or do nothing.

Then I looked at him as he seated himself in a rose-colored velvet chair near to me, and his eyes were filled with the light from the nearby electric lamp. Whereas Merrick had something of a mild challenge in even her most casual expression, his eyes were patient, restful, like the eyes in a painting, fixed and reliable.

"Did you hear it?" I asked.

"What, precisely?" he asked.

"Oh, my God, it's started," I said softly. "You remember. Think back, man. You remember, what Jesse Reeves told you. Think."

Then it came out of me in a bit of a gush—the harpsichord music and the sound of the birds. Decades ago it had come upon Jesse, on the night she'd found Claudia's diary in a secret place in a broken wall. It had come upon her with a vision of oil lamps and moving figures. And in terror she had fled the flat, taking with her a doll, a rosary, and the diary, and never coming back.

The ghost of Claudia had pursued her to a darkened hotel room. And from there Jesse had been taken ill, sedated, hospitalized, and finally taken home to England, never to return to this place, insofar as I knew.

Jesse Reeves had become a vampire due to her destiny, not through the mistakes or failings of the Talamasca. And Jesse Reeves herself had told Louis this tale.

It was all quite familiar to both of us, but I had no recollection of Jesse ever identifying the piece of music which she'd heard in the shadows.

It was up to Louis to state now in a soft voice that, yes, his beloved Claudia had loved the early sonatas of Mozart, that she had loved them because he composed them while he'd still been a child.

Suddenly an uncontrollable emotion seized Louis and he stood up and turned his back to me, looking out, apparently, through the lace curtains, to whatever sky lay beyond the rooftops and the tall banana trees that grew against the courtyard walls.

I watched him in polite silence. I could feel my energy returning. I could feel the usual preternatural strength upon which I'd always counted since the first night that I'd been filled with the blood.

"Oh, I know it must be tantalizing," I said, finally. "It's so easy to conclude that we're coming close."

"No," he said, turning to me politely. "Don't you see, David? You heard the music. I haven't heard it. Jesse heard the music. I've never heard it. Never. And I've been years waiting to hear it, asking to hear it, wanting to hear it, but I never do."

His French accent was sharp and precise, as always happened when he was emotional, and I loved the richness it gave to his speech. I think we are wise, we English speakers, to savor accents. They teach us things about our own tongue.

I rather loved him, loved his lean graceful movements, and the way in which he responded wholeheartedly to things, or not at all. He had been gracious to me since the first moment we met, sharing this, his house, with me, and his loyalty to Lestat was without a doubt.

"If it's any consolation to you," I hastened to add, "I've seen Merrick Mayfair. I've put the request to her, and I don't think she means to turn us down."

His surprise amazed me. I forget how completely human he is, being the very weakest of us, and that he cannot read minds at all. I had assumed also that he'd been watching me of late, keeping his distance, but spying as only a vampire or an angel can, to see when this meeting would take place.

He came back around and sat down again.

"You must tell me about the whole thing," he said. His face flushed for an instant. It lost the preternatural whiteness and he seemed a young man of twenty-four—with sharply defined and beautiful features, and gaunt well-modeled cheeks. He might have been made by God to be painted by Andrea del Sarto, so deliberately perfect did he seem.

"David, please let me know everything," he pressed, due to my silence.

"Oh, yes, I mean to. But let me have a few moments more.

Something is going on, you see, and I don't know if it's her general wickedness."

"Wickedness?" he asked in utter innocence.

"I don't mean it so seriously. You see, she's such a strong woman and so strange in her ways. Let me tell you everything, yes."

But before I began I took stock of him once more, and made myself note that no one among us, that is, no one of the vampires or immortal blood drinkers whom I had encountered, was anything like him.

In the years since I'd been with him, we'd witnessed wonders together. We had seen the very ancient of the species and been thoroughly humbled by these visitations, which had made a weary mockery of Louis's long nineteenth-century quest for answers which did not exist.

During our recent convocations, many of the old ones had offered Louis the power of their ancient blood. Indeed, the very ancient Maharet, who was now perceived to be the twin of the absolute Mother of us all, had pressed Louis in the extreme to drink from her veins. I had watched this with considerable apprehension. Maharet seemed offended by one so weak.

Louis had refused her offer. Louis had turned her away. I shall never forget the conversation.

"I don't treasure my weaknesses," he'd explained to her. "Your blood conveys power, I don't question that. Only a fool would. But I know from what I've learnt from all of you that the ability to die is key. If I drink your blood I'll become too strong for a simple act of suicide just as you are now. And I cannot allow that. Let me remain the human one among you. Let me acquire my strength slowly, as you once did, from time and from human blood. I wouldn't become what Lestat has become through his drinking from the ancients. I would not be that strong and that distant from an easy demise."

I had been amazed at Maharet's obvious displeasure. Nothing about Maharet is simple precisely because everything is. By that I mean that she is so ancient as to be divorced utterly from the common expression of tender emotions, except perhaps by deliberate merciful design.

She had lost all interest in Louis when he'd refused her, and to the best of my knowledge she never looked at him, or mentioned him, ever again. Of course she didn't harm him, and she had plenty of opportunity. But he was no longer a living being for her, no longer one of *us*, for her. Or so I had divined.

But then who was I to judge such a creature as Maharet? That I had seen her, that I'd heard her voice, that I'd visited with her for a time in her own sanctuary—all that was reason for thanks.

I myself had felt a great respect for Louis's disinclination to drink the absolute elixir of the dark gods. Louis had been made a vampire by Lestat when Lestat had been very young, indeed. And Louis was considerably stronger than humans, well able to spell-bind them, and could outmaneuver the most clever mortal opponent with ease. Though he was still bound by the laws of gravity to a far greater extent than I was, he could move about the world very rapidly, attaining a brand of invisibility which he very much enjoyed. He was no mind reader, and no spy.

However, Louis would very likely die if exposed to sunlight, though he was well past the point where sunlight would reduce him to pure ash, as it had done Claudia only seventy years or so after her birth. Louis still had to have blood every night. Louis could very probably seek oblivion in the flames of a pyre.

I shuddered now, as I reminded myself of this creature's deliberate limitations, and of the wisdom he seemed to possess.

My own blood was quite remarkably strong because it came from Lestat who had drunk not only from the elder Marius, but from the Queen of the Damned, the progenital vampire herself. I didn't know precisely what I might have to do to terminate my existence, but I knew it would not be an easy thing. As for Lestat, when I thought of his adventures and his powers, it seemed impossible by any means for him to exit this world.

These thoughts so disturbed me that I reached out and clasped Louis's hand.

"This woman is very powerful," I said, as I made to begin. "She's been playing a few tricks on me this evening, and I'm not sure why or how."

"It has you exhausted," he said considerately. "Are you sure you don't want to rest?"

"No, I need to talk to you," I said. And so I began by describing our meeting in the café, and all that had passed between us, including my memories of the child Merrick from years ago.

5

INDEED I TOLD HIM everything which I have told you so far.

I described even my scant memories of my first meeting with the girl Merrick, and my repressed fear when I was quite certain that the ancestors in the daguerreotypes had been passing approval on Aaron and me.

He was very startled when I laid down this part of the story, but wouldn't have me pause just yet but encouraged me to go on.

I told him briefly of how the meeting had triggered other, more erotic memories of Merrick, but that Merrick had not refused his request.

Merrick had seen him, I explained to him, and she knew who he was and what he was long before any intelligence on the vampires had been given to her by the Talamasca. In fact, to the best of my knowledge *no* information on the vampires had *ever* been given to Merrick.

"I remember more than one encounter with her," he said. "I should have told you, but by now you must know my manner."

"How do you mean?"

"I tell only what's necessary," he said with a little sigh. "I want to believe in what I say, but it's hard. Well, in truth I did have an encounter with Merrick. That's true. And yes, she did fling a curse at me. It was more than sufficient for me to turn away from her. However, I wasn't afraid. I'd misunderstood something about her altogether. If I could read minds as you can read them, the misunderstanding would never have occurred."

"But you must explain this to me," I said.

"It was in a back street, rather dangerous," he said. "I thought she wanted to die. She was walking alone in utter darkness, and when she heard my deliberate footfall behind her, she didn't even bother to glance over her shoulder or speed her pace. It was very reckless behavior and unusual for any woman of any sort at all. I thought she was weary of life."

"I understand you."

"But then, when I drew close to her," he said, "her eyes flashed on me violently, and she sent out a warning that I heard as distinctly as a spoken voice: 'Touch me and I'll shatter you.' That's about the best translation of it from the French that I can make. She uttered other curses, names, I'm not sure what they meant. I didn't withdraw from her in fear. I simply didn't challenge her. I had been drawn to her in my thirst because I thought she wanted death."

"I see," I said. "It checks with what she told me. Other times, I believe she's seen you from afar."

He pondered this for a moment. "There was an old woman, a very powerful old woman."

"Then you knew of her."

"David, when I came to you to ask you to speak with Merrick, I knew something of her, yes. But that was a while ago that the old woman was alive, and the old woman did sometimes see me, most definitely, and the old woman knew what I was." He paused for a moment, then resumed. "Way back before the turn of the last century, there were Voodooiennes about who always knew us. But we were quite safe because no one believed what they said."

"Of course," I responded.

"But you see, I never much believed in those women. When I encountered Merrick, well, I sensed something immensely powerful and alien to my understanding. Now, please, do go on. Tell me what happened tonight."

I recounted how I'd taken Merrick back to the Windsor Court Hotel, and how the spell had then descended upon me with numerous apparitions, the most unwholesome and frightening of which was most definitely that of the dead grandmother, Great Nananne.

"If you could have seen the two figures speaking to one another in the carriageway, if you could have seen their absorbed and somewhat secretive manner, and the casual fearless way in which they regarded me, it would have given you chills."

"No doubt of it," he said. "And you do mean you actually saw them, as though they were truly there. It wasn't simply an idea."

"No, my dear fellow, I saw them. They looked real. Of course they didn't look entirely like other people, you must understand. But they were there!"

I went on to explain my return to the hotel, the altar, Papa Legba, and then my coming home, and, once again, I described the music of the harpsichord and the singing of the caged birds.

Louis grew visibly sad at this, but again, he did not interrupt.

"As I told you before," I said, "I recognized the music. It was Mozart's first sonata. And the playing was unrealistic and full of—."

"Tell me."

"But you must have heard it. It was haunting. I mean a long, long time ago you must have heard such music, when it was first played here, for hauntings only repeat what occurred once upon a time."

"It was full of anger," he said softly, as though the very word "anger" made him hush his tone.

"Yes, that was it, anger. It was Claudia playing, was it not?"

He didn't respond. He seemed stricken by his memories and considerations. Then finally he spoke.

"But you don't know that Claudia made you hear these sounds," he said. "It might have been Merrick and her spell."

"You're right on that score, but you see, we don't know that Merrick caused all the other things, either. The altar, the candle, even my blood upon the handkerchief—these things don't prove that Merrick sent the spirits after me. We have to think about the ghost of Great Nananne."

"You mean this ghost might have interfered with us, entirely on her own?"

I nodded. "What if this ghost wants to protect Merrick? What if this ghost does not want her granddaughter to conjure the soul of a vampire? How can we know?"

He seemed on the edge of total despair. He remained poised and somewhat collected, but his face was badly stricken, and then he seemed to pull himself together, and he looked to me to speak, as if no words could express what he felt.

"Louis, listen to me. I have only a tenuous understanding of what I'm about to say, but it's most important."

"Yes, what is it?" He seemed at once animated and humble, sitting upright in the chair, urging me to go on.

"We're creatures of this earth, you and I. We are vampires. But we're material. Indeed, we are richly entangled with Homo sapiens in that we thrive on the blood of that species alone. Whatever spirit inhabits our bodies, governs our cells, enables us to live—whatever spirit that does all those things is mindless and might as well be nameless, insofar as we know. You do agree on these points. . . ."

"I do," he said, obviously eager for me to go on.

"What Merrick does is magic, Louis. It is from another realm."

He made no response.

"It's magic that we're asking her to do for us. Voodoo is magic, so is Candomble. So is the Holy Sacrifice of the Mass."

He was taken aback, but fascinated.

"God is magic," I continued, "and so are the saints. Angels are magic. And ghosts, if they be truly the apparitions of souls who once lived on earth, are magic as well."

He absorbed these words respectfully and remained silent.

"You understand," I continued, "I don't say that all these magical elements are equal. What I am saying is that what they have in common is that they are divorced from materiality, divorced from the earth, and from the flesh. Of course they interact with matter. They interact with the flesh. But they partake of the realm of pure spirituality where other laws—laws unlike our physical earthly laws—might exist."

"I see your meaning," he said. "You're warning me that this woman can do things that will baffle us as easily as they might baffle mortal men."

"Yes, that is my intent here, partly," I answered. "However, Merrick may do more than simply baffle us, you understand me. We must approach Merrick and what she will do with the utmost respect."

"I do understand you," he said. "But if human beings have souls that survive death, souls that can manifest as spirits to the living, then human beings have magical components as well."

"Yes, a magical component, and you and I still possess this magical component, along with some additional vampiric component, but when a soul truly leaves its physical body? Then it is in the realm of God."

"You believe in God," he murmured, quite amazed.

"Yes, I think so," I answered. "Indeed, I know so. What's the point of hiding it as if it were an unsophisticated or foolish frame of mind?"

"Then you do indeed have great respect for Merrick and her

magic," he said. "And you believe that Great Nananne, as you call her, might be a very powerful spirit indeed."

"Precisely," I said.

He settled back in the chair, and his eyes moved back and forth a little too rapidly. He was quite excited by all I'd told him, but his general disposition was one of profound sorrow, and nothing made him look happy or glad.

"Great Nananne might be dangerous, that's what you're saying," he murmured. "Great Nananne might want to protect Merrick from . . . you and me."

He looked rather splendid in his sorrow. Again he made me think of the paintings of Andrea del Sarto. There was something lush in his beauty, for all the sharp and clear well-drawn lines of his eyes and mouth.

"I don't expect my faith to make a particle of difference to you," I said. "But I want to emphasize these feelings, because this Voodoo, this matter of spirits, is indeed a dangerous thing."

He was perturbed but hardly frightened, perhaps not even cautious. I wanted to say more. I wanted to tell him of my experiences in Brazil, but it wasn't the time or place.

"But David, on the matter of ghosts," he said finally, again maintaining a respectful tone, "surely there are all kinds of ghosts."

"Yes, I think I know what you mean," I responded.

"Well, this Great Nananne, if indeed she appeared of her own volition, from where precisely did she come?"

"We can't expect to know that, Louis, about any ghost."

"Well surely some ghosts are manifestations of earthbound spirits, don't students of the occult maintain this truth?"

"They do."

"If these ghosts are the spirits of the dead who are earthbound, how can we say they are purely magical? Aren't they still within the atmosphere? Aren't they struggling to reach the living? Aren't they divorced from God? How else can one interpret Claudia's haunting of Jesse? If it was Claudia, then Claudia has not gone on into a purely spiritual realm. Claudia is not a partaker of the laws beyond us. Claudia is not at peace."

"Ah, I see," I answered. "So that is why you want to attempt the ritual." I felt foolish for not having seen it all along. "You believe that Claudia's suffering."

"I think it's entirely possible," he said, "if Claudia did appear to Jesse as Jesse seemed to think." He looked miserable. "And frankly, I hope that we can't rouse Claudia's spirit. I hope that Merrick's power doesn't work. I hope that if Claudia had an immortal soul, that soul has gone to God. I hope for things in which I can't believe."

"So this is why the story of Claudia's ghost has so tormented you. You don't want to speak to her. You want to know that she's at peace."

"Yes, I want to do this thing because she may be a restless and tormented spirit. I can't know from the stories of others. I myself have never been haunted, David. As I've told you, I have never heard this harpsichord music, nor the singing of caged birds here. I have never witnessed anything to indicate that Claudia exists anywhere in any form any longer at all. I want to try to reach Claudia so that I will know."

This confession had cost him dearly, and he sat back again and looked away, perhaps into some private corner of his soul.

Finally, his eyes still fixed on some invisible spot in the shadows, he spoke:

"If only I had seen her, I could make some assessment, no matter how poor that assessment might be. I tell myself no vagrant spirit could ever fool me into believing it was Claudia, but I've never seen a vagrant spirit, either. I have never seen anything like it. I have only Jesse's story of what happened, which Jesse herself sought to soften on account of my feelings, and of course Lestat's ramblings, that he was sure Claudia came to him, that past experiences quite literally engulfed him when he was suffering his adventures with the Body Thief."

"Yes, I've heard him talk of it."

"But with Lestat, one never knows . . ." he said. "Lestat may have been characterizing his conscience in those stories. I don't know. What I do know is that I want desperately for Merrick Mayfair to try to raise Claudia's spirit, and I'm prepared for whatever might come."

"You think you're prepared," I said hastily, perhaps unfairly.

"Oh, I know. The spell tonight has shaken you."

"You can't imagine," I said.

"Very well, I admit it. I can't imagine. But tell me this. You speak of a realm beyond the earth and that Merrick is magical when she reaches for it. But why does it involve blood? Surely her spells will involve blood." He went on, a little angrily. "Voodoo almost always involves blood," he averred. "You speak of the Holy Sacrifice of the Mass as magical, and I understand you, because if the Bread and Wine are transformed into the Holy Sacrifice of the Crucifixion, it is magical, but why does it involve blood? We are earthly beings, yes, but a small component of us is magical, and why does that component demand blood?"

He became quite heated as he finished, his eyes fixing on me severely almost, though I knew his emotions had little to do with me.

"What I'm saying is, we might compare rituals the world over in all religions and all systems of magic, forever, but they always involve blood. Why? Of course I know that human beings can not live without blood; I know that 'the blood is the life,' saith Dracula; I know that humankind speaks in cries and whispers of blood-drenched altars, of bloodshed and blood kin, and blood will have blood, and those of the finest blood. But why? What is the quintessential connection that binds all such wisdom or superstition? And above all, why does God want blood?"

I was taken aback. Surely I wasn't going to hazard a hasty answer. And I didn't have one, besides. His question went too deep. Blood was essential to Candomble. It was essential to real Voodoo as well.

He went on:

"I don't speak of your God in particular," he said kindly, "but the God of the Holy Sacrifice of the Mass has demanded blood, and indeed the Crucifixion has come down to us as one of the most renowned blood sacrifices of all time. But what of all the other gods, the gods of old Rome for whom blood had to be shed in the arena as well as on the altar, or the gods of the Aztecs who were still demanding bloody murder as the price of running the universe when the Spanish arrived on their shores?"

"Maybe we're asking the wrong question," I said finally. "Maybe blood does not matter to the gods. Maybe blood matters to us. Maybe we've made it the vehicle of Divine transmission. Maybe that's something which the world can move beyond."

"Hmmm, it's not a mere anachronism," he said. "It's a genuine mystery. Why should the natives of ancient South America have but one word in their language for both flowers and blood?"

He rose from the chair again, looking altogether restless, and went to the window once more and looked out through the lace.

"I have my dreams," he said in a whisper. "I dream she will come, and she will tell me that she is at peace and she will show me the courage to do what I must do."

These words saddened and disturbed me.

"The Everlasting has not fixed his canon against *my* self-slaughter," he said, paraphrasing Shakespeare, "because all I need do to accomplish it is not seek shelter at the rising of the sun. I dream she may warn me of hellfires and of the need for repentance. But then, this is a little miracle play, isn't it? If she comes, she may be groping in darkness. She may be lost among the wandering dead souls whom Lestat saw when he traveled out of this world."

"Absolutely anything is possible," I answered.

A long interval occurred during which I went quietly up to him and laid my hand on his shoulder, to let him know in my way that I respected his pain. He didn't acknowledge this tiny intimacy. I made my way back to the sofa and I waited. I had no intention of leaving him with such thoughts in his mind.

At last he turned around.

"Wait here," he said quietly, and then he went out of the room and down the passage. I heard him open a door. Within a brief moment he was back again with what appeared to be a small antique photograph in his hand.

I was immensely excited. Could it be what I thought?

I recognized the small black gutter perche case into which it was fitted, so like the ones that framed the daguerreotypes belonging to Merrick. It appeared intricate and well preserved.

He opened the case and looked at the image, and then he spoke:

"You mentioned those family photographs of our dearly beloved witch," he said reverently. "You asked if they were not vehicles for guardian souls."

"Yes, I did. As I told you, I could have sworn those little pictures were looking at Aaron and at me."

"And you mentioned that you could not imagine what it had meant to us to see daguerreotypes—or whatever they might be called—for the first time so many years ago."

I was filled with a sort of amazement as I listened to him. He had been there. He had been alive and a witness. He had moved from the world of painted portraits to that of photographic images. He had drifted through those decades and was alive now in our time.

"Think of mirrors," he said, "to which everyone is accustomed. Think of the reflection suddenly frozen forever. That is how it was. Except the color was gone from it, utterly gone, and there lay the horror, if there was one; but you see, no one thought it was so remarkable, not while it was happening, and then it was so common. We didn't really appreciate such a miracle. It went popular too very fast. And of course when it first started, when they first set up their studios, it was not for us."

"For us?"

"David, it had to be done in daylight, don't you see? The first photographs belonged to mortals alone."

"Of course, I didn't even think of it."

"She hated it," he said. He looked again at the image. "And one night, unbeknownst to me, she broke the lock of one of the new studios—and there were many of them—and she stole all the pictures she could find. She broke them, smashed them in a fury. She said it was ghastly that we couldn't have our pictures made. 'Yes, we see ourselves in mirrors, and old tales would have it not,' she screamed at me. 'But what about this mirror? Is this not some threat of judgment?' I told her absolutely it was not.

"I remember Lestat laughed at her. He said she was greedy and foolish and ought to be happy with what she had. She was past all tolerance of him, and didn't even answer him. That's when he had the miniature painted of her for his locket, the locket you found for him in a Talamasca vault."

"I see," I answered. "Lestat never told me such a story."

"Lestat forgets many things," he said thoughtfully and without judgment. "He had other portraits of her painted after that. There was a large one here, very beautiful. We took it with us to Europe. We took trunks of our belongings, but that time I don't want to remember. I don't want to remember how she tried to hurt Lestat."

I was silent out of respect.

"But the photographs, the daguerreotypes, that's what she wanted, the real image of herself on glass. She was furious, as I told you. But then years later, when we reached Paris, in those lovely nights before we ever happened upon the Théâtre des Vampires and the monsters who would destroy her, she found that the magic pictures could be taken at night, with artificial light!"

He seemed to be reliving the experience painfully. I remained quiet.

"You can't imagine her excitement. She had seen an exhibit by the famous photographer Nadar of pictures from the Paris catacombs. Pictures of cartloads of human bones. Nadar was quite the man, as I'm sure you know. She was thrilled by the pictures. She went to his studio, by special appointment, in the evening, and there this picture was made."

He came towards me.

"It's a dim picture. It took an age for all the mirrors and the artificial lamps to do their work. And Claudia stood still for so long, well, only a vampire child might have worked such a trick. But she was very pleased with it. She kept it on her dressing table in the Hotel Saint-Gabriel, the last place that we ever called our home. We had such lovely rooms there. It was near to the Opera. I don't think she ever unpacked the painted portraits. It was this that mattered to her. I'd actually thought she would come to be happy in Paris. Maybe she would have been . . . But there wasn't time. This little picture, she felt it was only the beginning, and planned to return to Nadar with an even lovelier dress."

He looked at me.

I stood up to receive the picture, and he placed it in my hands most carefully, as though it were about to shatter of its own accord.

I was dumbfounded. How small and innocent she seemed, this irretrievable child of fair locks and chubby cheeks, of darkened Cupid's bow lips and white lace. Her eyes veritably blazed from the shadowy glass as I looked at her. And there came back that very suspicion of years ago, that I'd suffered so strongly with Merrick's pictures, that the image was gazing at me.

I must have made some small sound. I don't know. I shut the little case. I even worked the tiny gold clasp into the lock.

"Wasn't she beautiful?" he asked. "Tell me. It's past a matter of opinion, isn't it? She was beautiful. One cannot deny that simple fact."

I looked at him, and I wanted to say that she was, indeed she was, she was lovely, but no sound would come out of my mouth.

"We have this," he said, "for Merrick's magic. Not her blood, nor an article of clothing, nor a lock of hair. But we have this. After her death, I went back to the hotel rooms where we'd been happy and I retrieved it, and all the rest I left."

He opened his coat and slipped the picture into his breast pocket. He looked a little shocked, his eyes purposefully blank, and then he gave a little shake of the head.

"Don't you think it will be powerful for the magic?" he asked.

"Yes," I said. There were so many comforting words tumbling through my mind, but all seemed poor and stiff.

We stood looking at one another, and I was surprised at the feeling in his expression. He seemed altogether human and passionate. I could scarce believe the despair with which he endured.

"I don't really want to see her, David," he said. "You must believe me on that score. I don't want to raise her ghost, and frankly, I don't think we can."

"I believe you, Louis," I said.

"But if she does come, and she is in torment . . ."

"Then Merrick will know how to guide her," I said quickly. "I'll know how to guide her. All mediums in the Talamasca know how to guide such spirits. All mediums know to urge such spirits to seek the light."

He nodded. "I was counting on it," he said. "But you see, I don't think Claudia would ever be lost, only wanting to remain. And then, it might take a powerful witch like Merrick to do the convincing that beyond this pale there lies an end to pain."

"Precisely," I said.

"Well, I've troubled you enough for one evening," he said. "I have to go out now. I know that Lestat is uptown in the old orphanage. He's listening to his music there. I want to make certain that no intruders have come in."

I knew this was fanciful. Lestat, regardless of his frame of mind, could defend himself against almost anything, but I tried to accept the words as a gentleman should.

"I'm thirsting," he added, glancing at me, with just the trace of a smile. "You're right on that account. I'm not really going to see to Lestat. I've already been to St. Elizabeth's. Lestat is alone with his music as he chooses to be. I'm thirsting very much. I'm going to feed. And I have to go about it alone."

"No," I said softly. "Let me go with you. After Merrick's spell, I don't want you to go alone."

This was most decidedly not Louis's way of doing things; however, he agreed.

6

WE WENT OUT TOGETHER, walking quite rapidly until we were well away from the lighted blocks of the Rue Bourbon and the Rue Royale.

New Orleans soon opened up her underbelly to us, and we went deep into a ruined neighborhood, not unlike the neighborhood in which I'd long ago met Merrick's Great Nananne. But if there were any great witches about, I found no hint of them on this night.

Now, let me say here a few words about New Orleans and what it was to us.

First and foremost it is not a monstrous city like Los Angeles or New York. And even though it has a sizable underclass of dangerous individuals, it is, nevertheless, a small place.

It cannot really support the thirst of three vampires. And when great numbers of blood drinkers are drawn to it, the random blood lust creates an unwanted stir.

Such had recently happened, due to Lestat publishing his memoirs of Memnoch the Devil, during which time many of the very ancient came to New Orleans, as well as rogue vampires—creatures of powerful appetite and little regard for the species and the subterranean paths which it must follow to survive in the modern world.

During that time of coming together, I had managed to persuade Armand to dictate his life story to me; and I had circulated, with her permission, the pages which the vampire Pandora had given me sometime before.

These stories attracted even more of the maverick blood drinkers—those creatures who, being masterless and giving out lies as to their beginnings, often taunt their mortal prey and seek to bully them in a way that can only lead to trouble for all of us.

The uneasy convocation did not last long.

But though Marius, a child of two millennia, and his consort, the lovely Pandora, disapproved of the young blood drinkers, they would not lift a hand against them to put them to death or to flight. It was not in their nature to respond to such a catastrophe, though they were outraged by the conduct of these baseborn fiends.

As for Lestat's mother, Gabrielle, one of the coldest and most fascinating individuals whom I have ever encountered, it was of absolutely no concern to her at all, as long as no one harmed her son.

Well, it was quite impossible for anyone to harm her son. He is unharmable, as far as we all know. Or rather, to speak more plainly, let me say that his own adventures have harmed Lestat far more than any vampire might. His trip to Heaven and Hell with Memnoch, be it delusion or supernatural journey, has left him stunned spiritually to such a point that he is not ready to resume his antics and become the Brat Prince whom we once adored.

However, with vicious and sordid blood drinkers breaking down the very doors of St. Elizabeth's and coming up the iron stairs of our very own town house in the Rue Royale, it was Armand who was able to rouse Lestat and goad him into taking the situation in hand.

Lestat, having already waked to listen to the piano music of a fledgling vampire, blamed himself for the tawdry invasion. It was he who had created the "Coven of the Articulate," as we had come to be called. And so, he declared to us in a hushed voice, with little or no enthusiasm for the battle, that he would put things right.

Armand—given in the past to leading covens, and to destroying them—assisted Lestat in a massacre of the unwelcome rogue vampires before the social fabric was fatally breached.

Having the gift of fire, as the others called it—that is, the means to kindle a blaze telekinetically—Lestat destroyed with flames the brash invaders of his own lair, and all those who had violated the privacy of the more retiring Marius and Pandora, Santino, and Louis and myself. Armand dismembered and obliterated those who died at his hand.

Those few preternatural beings who weren't killed fled the city, and indeed many were overtaken by Armand, who showed no mercy whatsoever to the misbegotten, the heartlessly careless, and the deliberately cruel.

After that, when it was plain to one and all that Lestat had returned to his semi-sleep, absorbed utterly in recordings of the finest music provided for him by me and by Louis, the elders—Marius, Pandora, Santino, and Armand, with two younger companions—gradually went their way.

It was an inevitable thing, that parting, because none of us could really endure the company of so many fellow blood drinkers for very long.

As it is with God and Satan, humankind is our subject matter. And so it is that, deep within the mortal world and its many complexities, we choose to spend our time.

Of course, we will all come together at various times in the future. We know well how to reach one another. We are not above writing letters. Or other means of communication. The eldest know telepathically when things have gone terribly wrong with the young ones, and vice versa. But for now, only Louis and Lestat and I hunt the streets of New Orleans, and so it will be for some time.

That means, strictly speaking, that only Louis and I hunt, for Lestat simply does not feed at all. Having the body of a god, he has subsumed the lust which still plagues the most powerful, and lies in his torpor as the music plays on.

And so New Orleans, in all her drowsy beauty, is host to only two of the Undead. Nevertheless, we must be very clever. We must cover up the deeds that we do. To feed upon the evildoer, as Marius has always called it, is our vow; however, the blood thirst is a terrible thing.

But before I return to my tale—of how Louis and I went out on this particular evening, allow me a few more words about Lestat.

I personally do not think that things are as simple with him as the others tend to believe. Above, I have given you pretty much "the party line," as the expression goes, as to his coma-like slumber and his music. But there are very troubling aspects to his presence which I cannot deny or resolve.

Unable to read his mind, because he made me a vampire and I am therefore his fledgling and far too close to him for such communication, I, nevertheless, perceive certain things about him as he lies by the hour listening to the brilliant and stormy music of Beethoven, Brahms, Bach, Chopin, Verdi, and Tchaikovsky, and the other composers he loves.

I've confessed these "doubts" about his well-being to Marius and to Pandora and to Armand. But no one of them could penetrate the veil of preternatural silence which he has drawn about his entire being, body and soul.

"He's weary," say the others. "He'll be himself soon." And "He'll come around."

I don't doubt these things. Not at all. But to put it plainly, something is more wrong with him than anyone has guessed. There are times when he is not *there* in his body.

Now this may mean that he is projecting his soul up and out of his body in order to roam about, in pure spirit form, at will. Certainly Lestat knows how to do this. He learnt it from the most ancient of the vampires; and he proved that he could do it, when with the evil Body Thief he worked a switch.

But Lestat does not like that power. And no one who has had his body stolen is likely to use it for more than a very short interval in any one night.

I feel something far more grave is wrong there, that Lestat is not always in control of either body or soul, and we must wait to discover the terms and outcome of a battle which might still be going on.

As for Lestat's appearance, he lies on the Chapel floor, or on the four-poster bed in the town house, with his eyes open, though they appear to see nothing. And for a while after the great cleansing battle, he did periodically change his clothes, favoring the red velvet jackets of old, and his lace-trimmed shirts of heavy linen, along with slim pants and plain black boots.

Others have seen this attention to wardrobe as a good sign. I believe Lestat did these things so that we would leave him alone.

Alas, I have no more to say on the subject in this narrative. At least I don't think so. I can't protect Lestat from what is happening, and no one really has ever succeeded in protecting him or stopping him, no matter what the circumstances of his distress.

Now, let me return to my record of events.

Louis and I had made our way deep into a forlorn and dreadful part of the city where many houses stood abandoned, and those few which still showed evidence of habitation were locked up tight with iron bars upon their windows and doors.

As always happens with any neighborhood in New Orleans, we came within a few blocks to a market street, and there we found many desolate shops which had long ago been shut up with nails and boards. Only a "pleasure club," as it was called, showed signs of habitation and those inside were drunk and gambling the night away at card games and dice.

However, as we continued on our journey, I following Louis, as this was Louis's hunt, we soon came to a small dwelling nestled between the old storefronts, the ruins of a simple shotgun house, whose front steps were lost in the high weeds.

There were mortals inside, I sensed it immediately, and they were of varying dispositions.

The first mind which made itself known to me was that of an aged woman, keeping watch over a cheap little bassinet with a baby inside of it, a woman who was actively praying that God deliver her from her circumstances, those circumstances pertaining to two young people in a front room of the house who were entirely given over to drink and drugs.

In a quiet and efficient manner, Louis led the way back to the overgrown alley to the rear of this crooked little shack, and without a sound he peered through the small window, above a humming air conditioner, at the distraught woman, who wiped the face of the infant, who did not cry.

Again and again I heard this woman murmur aloud that she didn't know what she would do with those young people in the front room, that they had destroyed her house and home and left her this miserable little infant who would starve to death or die of other neglect if the young mother, drunk and dissolute, was forced to care for the child alone.

Louis seemed an angel of death come to this window.

On closer inspection over Louis's shoulder, I gained a better perspective on the old one, and discovered that she was not only caring for the infant, but ironing clothes on a low board which allowed her to sit as she did it, and reach again and again to comfort the baby in its wicker crib.

The smell of the freshly ironed clothes was somewhat delicious, a burnt smell but a good one, of heat against cotton and linen.

And I saw now that the room was full of these garments, and conjectured that this woman did this work for hire.

"God help me," she muttered in a little singsong voice, shaking her head as she ironed, "I wish you would take that girl from me, take her and her friends. God help me, I wish you would deliver me from this Valley, O Lord, where I have been for so long."

The room itself had comfortable furnishings and touches of domestic care, such as lace doilies on the backs of its chairs and a clean linoleum floor which shone as though it had been recently waxed.

The woman herself was heavy of build and wore her hair in a knot on the back of her head.

As Louis passed on to view the back rooms of the house, the old woman was quite unaware of it, and her singsong prayers for deliverance went on.

The kitchen, also immaculate, revealed the same shining linoleum and all its dishes washed and set out to drain beside the sink.

The front rooms of the house were another story. Here the young people reigned in positive squalor, one stretched out on a bed without a sheet to cover its dirty mattress, and the other pitiful creature, alone, in the living room, so full of narcotics as to be in a swoon.

Both these hopeless beings were women, though one could not tell this at first glance. On the contrary, their brutally clipped hair, their emaciated bodies, and their denim-clad limbs gave them a desolate sexless appearance. And the piles of clothing strewn everywhere about them gave no clue of a predilection for either feminine or masculine attire.

I found this spectacle unendurable.

Of course, Marius had cautioned us in no uncertain terms before he departed New Orleans that if we did not hunt the evildoer almost exclusively, we would very soon go mad. To feed upon the innocent is sublime, but leads inevitably to such a love of human life that the vampire who does it cannot endure for very long.

I am not sure I agree with Marius on this score, and I do think that other blood drinkers have survived very well by feeding on the innocent. But the idea of hunting the evildoer is one which I personally embraced for my own peace of mind. The intimacy with evil is something which I must bear.

Louis made his way into the house by means of a side door, one which is quite typical in shotgun houses of this kind which have no hallway but merely a chain of rooms.

I remained in the fresher air of the weedy garden, glancing at the stars now and then for comfort, and overcome suddenly by the unwelcome reek of vomit and feces which came from the house's small bathroom, another miracle of order and cleanliness except for the recent filth deposited on the floor.

Indeed, the two young women were in need of immediate intervention, it seemed, were they to be saved from themselves, but Louis had not come to provide such, but as a vampire, so hungry that even I could feel it, and he made his way into the bedroom first, and seated himself beside the wraith of a being on the stripped mattress, and very quickly, ignoring her giggles at the sight of him, embraced her with his right arm, and sank his teeth for the fatal drink.

On and on, the old woman prayed in the back room.

I had thought Louis would be finished with the place, but no such luck.

As soon as the scrawny body of the woman had been allowed to fall to one side and against the mattress, he rose and stood for a moment in the light of the room's few scattered lamps.

He looked splendid with the light glinting on his black curly hair and flaring in his dark-green eyes. The blood inside him had colored his face naturally and brilliantly. In the buff-colored velvet coat with its gold buttons, he appeared an apparition among the soiled tints and roughened textures of the place.

It took my breath away to see him focus his eyes slowly and then walk into the front room.

The remaining woman gave a whooping cry of dazed merriment when she saw him, and for a long moment he stood merely regarding her as she slumped in an overstuffed chair, with her legs wide apart and her naked arms, covered in sores, dangling at her sides.

It seemed he was quite undecided as to what to do. But then I saw his seemingly thoughtful face grow blank with hunger. I watched him approach, losing all the grace of a contemplative human, appearing to be driven only by hunger, and lift up this ghastly young creature, and close his lips against her neck. No glimpse of teeth, no moment of cruelty. Merely the final kiss.

There followed the swoon, which I could more fully appreciate while peering through the front window. It lasted only a few moments; then the woman was dead. He laid her down again on her soiled chair, positioning her limbs with some care. I watched as he used his blood to seal up the puncture wounds in her throat. No doubt he had done the same for the victim in the other room.

I felt a wave of sorrow come over me. Life seemed simply unendurable. I had the feeling I would never know safety or happiness again. I had no right to either. But for what it was worth, Louis was feeling what the blood could give a monster, and he had chosen his victims well.

He stepped out of the front door of the house, which was unlatched and unattended in any way, and came round to meet me in the side yard. The transformation of his face was now complete. He appeared the handsomest of men, his eyes utterly unclouded and almost fierce, and his cheeks beautifully flushed.

It would all seem routine to the authorities, the deaths of these two unfortunates, that they had died by the drugs they were ingesting. As for the old woman in the back room, she continued with her prayers, though she was making them now into a song for the baby, who had begun to utter small cries.

"Leave her something for the funerals," I said in a hushed voice to Louis. This seemed to confuse him.

I quickly went around to the front door, slipped inside, and left a substantial offering of money on the top of a broken table which was littered with overflowing ashtrays and glasses half filled with stale wine. I put some more money atop an old bureau as well.

Louis and I made our way home. The night was warm and damp, yet felt clean and lovely, and the smell of ligustrum filled my lungs.

We were soon walking back towards the lighted streets we loved.

His step was brisk and his manner entirely human. He stopped to pick the flowers that grew over the fences or out of the little gardens. He sang to himself something soft and unobtrusive. Now and then he looked up at the stars.

All of this was pleasant to me, though I wondered how in the name of Heaven I would have the courage to feed upon the evildoer only, or to answer a prayer as Louis had just done. I saw the fallacy in all of it. Another wave of desolation passed over me, and I felt a terrible need to explain my various points of view, but this did not seem the time.

It struck me very heavily that I had lived to an old age as a mortal man, and so had ties with the human race that many another blood drinker simply did not possess. Louis had been twenty-four when he had struck his bargain with Lestat for the Dark Blood. How much can a man learn in that time, and how much can he later forget?

I might have continued to think in this vein and indeed to start some conversation with Louis, however I was once again bothered by something outside of myself, and that is that a black cat, a very huge black cat, shot out of the shrubbery ahead of us and stopped in our path.

I stopped in my tracks. So did Louis, only because I had.

A passing car then sent its beams into the eyes of the cat, and for a moment they were purely golden; then the animal, truly one of the largest domestic cats I've ever beheld, and a most unwholesome specimen, shot away into the shadows as swiftly as it had come.

"Surely you don't take that as a bad omen," said Louis, smiling at me, almost teasing me. "David, you're not superstitious, as mortals would say."

I loved the bit of levity in his voice. I loved seeing him so full of the warm blood that he might have been human. But I couldn't respond to the words.

I didn't like the cat at all. I was furious at Merrick. I could have blamed the rain on Merrick had it started to pour. I felt challenged by Merrick. I was working myself up to a little fit of pique. I didn't say a word.

"When will you let me meet Merrick?" he asked.

"First her story," I said, "or that part of it which I know. Tomorrow, feed early, and when I come to the flat I'll tell you the things you need to know."

"And then we speak of a meeting?"

"Then you can make up your mind."

7

T HE FOLLOWING NIGHT, I rose to find the sky uncommonly clear and full of visible stars. A good omen to all those in a state of grace. This is not the normal thing for New Orleans, as the air is very filled with moisture, and frequently the sky has a veiled appearance and little spectacle of cloud and light.

Having no need to feed, I went directly to the Windsor Court Hotel, once again entering its very lovely modern lobby, a space which has all the usual elegance of an older establishment, and went up to Merrick's suite.

She had only just left, I was informed, and a maid was engaged in preparing the rooms for a next guest.

Ah, she had stayed longer than I had expected, but not as long as I'd hoped. However, imagining her to be safely on her way back to Oak Haven, I checked with the desk to see if she had left any message for me. She had.

I waited until I was alone outside to read the short note:

"Have gone to London to retrieve from the vault those few items which we know are connected with the child."

So things had progressed so far!

Of course, she was referring to a rosary and a diary which our field-worker Jesse Reeves had found in the flat in the Rue Royale over ten years before. And if memory served me correctly, there were a few other things which had been collected a century earlier from an abandoned hotel room in Paris where rumor had led us to believe that vampires had lodged.

I was alarmed.

But what had I expected? That Merrick would resist my request?

Nevertheless, I'd never anticipated that she would act so quickly. Of course I knew that she could obtain the items in question. She was quite powerful within the Talamasca. She had unlimited access to the vaults.

It occurred to me to try to call her at Oak Haven, to tell her that we must discuss the matter a little further. But I couldn't risk it.

The members of the Talamasca there were only a small number, but each was gifted psychically and in a different way. The phone can be a powerful connecter between souls, and I simply could not have someone there sensing something "strange" about the voice on the other end of the line.

There I left the matter, and I set out for our flat in the Rue Royale.

As I entered the carriageway, something soft moved past my leg. I stopped and searched the darkness until I made out the shape of another giant black cat. Surely it had to be another. I couldn't imagine the creature I had seen the night before having followed us home with no incentive of food or milk.

The cat vanished in the rear courtyard garden and was gone when I reached the back iron stairs. But I didn't like this. I didn't like this cat. No, not at all. I took my time in the garden. I walked about the fountain, which had recently been cleaned and stocked with large goldfish, and I spent more than a few moments gazing at the faces of the stone cherubs, with their conches held high, now quite overrun with lichen, and then looking about at the overgrown flower patches along the brick walls.

The yard was kept, yet out of hand, its flagstones swept, but its plants gone wild. Lestat probably wanted it that way, insofar as he cared. And Louis loved it.

Suddenly, when I had just about resolved to go upstairs, I saw the cat again, a huge black monster of a thing in my book, but then I don't like cats, creeping on the high wall.

A multitude of thoughts crowded my mind. I felt an ever increasing excitement about this project with Merrick and a certain foreboding which seemed a necessary price. It frightened me suddenly that she had left so abruptly for London, that I had worked such a distraction upon her that she had abandoned whatever projects in which she might have been engaged.

Should I tell Louis what she had set out to do? It would certainly bring about a finality to our plans.

Entering the flat, I turned on all the electric lights in every room, a detail which was our custom by this time, and one upon which I depended heavily for some sense of normality, no matter that it was a mere illusion, but then, perhaps normality is always an illusion. Who am I to say?

Louis arrived almost immediately after, coming up the rear stairs with his usual silken step. It was the heartbeat I heard in my alert state, not the footfall at all.

Louis found me in the rear parlor, the one more distant from the noises of the tourists in the Rue Royale, and with its windows open to the courtyard below. I was in fact looking out the window, looking for the cat again, though I didn't tell myself so, and observing how our bougainvillea had all but covered the high walls that enclosed us and kept us safe from the rest of the world. The wisteria was also fierce in its growth, even reaching out from the brick walls to the railing of the rear balcony and finding its way up to the roof.

I could never quite take for granted the lush flowers of New Orleans.

Indeed, they filled me with happiness whenever I stopped to really look at them and to surrender to their fragrance, as though I still had the right to do so, as though I still were part of nature, as though I were still a mortal man.

Louis was carefully and thoughtfully dressed, as he had been the night before. He wore a black linen suit of exquisite cut around the waist and the hips, an unusual thing with linen, and another pristine white shirt and dark silk tie. His hair was the usual mass of waves and curls, and his green eyes were uncommonly bright.

He had fed already this evening, it was plain. And his pale skin was once more suffused with the carnal color of blood.

I wondered at all this seductive attention to detail, but I liked it. It seemed to betoken some sort of inner peace, this fastidious dressing, or at least the cessation of inner despair.

"Sit down there on the couch, if you will," I said.

I took the chair which had been his last night.

The little parlor surrounded us with its antique glass lamps, the vivid red of its Kirman carpet, and the glinting polish of its floor. I was vaguely aware of its fine French paintings. It seemed the smallest details were a solace.

It struck me that this was the very room in which Claudia had tried to murder Lestat well over a century ago. But Lestat himself had recently reclaimed this space, and for several years we were wont to gather here, and so it did not seem to matter so very much.

Quite suddenly I realized that I had to tell Louis that Merrick had gone to England. I had to tell him that which made me most uncomfortable, that the Talamasca, in the 1800s, had gathered his possessions from the Hotel Saint-Gabriel in Paris, which he himself had abandoned, as he'd described last night.

"You knew of our presence in Paris?" he asked. I saw the blood flash in his cheeks.

I reflected for a long moment before answering.

"We didn't really know," I said. "Oh, we knew of the Théâtre des Vampires, yes, and we knew that the players weren't human. As for you and Claudia, it was more or less the supposition of a lone investigator that you were connected. And when you abandoned everything in your hotel, when you were seen leaving Paris one evening in the company of another vampire, we moved in cautiously to purchase all that you'd left behind."

He accepted this quietly. Then he spoke up.

"Why did you never try to harm or expose the vampires of the theater?" he asked.

"We would have been laughed at if we'd tried to expose them," I said. "Besides, that is simply not what we do. Louis, we've never really talked of the Talamasca. For me, it's like speaking of a country to which I've become a traitor. But surely you must understand, the Talamasca watches, truly watches, and counts its own survival over the centuries as its primary goal."

There was a brief pause. His face was composed and appeared only a little sad.

"So Claudia's clothing, well, Merrick will have it when she returns."

"Insofar as we took ownership of it, yes. I myself am not certain what's in the vault." I stopped. I had once brought Lestat a present from the vault. But I'd been a man then. I could not conceive of trying to rob the Talamasca of anything just now.

"I've often wondered about those archives," Louis said. Then again in the most tender voice: "I've never wanted to ask. It's Claudia I want to see, not those things which we left behind."

"I understand your meaning."

"But it counts for magic, doesn't it?" he asked.

"Yes. You'll understand that better perhaps when I tell you about Merrick."

"What do you want me to know about Merrick?" he asked earnestly. "I'm eager to hear it. You told me last night about your first meeting. You told me how she'd showed you the daguerreotypes—."

"Yes, that was the very first encounter. But there is much, much more. Remember what I said last night. Merrick is a magician of sorts, a witch, a veritable Medea, and we can be as overwhelmed by magic as any earthly creature can."

"My desires are singular and pure," Louis said. "I only want to see Claudia's ghost."

I couldn't help but smile. I think I wounded him. I was immediately sorry.

"Surely you must recognize some danger is opening the way to the supernatural," I insisted. "But let me tell you what I know of Merrick, what I feel I can tell."

I began to recount to him my recollections in order.

Only a few days after Merrick had come to Oak Haven, some twenty years ago, Aaron and I had set out with Merrick to drive to New Orleans and to visit Merrick's Great Nananne.

My memories were vivid.

The last cool days of spring had passed and we were plunged into a hot and damp weather, which, loving the tropics as I did, and do, had been very pleasing to me. I had no regrets about having left London at all.

Merrick still had not revealed to us the day of Great Nananne's death as it had been confided to her by the old woman. And Aaron, though he'd been the personage in the dream who gave the fatal date to Great Nananne, had no knowledge whatever of this dream.

Though Aaron had prepared me for the old section of New Orleans to which we were going, I had nevertheless been astonished to see the neighborhood of tumbledown houses of all different sizes and styles, steeped in its overgrown oleander, which bloomed profusely in the moist heat, and most surprised of all to come upon the old raised cottage of a house which belonged to Great Nananne.

The day, as I've said, was close and warm, with violent and sudden showers of rain, and though I have been a vampire now for five years, I can vividly remember the sunshine coming through the rain to strike the narrow broken pavements, and everywhere the weeds rising out of gutters which were in fact no more than open ditches, and the snarls of oak and rain tree, and cottonwood, which sprang up all around us as we made our way to the residence which Merrick was now to leave behind.

At last we came to a high iron picket fence, and a house much larger than those around it, and of much earlier date.

It was one of those Louisiana houses which stands upon brick foundation post pillars of about five feet in height, with a central wooden stair rising to its front porch. A row of simple square pillars held up its Greek Revival porch roof, and the central door was not unlike the grander doors of Oak Haven in that it had a small fanlight intact above.

Long windows went from floor to ceiling on the front of the house, but these were all pasted over with newspaper, which made the house look derelict and uninhabited. The yew trees, stretching their scrawny limbs to Heaven on either side of the front porch, added a note of grimness, and the front hall into which we entered was empty and shadowy, though it went clear through to an open door at the back. There were no stairs to the attic, and an attic there must have been, I conjectured, for the main body of the house had a deeply pitched roof. Beyond that rear open door all was tangled and green.

The house was three rooms in depth from front to back, giving it six rooms in all on the main floor, and in the first of these, to the left of the hallway, we found Great Nananne, under a layer of hand-sewn quilts in an old plantation four-poster, without a canopy, of simple mahogany design. I say plantation bed when I refer to this species of furniture because the pieces are so huge, and so often crammed into small city rooms that one immediately envisions more space in the country for which this kind of furnishing must have been designed. Also, the mahogany posts, though artfully tapered, were otherwise plain.

As I looked at the little woman, dried-up upon the heavily stained pillow, her frame completely invisible beneath the worn quilts, I thought for a moment she was dead.

In fact, I could have sworn by all I knew of spirits and humans that the dried little body in the bed was empty of its soul. Maybe she'd been dreaming of death and wanted it so badly she'd left her mortal coil for but a few moments.

But when little Merrick stood in the doorway, Great Nananne came back, opening her small crinkled and yellow eyes. Her ancient skin had a beautiful gold color to it, faded though she must have been. Her nose was small and flat, and her mouth fixed in a smile. Her hair was wisps of gray.

Electric lamps, quite shabby and makeshift, were the only illumination save for a wealth of candles on an immense nearby shrine. I could not quite make out the shrine, as it seemed shrouded in dimness, being against the papered shut windows of the front of the house. And the people drew my attention at first.

Aaron brought up an old cane-backed chair, to sit beside the woman in the bed.

The bed reeked of sickness and urine.

I saw that newspapers and large brilliantly colored Holy Pictures papered all of the decaying walls. Not a bit of plaster was left bare save for the ceiling, which was full of cracks and chipped paint and seemed a threat to us all. Only the side windows had their curtains, but much glass was broken out and here and there newspaper patches had been applied. Beyond loomed the eternal foliage.

"We'll bring nurses for you, Great Nananne," said Aaron, in a kindly and sincere voice. "Forgive me that it took me so long to come." He leant forward. "You must trust in me implicitly. We'll send for the nurses as soon as we leave you this afternoon."

"Come?" asked the old woman sunk down into the feather pillow. "Did I ever ask you—either of you—to come?" She had no French accent. Her voice was shockingly ageless, low in pitch and strong. "Merrick, sit by me here for a little while, *chérie*," she said. "Be still, Mr. Lightner. Nobody asked you to come."

Her arm rose and fell like a branch on the breeze, so lifeless in shape and color, fingers curled as they scratched at Merrick's dress.

"See what Mr. Lightner bought for me, Great Nananne?" said Merrick beside her, gesturing with open arms as she looked down on her new clothes.

I had not noticed before that she was in Sunday Best, with a dress of white pique and black patent leather shoes. The little white socks looked incongruous on such a developed young woman, but then Aaron saw her completely as an innocent child.

Merrick leant over and kissed the old woman's small head. "Don't you be afraid of anything on my account any longer," she said. "I'm home now with them, Great Nananne."

At that point, a priest came into the room, a tall sagging man as old as Nananne was, it seemed to me, slow moving and scrawny in his long black cassock, the thick leather belt drooping over shrunken bones, rosary beads knocking softly against his thigh.

He seemed blind to our presence, only nodding at the old woman, and he slipped away without a word. As to what his feelings might have been about the shrine to the left of us, against the front wall of the house, I couldn't guess.

I felt an instinctive wariness, and an apprehension that he might try to prevent us—with good reason—from taking the child Merrick away.

One never knew which priest might have heard of the Talamasca, which priest might have feared it or despised it, under the guidance of Rome. To those within the hierarchy of the Church, we were alien and mysterious. We were maverick and controversial. Claiming to be secular, yet ancient, we could never hope for the cooperation or the understanding of the Church of Rome.

It was after this man disappeared, and as Aaron continued his polite and subdued conversation with the old woman, that I had a chance to view the shrine in full.

It was built up of bricks, from the floor, in stair steps to a high wide altar where perhaps special offerings were placed. Huge plaster saints crowded the top of it in long rows to the left and right.

At once I saw St. Peter, the Papa Legba of Haitian Voodoo, and a saint on a horse who appeared to be St. Barbara, standing in for Chango of Xango in Candomble, for whom we had always used St. George. The Virgin Mary was there in the form of Our Lady of Carmel, standing in for Ezilie, a goddess of Voodoo, with heaps of flowers at her feet and perhaps the most candles before her, all of them aflicker in their deep glasses as a breeze stirred the room.

There stood St. Martin de Porres, the black saint of South America, with his broom in hand, and beside him, St. Patrick stood gazing down, his feet surrounded by fleeing snakes. All had their place in the underground religions which the slaves of the Americas had nourished for so long.

There were all kinds of obscure little mementos on the altar before these statues, and the steps below were covered with various objects, along with plates of birdseed, grain, and old cooked food which had begun to rot and to smell.

The more I studied the entire spectacle, the more I saw things, such as the awesome figure of the Black Madonna with the white Infant

Jesus in her arms. There were many little sacks tied shut and kept there, and several expensive-looking cigars still in their wrapping, perhaps held for some future offering, I couldn't know for sure. At one end of the altar stood several bottles of rum.

It was certainly one of the largest such altars I'd ever seen, and it did not surprise me that the ants had overrun some of the old food. It was a frightening and disturbing sight, infinitely more than Merrick's recent little makeshift offering in the hotel. Even my Candomble experiences in Brazil did not make me immune to the solemn and savage spectacle of it. On the contrary, I think these experiences in every regard make me more afraid.

Perhaps without realizing I was doing it, I came deeper into the room, close to the altar, so that the woman and her sickbed were out of my sight, behind my back.

Suddenly the voice of the woman in the bed startled me out of my studies.

I turned to see that she had sat up, which seemed almost impossible due to her frailty, and that Merrick had adjusted her pillows so that she might rest in this position as she spoke.

"Candomble priest," she said to me, "sacred to Oxalá." There it was, the very mention of my god.

I was too astonished to respond.

"I didn't see you in my dream, English man," she went on. "You've been in the jungles, you've hunted treasure."

"Treasure, Madam?" I responded, thinking only as quickly as I spoke. "Indeed not treasure in the conventional sense. No, never that at all."

"I follow my dreams," said the old woman, her eyes fixed on me in a manner that suggested menace, "and so I give you this child. But beware of her blood. She comes down from many magicians far stronger than you."

Once again I was amazed. I stood opposite her. Aaron had forsaken his chair to get out of the way.

"Call up The Lonely Spirit, have you?" she asked me. "Did you frighten yourself in the jungles of Brazil?"

It was quite impossible that this woman could have had this intelligence of me. Not even Aaron knew all of my story. I had always passed over my Candomble experiences as though they were slight.

As for "The Lonely Spirit," of course I knew her meaning. When one calls The Lonely Spirit, one is calling some tortured soul, a soul in Purgatory, or earthbound in misery, to ask that soul for its help in reaching gods or spirits who are further on. It was an old legend. It was as old as magic under other names and in other lands.

"Oh, yes, you are some scholar," said the old woman, smiling at me so that I could see her perfect false teeth, yellow as she was, her eyes seemingly more animate than before. "What is the state of your own soul?"

"We are not here to deal with such a matter," I fired back, quite shaken. "You know I want to protect your godchild. Surely you see that in my heart."

"Yes, Candomble priest," she said again, "and you saw your ancestors when you looked into the chalice, didn't you?" She smiled at me. The low pitch of her voice was ominous. "And they told you to go home to England or you would lose your English soul."

All this was true and untrue. Suddenly I blurted out as much.

"You know something but not everything," I declared. "One has to have a noble use for magic. Have you taught Merrick as much?" There was anger in my voice, which this old woman did not deserve. Was I jealous of her power suddenly? I couldn't control my tongue. "How has your magic brought you to this disaster!" I said, gesturing to the room about me. "Is this the place for a beautiful child?"

At once Aaron begged me to be silent.

Even the priest came forward and peered into my eyes. As if minding a child, he shook his head, frowning most sadly, and wagged his finger in my eye.

The old woman laughed a short dry little laugh.

"You find her beautiful, don't you English man," she said. "You English like children."

"Nothing could be further from the truth with me!" I declared, offended by her suggestion. "You don't believe what you're saying. You speak to dazzle others. You sent this girl unaccompanied to Aaron." At once I regretted it. The priest would certainly come to object when it was time to take Merrick away.

But I saw now he was too shocked by my audacity to protest it further.

Poor Aaron was mortified. I was behaving like a beast.

I had lost all my self-possession and was angry with an old woman who was dying before my eyes.

But when I looked at Merrick I saw nothing but a rather clever amusement in her expression, possibly even a little pride or triumph, and then she locked eyes with the old woman and there was some silent message exchanged there for which all assembled would have to wait.

"You'll take care of my godchild, I know it," said the old woman. Her wrinkled lids came down over her eyes. I saw her chest heave beneath the white flannel nightgown, and her hand trembled loosely on the quilt. "You won't be afraid of what she can do."

"No, never will I be afraid," I said reverently, eager to make the peace. I drew closer to the bed. "She's safe from everyone with us, Madam," I said. "Why do you try to frighten me?"

It didn't seem she could open her eyes. Finally she did and once again she looked directly at me.

"I'm in peace here, David Talbot," she said. I could not recall any- one having given her my name. "I'm as I want to be, and as for this child, she was always happy here. There are many rooms to this house."

"I'm sorry for what I said to you," I answered quickly. "I had no right." I meant it from my heart.

She gave a rattling sigh as she looked at the ceiling.

"I'm in pain now," she said. "I want to die. I'm in pain all the time. You'd think I could stop it, that I had charms that could stop it. I have charms for others, but for me, who can work the magic? Besides, the time has come, and it's come in its own fashion. I've lived a hundred years."

"I don't doubt you," I said, violently disturbed by her mention of her pain and her obvious veracity. "Please be assured you can leave Merrick with me."

"We'll bring you nurses," said Aaron. It was Aaron's way to pursue the practical, to deal with what could be done. "We'll see to it that a doctor comes this very afternoon. You mustn't be in pain, it isn't neces- sary. Let me go now to make the proper calls. I won't be long."

"No, no strangers in my house," she said as she looked at him and then up at me. "Take my godchild, both of you. Take her and take all that I have in this house. Tell them, Merrick, everything that I told you. Tell them all your uncles taught, and your aunts, and your great- grandmothers. This one, this tall one with the dark hair—," she looked at me, "—he knows about the treasures you have from Cold Sandra, you trust in him. Tell him about Honey in the Sunshine. Sometimes I feel bad spirits around you, Merrick. . . ." She looked at me. "You keep the bad spirits from her, English man. You know the magic. I see now the meaning of my dream."

"Honey in the Sunshine, what does it mean?" I asked her.

She shut her eyes bitterly and tightened her lips. It was extraordinarily expressive of pain. Merrick appeared to shudder, and for the first time to be about to cry.

"Don't you worry, Merrick," said the old woman finally. She pointed with her finger, but then dropped her hand again as if she was too weak to go on.

I tried suddenly with all of my might and main to penetrate the old woman's thoughts. But nothing came of it, except perhaps that I startled her when she should have been in peace.

Quickly I tried to make up for my little blunder.

"Have faith in us, Madam," I said again adamantly. "You sent Merrick on the right path."

The old woman shook her head.

"You think magic is simple," the old woman whispered. Once more our eyes met. "You think it's something you can leave behind when you cross an ocean. You think les mystères aren't real."

"No, I don't."

Once again she laughed, a low and mocking laugh.

"You never saw their full power, English man," she said. "You made things shake and shiver, but that was all. You were a stranger in a strange land with your Candomble. You forgot Oxalá, but he never forgot you."

I was fast losing all composure.

She closed her eyes and her fingers curled around Merrick's small-boned wrist. I heard the rattle of the priest's rosary, and then came the fragrance of fresh-brewed coffee mingled with the sweetness of newly falling rain.

It was an overwhelming and soothing moment—the close moist air of the New Orleans springtime, the sweetness of the rain coming down all around us, and the soft murmur of thunder far off to the right. I could smell the candle wax and the flowers of the shrine, and then again there came the human scents of the bed. It seemed a perfect harmony suddenly, even those fragrances which we condemn as sour and bad.

The old woman had indeed come to her final hour and it was only natural, this bouquet of fragrances. We must penetrate it and see her and love her. That was what had to be done.

"Ah, you hear it, that thunder?" asked Great Nananne. Once again her little eyes flashed to me. She said, "I'm going home."

Now, Merrick was truly frightened. Her eyes were wild and I could see her hand shaking. In fact, as she searched the old woman's face she appeared terrified.

The old woman's eyes rolled and she appeared to arch her back against the pillow, but the quilts seemed far too heavy for her to gain the space she craved.

What were we to do? A person can take an age to die, or die in one second. I was afraid too.

The priest came in and moved ahead of us so that he could look down at her face. His hand was easily as withered as her own.

"Talamasca," the old woman whispered. "Talamasca, take my child. Talamasca, keep my child."

I thought I myself would give way to tears. I had been at many a deathbed. It is never easy but there is something crazily exciting about it, some way in which the total fear of death kindles excitement, as if a battle were beginning, when indeed, it is coming to an end.

"Talamasca," she said again.

Surely, the priest heard her. But the priest paid no attention at all. His mind was not difficult to penetrate. He was only here to give the rites to a woman he knew and respected. The shrine was no shock to him.

"God's waiting on you, Great Nananne," said the priest softly, in a strong local accent, rather rural sounding. "God's waiting and maybe Honey in the Sunshine and Cold Sandra are there too."

"Cold Sandra," said the old woman with a long sigh and then an unintentional hiss. "Cold Sandra," she repeated as though praying, "Honey in the Sunshine . . . in God's hands."

This was violently disturbing to Merrick. It was plain from her face. Merrick began to cry. This girl, who had seemed so strong throughout, now appeared quite fragile, as if her heart would be crushed.

The old woman wasn't finished.

"Don't you spend your time looking for Cold Sandra," she said, "or Honey in the Sunshine, either." She gripped Merrick's wrist all the harder. "You leave those two to me. That's a woman who left her baby for a man, Cold Sandra. Don't you cry for Cold Sandra. You keep your candles burning for the others. You cry for me."

Merrick was distraught. She was crying without a sound. She bent down and laid her head on the pillow beside that of the old woman, and the old woman wrapped her withered arm around the child's shoulders, which appeared to droop.

"That's my baby," she said, "my baby girl. Don't you cry over Cold Sandra. Cold Sandra took Honey in the Sunshine with her on the road to Hell."

The priest moved away from the bed. He had begun to pray in a soft voice, the Hail Mary in English, and when he came to the words "Pray for us sinners, *now and at the hour of our death*," he timidly and gently raised his voice.

"I'll tell you if I find those two," said Great Nananne in a murmur. "St. Peter, let me through the gates. St. Peter, let me through."

I knew she was calling on Papa Legba. Possibly they were one and the same for her, Papa Legba and St. Peter. The priest probably knew all about it too.

The priest drew near again. Aaron stood back out of respect. Merrick remained with her head down on the pillow, her face buried in it, her right hand against the old woman's cheek.

The priest raised his hands to give the blessing in Latin, *In Nomine Patris, et filie, et spiritu sanctum, Amen.*

I felt I should leave, out of decency, but Aaron gave me no signal. What right had I to remain?

I looked again at the gruesome altar, and at the huge statue of St. Peter with his Heavenly keys, very like the one I was to see years later—only a night ago—in Merrick's hotel suite.

I stepped back and into the hallway. I looked out the back door, though why, I was uncertain, perhaps to see the foliage darkening as the rain fell. My heart was pounding. The big noisy wet drops came in the back door and in the front, and left their mark on the soiled old wooden floor.

I heard Merrick crying aloud. Time stood still, as it can on a warm afternoon in New Orleans. Suddenly, Merrick cried all the more miserably, and Aaron had put his arm around her.

It had been an awakening, to realize that the old woman in the bed had died.

I was stunned. Having known her for less than an hour, having heard her revelations, I was stunned. I could make no sense of her powers, except that too much of my Talamasca experience had been academic, and, faced with true magic, I was as easily shaken as anyone else.

We remained near the door of the bedroom for three quarters of an hour. It seemed that the neighbors wanted to come in.

Merrick was at first against it, leaning against Aaron and crying that she'd never find Cold Sandra, and Cold Sandra ought to have come home.

The child's palpable misery was dreadful to us all, and the priest again and again came to Merrick and kissed her and patted her.

At last, two young women of color, both very fair and with obvious signs of African blood, came in to attend to the body in the bed. One woman took Merrick in hand and told her to close her godmother's eyes. I marveled at these women. It wasn't only their gorgeous colored skin or their pale eyes. It was their old-fashioned formal manner, the way they were dressed in shirtwaist dresses of silk, with jewelry, as if to come calling, and the importance of this little ceremony in their minds.

Merrick went to the bed and did her duty with two fingers of her right hand. Aaron came to stand beside me in the hall.

Merrick came out, asked Aaron through her sobs if he would wait while the women cleaned up Great Nananne and changed the bed, and of course Aaron told her that we would do as she wished.

We went into a rather formal parlor on the other side of the hall. The old woman's proud statements came back to me. This parlor opened by means of an arch into a large dining room, and both rooms contained many fine and costly things.

There were huge mirrors over the fireplaces, and these had their heavily carved white marble mantels; and the furniture, of rich mahogany, would fetch a good price.

Darkened paintings of saints hung here and there. The huge china cabinet was crowded with old patterned bone china; and there were a few huge lamps with dim bulbs beneath dusty shades.

It would have been rather comfortable except it was suffocatingly hot, and though there were broken windowpanes, only the dampness seemed to penetrate the dusty shadows where we sat down.

At once, a young woman, another rather exotically colored creature, lovely and as primly dressed as the others, came in to cover the mirrors. She had a great deal of folded black cloth with her, and a small ladder. Aaron and I did what we could to assist.

After that she closed the keyboard of an old upright piano which I had not even noticed. Then she went to a large casement clock in the corner, opened the glass, and stopped the hands. I heard the ticking for the first time only when it actually ceased.

A large crowd of people, black, white, and of different racial blending, gathered before the house.

At last the mourners were allowed to come in and there was a very long procession, during which time Aaron and I retired to the sidewalk, as it was perfectly plain that Merrick who had taken up a position at the head of the bed, was no longer so badly shaken, only merely terribly sad.

People stepped into the room, as far as the foot of the bed, and then went out the back door of the house, reappearing again along the side as they opened a small secondary gate to the street.

I remember being very impressed by the sobriety and silence that reigned, and being somewhat surprised as cars began to arrive and smartly dressed people—again, of both races, and of obvious mixture—went up the steps.

My clothes became uncomfortably limp and sticky from the drowsy heat, and several times I went inside the house to assure myself that Merrick was all right. Several window air conditioning units in the bedroom, living room, and dining room had been pressed into service, and the rooms were growing cool.

It was on my third visit that I realized a collection was being taken for the funeral of Great Nananne. Indeed a china bowl on the altar was overflowing with twenty-dollar bills.

As for Merrick, her face showed little or no emotion as she gave a little nod to each person who came to call. Yet she was obviously numb and miserable.

Hour followed hour. Still people came, drifting in and out in the same respectful silence, only giving in to conversation when they were well away from the house.

I could hear the more formally dressed women of color speaking to one another with the most genteel southern accents, very far from the African which I have heard.

Aaron assured me in a whisper that this was hardly typical of funeral affairs in New Orleans. The crowd was altogether different. It was too quiet.

I could sense the problem with no difficulty. People had been afraid of Great Nananne. People were afraid of Merrick. People made sure that Merrick saw them. People left lots of twenty-dollar bills. There wasn't to be a funeral mass, and people didn't know what to make of it. People thought there ought to be a mass, but Merrick said Great Nananne herself had said no.

At last, as we stood in the alleyway once more, enjoying our cigarettes, I saw a look of concern on Aaron's face. He made a very subtle gesture, that I was to look at an expensive car which had just come to the curb.

Several obviously white persons got out of the car—a rather handsome young man, and an austere woman with a pair of wire-rimmed glasses on her nose. They went directly up the steps, deliberately avoiding the gaze of those who hung about.

"Those are white Mayfairs," said Aaron under his breath. "I can't be noticed here." Together we moved deeper into the alleyway and towards the back of the house. Finally, when the way became impassable due to the magnificent wisteria, we stopped.

"But what does it mean?" I asked. "The white Mayfairs. Why have they come?"

"Obviously, they feel some obligation," said Aaron in a whisper. "Truly, David, you must be quiet. There isn't a member of the family who doesn't have some psychic power. You know I've tried in vain to make contact. I don't want us to be seen here."

"But who are they?" I pressed. I knew a voluminous file existed on the Mayfair Witches. I knew Aaron had been assigned to it for years. Yes, I knew, but for me as Superior General it was one story among thousands.

And the exotic climate, the strange old house, the clairvoyance of the old woman, the rising weeds, and the sunshiney rainfall had all gone to my head. I was as stimulated as if we were seeing ghosts.

"The family lawyers," he said in a hushed voice, trying to hide his annoyance with me. "Lauren Mayfair and young Ryan Mayfair. They don't know anything, not about Voodoo or witches, here or uptown, but clearly they know the woman is related to them. They don't shirk a family responsibility, the Mayfairs, but I never expected to see them here."

At this juncture, as he cautioned me again to be quiet and stay out of the way, I heard Merrick speaking within. I drew close to the broken windows of the formal parlor. I couldn't make out what was being said.

Aaron, too, was listening. Very shortly the white Mayfairs emerged from the house and went away in their new car.

Only then did Aaron go up to the steps. The last of the mourners was just leaving. Those out on the pavement had already paid their respects. I followed Aaron into Great Nananne's room.

"Those uptown Mayfairs," said Merrick in a low voice, "You saw them? They wanted to pay for everything. I told them we had plenty. Look there, we have thousands of dollars, and the undertaker is already coming. We'll wake the body tonight and tomorrow it will be buried. I'm hungry. I need something to eat."

Indeed the elderly undertaker was also a man of color, quite tall and completely bald. He arrived along with his rectangular basket in which he would place the body of Great Nananne.

As for the house, it was now left to the undertaker's father, a *very* elderly colored man, much the same hue as Merrick, except that he had tight curly white hair. Both of the aforementioned old men had a distinguished air, and wore rather formal clothes, when one considered the monstrous heat.

They also believed that there should be a Roman Catholic mass at Our Lady of Guadalupe Church, but Merrick again explained that they didn't need that for Great Nananne.

It was amazing how well this settled the whole affair.

Now Merrick went to the bureau in Great Nananne's room and removed from the top drawer a bundle wrapped in white sheeting, and gestured for us to leave the house.

Off we went to a restaurant, where Merrick, saying nothing, and keeping the bundle on her lap, devoured an enormous fried shrimp sandwich and two diet Cokes. She had obviously grown tired of crying, and had the weary sad-eyed look of those who are deeply and irreparably hurt.

The little restaurant struck me as exotic, having a filthy floor and obviously dirty tables, but the happiest waiters and waitresses as well as clientele.

I was hypnotized by New Orleans, hypnotized by Merrick, though she was saying nothing; but little did I know that stranger things were yet to come.

In a dream, we went back to Oak Haven, to bathe and to change for the wake. There was a young woman there, a good member of the Talamasca whom I shall not name for obvious reasons, who assisted Merrick and saw to it that she was turned out beautifully in a new navy blue dress and broad-brimmed straw hat. Aaron himself gave a quick buffing to her patent leather shoes. Merrick had a rosary with her and a Catholic prayer book with a pearl cover.

But before she would have us return to New Orleans, she wanted to show us the contents of the bundle she had taken from the old woman's room.

We were in the library, where I first met Merrick only a short time before. The Motherhouse was at supper, so we had the room entirely to ourselves, with no special request.

When she unwrapped the sheeting, I was astonished to see an ancient book or codex, with brilliant illustrations on its wooden cover, a thing in tatters, which Merrick handled as carefully as she could.

"This is my book from Great Nananne," she said, looking at the thick volume with obvious respect. She let Aaron lift the book in its swaddling to the table under the light.

Now vellum or parchment is the strongest material ever invented for books, and this one was clearly so old that it would never have survived had it been written on anything else. Indeed, the wooden cover was all but in pieces. Merrick herself took the initiative to move it to the side so that the title page of the book could be read.

It was in Latin, and I translated it as instantly as any member of the Talamasca could do.

HEREIN LIE ALL SECRETS

OF THE MAGICAL ARTS

AS TAUGHT TO HAM,

SON OF NOAH,

BY THE WATCHERS

AND PASSED DOWN TO HIS ONLY SON,

Mesran

Carefully lifting this page, which was bound as all the others were by three different ties of leather thong, Merrick revealed the first of many pages of magic spells, written in faded but clearly visible and very crowded Latin script.

It was as old a book of magic as I have ever beheld, and of course its claim—the claim of its title page—was to the very earliest of all black magic ever known since the time of The Flood.

Indeed, I was more than familiar with the legends surrounding Noah, and his son, Ham, and the even earlier tale, that the Watcher Angels had taught magic to the Daughters of Men when they lay with them, as Genesis so states.

Even the angel Memnoch, the seducer of Lestat, had revealed a version of this tale in his own fashion, that is, of being seduced during his earthly wanderings by a Daughter of Man. But of course I knew nothing of Memnoch back then.

I wanted to be alone with this book! I wanted to read every syllable of it. I wanted to have our experts test its paper, its ink, as well as peruse its style.

It will come as no surprise to most readers of my narrative that people exist who can tell the age of such a book at a glance. I was not one such person, but I believed firmly that what I held had been copied out in some monastery somewhere in Christendom, somewhere before William the Conqueror had ever come to the English shores.

To put it more simply, the book was probably eighth or ninth century. And as I leant over to read the opening page I saw that it claimed to be a "faithful copy" of a much earlier text that had come down, of course, from Noah's son, Ham, himself.

There were so many rich legends surrounding these names. But the marvelous thing was that this text belonged to Merrick and that she was revealing it to us.

"This is my book," she said again. "And I know how to work the charms and spells in it. I know them all."

"But who taught you to read it?" I asked, unable to conceal my enthusiasm.

"Matthew," she answered, "the man who took me and Cold Sandra to South America. He was so excited when he saw this book, and the others. Of course I could already read it a little, and Great Nananne could read every word. Matthew was the best of the men my mother ever brought home. Things were safe and cheerful when Matthew was with us. But we can't talk about these matters now. You have to let me keep my book."

"Amen, you shall," said Aaron quickly. I think he was afraid that I meant to spirit away the text but nothing of the sort was true. I wanted time with it, yes, but only when the child would permit.

As for Merrick's mention of her mother, I had been more than curious. In fact, I felt we should question her on that point immediately, but Aaron shook his head sternly when I started to inquire.

"Come on, let's us go back now," said Merrick. "The body will be laid out."

Leaving the precious book in Merrick's upstairs bedroom, back we went to the city of dreams once more.

The body had been brought back in a dove-gray casket lined in satin, and set upon a portable bier in the grim front parlor which I described before. By the light of numerous candles—the overhead chandelier was naked and harsh and therefore turned off—the room was almost beautiful, and Great Nananne was now dressed in a fine gown of white silk with tiny pink roses stitched to the collar, a favorite from her own chifforobe.

A beautiful rosary of crystal beads was wound around her clasped fingers, and above her head, against the satin of the lid of the coffin, there hung a gold crucifix. A prie-dieu of red velvet, furnished no doubt by the undertaker, stood beside the coffin, and many came up to kneel there, to make the Sign of the Cross, and to pray.

Once again there came hordes of people, and indeed they did tend to break into groups according to race, just as if someone had commanded them to do so, the light of skin clumping together, as well as whites clumped with whites, and blacks with blacks.

Since this time I have seen many situations in the city of New Orleans in which people self-segregate according to color in a most marked way. But then, I didn't know the city. I knew only that the monstrous injustice of Legal Segregation no longer existed, and I marveled at the way color seemed to dominate the separation in this group.

On tenterhooks, Aaron and I waited to be questioned about Merrick, and what was to happen to her, but no one spoke a single word. Indeed, people merely embraced Merrick, kissed her and whispered to her, and then went their way. Once more there was a bowl, and money was put in it, but for what I did not know. Probably for Merrick, because surely people knew she had no mother or father there.

Only as we prepared to go to sleep on cots in a rear room (the body

would remain exposed all night), which was totally unfurnished otherwise, did Merrick bring in the priest to speak to us, saying to him in
very good and rapid French that we were her uncles and she would live
with us.

"So that is the story," I thought. We were uncles of Merrick. Merrick was definitely going away to school.

"It's exactly what I meant to recommend to her," said Aaron. "I
wonder how she knew it. I thought she would quarrel with me about
such a change."

I didn't know what I thought. This sober, serious, and beautiful
child disturbed me and attracted me. The whole spectacle made me
doubt my mind.

That night, we slept only fitfully. The cots were uncomfortable, the
empty room was hot, and people were going and coming and forever
whispering in the hall.

Many times I went into the parlor to find Merrick dozing quietly in
her chair. The old priest himself went to sleep sometime near morning. I could see out the back door into a yard shrouded in shadow
where distant candles or lamps flickered wildly. It was disturbing. I fell
asleep while there were still a few stars in the sky.

At last, there came the morning, and it was time for the funeral service to begin.

The priest appeared in the proper vestments, and with his altar boy,
and intoned the prayers which the entire crowd seemed to know. The
English language service, for that is what it was, was no less awe inspir-
ing than the old Latin Rite, which had been cast aside. The coffin was
closed.

Merrick began to shake all over and then to sob. It was a dreadful
thing to behold. She had pushed away her straw hat, and her head was
bare. She began to sob louder and louder. Several well-dressed women
of color gathered around her and escorted her down the front steps.
They rubbed her arms vigorously and wiped her forehead. Her sobs
came like hiccups. The women cooed to her and kissed her. At one
point Merrick let out a scream.

To see this composed little girl now near hysterics wrenched my
heart.

They all but carried her to the funeral service limousine. The coffin
came behind her, accompanied by solemn pallbearers to the hearse,
and then off to the cemetery we rode, Aaron and I in the Talamasca car,

uncomfortably separated from Merrick but resigned that it was for the best.

The sorrowful theatricality was not diminished as the rain came steadily down upon us, and the body of Great Nananne was carried through the wildly overgrown path of St. Louis No. 1 amid high marble tombs with pointed roofs, to be placed in an oven-like vault of a three-story grave.

The mosquitoes were almost unbearable. The weeds seemed alive with invisible insects, and Merrick, at the sight of the coffin being put in its place, screamed again.

Once more the genteel women rubbed her arms and wiped her head, and kissed her cheeks.

Then Merrick let out a terrible cry in French.

"Where are you, Cold Sandra, where are you, Honey in the Sunshine? Why didn't you come home!"

There were rosary beads aplenty, and people praying aloud, as Merrick leant against the grave, with her right hand on the exposed coffin.

Finally, having spent herself for the moment, she grew quiet and turned and moved decisively, with the help of the women, towards Aaron and me. As the women patted her, she threw her arms around Aaron and buried her head in his neck.

I could see nothing of the young woman in her now. I felt utter compassion for her. I felt the Talamasca must embrace her with every conceivable element of fantasy that she should ever desire.

The priest meanwhile insisted the cemetery attendants bolt the stone into place NOW, which caused some argument, but eventually this did happen, the stone thereby sealing up the little grave slot and the coffin now officially removed from touch or view.

I remember taking out my handkerchief and wiping my eyes.

Aaron stroked Merrick's long brown hair and told her in French that Great Nananne had lived a marvelous and long life, and that her one deathbed wish—that Merrick be safe—had been fulfilled.

Merrick lifted her head and uttered only one sentence. "Cold Sandra should have come." I remember it because when she said it several of the onlookers shook their heads and exchanged condemnatory glances with one another.

I felt rather helpless. I studied the faces of the men and women around me. I saw some of the blackest people of African blood I have ever beheld in America, and some of the lightest as well. I saw people of extraordinary beauty and others who were merely simple. Almost no one was ordinary, as we understand that word. It seemed quite impossible to guess the lineage or racial history of anyone I saw.

But none of these people were close to Merrick. Except for Aaron and for me, she was basically alone. The well-dressed genteel women had done their duty, but they really did not know her. That was plain. And they were happy for her that she had two rich uncles who were there to take her away.

As for the "white Mayfairs" whom Aaron had spotted yesterday, none had appeared. This was "great luck," according to Aaron. If they had known a Mayfair child was friendless in the wide world, they would have insisted upon filling the need. Indeed, I realize now, they had not been at the wake, either. They had done their duty, Merrick had told them something satisfactory, and they had gone their way.

Now it was back towards the old house.

A truck from Oak Haven was already waiting for the transport of Merrick's possessions. Merrick had no intention of leaving her aunt's dwelling without everything that was hers.

Sometime or other before we reached the house, Merrick stopped crying, and a somber expression settled over her features which I have seen many times.

"Cold Sandra doesn't know," she said suddenly without preamble. The car moved sluggishly through the soft rain. "If she knew, she would have come."

"She is your mother?" Aaron asked reverently.

Merrick nodded. "That what's she always said," she answered, and she broke into a fairly playful smile. She shook her head and looked out the car window. "Oh, don't you worry about it, Mr. Lightner," she said. "Cold Sandra didn't really leave me. She went off and just didn't come back."

That seemed to make perfect sense at the moment, perhaps only because I wanted it to make sense, so that Merrick would not be deeply hurt by some more commanding truth.

"When was the last time you saw her?" Aaron ventured.

"When I was ten years old and we came back from South America. When Matthew was still alive. You have to understand Cold Sandra. She was the only one of twelve children who didn't pass."

"Didn't pass?" asked Aaron.

"For white," I said before I could stop myself.

Once again, Merrick smiled.

"Ah, I see," said Aaron.

"She's beautiful," said Merrick, "no one could ever say she wasn't, and she could fix any man she wanted. They never got away."

"Fix?" asked Aaron.

"To fix with a spell," I said under my breath.

Again, Merrick smiled at me.

"Ah, I see," said Aaron again.

"My grandfather, when he saw how tan my mother was, he said that wasn't his child, and my grandmother, she came and dumped Cold Sandra on Great Nananne's doorstep. Her sisters and brothers, they all married white people. 'Course my grandfather was a white man too. Chicago is where they are all are. That man who was Cold Sandra's father, he owned a jazz club up in Chicago. When people like Chicago and New York, they don't want to stay down here anymore. Myself, I didn't like either one."

"You mean you've traveled there?" I asked.

"Oh, yes, I went with Cold Sandra," she said. " 'Course we didn't see those white people. But we did look them up in the book. Cold Sandra wanted to set eyes on her mother, she said, but not to talk to her. And who knows, maybe she did her bad magic. She might have done that to all of them. Cold Sandra was so afraid of flying to Chicago, but she was more afraid of driving up there too. And drowning? She had nightmares about drowning. She wouldn't drive across the Causeway for anything in this world. Afraid of the lake like it was going to get her. She was so afraid of so many things." She broke off. Her face went blank. Then, with a small touch of a frown, she went on:

"I don't remember liking Chicago very much. New York had no trees that I ever saw. I couldn't wait to come back home. Cold Sandra, she loved New Orleans too. She always came back, until the last time."

"Was she a smart woman, your mother?" I asked. "Was she bright the way you are?"

This gave her pause for thought.

"She's got no education," said Merrick. "She doesn't read books. I myself, I like to read. When you read you can learn things, you know. I read old magazines that people left lying around. One time I got stacks and stacks of *Time* magazine from some old house they were tearing down. I read everything I could in those magazines, I mean every one of them; I read about art and science and books and music and politics and every single thing till those magazines were falling apart. I read books from the library, from the grocery store racks; I read the newspaper. I read old prayer books. I've read books of magic. I have many books of magic that I haven't even showed you yet."

She gave a little shrug with her shoulders, looking small and weary but still the child in her puzzlement of all that had happened.

"Cold Sandra wouldn't read anything," she said. "You'd never see Cold Sandra watching the six o'clock news. Great Nananne sent her to the nuns, she always said, but Cold Sandra misbehaved and they were always sending her home. Besides, Cold Sandra was plenty light enough to not like dark people herself, you know. You'd think she knew better, with her own father dumping her, but she did not. Fact is she was the color of an almond, if you see the picture. But she had those light yellow eyes, and that's a dead giveaway, those yellow eyes. She hated it when they started calling her Cold Sandra too."

"How did the nickname come about?" I asked. "Did the children start it?"

We had almost reached our destination. I remember there was so much more I wanted to know about this strange society, so alien to what I knew. At that moment, I felt that my opportunities in Brazil had been largely wasted. The old woman's words had stung me to the heart.

"No, it started right in our house," said Merrick. "That's the worst kind of nickname, I figure. When the neighbors and the children heard it, they said 'Your own Nananne calls you Cold Sandra.' But it stuck on account of the things she did. She used all the magic to fix people, like I said. She put the Evil Eye on people. I saw her skin a black cat once and I never want to see that again."

I must have flinched because a tiny smile settled on her lips for a moment. Then she went on.

"By the time I was six years old, she started calling herself Cold Sandra. She'd say to me, 'Merrick, you come here to Cold Sandra.' I'd jump in her lap."

There was a slight break in her voice as she continued.

"She was nothing like Great Nananne," Merrick said. "And she smoked all the time and she drank, and she was always restless, and when she drank she was mean. When Cold Sandra came home after being gone for a long time, Great Nananne would say, 'What's in your cold heart this time, Cold Sandra? What lies are you going to tell?'

"Great Nananne used to say there was no time for black magic in this world. You could do all you had to do with good magic. Then Matthew came, and Cold Sandra was the happiest she'd ever been."

"Matthew," I said coaxingly, "the man who gave you the parchment book."

"He didn't give me that book, Mr. Talbot, he taught me to read it," she answered. "That book we already had. That book came from Great-Oncle Vervain, who was a terrible Voodoo Man. They called him Dr. Vervain from one end of the city to the other. Everybody wanted his spells. That old man gave me lots of things before he passed on. He was Great Nananne's older brother. He was the first person I ever saw just up and die. He was sitting at the dining room table with the newspaper in his hand."

I had more questions on the tip of my tongue.

In all of this long unfolding tale there had been no mention of that other name which Great Nananne had uttered: Honey in the Sunshine.

But we had arrived at the old house. The afternoon sun was quite strong but the rain had thinned away.

8

I WAS SURPRISED to see so many people standing about. Indeed they were everywhere, and a very subdued but attentive lot. I observed at once that not one, but two small paneled trucks had come from the Motherhouse, and that there stood guard a small group of Talamasca acolytes, ready to pack up the house.

I greeted these youngsters of the Order, thanking them in advance for their care and discretion, and told them to wait quietly until they were given the signal to begin their work.

As we went up the stairs and walked through the house, I saw, where the windows permitted me to see anything, that people were loitering in the alleyways, and as we came into the backyard, I noticed many persons gathered far off to the right and to the left beyond the heavy growth of the low-limbed oaks. I could see no fences anywhere. And I do not believe there were any at that time.

All was dimness beneath a canopy of luxuriant leaf, and we were surrounded by the sound of softly dripping water. Wild red hyacinth grew where the sun could penetrate the precious gloom. I saw thin yew trees, the species so sacred to the dead and to the magician. And I saw many lilies lost in the choking grass. It could not have been more lulling and dreamy had it been a purposeful Japanese garden.

As my eyes became accustomed to the light, I realized that we were standing on a flagstone patio of sorts, punctuated by several twisted yet flowering trees, and much cracked and overwhelmed by slippery shining moss. Before us stood a huge open shed with a central pillar holding its corrugated tin roof.

The pillar was brightly painted red to the midpoint and green to the top, and it rose from a huge altar stone quite appropriately heavily stained. Beyond in the darkness stood the inevitable altar, with saints even more numerous and magnificent than those in Great Nananne's bedroom.

There were banks upon banks of lighted candles.

It was, I knew from my studies, a common Voodoo configuration— the central pillar and the stone. One could find it all over the island of Haiti. And this weedy flagstone spot was what a Haitian Voodoo doctor might have called his peristyle.

Cast to the side, among the close and straggling yew trees, I saw two iron tables, small and rectangular in shape, and a large pot or cauldron, as I suppose it is properly called, resting upon a brazier with tripod legs. The cauldron and the deep brazier disturbed me somewhat, possibly more than anything else. The cauldron seemed an evil thing.

A humming sound distracted me somewhat, because I was afraid that it came from bees. I have a very great fear of bees, and like many members of the Talamasca, I fear some secret regarding bees which has to do with our origins, but there is not room enough to explain here.

Allow me to continue by saying only that I quickly realized that the sound came from hummingbirds in this vast overgrown place, and when I stood quite still beside Merrick, I fancied I saw them hovering as they do, near the fiercely sprawling flower-covered vines of the shed roof.

"Oncle Vervain loved them," said Merrick to me in a hushed voice. "He put out the feeders for them. He knew them by their colors and he called them beautiful names."

"I love them, too, child," I said. "In Brazil they had a beautiful name in Portuguese, 'the kisser of flowers,' " I said.

"Yes, Oncle Vervain knew those things," she told me. "Oncle Vervain had been all over South America. Oncle Vervain could see the ghosts in the middle air all around him all the time."

She left off with these words. But I had the distinct feeling that it was going to be very difficult for her to say farewell to this, her home. As for her use of the phrase "ghosts in the middle air," I was suitably impressed, as I had been by so much else. Of course we would keep this house for her, of that I'd make certain. We'd have the place entirely restored if she so wished.

She looked about herself, her eyes lingering on the iron pot on its tripod.

"Oncle Vervain could boil the cauldron," she said softly. "He put coals under it. I can still remember the smell of the smoke. Great Nananne would sit on the back steps to watch him. Everybody else was afraid."

She went forward now and into the shed, and stood before the saints, staring at the many offerings and glittering candles. She made the Sign of the Cross quickly and laid her right two fingers on the naked foot of the tall and beautiful Virgin.

What were we to do?

Aaron and I stood a little behind her, and at her shoulders, like two rather confused guardian angels. There was fresh food in the dishes on the altar. I smelled sweet perfume and rum. Obviously some of those people crowded about in the shrubbery had brought these mysterious offerings. But I shrank back when I realized that one of the curious objects heaped there in seeming disarray was in fact a human hand.

It was cut right before the wrist bone, and it had dried into a dreadful clench of sorts, but that was not the full horror. It was overrun with ants, who had made a little massacre of the entire feast.

When I realized that the loathsome insects were everywhere, I felt a peculiar horror that only ants can bring.

Merrick, much to my amazement, picked up this hand rather daintily in her thumb and forefinger, and shook off the hoodlum ants with several small fierce gestures.

I heard nothing from the audience in the crowd beyond, but it seemed to me that they pressed closer. The humming of the birds was becoming hypnotic, and again there came a low hiss of rain.

Nothing penetrated the canopy. Nothing struck the tin of the roof.

"What do you want us to do with these things?" asked Aaron gently. "You don't want anything left, as I understand it."

"We're going to take it down," said Merrick, "if it's all right with you. It's past its time. This house should be closed up now, if you will keep your promises to me. I want to go with you."

"Yes, we'll have everything dismantled."

She suddenly looked at the shriveled hand which she held in her own. The ants were crawling onto her skin.

"Put it down, child," I said suddenly, startling myself.

She gave it a wring or two again and then did what I said. "It must come with us, everything must," she said. "Some day, I'll take out all these things and I'll see what they are." She brushed off the unwelcome ants.

Her dismissive tone filled me with relief, I must confess it.

"Absolutely," said Aaron. He turned and gave a signal to the Talamasca acolytes who had come as far as the edge of the patio behind us. "They will begin packing everything," he told Merrick.

"There's one thing in this backyard that I have to take myself," she said, glancing at me and then at Aaron. She seemed not purposefully or playfully mysterious as much as troubled.

She backed away from us and moved slowly towards one of the gnarled fruit trees that sprang up in the very middle of the patio flagstones. She dipped her head as she moved under the low green branches, and lifted her arms almost as if she was trying to embrace the tree.

In a moment, I saw her purpose. I should have guessed it. A huge snake had descended, coiling itself about her arms and her shoulders. It was a constrictor.

I felt a helpless shudder and a total revulsion. Not even my years in the Amazon had made me a patient liker of snakes. Quite to the contrary. But I knew what they felt like; I knew that eerie silky weight, and the strange current of feeling they sent through one's skin as they moved very rapidly to encoil one's arms.

I could feel these things as I watched her.

Meanwhile, out of the overgrown tangle of green there came low whispers from those who watched her as well. This is what they had gathered to see. This was the moment. The snake was a Voodoo god, of course. I knew it. But I was still amazed.

"It's definitely harmless," Aaron said to me hastily. As if he knew! "We'll have to feed it a rat or two, I suppose, but to us, it's quite—."

"Never mind," I said with a smile, letting him off the hook. I could see he was quite uncomfortable. And then to tease him a little, and to fend off the deep melancholy of the place, I said, "You know of course the rodents must be alive."

He was appropriately horrified and gave me a reproving glance, as if to say, you needn't have told me that! But he was far too polite to say a word.

Merrick was talking to the snake in a low voice in French.

She made her way back to the altar, and there found a black iron box with barred windows on all sides—I know no other words for it—which she opened with one hand, the hinges of its lid creaking loudly; and into this box she let the serpent slowly and gracefully settle itself, which fortunately for all of us, it did.

"Well, we'll see what stalwart gentlemen want to carry the snake," Aaron said to the closest of the assistants who stood speechless, watching.

Meanwhile, the crowd had begun to break up and slip away. There was much rustling in the trees. Leaves fell all around us. Somewhere, unseen in the lush garden, the birds continued to hover, beating the air with their tiny busy wings.

Merrick stood for a long moment looking up, as though she'd found a chink in the rooftop of foliage.

"I'll never be coming back here, I don't think," she said softly to both of us or to no one.

"Why do you say that, child?" I asked. "You can do as you like, you can come every day if you wish. There are so many things we must talk over together."

"It's ruined, this whole place," she said, "and besides, if Cold Sandra ever comes back, I don't want her to find me." She looked at me in a level manner. "You see, she is my mother and she could take me away, and I don't want that ever to happen."

"It won't happen," I responded, though no one on earth could give the child such a guarantee against a mother's love, and Merrick knew it. I could only do my best to see that we did what Merrick wanted.

"Now, come," she said, "there are some things up in the attic that only I want to move."

The attic was in fact the second story of the house, a very deep sloped roof affair, as I have described, with four dormer windows, one for each point of the compass, assuming the house was correctly oriented. I had no idea whether it was or not.

We made our way up by a narrow back stairs that doubled once upon itself and then entered a place of such delicious woody fragrances that I was caught off guard. It had a snugness and a cleanness about it, despite the dust.

Merrick turned on a grim electric bulb and we soon found ourselves amid suitcases, ancient trunks, and leather-bound packing cases. It was vintage luggage. An antiques dealer would have loved it. And I, having seen one book of magic, was very much ready for more.

Merrick had but one suitcase that mattered above all else, she explained, and she set this down on the dusty rafters beneath the dangling light.

It was a canvas bag with leathered patched corners. She opened it with ease, as it wasn't locked, and stared down at a series of loosely wrapped cloth bundles. Once again, white sheeting had been used for these items, or perhaps to put it more simply, cotton pillowcases past their time.

It was obvious that the contents of this case were of very special importance, but how special I could not have guessed.

I was astonished now as Merrick, whispering a little prayer, an Ave, if I'm correct, lifted one bundle and moved back the cloth to reveal a startling object—a long green axe blade, heavily incised with figures on both sides.

It was easily two feet in length and quite heavy, though Merrick held it easily. And Aaron and I both could see the likeness of a face in profile carved deeply into the stone.

"Pure jade," said Aaron reverently.

It had been highly polished, this object, and the face in profile wore an elaborate and beautifully realized headdress, which if I'm not mistaken, involved both plumage and ears of corn.

The carved portrait or ritual image, whichever it might be, was as large as a human face.

As Merrick turned the object, I saw that a full figure was etched into the other side. There was a small hole near the narrow tapering end of the object, perhaps to allow suspension from a belt.

"My God," said Aaron under his breath. "It's Olmec, isn't it? It must be priceless."

"Olmec, if I have any guess," I answered. "Never have I seen such a large and exquisitely decorated object outside of a museum."

Merrick showed no surprise.

"Don't say things you don't mean, Mr. Talbot," she said gently. "You have some like this in your own vault." She locked her eyes on me for a long dreamy moment.

I could scarcely breathe. How could she know such a thing? But then I told myself she might have learnt such information from Aaron. Only, a glance at him let me know I was quite wrong.

"Not as beautiful, Merrick," I answered her quite truthfully. "And ours are fragments, as well."

When she gave me no reply, when she merely stood there holding the gleaming axe blade with both hands out before her, as if she liked to look at the light on it, I went on.

"It's worth a fortune, child," I said, "and I never expected to see such a thing in this place."

She thought for a long second, and then gave me a solemn forgiving nod.

"In my opinion," I went on, struggling to redeem myself, "it comes from the oldest known civilization in Central America. And I can feel my heart thumping as I look at it."

"Maybe even older than Olmec," she said, looking up at me again. Her wide gaze swept lazily over Aaron. The gold light of the bulb spilled down upon her and the elaborately dressed figure. "That's what Matthew said after we took it from the cave beyond the waterfall. That's what Oncle Vervain said when he told me where to look."

I looked down again on the splendid face of shining green stone with its blank eyes and flattened nose.

"You don't need me to tell you," I said, "that it's all very likely so. The Olmec come from nowhere, or so the textbooks tell us."

She nodded.

"Oncle Vervain was born from one of those Indians who knew the deepest magic. Colored man and red woman made Oncle Vervain and Great Nananne, and Cold Sandra's mother was Great Nananne's grandchild, so it's inside of me."

I couldn't speak. There weren't any words to express my trust or my wonder.

Merrick set the axe blade to one side, on top of the many bundles, and reached for another with equal care. This was a smaller, longer bundle, and when she unwrapped it, I was again too breathless for words.

It was a tall figure, richly carved, and obviously a god or king, I could not say which. As with the axe blade, the size alone was impressive, not to mention the gloss of the stone.

"Nobody knows," the child said, speaking to my thoughts very directly. "Only, you see this scepter, it's magic. If he's a king, he's a priest and god too."

Humbled, I studied the detailed carving. The long narrow figure wore a handsome headdress which came low over his fierce, wide eyes, and down to his shoulders all around. On his naked chest was a disc suspended from the radial collar about his shoulders and neck.

As for the scepter, he seemed about to be striking the open palm of his left hand with it, as though preparing to do violence with it when his enemy or victim approached. It was chilling in its menace and beautiful in its sincerity and intricacy. It was polished and seemed to glow, as did the mask.

"Shall I stand him up or lay him down?" Merrick asked, looking at me. "I don't play with these creatures. No, I would never do such a thing. I can feel the magic in them. I've conjured with them. I don't play. Let me cover him once more so he can be quiet."

Having rewrapped the idol, she reached for yet a third bundle. I could not calculate the number that remained in the closely packed case.

I could see that Aaron was speechless. One did not have to be an expert in Mesoamerican antiquities to realize what these artifacts were.

As for Merrick, she began to talk as she unwrapped this third wonder . . .

"We went down there, and followed the map that Oncle Vervain had given us. And Cold Sandra kept praying to Oncle Vervain to tell us where to go. It was Matthew and Cold Sandra and me. Cold Sandra kept saying, 'Aren't you happy now, you never went to school? You're always complaining. Well, you're getting to go on a great adventure.' And to tell the truth, that's what it was."

The cloth fell away from the long sharp pointed pick in her hands. It was all of a piece of green jade, and its handle bore the distinct feathers of the hummingbird and two small deeply carved eyes. I had seen its type before in museums, but never such a fine example. And now I understood Oncle Vervain's love of the birds in the yard beyond.

"Yes, sir," said Merrick. "He said those birds were magic. He was the one to put the feeders out. I told you. Who's going to fill the feeders when I leave this place behind?"

"We'll care for the place," said Aaron in his comforting fashion. But I could see he was greatly concerned about Merrick. She went on talking.

"The Aztecs believed in hummingbirds. They hover in the air like magic. They turn this way and that and make another color. There's a legend that Aztec warriors became hummingbirds when they died.

Oncle Vervain said magicians need to know everything. Oncle Vervain said our kind were all magicians, that we came four thousand years before the Aztecs. He told me about the paintings on the cave wall."

"And you know where this cave is?" Aaron asked her. He was quick to clarify his meaning. "Darling, you must tell no one. Men lose common sense over secrets such as these."

"I have Oncle Vervain's pages," Merrick answered in the same dreamy voice. She laid the sharp blade of this knife back down on the bed of cotton parcels. Offhandedly, she laid bare a fourth object, a small squat idol as beautifully carved as the one already revealed. Her hand went back to the perforator with its round, hummingbird handle. "They used this to draw blood in their magic. That's what Oncle Vervain told me I would find, a thing for drawing blood; that's what Matthew said this was."

"This suitcase is filled with such objects, isn't it?" I asked. "These are by no means the most significant of the lot?" I glanced about. "What else is hidden in this attic?"

She shrugged. For the first time she looked hot and uncomfortable under the low roof.

"Come on," she said politely, "let's us pack up the suitcase and go down to the kitchen. Tell your people not to open all those boxes, just to move them to where they will be safe. I'll make you some good coffee. I make the best coffee. I make better coffee than Cold Sandra or Great Nananne. Mr. Talbot, you're about to faint from the heat, and Mr. Lightner, you're too worried. No one's going to break into this house any time ever, and your house has guards all over night and day."

She rewrapped the axe blade, the idol, and the perforator carefully, then closed the suitcase and snapped its two rusted locks. Now, and only now, did I see the withered old cardboard tag on it listing an airport in Mexico, and the stamps that indicated the suitcase had traveled many miles beyond that.

I held my questions until we had come down into the cooler air of the kitchen. I realized that what she'd said about my failing in the heat above had been perfectly true. I was almost ill.

She set the suitcase down, took off her white pantyhose and her shoes, and turned on a rusted round fan above the refrigerator, which oscillated drowsily, and set to work to make the coffee, as she had said.

Aaron rummaged for sugar, and in the old "ice box," as she called it, found the pitcher of cream still fresh and quite cold. That didn't much matter to Merrick, however, because it was milk she wanted for coffee and she heated it to just below a boil.

"This is the way to do it," she told us both.

At last we were settled at a round oak table, whose white painted surface had been wiped quite clean.

The café au lait was strong and delicious. Five years among the Undead can't kill the memory. Nothing ever will. I piled the sugar into it, just as she did, and I drank it in deep gulps, believing thoroughly that it was a restorative, and then I sat back in the creaky wooden chair.

All around me, the kitchen was in good order, though a relic of former times. Even the refrigerator was some sort of antique with a humming motor on top of it, beneath the creaking fan. The shelves over the stove and along the walls were covered by glass doors, and I could see all the accouterments of a place where people regularly take their meals. The floor was old linoleum and very clean.

Suddenly, I remembered the suitcase. I jumped and looked about. It was right beside Merrick on the empty chair.

When I looked at Merrick I saw tears in her eyes.

"What is it, darling?" I asked. "Tell me and I'll do my level best to make it right."

"It's just the house and everything that ever happened, Mr. Talbot," she answered. "Matthew died in this house."

This was the answer to a rather momentous question, and one which I had not dared to voice. I can't say I was relieved to hear it, but I couldn't help but wonder who might lay claim to the treasures which Merrick regarded as her own.

"Don't you worry about Cold Sandra," said Merrick, directly to me. "If she was going to come back for these things, she would have come back a long time ago. There was never enough money in the world for Cold Sandra. Matthew really loved her, but he had plenty of money, and that made all the difference in the world."

"How did he die, darling?" I asked.

"Of a fever from those jungle places. And he'd made us all get all our shots too. I don't like needles. We got shots for every disease you can imagine. Yet still he came back sick. Some time afterwards, when Cold Sandra was screaming and hollering and throwing things, she said that the Indians down there in the jungles had put a curse on him, that he never should have gone up the waterfall to the cave. But Great Nananne said it was too strong a fever. He died over there, in the back room."

She pointed to the hallway that separated us from the room in which Aaron and I had spent our uncomfortable night.

"After he was gone and she went away, I took out the furniture. It's in the front bedroom next to Great Nananne's. That's where I've slept ever since."

"I can imagine why," said Aaron comfortingly. "It must have been dreadful for you to lose them both."

"Now Matthew was always good to us all," she continued, "I wish he had been my father, lot of good it would do me now. He was in the hospital and out of it, and then the doctors stopped coming because he was drunk all the time and shouted at them, and then he just choked out his last."

"And had Cold Sandra already gone?" Aaron asked gently. He had laid his hand on the table beside her own.

"She was out all the time at the barroom down on the corner, and after they threw her out of that one, she went to the one on the big street. The night he started to go, I ran down two blocks and over there to get her, and banged on the back screen door for her to come out. She was too drunk to walk.

"She was sitting there with this handsome white man, and he was just in love with her, you know, adoring her. I could see it. And she was so drunk she couldn't stand up. And then it hit me. She didn't want to see Matthew go. She was afraid to be at his side when it happened. She wasn't being hard-hearted. She was just really scared. So I came running back.

"Great Nananne was washing his face and giving him his Scotch, that's what he drank all the time, he wouldn't have any other kind of drink, and he was choking and choking, and we just sat by him till sometime about dawn, the choking stopped, and his breathing got very steady, so steady you could have set a clock by it, just up and down, up and down.

"It was a real relief that he wasn't choking. But Great Nananne shook her head to mean no good. Then his breathing got so low you couldn't see or hear it. His chest stopped moving. And Great Nananne told me he was dead."

She paused long enough to drink the rest of her coffee, then she stood up, pushing the chair back carelessly, and took the pot from the stove and gave us all some more of the heavy brew to drink.

She sat down again and ran her tongue along her lip, a habit with her. She seemed a child in all these gestures, perhaps because of the convent-school way in which she sat up straight in her chair and folded her arms.

"You know, it's nice having you listen to this," she said looking from me to Aaron. "I never told anyone all about it. Just the little things. He left Cold Sandra plenty of money.

"She came home around noon the next day and demanded to know where they'd taken him, and started screaming and throwing things and saying we never should have called for the morgue to take him away.

" 'And what did you think we were going to do with him?' Great Nananne asked. 'You don't think they have a law in this town about dead bodies? You think we can just take him out and bury him in the backyard?' Turned out his people in Boston came and got him, and soon as Cold Sandra saw that check, you know, the money he'd left her, she was out of this house and gone.

"Of course I didn't know it was going to be the last time I ever saw her. All I knew was that she had packed up some of her clothes in a new red leather suitcase, and she was dressed like a model from a magazine, in a white silk suit. Her hair was pulled back to a bun on the back of her head. She was so beautiful she didn't need any makeup, but she had put some dark-violet eye shadow above her eyelashes and a dark color, like violet, too, I think, on her lips. I knew that dark violet meant trouble. She looked so beautiful.

"She kissed me and she gave me a bottle of Chanel No. 22 perfume. She said that was for me. She told me she'd be coming back for me. She told me she was going out to buy a car, she was driving out of here. She said, 'If I can just get across that spillway without drowning, I can get out of this town.' "

Merrick broke off for a moment, her eyebrows knitted, her mouth slightly open. Then she began again.

" 'The hell you'll come back for her.' That's what Great Nananne told her. 'You've never done anything except run wild and let that child run wild, well, she's staying here with me, and you go to Hell.' "

Once again, she stopped. Her girlish face grew quiet. I was afraid she was going to cry. I think that she swallowed the tears very deliberately. Then she spoke again, clearing her throat a little. I could hardly make out the words.

"Think she went to Chicago," she said.

Aaron waited respectfully while the silence filled the old kitchen. I picked up my coffee and drank deeply again, savoring the taste of it, as much out of respect for her as for the pleasure.

"You're ours, darling," I said.

"Oh, I know, Mr. Talbot," she answered in a small voice, and, without moving the focus of her eyes from some distant point, she lifted her right hand and laid it on mine. I never forgot the gesture. It was as if she was comforting me.

Then she spoke. "Well, Great Nananne knows now. She knows whether my mother is alive or dead."

"Yes, she knows," I answered, avowing my belief before I could think the better of it. "And whatever she knows, she's at peace."

There was a quiet interval in which I became painfully conscious of Merrick's suffering, and of the noises of the Talamasca acolytes who were moving every object in the place. I heard the grinding noise of the large statues being dragged or pushed. I heard the sound of packing tape being stretched and torn.

"I loved that man, Matthew," said Merrick softly. "I really loved him. He taught me how to read the Book of Magic. He taught me how to read all the books that Oncle Vervain had left. He liked to look at the pictures I showed you. He was an interesting man."

There was another long pause. Something in the atmosphere of the house disturbed me. I was confused by what I was feeling. It had nothing to do with normal noises or activity. And it seemed imperative suddenly that I conceal this disturbance from Merrick, that such a thing, whatever it was, not trouble her at this time.

It was as if someone altogether new and different had entered the house, and one could hear that person's stealthy movements. It was the sense of a coherent presence. I wiped it from my mind, never for a moment fearing it, and keeping my eyes on Merrick, when, in a daze of sorts, she began to speak rather rapidly and tonelessly again.

"Up in Boston, Matthew had studied history and science. He knew all about Mexico and the jungles. He told me the story of the Olmec. When we were in Mexico City he took me to the museum. He was going to see to it that I went to school. He wasn't afraid in those jungles. He thought those shots protected us. He wouldn't let us drink the water, you know, all of that. And he was rich, like I told you, and he would have never tried to steal these things from Cold Sandra or me."

Her eyes remained steady.

I could still feel this distinct entity within the house, and I realized that she did not feel it. Aaron did not know it was there, either. But it was there. And it was not far from where we sat. With all my soul I listened to Merrick.

"Oncle Vervain left lots of things. I'll show you. Oncle Vervain said we had our roots in the jungle land down there, and in Haiti before our people ever came up here. He said we weren't like American black people, though he never said the word 'black,' he always said colored. He thought it was polite to say colored. Cold Sandra used to laugh at him. Oncle Vervain was a powerful magician, and before him there had been his grandfather, and Oncle Vervain told tales of what the Old Man could do."

I realized her soft speech was becoming more rapid. The history was pouring out from her.

"The Old Man, that's all I ever called him. He was a Voodoo man in the Civil War. He went back to Haiti to learn things and when he came back to this town they said he took it by storm. Of course, they talk about Marie Laveau, but they talk of the Old Man too. Sometimes I can feel them near me, Oncle Vervain and the Old Man, as well as Lucy Nancy Marie Mayfair, who's in the photograph, and another one, a Voodoo queen whom they called Pretty Justine. They said everybody was afraid of Pretty Justine."

"What do you want for yourself, Merrick," I asked her suddenly, desperate to stop the ever increasing speed of her words.

She looked at me sharply, and then she smiled. "I want to be educated, Mr. Talbot. I want to go to school."

"Ah, how marvelous," I whispered.

"I told Mr. Lightner," she continued, "and he said you could do it. I want to be in a high-quality school where they teach me Greek and Latin and which fork to use for my salad or my fish. I want to know all about magic, the way Matthew did, telling me things out of the Bible, and reading over those old books and saying what was tried and true. Matthew never had to make a living. I expect I will have to make a living. But I want to be educated, and I think you know what I mean."

She fixed her gaze on me. Her eyes were dry and clear, and it was then perhaps more than at any other time that I noticed their beautiful coloration of which I've spoken before. She went on talking, her voice a little slower now, and calmer and almost sweet.

"Mr. Lightner says all your members are educated people. That's what he told me right before you came. I can see those manners in the people at the Motherhouse and I hear the way they talk. Mr. Lightner says it's the tradition of the Talamasca. You educate your members, because it's a lifelong thing to be a member, and you all live under the same roof."

I smiled. It was true. Very true. "Yes," I said, "we do this with all who come to us, insofar as they are willing and able to absorb it, and we'll give it to you."

Merrick leant forward and kissed me on the cheek.

I was quite startled by this affection, and at a loss as to the proper thing to do. I spoke from the heart.

"Darling, we'll give you everything. We have so much to share, it would be our duty if it weren't . . . if it weren't such a pleasure for us to do."

Something invisible was suddenly gone from the house. I felt it as if a being had snapped its fingers and simply disappeared. Merrick showed no consciousness of this.

"And what will I do for you in exchange?" she asked in a calm sure voice. "You can't give me everything for nothing, Mr. Talbot. Tell me what you want from me."

"Teach us what you know about magic," I answered, "and grow up to be happy, to be strong, and never to be afraid."

9

I T WAS GROWING DARK when we left the house.

Before leaving New Orleans, we dined together at Galatoire's, a venerable old New Orleans restaurant where I found the food to be delicious, but Merrick was by this time so exhausted that she turned quite pale and fell sound asleep in her chair.

The transformation in her was remarkable. She murmured that Aaron and I must care for the Olmec treasures. "Look at them but be careful," she said, as a matter of fact. And then came the sudden slumber which left her pliant but unconscious, as far as I could see.

Aaron and I all but carried her to the car—she could walk in her sleep if propelled—and much as I wanted to talk with Aaron I didn't dare risk it, though Merrick slept between us, quite soundly, during the entire ride home.

When we reached the Motherhouse, that good female member of the Order whom I've mentioned before, and will now for the sake of this account call Mary, helped us to carry Merrick up to her room and lay her on the bed.

Now, I remarked a little while ago that I wanted the Talamasca to envelop her in fantasy, to give her everything that she should desire.

Let me explain that we had already begun this process by creating an upstairs corner bedroom for her, which we believed to be a young woman's dream. The fruit-wood bed, its posts and canopy decorated with carved flowers and trimmed in fancy lace, the dressing table with its little satin bench and huge round mirror, its small fancy twin lamps and myriad bottles, all of this was part of the fantasy, along with a pair of frilly boudoir dolls, as they are called, which had to be moved aside to lay down the poor darling on her pillow for the night.

And lest you believe we were misogynist imbeciles, allow me to explain that one wall of the room, the wall that was not punctuated by floor-length windows to the porch, was filled with a fine general assortment of books. There was also a corner table and chairs for reading, many other pretty lamps here and there, and a bathroom filled with perfumed soaps, varicolored shampoos, and countless bottles of scented cologne and oil. In fact, Merrick herself had bought any number of products scented with Chanel No. 22, a particularly wonderful scent.

By now, as we left her fast asleep and in the gentle care of Mary, I believe that Aaron and I both had fallen in love with her, completely in a parental sense, and I meant to allow nothing in the Talamasca to distract me from her case.

Of course Aaron, not being the Superior General of the Order, would have the luxury of remaining here with her long after I had been forced back to my desk in London. And I envied him that he would have the pleasure of watching this child meet her first tutors and pick out her own school.

As for the Olmec treasures, we took them now to the small Louisiana vault for safekeeping, and once inside, after some debate, opened the suitcase and examined what was there.

The cache was quite remarkable. There were close to forty idols, at least twelve of the perforator knives, numerous axe blades, and many smaller blade-shaped objects which we commonly call celts. Every single item was exquisite in its own right. There was also a handwritten inventory, apparently the work of the mysterious and doomed Matthew, listing each item and its size. The note was appended:

> There are many more treasures within this tunnel, but they must wait for later excavation. I am already sick and must return home as soon as possible. Honey and Sandra are highly argumentative on this point. They want to take everything out of the cave. But I am getting weaker even as I write. As for Merrick, my illness is scaring her. I need to take her home. It is worth noting while I have the strength in my right hand that nothing else scares any of my ladies, not the jungles, not the villages, not the Indians. I have to go back.

It was more than poignant, these words of the dead man, and my curiosity about "Honey" was all the more strong.

We were in the process of wrapping everything and restoring it to its old order, when there came a knock on the outside door of the room in which the vault is situated.

"Come quickly," Mary said through the door. "She's become hysterical. I don't know what to do."

Up the stairs we headed, and before we'd reached the second floor we could hear her desperate sobs.

She sat on the bed, still in her navy blue dress from the funeral, her feet bare again, and her hair in tangles, sobbing over and over again that Great Nananne was dead.

It was all entirely understandable, but Aaron had a near magical effect upon people in such states, and he soon quieted her with his words, while Mary assisted when she could.

Merrick then asked through her tears if she could please have a glass of rum.

Of course no one was in favor of this remedy, but on the other hand, as Aaron judiciously pointed out, the liquor would quiet her, and she would go to sleep.

Several bottles were found in the bar downstairs, and Merrick was given a glass of the rum, but asked for more.

"This is a sip," she said through her tears, "I need a glassful." She looked so perfectly unhappy and distraught that we couldn't deny her. At last, after imbibing, her sobs became softer.

"What am I going to do, where will I go?" she asked piteously, and once again we made our assurances, though her grief was something which I felt she had to express with tears.

As for doubts about her future, that was a different matter. I sent Mary out of the room. I sat down on the bed beside Merrick.

"My dear, listen to me," I said to her. "You're rich in your own right. Those books of Oncle Vervain's. They're worth enormous amounts of money. Universities and museums would bid on them at auction. As for the Olmec treasures, I cannot calculate their worth. Of course you don't want to part with these things, and we don't want you to do it, but rest assured you are secure, even without us."

This seemed to quiet her somewhat.

Finally, after she had cried softly against my chest for the better part of an hour, she put her arms around Aaron, laid her head on his shoulder, and said that if she knew we were in the house, that we would not leave it, then she could go to sleep.

"We'll be waiting for you downstairs in the morning," I told her. "We want you to make that coffee for us. We've been fools, drinking the wrong coffee. We refuse to have breakfast without you. Now you must sleep."

She gave me a grateful and kindly smile, even though the tears were still spilling onto her cheeks. Then, asking no one's permission, she went to the frilly dressing table, where the bottle of rum stood quite incongruously among the other fancy little bottles, and took a good slug of the drink.

As we rose to go, Mary answered my call with a nightgown ready for Merrick, and I took the bottle of rum, nodded to Merrick to make certain that she had seen me do it, so there would be some civil pretense of her permission, and Aaron and I retired to the library below.

I don't remember how long we talked.

Possibly it was an hour. We discussed tutors, schools, programs of education, what Merrick should do.

"Of course there can be no question of asking her to display her psychic powers to us," Aaron said firmly, as though I was going to overrule him. "But they're considerable. I've sensed it all day and yesterday as well."

"Ah, but there's another matter," I said, and I was about to broach the subject of the weird "disturbance" which I had felt in Great Nananne's house while we had sat in the kitchen. But something stopped me from speaking.

I realized that I sensed the same presence now, under our Mother-house roof.

"What's the matter, man?" asked Aaron, who knew my every facial expression and who could probably read my mind if he really chose to do it.

"Nothing," I said, and then, instinctively, and perhaps selfishly, with some desire to be heroic, I added, "I want you to stay where you are."

I rose and went through the open doors of the library out into the hallway.

From above, from the upstairs rear of the house, there came a sardonic and ringing laugh. It was a woman's laugh, there was no doubt about it, only I could not attach it to Mary or to the female members of the Order who were then living in the house. Indeed Mary was the only one in the main building. The others had gone to sleep some time ago in the "slave quarters" and cottages which made up part of the out-buildings some distance from the rear doors of the house.

Once again, I heard the laugh. It seemed an answer to my very query.

Aaron appeared at my shoulder. "That's Merrick," he said warily.

This time, I didn't tell him to remain behind. He followed me as I went up the stairs.

The door to Merrick's room was open, and the lights were on, caus-ing a brilliant glow to spill into the long broad center hallway.

"Well, come on in," said a womanish voice as I hesitated, and when I did, I was quite alarmed by what I saw.

In a haze of cigarette smoke, there was a young woman sitting in a highly seductive posture at the dressing table, her youthful and fast-ripening body clothed only in a scant white cotton petticoat, its thin cloth hardly disguising her full breasts and pink nipples, or the dark shadow between her legs.

Of course it was Merrick, but then it wasn't Merrick at all.

With her right hand she put the cigarette to her lips and drew on it, deeply, with the casual air of an accustomed smoker, and let her breath out with ease.

Her eyebrows were raised as she looked at me, and her lips were drawn back in a beautiful sneer. Indeed, the expression was so alien to the Merrick I had come to know that it was very simply terrifying all to itself. One couldn't imagine a skilled actress so successfully altering her features. As for the voice which came out of the body, it was sultry and low.

"Good cigarettes, Mr. Talbot. Rothmans, aren't they?" The right hand toyed with the little box which she had taken from my room. The woman's voice continued, cold, utterly without feeling, and with a faint tone of mockery. "Matthew used to smoke Rothmans, Mr. Talbot. He went to the French Quarter to buy them. You don't find them at the corner store. Smoked them right up until he died."

"Who are you?" I asked.

Aaron said nothing. He relinquished command to me at this moment completely, but he stood his ground.

"Don't be so hasty, Mr. Talbot," came the hard-toned answer. "Ask me a few questions." She gave more of her weight to the left elbow on the dressing table, and the petticoat gaped to reveal more of her full breasts.

Her eyes positively sparkled in the light of the dressing table lamps. It seemed her lids and eyebrows were governed exclusively by a new personality. She was not even Merrick's twin.

"Cold Sandra?" I asked.

A burst of laughter came out of her that was ominous and shocking. She tossed her black hair and drew on the cigarette again.

"She never told you one word about me, did she?" she asked, and once again came that sneer, beautiful yet full of venom. "She was always jealous. I hated her from the day she was born."

"Honey in the Sunshine," I said calmly.

She nodded, grinning at me, letting go of the smoke.

"That's a name that's always been good enough for me. And there she goes, leaving me out of the story. Well, don't you think I'll settle for so little, Mr. Talbot. Or should I call you David? I think you look like a David, you know, righteous and clean living and all of that." She crushed out the cigarette right into the tabletop. And with one hand now, she took another, and lighted it with the gold lighter which I had also left in my room.

She turned the lighter over now, the cigarette dangling from her lip, and through the little coil of smoke she read the inscription. "To David, my Savior, from Joshua." Her eyes flashed on my face, and she smiled.

The words she'd read cut deep into me, but I would have none of it. I merely stared at her. This would take a little time.

"You're damned right," she said, "it's going to take time. Don't you think I want some of what she's getting. But let's talk about this here, Joshua, he was your lover, wasn't he? You were lovers with him and he died."

The pain I felt was exquisite, and for all my claim to enlightenment and self-knowledge, I was mortified that these words were spoken in Aaron's presence. Joshua had been young, and one of us.

She laughed a low, carnal laugh. "Course you can do women, too, if they're young enough, can't you?" she asked viciously.

"Where do you come from, Honey in the Sunshine?" I demanded.

"Don't call her by name," Aaron whispered.

"Oh, that's good advice, but it don't matter. I'm staying right where I am. Now let's talk about you and that boy, Joshua. Seems he was mighty young when you—."

"Stop it," I said sharply.

"Don't talk to it, David," said Aaron under his breath. "Don't address it. Every time you talk to it, you give it strength."

A high pealing laughter erupted from the little woman at the dressing table. She shook her head and turned her body to face us completely, the hem of the slip riding up on her naked thighs.

"I'd say he was eighteen maybe," she said, looking at me with blazing eyes as she took the cigarette off her lip. "But you didn't know for sure, did you, David? You just knew you had to have him."

"Get out of Merrick," I said. "You don't belong in Merrick."

"Merrick's my sister!" she flashed. "I'll do what I want with her. She drove me crazy from the cradle, always reading my mind, telling me what I thought, telling me I made my own trouble, always blaming everything on me!"

She scowled at me and leant forward. I could see her nipples.

"You give yourself away for what you are," I said. "Or is it what you were?"

Suddenly she rose from the dressing table, and the left hand, free of the cigarette, swept all the bottles and the lamp off the right side of the table, with one fine blow.

There was a roar of shattered glass. The lamp went out with a loud spark. Two or more of the bottles were broken. The carpet was littered with sharp fragments. The room was filled with a powerful perfume.

She stood before us, her hand on her hip, the cigarette held high. She looked down at the bottles.

"Yeah, she likes those things!" she said.

Her posture became ever more suggestive, mocking. "And you do like what you see, don't you, David? She's just young enough for you. She's got some of the little boy left in her, don't she? Great Nananne knew you and what you wanted. And I know you too."

Her face was full of anger and very beautiful.

"You killed Joshua, didn't you?" she said in a low voice, eyes suddenly narrow, as if she was peering into my soul. "You let him go on that climb in the Himalayas—." She pronounced the word as I would have said it. "And you knew it was dangerous but you loved him so much, you couldn't say no."

I could say nothing. The pain in me was too intense. I tried to banish all thoughts of Joshua. I tried not to think of the day when they had brought his body back to London. I tried to focus on the girl before me.

"Merrick," I said with all the strength I could muster, "Merrick, drive her out."

"You want me, and so do you, Aaron," she continued, the grin making her cheeks supple, her face flushing. "Either one of you'd tack me to that mattress if you thought you could."

I said nothing.

"Merrick," said Aaron loudly. "Cast her out. She means you no good, darling, cast her out!"

"You know what Joshua was thinking about you when he fell off that cliff?" she said.

"Stop it!" I cried.

"He was hating you for sending him, hating you for saying yes, he could go!"

"Liar!" I said. "Get out of Merrick."

"Don't you shout at me, Mister," she blazed back. She glanced down at the broken glass and tapped her ashes into it. "Now let's just see about fixing her good."

She took a step forward, right into the mess of broken glass and overturned bottles that lay between us.

I advanced on the figure.

"Stay back."

I seized her by the shoulders and forced her backwards. But it took all of my strength. Her skin was moist with sweat, and she squirmed out of my grasp.

"You don't think I can walk on glass in bare feet?" she said right in my face as she struggled to resist me. "You stupid old man," she went on, "now why would I want to cut Merrick's foot?"

I took hold of her, crushing the glass under my shoes.

"You're dead, aren't you, Honey in the Sunshine? You're dead, and you know it, and this is all the life you can get!"

For one moment the beautiful face went blank. The girl appeared to be Merrick. Then the eyebrows were raised again. The lids assumed their languid expression, making the eyes glitter.

"I'm here and I'm staying here."

"You're in the grave, Honey in the Sunshine," I answered. "That is, the body you want is in the grave, and all you've got is a vagrant spirit, now isn't that so!"

A look of fear flittered across her expression, and then the face hardened once more, as she freed herself from my hands.

"You know nothing about me, Mister," she said. She was baffled, as spirits often are. She couldn't keep the cocky expression on Merrick's face. Indeed, the whole body shuddered suddenly. The true Merrick was struggling.

"Come back, Merrick, throw her off, Merrick," I said. I stepped forward once again.

She moved back and towards the foot of the high bed. She turned the cigarette in her hand. She meant to jab me with it.

"You bet your life I do," she said, reading my thoughts. "I wish I had something I could really hurt you with. But I guess I'll have to settle for hurting her!"

She glanced about the room.

It was all I needed. I advanced on her and caught her by the shoulders, desperate to keep hold of her in spite of the sweat that covered her and her writhing to escape.

She shrieked. "You stop that, lemme go!" And she managed to grind the cigarette into the side of my face.

I reached for her hand, grabbed it and twisted it until she dropped the cigarette. She slapped me hard, so that for one moment I felt faint. Nevertheless, I held on to her slippery shoulders.

"That's it," she cried. "Hurt her, break her bones, why don't you just do that? Think it will make Joshua come back? Think he'll be any older for you, David, think it will make everything right?"

"Get out of Merrick!" I shouted. I could still hear the broken glass under my shoes. She was perilously close to it. I shook her hard, her head flopping from side to side.

She convulsed, wrenching free, and again there came a slap of awesome strength that all but knocked me off balance. For one split second I couldn't see.

I lunged at her and lifted her under the arms and threw her back on the bed. I knelt on the bed over her, gripping her still. She was struggling to reach my face.

"Let her go, David," Aaron cried out behind me. And I heard the voice of Mary, suddenly, that other loyal member, begging me not to twist her wrist so hard.

Her fingers struggled to reach my eyes.

"You're dead, you know you are, you've got no right here," I roared at her. "Say it, you're dead, you're dead, and you've got to let Merrick go."

I felt her knee against my chest.

"Great Nananne, get her out!" I said.

"How dare you!" she screamed. "You think you can use my god-mother against me." She caught my hair with her left hand and yanked at it.

Still I shook her.

And then I drew back, I let her go, and I called upon my own spirit, my own soul to make itself into a powerful instrument, and it was with that invisible instrument that I plunged towards her, striking her at the heart so that she lost her breath.

Get out, get out, get out! I commanded her with all the strength of my soul. I felt myself against her. I felt her collective power, as though there were no body to house it. I felt her resist. I had lost all contact with my own body. *Get out of Merrick. Go!*

A sob broke loose from her.

"There's no grave for us, you bastard, you devil," she cried. "There's no grave for me or my mother! You can't make me leave here!"

I looked down into her face, though where my own body had fallen—onto the floor or onto the bed—I didn't know.

Call on God under any name and go towards him! I told her. *Leave those bodies wherever they lie, do you hear me, leave them and go on. Now! It's your chance!*

Suddenly the strength that was resisting me contracted, and I felt its intense pressure dissolve. For one moment I thought I saw it, an amorphous shape rising above me. Then I realized I was lying on the floor.

I was staring up at the ceiling. And I could hear Merrick, our Merrick crying once more.

"They're dead, Mr. Talbot, they're dead, Cold Sandra's dead and so is Honey in the Sunshine, my sister, Mr. Talbot, they're both dead, they've been dead since they left New Orleans, Mr. Talbot, all those four years of waiting, and they were dead the first night in Lafayette, Mr. Talbot, they're dead, dead, dead."

Slowly I climbed to my feet. There were cuts from the broken glass on my hands. I was physically sick.

The child on the bed had shut her eyes. Her lips weren't sneering, they were stretched back as she continued her plaintive wails.

Mary was quick to lay a thick robe over her. Aaron was at her side. She rolled on her back and made a face suddenly.

"I'm sick, Mr. Talbot," she said hoarsely.

"This way," I turned her over, away from the perilous glass, and lifted her and carried her into the bathroom in my arms. She leant over the sink, and the vomit poured out of her.

I was shuddering all over. My clothes were drenched.

Mary urged me to step aside. It seemed quite outrageous to me for a moment, and then I realized how it must have seemed to Mary.

And so I withdrew.

When I glanced at Aaron I was amazed at the expression on his face. He had seen many cases of possession. They are all terrible, each in its own way.

We waited in the hallway until Mary told us we might come in.

Merrick was dressed in a white cotton gown to receive us, her hair brushed to a marvelous brown luster, and her eyes rimmed in red, but otherwise quite clear. She was in the armchair in the corner, under the light of the tall lamp.

Her feet were safely protected with white satin slippers. But all the glass was gone. Indeed the dressing table looked quite fine with only one lamp and all of its intact bottles.

Merrick was still trembling, however, and when I approached her, she reached out and clasped my hand.

"Your shoulders will hurt for a little while," I said apologetically.

"Here's how they died," she said, looking at me and then at Aaron. "They went with all that money to buy a new car. The man who sold it to them picked them up, you know, and he went with them to Lafayette, and there he killed them for the cash they had. He knocked them both hard over the head."

I shook my head.

"Four years ago, it happened," she said, going on intently, her mind on her story and nothing else. "It happened the very next day after they left. He beat them in a motel room in Lafayette and put their bodies in that car and drove it into the swamps. That car just filled up with water. If they woke up, they drowned. There's nothing left of either one of them now."

"Dear God," I whispered.

"And all this time," she said, "I was so guilty for being jealous, jealous that Cold Sandra had taken Honey in the Sunshine and left me behind. I was guilty and jealous, guilty and jealous. Honey in the Sunshine was my older sister. Honey in the Sunshine was sixteen and she was 'no trouble,' that's what Cold Sandra told me. I was too little and she'd come back for me soon."

She closed her eyes for a moment and took a deep breath.

"Where is she now?" I asked. Aaron let me know he had not been prepared for that. But I had to put the question to her.

For a very long time she made no response. She lay staring, her body shivering violently, and then finally, she said:

"She's gone."

"How did she come through?" I demanded.

Mary and Aaron shook their heads. "David, leave her for the moment," said Aaron as politely as he could. I had no intention of dropping the matter. I had to know.

Again, there was no immediate answer. And then Merrick heaved a sigh and turned to one side.

"How did she come through?" I asked again.

Merrick's face crumpled. She began very softly to cry.

"Please, Sir," said Mary, "let her alone just now."

"Merrick, how did Honey in the Sunshine come through?" I demanded. "Did you know she wanted to come through?"

Mary took a stand to Merrick's left and glared at me.

I kept my eyes on the shivering girl.

"Did you ask her to come through?" I demanded softly.

"No, Mr. Talbot," she said softly, her eyes drifting up to me again. "I prayed to Great Nananne. I prayed to her spirit while it was still near earth to hear me." Her tired voice could barely carry the words. "Great Nananne sent her to tell me. Great Nananne will take care of them both."

"Ah, I see."

"You know what I did," she continued. "I called on a spirit that had only just died. I called on a soul that was still close enough to help me, and I got Honey, I got more than I ever wanted to get. But that's how it works sometimes, Mr. Talbot. When you call on *les mystères* you don't always know what you're going to get."

"Yes," I responded. "I know. Do you remember all that happened?"

"Yes," she said, "and no. I remember your shaking me and I remember knowing what had happened, but I don't really remember all the time that ticked by while she was in me."

"I see," I said gratefully. "What do you feel now, Merrick?"

"Afraid of myself a little," she answered. "And I'm sorry she hurt you."

"Oh, darling, for the love of Heaven, don't think about me," I answered. "I'm only concerned with you."

"I know that, Mr. Talbot, but if it's any consolation to you, Joshua went into the Light when he died. He didn't hate you when he was falling down the mountain. Honey just made that up."

I was stunned. I could feel Mary's sudden embarrassment. I could see that Aaron was amazed.

"I'm sure of it," Merrick said. "Joshua's in Heaven. Honey just read all those things from your mind."

I couldn't answer her. At the risk of more suspicion and condemnation from the vigilant Mary, I leant over and kissed Merrick on the cheek.

"The nightmare's over," she said. "I'm free of them all. I'm free to begin."

And so our long journey with Merrick began.

10

I T HAD NOT BEEN EASY for me to tell this story to Louis, and it was not finished. I had much more to say.

But as I paused, it was as if I had wakened to the parlor around me, and to Louis's attentive presence, and I felt both immediate comfort and crushing guilt. For a moment I stretched my limbs and I felt my vampiric strength in my veins.

We sat like two wholesome beings together, in the comfort of the glass-shaded lamps.

For the first time since I'd begun the story, I stared up at the paintings along the walls of the room. These were all wonderfully colored Impressionist treasures which Louis had long ago collected and once kept in a small uptown house, where he lived until Lestat burnt that house, and, in reconciliation, begged Louis to come and join him here.

I looked at a painting by Monet—one I'd come to neglect of late due to familiarity—a painting full of sunshine and greenery, of a woman at work on her needlepoint by a window under the limbs of delicate indoor trees. Like so many Impressionist paintings it was both highly intellectual, with its obvious brush strokes, and flagrantly domestic. And I let its stalwart sanctification of the ordinary soothe my suffering heart.

I wanted to feel our domesticity here in the Rue Royale. I wanted to feel morally safe, which of course I would never feel again.

It had exhausted my soul to revisit those times when I was a living mortal being, when I had taken the wet daytime heat of New Orleans for granted, when I'd been a trusted friend to Merrick, for that is what I had been, regardless of what Honey in the Sunshine had condemned me for being—with a boy named Joshua who had lived many, many years before.

As for that matter, Aaron and Mary never questioned me about it. But I knew that neither of them would ever look at me in the same way again. Joshua had been too young and I had been too old for the relationship. And I had only confessed my transgressions—a precious few nights of love—to the Elders long after Joshua was dead. They had condemned me for it and charged me never to let such a thing occur again.

When I'd been appointed Superior General, the Elders had exacted a confirmation that I was well beyond such breaches of morality, and I had given it, humiliated that it had been mentioned again.

As for Joshua's death, I did blame myself for what happened to him. He had begged me to go on the climb, which itself was not terribly dangerous, to visit a shrine in the Himalayas which had been part of his study in Tibetan lore. Other members of the Order were with him and they came home safe. The fall had been the result of a small but sudden avalanche, as I understood it, and Joshua's body had not been recovered for several months.

Now as I reviewed these things for Louis, now as I pondered that I had approached the woman Merrick in my dark and eternal guise as a vampire, I felt the sharpest and most profound guilt. It wasn't something for which I could ever seek absolution. And it wasn't something that could prevent me from seeing Merrick again.

It had been done. I had asked Merrick to raise Claudia's ghost for us. And I had much more to tell Louis before the two could come together, and more within myself that had to be resolved.

All this while, Louis had listened without saying a word. With his finger curled under his lip, his elbow on the arm of the couch, he had merely studied me as I recounted the memories, and now he was eager for the tale to go on.

"I knew this woman was powerful," he said gently. "What I didn't know was how much you loved her."

I marveled at his customary manner of speaking, the melting quality of his voice and the way his words seemed barely to disturb the air.

"Ah, well, neither did I," I replied. "There were so many of us, bound together by love, in the Talamasca, and each one is a special case."

"But this woman, you truly love her," he pressed gently. "And I've asked you to go against your heart."

"Oh, no, you haven't," I confessed. I faltered. "It was inevitable that I contact the Talamasca," I insisted. "But it should have been contact with the Elders, in writing, and not this."

"Don't condemn yourself so much for contacting her," he said with an uncommon self-confidence. He seemed earnest and, as always, forever young.

"Why not?" I asked. "I had thought you were a specialist in guilt?"

He laughed politely at this, and then again made a silent chuckle. He shook his head.

"We have hearts, don't we?" he replied. He shifted a little against the pillows of the couch. "You tell me you believe in God. That's more than the others have ever said to me. Quite truly it is. What do you think God has planned for us?"

"I don't know that God plans anything," I said a little bitterly. "I know only that He's there."

I thought of how much I loved Louis, and had ever since I had become Lestat's fledgling. I thought of how deeply I depended upon him, and what I would do for him. It was the love of Louis which had at times crippled Lestat, and enslaved Armand. Louis need have no consciousness of his own beauty, of his own obvious and natural charm.

"David, you have to forgive me," he said suddenly. "I want so desperately to meet this woman myself that I urge you on for selfish reasons, but I mean it when I say that we do have hearts in every sense of the word."

"Of course, you do," I replied. "I wonder if angels have hearts," I whispered. "Ah, but it doesn't matter, does it? We are what we are."

He didn't answer me, but I saw his face darken for a moment and then he fell into reverie, with his habitual expression of curiosity and quiet grace.

"But when it comes to Merrick," I said, "I have to face that I've contacted her because I need her desperately. I could not have gone on for long without contacting her. Every night that I spend in New Orleans, I think of Merrick. Merrick haunts me as though she was a ghost herself."

"Tell me the rest of your story," Louis prodded. "And, if when you're finished you wish to conclude the matter with Merrick—end the contact, so to speak—then I shall accept it without another word."

11

I WENT ON with my tale, flashing back once more some twenty years, to the summer of Merrick's fourteenth year.

It wasn't hard for the Talamasca to enfold such a friendless orphan as one could easily see.

In the days following Great Nananne's funeral, we discovered that Merrick had no legal identity of any kind, save for a valid passport obtained through the testimony of Cold Sandra that Merrick was her daughter. The last name was an assumed name.

Where and how Merrick's birth might have been recorded eluded our most diligent efforts. No baptism of Merrick Mayfair was recorded in any parish church in New Orleans for the year of Merrick's birth. Few pictures of her existed in the boxes which she had brought with us.

And indeed, no record of Cold Sandra or Honey in the Sunshine existed other than passports which were both under assumed names. Though we calculated a year of death for the two unfortunates, we could find nothing in the newspapers of Lafayette, Louisiana, or anywhere near it to indicate that murdered bodies had been found.

In sum, the Talamasca began with a blank slate for Merrick Mayfair, and using its immense resources it soon created for her the documentation of birth and age which the modern world requires. As for the matter of Catholic baptism, Merrick was adamant that she had indeed been given the sacrament as an infant—Great Nananne had "carried her to church"—and as late as only a few years before I left the Order, Merrick still combed church records, in vain, for proof of this herself.

I never fully understood the significance of this baptism to Merrick, but then there were many things about Merrick which I never came to understand. One thing I can say for certain, however. Magic and

Roman Catholicism were completely intermingled for Merrick and this remained so all her life.

As for the gifted and kindhearted man named Matthew, he was not difficult to trace at all.

Matthew had been, in fact, an Olmec archaeologist, and when polite inquiries were made among his survivors in Boston, it was quickly ascertained that a woman named Sandra Mayfair had lured him to New Orleans by means of a letter some five years before regarding some Olmec treasure for which the woman claimed to have directions and a rough hand-drawn map. Cold Sandra claimed to have been given an article about Matthew's amateur adventures by her daughter Merrick, who came upon it in *Time* magazine.

Though Matthew's mother was seriously ill at the time, Matthew had made the journey south with her blessing, and had set out on a private expedition beginning in Mexico. He was never seen by anyone in the family alive again.

As for the expedition, Matthew had kept a journal by means of long impassioned letters addressed to his mother, which he had mailed all in a batch upon his return to the States.

After Matthew's death, in spite of the woman's determined efforts, no scholars in the field of Olmec studies could be interested in what Matthew claimed to have seen or found.

The mother had died, leaving all these papers to her sister, who did not know what to make of "the responsibility" and quickly decided to sell Matthew's papers to us for a liberal sum. Those papers included a small box of vivid color photographs sent to the mother, many of which included Cold Sandra and Honey in the Sunshine, both extraordinarily beautiful women, as well as the ten-year-old child, Merrick, who did not resemble the other two.

As Merrick had risen from a week of torpor and was deep in her studies, and fascinated with her education in etiquette, it was no great pleasure for me to give her these photographs and letters for her private store.

She showed no emotion, however, when confronted with the snapshots of her mother and her sister. And preserving her usual silence on the question of Honey in the Sunshine, who appeared to be about sixteen in the pictures, she put all of this aside.

As for me, I spent some time with the pictures.

Cold Sandra was tall and tawny with very black hair and light eyes.

As for Honey in the Sunshine, she appeared to fulfill all the expectations engendered by that name. Her skin in the photographs did appear to be the color of honey, her eyes were yellow as were her mother's, and her hair, light blond and tightly curly, fell down around her shoulders like foam. Her facial features appeared entirely Anglo-Saxon. The same was true of Cold Sandra.

As for Merrick in the photographs, she appeared very much as she did when she came to our door. She was already the budding woman at the age of ten, and appeared somehow to be of a quieter nature, the other two often hanging upon Matthew and smiling as they embraced him for the eager lens. Merrick was frequently captured with a solemn face, and most often alone.

Of course these pictures revealed much of the rain forest into which they'd penetrated, and there were even poor-quality flash shots of bizarre cave paintings which appeared neither Olmec nor Maya, though my opinion might very well have been wrong. As for the exact location, Matthew refused to reveal it, using terms such as "Village One" and "Village Two."

Given Matthew's lack of specificity, and the bad condition of the photographs, it wasn't difficult to see why archaeologists had not been interested in his claims.

With Merrick's consent, and in secrecy, we enlarged every photograph of any value, but the quality of the originals defeated us. And we lacked concrete information as to how the journey could be made again. But of one thing I was fairly sure. The initial flight might have been to Mexico City, but the cave was not in Mexico at all.

There was a map, yes, drawn with an unsteady hand in black ink on common modern parchment paper, but it gave no place names, only a diagram involving "The City" and the aforementioned Village One and Village Two. We had it copied for preservation's sake, as the parchment paper was badly damaged and torn at the edges. But it was hardly a significant clue.

It was tragic to read the enthusiastic letters which Michael had sent home.

I shall never forget the first letter he wrote to his mother after the discovery. The woman was very ill, and had only just learnt that her case was terminal, news which had reached Matthew somewhere along the route, though we had no indication of where precisely, and Matthew had begged her please to wait for him to come home. Indeed, it was on that account that he had cut the journey short, taking only some of the treasure, a great deal of which remained.

"If only you'd been with me," he wrote, or words to that effect.

And can you imagine me, your gangly and awkward son, plunging into the pure darkness of a ruined temple and finding these strange murals which defy classification? Not Maya, certainly not Olmec. But by and for whom? And in the very midst of this, my flashlight slips out of my hands as if someone snatched it from me. And darkness shrouds the most splendid and unusual paintings I've ever seen.

But no sooner had we left the temple, than we must climb the rocks beside the waterfall, with Cold Sandra and Honey leading the way. It was in back of the waterfall that we found the cave, though I suspect it might have been a tunnel, and there was no mistaking it because the mammoth volcanic boulders around it had been carved into a giant face with an open mouth.

Of course we had no light with us—Cold Sandra's flashlight was drenched—and we were near to fainting from the heat when we got inside. Cold Sandra and Honey were fearful of spirits and claimed to be "feeling" them. Merrick has even spoken up on this subject, blaming the spirits for a bad fall she took on the rocks.

Yet tomorrow, we'll be making the entire trek again. For now, let me say again what I saw by the sunshine that made its way into temple and cave. Unique paintings, I tell you, in both places, which must be studied at once. But in the cave there were also hundreds of glistening jade objects, just waiting for a scoop of the hand.

How in the world such treasures have survived the usual thievery in these parts, I can't guess. Of course the local Maya deny all knowledge of such a place, and I'm not eager to enlighten them. They are kind to us, offering us food and drink and hospitality. But the shaman appears angry with us, but will not tell us the reason. I live and breathe only to go back.

Matthew never did go back. During the night he had grown feverish and his very next letter recorded the regret with which he set out for civilization, thinking his illness was something that could easily be cured.

How awful it was that this curious and generous man had fallen ill.

A mysterious insect bite had been the culprit, but that was not discovered until he'd reached "The City," as he called it, careful to use no key description or name. His last batch of letters was written from the hospital in New Orleans, and mailed by the nurses at his request.

"Mother, there is nothing that can be done. No one is even certain of the nature of the parasite, except that it has made its way throughout my internal organs, and has proved itself refractory to every medicine known to man. I wonder sometimes if the local Maya might have helped me with this ailment. They were so very kind. But then the natives have probably long been immune."

His very last letter was completed on the day he prepared to return to Great Nananne's house. The script had degenerated, as Matthew was suffering one violent chill after another, but obviously determined to write. His news was marked by the same strange mixture of resignation and denial which so often afflicts the dying:

"You cannot believe the sweetness of Sandra and Honey and Great Nananne. Of course, I've done everything I can to lighten their burden. All of those artifacts which we discovered on the expedition are by right the property of Sandra, and I will attempt a revised catalog once I reach the house. Perhaps Great Nananne's nursing will work some miracle. I'll write to you when I have good news."

The only remaining letter in the collection was from Great Nananne. It was in beautiful convent script, written with a fountain pen, and stated that Matthew had died "with the Sacraments," and that his suffering had not been very great at the end. She signed herself Irene Flaurent Mayfair.

Tragic. I can find no better word.

Indeed, there seemed a ring of tragedy surrounding Merrick, what with the murders of Cold Sandra and Honey, and I could well understand why Matthew's collected papers did not tear her away from her studies, or away from her frequent lunches and shopping trips in town.

She was also indifferent to the renovation of Great Nananne's old house, which did indeed belong to Great Nananne with proper title, and was passed on to Merrick by means of a handwritten will, which was handled for us by a skilled local lawyer with no questions asked.

The renovation was historically accurate and quite extensive, involving two expert contractors in the field. Merrick did not want to visit the house at all. The house, to my knowledge, does belong to Merrick officially, right now.

By the end of that long ago summer, Merrick had an immense wardrobe, though she was growing taller with every passing day. She favored expensive well-made dresses with lots of stitching, and visibly worked fabrics such as the white pique which I already described. When she began to appear at supper in graceful high heeled shoes, I was personally and secretly distraught.

I am not a man who loves women of any age, but the sight of her foot, its arch so delicately stretched by the height of the heel, and of her leg, so taut from the pressure, was quite enough to send the most unwelcome and erotic thoughts through my brain.

As for her Chanel No. 22, she had begun to wear it daily. Even those who claimed to be annoyed by perfume rather liked it and came to associate it with her ever genial presence, her questions and steady conversation, her hunger for knowledge about all things.

She had a wondrous grasp of the fundamentals of grammar, which greatly assisted her in learning to read and write French, after which learning Latin was something of a snap. As for mathematics, she detested it, and suspected it somewhat—the theory was simply beyond her—but she was clever enough to absorb the fundamentals. Her enthusiasm for literature was as great as that of anyone I've ever known. She ripped through Dickens and Dostoyevsky, talking about the characters with easy familiarity and endless fascination as though they lived down the street from her house. As for magazines, she was enthralled by the art and archaeology periodicals to which we subscribed routinely, and went on to devour the standards of pop culture, as well as the news magazines she'd always loved.

Indeed, Merrick remained convinced all her young years, as I knew her, that reading was the key to all things. She claimed to understand England simply because she read the London *Times* every day. As for the history of Mesoamerica, she fell in love with it, though she never asked to see the suitcase of her own treasures at all.

With her own writing she made wondrous progress, soon developing something of an old-fashioned hand. It was her aim to shape her letters as Great Nananne had shaped hers. And Merrick succeeded, being able to keep copious diaries with ease.

Understand, she was not a genius of a child, but merely one of considerable intelligence and talent, who after years of frustration and boredom had seized her opportunity at last. There was no impediment in her to knowledge. She resented no one's seeming superiority. Indeed, she absorbed every influence that she could.

Oak Haven, having no other child in its midst, delighted in her. The giant boa constrictor became a favorite pet.

Aaron and Mary took Merrick into the city frequently to the local municipal museum, and often made the short flight to Houston to expose her to the splendid museums and galleries of that southern capital as well.

As for me, I had to go back to England several times during that fateful summer. I much resented it. I had come to love the New Orleans Motherhouse, and I did seek every excuse to remain. I wrote long reports to the Elders of the Talamasca, admitting to this weakness, but explaining, well, pleading perhaps, that I needed to become better acquainted with this strange part of America which didn't seem American at all.

The Elders were indulgent. I had plenty of time to spend with Merrick. However, one letter from them cautioned me not to become overly fond of this "little girl." This stung me because I misinterpreted it. I made an avowal of my purity. The Elders wrote back: "David, we don't doubt your purity; children can be fickle; we were thinking of your heart."

Aaron, meantime, cataloged all Merrick's possessions and eventually established a full room in one of the outbuildings to contain the statues which had been taken from her shrines.

Not one but several medieval codices made up the legacy of Oncle Vervain. There was no explanation as to how he had acquired these books. But there was evidence that he had used them, and in some we found his notes in pencil along with certain dates.

In one carton from Great Nananne's attic were a whole cache of printed books on magic, all published in the 1800s, when the "paranormal" had been such the rage in London and on the Continent, what with mediums and séances and such. These had their pencil markings as well.

We found also a great disintegrating scrapbook crammed with brittle yellowed newspaper clippings, all from New Orleans, which told tales of Voodoo attributed to "the local Doctor of much renown, Jerome Mayfair," whom Merrick identified for us as Oncle Vervain's grandfather, The Old Man. Indeed, all of New Orleans had known about him and there were many quaint little stories of Voodoo meetings broken up by the local police at which many "white ladies" were arrested, as well as women of color, and blacks.

The most tragic of all discoveries, however, and the one which was of the least use to us as an Order of Psychic Detectives—if that is what we are—was the diary of the colored daguerreotypist who was too far back in the lineage for a direct connection in Merrick's account. It was a quiet, friendly document, created by one Laurence Mayfair, mentioning, among other things, the daily weather in the city, the number of customers at the studio, and other small local events.

It recorded a happy life, I felt certain, and we took the time to copy it very carefully and send that copy to the local university, where such a document by a man of color before the Civil War would be given its just due.

In time, many similar documents, as well as copies of photographs, were sent on to various Southern universities, but such steps were always taken—for Merrick's sake—with great care.

Merrick was absent from the accompanying letters. She really did not want the material traced to her personally because she did not want to explain her family to those outside the Order, and I think she feared, and perhaps rightly, that her presence with us might be questioned as well.

"They need to know about our people," she'd say at table, "but they don't need to know about me."

She was greatly relieved that we did what we did, but she was launched now into another world. She would never be that tragic child again who had showed the daguerreotypes to me the first evening.

She was Merrick the student who pored over her books for hours, Merrick the passionate arguer of politics, before, during, and after the television news. She was Merrick who owned seventeen pairs of shoes, and changed them three times a day. She was Merrick, the Catholic, who insisted on going to Mass every Sunday even if a Biblical inundation were falling upon the plantation and the nearby church.

Of course I was pleased to see these things, though I knew many recollections lay dormant inside her and must someday be resolved.

Finally, it was late fall, and I had no choice but to return to London for good. Merrick had another six months of study planned before she'd be sent to Switzerland, and our parting was tearful to say the least.

I was no longer Mr. Talbot, but David, as I was to many other members, and, as we waved goodbye to each other at the doorway of the plane, I saw Merrick cry again for the first time since that awful night when she'd cast off the ghost of Honey in the Sunshine and broken into sobs.

It was dreadful. I couldn't wait for the plane to land so that I could write her a letter.

And for months her frequent letters were the most interesting aspect of my life.

By February of the following year, Merrick was on a plane with me for Geneva. Though the weather made her hopelessly forlorn, she studied diligently at school, dreaming of summers spent in Louisiana, or of the many vacation trips which took her to the tropics which she loved.

One year she went back to Mexico, during the worst of all seasons, to see the Maya ruins, and it was that summer that she confided to me that we had to make the return trip to the cave.

"I'm not ready to retrace my steps," she said, "but the moment will come. I know that you've saved everything that Matthew wrote on the subject, and understand that I may be guided on that journey by others besides Matthew. But do not worry. It's too soon for us to go."

The next year she visited Peru, then after that Rio de Janeiro, and always back to school when fall came. She did not make friends easily in Switzerland, and we did all we could to convey upon her a sense of normality, but the very nature of the Talamasca is unique and secretive and I'm not sure we were always successful at making her feel at ease with others at school.

At age eighteen, Merrick informed me by official letter that she was more than positive that she wished to spend her life in the Talamasca, even though we assured her that we would educate her no matter what her choice. She was admitted as a postulant, which is for us a very young member, and she went to Oxford to begin her university years.

I was thrilled to have her in England. I met her plane and was astonished by the tall graceful young woman who flew into my arms.

She lodged at the Motherhouse every weekend. Once again the chilly weather oppressed her dreadfully, but she wanted to remain.

On weekends we would take side trips to Canterbury Cathedral or Stonehenge or Glastonbury, whatever her fancy. It was interesting talk all the way. Her New Orleans accent—I call it that for want of a better term—had left her completely, she had surpassed me utterly in her knowledge of the Classics, her Greek was perfect, and she could speak Latin with other members of the Order, a rare talent in one of her time.

She became a specialist in Coptic, translating volumes of Coptic magical texts which the Talamasca had owned for centuries. She was deep into the history of magic, assuring me of the obvious, that magic all over the world and in every era is pretty much the same.

She often fell asleep in the Motherhouse library, her face on her book on the table. She'd lost her interest in clothes except for a few very pretty and ultrafeminine garments, and, intermittently, she bought and wore those fatal very high heeled shoes.

As for her liking for Chanel No. 22, nothing ever inhibited her from wearing a great deal of the scent in her hair and on her skin and her clothing. Most of us found it very delicious, and no matter where I was in the Motherhouse, I knew, by the rise of this delightful scent, when Merrick had come through the front door.

On her twenty-first birthday, my personal gift to Merrick was a triple string of natural and perfectly matched white pearls. Of course it cost a fortune, but I didn't care. I had a fortune. She was deeply touched by it, and to all important functions within the Order she always wore the necklace, whether attired in a black silk shirtwaist dress of magnificent angles and fullness—her favorite for such evenings—or a more casual dark wool suit.

Merrick was by this time a famous beauty, and the young members were always falling in love with her and complaining bitterly that she repelled their advances and even their praise. Merrick never spoke of love, or of men who were interested in her. And I had come to suspect that she was enough of a mind reader to feel very much isolated and alienated, even within our hallowed halls.

I was hardly immune to her appeal. At times, I found it downright difficult to be in her presence, so fresh and lovely and inviting did she seem. She had a way of looking luscious in austere garments, her breasts large and high, her legs rounded and tapered exquisitely beneath her modest hem.

There was one trip to Rome on which I became miserable in my desire for her. I cursed the fact that age had not yet delivered me from such torment, and did all that I could so that she might never guess. I think she knew it, however, and in her own way, she was merciless.

She once let slip, after a sumptuous dinner at the Hassler Hotel, that she found me the only truly interesting man in her life.

"Bad luck, wouldn't you say, David?" she had asked me pointedly. The return to the table of two other Talamasca comrades had cut the conversation short. I was flattered but deeply disturbed. I couldn't have her, it was quite out of the question, and that I wanted her so much came as a terrible surprise.

At some point, after that Roman trip, Merrick devoted some time in Louisiana to recording the entire history of her family—that is, what she knew of her people, quite apart from their occult powers, and, together with quality copies of all of her daguerreotypes and photographs, she made this available to several universities for whatever use they might desire. Indeed, the family history—without Merrick's name, and indeed minus several key names—is now part of several important collections concerning the *"gens de couleur libres,"* or the history of black families in the south.

Aaron told me that the project exhausted Merrick emotionally, but she had said *les mystères* were haunting her, and it had to be done. Lucy Nancy Marie Mayfair demanded it; indeed so did Great Nananne. So did white Oncle Julien Mayfair from uptown. But when Aaron prodded as to whether she was really being haunted, or merely respectful, Merrick said nothing except that it was time to go back to work overseas.

As for her own Afro-American blood, Merrick was always quite frank about it and sometimes surprised others by discussing it. But almost without exception, in every situation, she passed for white.

For two years, Merrick studied in Egypt. Nothing could lure her away from Cairo, until she began an impassioned investigation of Egyptian and Coptic documents throughout the museums and libraries of the globe. I remember going through the dim and grimy Cairo Museum with her, loving her inevitable infatuation with Egyptian mystery, and that trip ended with her getting completely drunk and passing out after supper in my arms. Fortunately I was almost as drunk as she was. I think we woke up together, each properly dressed, lying side by side on her bed.

In fact, Merrick had already become something of a famous though occasional drunk. And more than once she had wrapped her arms around me and kissed me in a way that thoroughly invigorated me and left me in despair.

I refused her seeming invitations. I told myself, and probably rightly so, that I was partly imagining her desire. Besides, I was old then obviously, and for a young person to think that she wants you when you're old is one thing; to actually follow through with it is quite another affair. What had I to offer her but a host of minor inevitable physical debilities? I did not dream then of Body Thieves who would bequeath to me the form of a young man.

And I must confess that, years later, when I did find myself in possession of this young man's corpus, I did think of Merrick. Oh, indeed, I did think of Merrick. But by then I was in love with a supernatural being, our inimitable Lestat, and he blinded me even to memories of Merrick's charms.

Enough said on that damned subject! Yes, I desired her, but my task is to return to the story of the woman I know today. Yes, Merrick, the brave and brilliant member of the Talamasca, that is the story I have to tell:

Long before computers were so very common, she had mastered them for her own writing and was soon heard to be tapping away at fantastical speed on her keyboard late into the night. She published hundreds of translations and articles for our members, and many, under a pseudonym, in the outside world.

Of course we are very careful in sharing all such learning. It is not our purpose to be noticed; but there are things which we do not feel we can keep to ourselves. We would never have insisted on a pseudonym, however; but Merrick was as secretive about her own identity as ever she was as a child.

Meanwhile, as regards the "uptown Mayfairs" of New Orleans, she showed little interest in them personally, hardly bothering with the few records we recommended that she read. They were never her people, really, no matter what she might have thought of "Oncle Julien" appearing in Great Nananne's dream. Also, no matter what one might observe about the "powers" of those Mayfairs, they have in this century almost no interest at all in "ritual magic," and that was Merrick's chosen field.

Of course nothing of Merrick's possessions had ever been sold. There was no reason to sell anything. It would have been absurd.

The Talamasca is so very rich that the expenses of one person, such as Merrick, mean virtually nothing, and Merrick, even when she was very young, was devoted to the projects of the Order and worked of her own free will in the archives to update records, make translations, and identify and label articles very similar to those Olmec treasures which belonged to her.

If ever a member of the Talamasca earned her own way, it was Merrick, almost to a degree which put us to shame. Therefore, if Merrick wanted a shopping spree in New York or Paris, no one was likely to deny it. And when she chose a black Rolls Royce sedan as her personal car, soon establishing a small worldwide collection of them, no one thought it a bad idea at all.

Merrick was some twenty-four years old before she approached Aaron about taking stock of the occult collection she had brought to the Order ten years before.

I remember it because I remember Aaron's letter.

"Never has she shown the slightest interest," he wrote:

and you know how this has worried me. Even when she made her family history and sent it off to various scholars, she did not touch upon the occult heritage at all. But this afternoon she confided to me that she has had several "important" dreams about her childhood, and that she must return to Great Nananne's house. Together with our driver we made the trip back to the old neighborhood, a sad journey indeed.

The district has sunk considerably lower, I think, than she could have imagined, and I believe the shattered ruin of the "corner bar" and the "corner store" took her quite by surprise. As for the house, it has been splendidly maintained by the man who lives on the premises, and Merrick spent almost an hour, alone by choice, in the rear yard.

There the caretaker had made a patio, and the shed is virtually empty. Nothing remains of the temple, naturally, except the brightly painted center post.

She said nothing to me afterwards, absolutely refusing to discuss these dreams of hers in any detail.

She expressed extreme gratitude to me that we'd kept the house for her, during her period of "negligence," and I hoped this might be the end of it.

But at supper, I was quite astonished to hear that she planned to move back into the house and spend part of her time there from now on. She wanted all the old furniture, she told me. She'd supervise the arrangements herself.

"What about the neighborhood?" I found myself asking weakly, to which she replied with a smile, "I was never afraid of the neighbors. You'll soon discover, Aaron, that the neighbors will become afraid of me." Not to be outdone, I quipped, "And suppose some stranger should try to murder you, Merrick," to which she fired back, "Heaven help the man or woman who would attempt such a thing."

Merrick was as good as her word, and did move back to the "old neighborhood," but not before building a caretaker's quarters above the old shed.

The two miserably rundown houses which flanked the house were purchased and demolished, and brick walls went up around three sides of the enormous lot and along the front, coming to meet the high iron picket fence directly before the facade. There was always to be a man on the property; some sort of alarm system was installed; flowers were planted. Feeders were put out for the hummingbirds once more. It all sounded quite wholesome, and natural, but having once seen that house, I was still chilled by frequent stories of how Merrick came and went.

The Motherhouse remained her true home, but many afternoons, according to Aaron, she disappeared into New Orleans and did not return for several days.

"The house is now quietly spectacular," Aaron wrote to me. "All the furniture was of course repaired and refinished, and Merrick has claimed Great Nananne's mammoth four-poster for her own. The floors of heart pine have been beautifully redone, giving the house a rather amber glow. Nevertheless, it worries me dreadfully that Merrick secludes herself there for days on end."

Naturally, I myself wrote to Merrick, broaching the subject of the dreams that had motivated her return to the house.

"I want to tell you about these things but it is too soon," Merrick replied immediately.

Let me say only that in these dreams it is Great-Oncle Vervain who talks with me. Sometimes I'm a child again as I was on the day he died. Other times we are adults together. And it seems, though I cannot with uniform success remember everything, in one dream we were both young.

For now, you mustn't worry. You must realize that it was inevitable that I should return to my childhood home. I am of an age when people become curious about the past, especially when it has been sealed off so successfully and abruptly as was mine.

Understand, I do not feel guilt for having abandoned the house where I grew up. It is only that my dreams are telling me that I must return. They tell me other things as well.

These letters worried me, but Merrick gave only brief responses to my queries.

Aaron had also become concerned. Merrick was spending less and less time at Oak Haven. Often he made the drive into New Orleans to call upon her at the old house, that is, until Merrick asked to be left alone.

Of course, such a manner of living is not uncommon among Talamasca members. Frequently they divide their time between the Motherhouse and a private family home. I had and still do have a home in the Cotswolds in England. But it is not a good sign when a Member absents herself from the Order for long periods of time. In Merrick's case it was particularly disturbing due to her frequent and cryptic mentions of her dreams.

During the fall of that fateful year, her twenty-fifth, Merrick wrote to me about a journey to the cave.

Let me continue with my reconstruction here of her words:

"David, I no longer sleep through the night without a dream of my Great-Oncle Vervain. Yet less and less am I able to recall the substance of these dreams. I know only that he wants me to return to the cave I visited in Central America when I was a child. David, I must do this. Nothing can prevent it. The dreams have become a form of obsession, and I ask that you not bombard me with logical objections to what you know I must do."

She went on to talk about her treasure.

I have been through all of the so-called Olmec treasures, and I know now they are not Olmec at all. In fact, I can't identify them, though I have every published book or catalog on antiquities in that part of the world. As for the destination itself, I have what I remember, and some writings by my Oncle Vervain, and the papers of Matthew Kemp, my beloved stepfather of years ago.

I want you to make this journey with me, though certainly we cannot attempt it without others. Please answer me as quickly as you can as to whether you are willing. If not, I will organize a party on my own.

Now, I was almost seventy years of age when I received this letter, and her words presented quite a challenge to me, and one which I didn't welcome at all. Though I longed for the jungles, longed for the experience, I was quite concerned that it was beyond my ability to make such a trip.

Merrick went on to explain that she had spent many hours going through the artifacts retrieved on her girlhood journey.

"They are indeed older," she wrote, "than those objects which archaeologists call Olmec, though they undoubtedly share many common traits with that civilization and would be called Olmec-oid due to their style. Elements we might call Asian or Chinese proliferate in these artifacts, and then there is the matter of the alien cave-paintings which Matthew managed to photograph as best he could. I must investigate these things personally. I must try to arrive at some conclusion regarding the involvement of my Oncle Vervain in this part of the world."

I called her that night from London.

"Look, I'm entirely too old to go off into that jungle," I said, "if it's even still there. You know they're cutting down the rain forests. It might be farmland by now. Besides, I'd slow you down no matter what the terrain."

"I want you to come with me," she said softly, coaxingly. "David, please do this. We can move at your pace, and when it comes time to make the climb in the waterfall, I can do that part alone.

"David, you were in the jungles of the Amazon years ago. You know this sort of experience. Imagine us now with every microchip convenience. Cameras, flashlights, camping equipment; we'll have every luxury. David, come with me. You can remain in the village if you like. I'll go on to the waterfall alone. With a modern four-wheel drive vehicle, it will be nothing at all."

Well it wasn't nothing at all.

A week later I arrived in New Orleans, determined to argue her out of the excursion. I was driven directly to the Motherhouse, a little disturbed that neither Aaron nor Merrick had come to meet my plane.

12

AARON GREETED ME at the door.

"Merrick's at her house in New Orleans. The caretaker says she's been drinking. She will not talk to him. I've called every hour since morning. The phone simply rings and rings."

"Why didn't you tell me this was happening?" I demanded. I was deeply concerned.

"Why? So you'd worry about it all the way across the Atlantic? I knew you were coming. I know you're the only one who can reason with her when she's in this state."

"Whatever in the world makes you think so?" I argued. But it was true. Sometimes I could talk Merrick into ending her binges. But not always.

Whatever the case, I bathed, changed clothes, as the early winter weather was unseasonably warm, and set out in a drowsy evening shower, with the car and driver, for Merrick's house.

It was dark when I got there, but even so, I could see that the neighborhood had deteriorated beyond my wildest speculation. It seemed as if a war had been lost in the district, and the survivors had no choice but to live among hopeless wooden ruins tumbling down into the eternal giant weeds. Here and there was a well-kept shotgun house with a bright coat of paint and some gingerbread trim beneath its roof. But dim lights shone through heavily barred windows. Abandoned cottages were being dismantled by the rampant greenery. The area was derelict and obviously dangerous as well.

It seemed to me that I could sense people prowling about in the darkness. I detested the feeling of fear which had been so uncommon in me in my youth. Old age had taught me to respect danger. As I said,

I hated it. I remember hating the thought that I wouldn't ever be able to accompany Merrick on this insane journey to the Central American jungles, and I'd be humiliated as the result.

At last the car stopped at Merrick's house.

The lovely old raised cottage, painted a fresh shade of tropical pink with white trim, appeared rather wonderful behind the high iron picket fence. The new brick walls were thick and very high as they embraced the property on either side. A bank of densely flowering oleander behind the iron pickets shielded the house somewhat from the squalor of the street.

As the caretaker greeted me, and brought me up the front steps, I saw that Merrick's long windows were well barred also, in spite of their white lace curtains and shades, and that lights were on throughout the house.

The porch was clean; the old square pillars were solid; the leaded glass sparkled within the twin windows of the polished double doors. A wave of remembrance passed over me, nevertheless.

"She won't answer the bell, Sir," said the caretaker, a man I scarcely noticed in my haste. "But the door's unlocked for you. I took her some supper at five o'clock."

"She asked for her supper?" I inquired.

"No, Sir, she never said anything. But she ate the food. I picked up the dishes at six."

I opened the door and found myself in the comfortable air-cooled front hall. I saw at once that the old parlor and dining room to my right had been splendidly refurnished with rather bright Chinese carpets. A modern sheen covered the old furniture. The old mirrors above the white marble mantels were as dark as they had ever been.

To my left lay the front bedroom; Great Nananne's bed was dressed with an ivory white canopy and a counterpane of heavy crocheted lace.

In a polished wooden rocking chair before the bed, facing the front windows, sat Merrick, a wobbling light easily illuminating her thoughtful face.

There was a bottle of Flor de Caña rum on the little candlestand table beside her.

She lifted the glass to her lips, drank from it, and then sat back, continuing to stare off as if she didn't know that I was there.

I stopped at the threshold.

"Darling," I said, "aren't you going to offer me a drink?"

Without so much as turning her head, she smiled.

"You never liked straight rum, David," she said softly. "You're a Scotch man like my old stepfather, Matthew. It's in the dining room. How about some Highland Macallan? Twenty-five years old. That good enough for my beloved Superior General?"

"I should say so, gracious lady," I replied. "But never mind that just now. May I step into your boudoir?"

She uttered a small pretty laugh. "Sure, David," she said, "come on in."

I was startled as soon as I looked to my left. A large marble altar had been erected between the two front windows, and I saw there the old multitude of sizable plaster saints. The Virgin Mary wore her crown and the vestments of Mount Carmel, holding the radiant Baby Jesus beneath her innocent smile.

Some elements had been added. I realized they were the Three Magi of Christian scripture and lore. The altar was no Christmas crèche, you understand. The Magi or Wise Men had merely been included in a large panoply of sacred figures, more or less on their own terms.

I spied several of the mysterious jade idols among the saints, including one very mean little idol which held its scepter quite ready for duty or attack.

Two other rather vicious little characters flanked the large statue of St. Peter. And there before them lay the green jade hummingbird perforator, or knife, one of the most beautiful artifacts in Merrick's large cache.

The gorgeous axe of obsidian which I had seen years ago was given a place of prominence between the Virgin Mary and the Arc Angel Michael. It had a lovely luster in the dim light.

But perhaps the most surprising contents of the altar were the daguerreotypes and old photographs of Merrick's people, ranged thickly as any display upon a parlor piano, the multitude of faces lost in the gloom.

A double row of candles burned before the entire array, and there were fresh flowers aplenty, in numerous vases. Everything appeared dusted and quite clean. That is, until I realized that the shriveled hand had its place among the offerings. It stood out against the white marble, curled and hideous, very much as it had seemed when I first saw it long ago.

"For old times' sake?" I asked, gesturing to the altar.

"Don't be absurd," she said under her breath. She lifted a cigarette to her lips. I saw by the box on the little table that it was Rothmans, Matthew's old brand. My old brand as well. I knew her to be a smoker now and then, rather like I was myself.

Nevertheless, I found myself looking hard at her. Was she really my beloved Merrick? My skin had begun to crawl, as they say, a feeling I detest.

"Merrick?" I asked.

When she looked up at me, I knew it was she and no one else inside her handsome young body, and I knew that she wasn't very drunk at all.

"Sit down, David, my dear," she said sincerely, almost sadly. "The armchair's comfortable. I'm really glad you came."

I was much relieved by the familiarity of her tone. I crossed the room, in front of her, and settled in the armchair from which I could easily see her face. The altar loomed over my right shoulder, with all those tiny photographic faces staring at me, as they had long ago. I found that I did not like it, did not like the many indifferent saints and the subdued Wise Men, though I had to admit that the spectacle was dazzling to my eyes.

"Why must we go off to these jungles, Merrick?" I asked. "Whatever made you decide to drop everything for such an idea?"

She didn't answer immediately. She took a drink of rum from her glass, her eyes focused on the altar.

This gave me time to note that a huge portrait of Oncle Vervain hung on the far wall beside the door through which I'd entered the room.

I knew it at once to be an expensive enlargement of the likeness Merrick had revealed to us years ago. The processing had been true to the sepia tones of the portrait, and Oncle Vervain, a young man in his prime, resting his elbow comfortably on the Greek column, appeared to be staring directly at me with bold brilliant light eyes.

Even in the shuddering gloom, I could see his handsome broad nose and beautifully shaped full lips. As for the light eyes, they gave the face a certain frightening aspect, though I wasn't certain whether or not I ought to have felt such a thing.

"I see you came to continue the argument," Merrick said. "There can be no argument for me, David. I have to go and now."

"You haven't convinced me. You know very well I won't let you journey into that part of the world without the support of the Tala-masca, but I want to understand—."

"Oncle Vervain is not going to leave me alone," she said quietly, her eyes large and vivid, her face somewhat dark against the low light of the distant hall. "It's the dreams, David. Truth is, I've had them for years, but never the way they come now. Maybe I didn't want to pay attention. Maybe I played, even in the dreams themselves, as if I didn't understand."

It seemed to me that she was three times as fetching as I had remembered. Her simple dress of violet cotton was belted tightly at the waist, and the hem barely covered her knees. Her legs were lean and exquisitely shaped. Her feet, the toenails painted a bright shiny violet to match the dress, were bare.

"When precisely did the onslaught of dreams begin?"

"Spring," she replied a little wearily. "Oh, right after Christmas. I'm not even sure. Winter was bad here. Maybe Aaron told you. We had a hard freeze. All the beautiful banana trees died. Of course they came right back up as soon as the spring warmth arrived. Did you see them outside?"

"I didn't notice, darling. Forgive me," I replied.

She resumed as if I hadn't answered.

"And that's when he came to me the most clearly," she said. "There was no past or future in the dream, then, only Oncle Vervain and me. We were in this house together, he and I, and he was sitting at the din-ing room table—." She gestured to the open door and the spaces beyond it, "—and I was with him. And he said to me, 'Girl, didn't I tell you to go back there and get those things?' He went into a long story. It was about spirits, awful spirits that had knocked him down a slope so that he cut his head. I woke up in the night and wrote down every-thing I remembered, but some of it was lost and maybe that was meant to be."

"Tell me what else you remember now."

"He said it was his mother's great-grandfather who knew of that cave," she responded. "He said that the old man took him there, though he himself was scared of the jungle. Do you know how many years back that would be? He said he never got to go back there. He came to New Orleans and got rich off Voodoo, rich as anybody can get off Voodoo. He said you give up your dreams the longer you live, until you've got nothing."

I think I winced at those choice and truthful words.

"I was seven years old," she said, "when Oncle Vervain died under this roof. His mother's great-grandfather was a *brujo* among the Maya. You know, that's a witch doctor, a priest of sorts. I can still remember Oncle Vervain using that word."

"Why does he want you to go back?" I asked her.

She had not removed her eyes from the altar. I glanced in that direction and realized that a picture of Oncle Vervain was there too. It was small, frameless, merely propped at the Virgin's feet.

"To get the treasure," she said in her low, troubled voice. "To bring it here. He says there's something there that will change my destiny. But I don't know what he means." She gave one of those characteristic sighs of hers. "He seems to think I'll need it, this object, this thing. But what do spirits know?"

"What *do* they know, Merrick?" I asked.

"I can't tell you, David," she replied raggedly. "I can only tell you that he haunts me. He wants me to go there and bring back those things."

"You don't want to do this," I said. "I can tell by your entire manner. You're being haunted."

"It's a strong ghost, David," she said, her eyes moving over the distant statues. "They're strong dreams." She shook her head. "They're so full of his presence. God, how I miss him." She let her eyes drift. "You know," she said, "when he was very old, his legs were bad. The priest came; he said Oncle Vervain didn't have to go to Sunday Mass anymore. It was too hard. Yet every Sunday, Oncle Vervain got dressed in his best three-piece suit, and always with his pocket watch, you know, the little gold chain in front and the watch in the little pocket— and he sat in the dining room over there listening to the broadcast of Mass on the radio and whispering his prayers. He was such a gentleman. And the priest would come and bring him Holy Communion in the afternoon.

"No matter how bad his legs were, Oncle Vervain knelt down for Holy Communion. I stood in the front door until the priest was gone and the altar boy. Oncle Vervain said that our church was a magic church because Christ's Body and Blood was in Holy Communion. Oncle Vervain said I was baptized: Merrick Marie Louise Mayfair— consecrated to the Blessed Mother. They spelled it the French way, you know: M-e-r-r-i-q-u-e. I know I was baptized. I know."

She paused. I couldn't bear the suffering in her voice or in her expression. If only we had located that baptismal certificate, I thought desperately, we might have prevented this obsession.

"No, David," she said aloud, sharply correcting me. "I dream of him, I tell you. I see him holding that gold watch." She settled back into her reverie, though it gave her no consolation. "How I loved that watch, that gold watch. I was the one who wanted it, but he left it to Cold Sandra. I used to beg him to let me look at it, to let me turn its hands to correct it, to let me snap it open, but no, he said, 'Merrick, it doesn't tick for you, *chérie*, it ticks for others.' And Cold Sandra got it. Cold Sandra took it with her when she left."

"Merrick, these are family ghosts. Don't we all have family ghosts?"

"Yes, David, but it's my family, and my family was never very much like anyone else's family, was it, David? He comes in the dreams and tells me about the cave."

"I can't bear to see you hurt, my darling," I said. "In London, behind my desk, I isolate myself emotionally from the Members all over the world. But from you? Never."

She nodded. "I don't want to cause you pain, either, boss," she said, "but I need you."

"You won't give up on this, will you?" I replied as tenderly as I could.

She said nothing. Then:

"We have a problem, David," she said, her eyes fixed on the altar, perhaps deliberately avoiding me.

"And what is that, darling?" I asked.

"We don't know exactly where to go."

"I'm hardly surprised," I responded, trying to remember what I could of Matthew's vague letters. I tried not to sound cross or pompous. "All Matthew's letters were mailed from Mexico City in a batch as I understand it, when you were making your way home."

She nodded.

"But what of the map that Oncle Vervain gave you? I know it has no names, but when you touched it, what happened?"

"Nothing happened when I touched it," she said. She smiled bitterly. She was silent for a long time. Then she gestured to the altar.

It was then that I saw the small rolled parchment, tied in black ribbon, sitting beside the small picture of Oncle Vervain.

"Matthew had help getting there," she said in a strange, almost hollow voice. "He didn't figure it out from that map, or on his own in any fashion."

"You're referring to sorcery," I said.

"You sound like a Grand Inquisitor," she replied, her eyes still very distant from me, her face devoid of feeling, her tone flat. "He had Cold Sandra to help him. Cold Sandra knew things from Oncle Vervain that I don't know. Cold Sandra knew the whole lay of the land. So did Honey in the Sunshine. She was six years older than me."

She paused. She was obviously deeply troubled. I don't think I had ever seen her so troubled in all her adult years.

"Oncle Vervain's mother's people had the secrets," she said. "I see so many faces in my dreams." She shook her head as if trying to clear her mind. On her voice went in a near whisper. "Oncle Vervain used to talk to Cold Sandra all the time. If he hadn't died when he did, maybe Cold Sandra would have been better, but then he was so old, it was his time."

"And in the dreams, Oncle Vervain doesn't tell you where the cave is located?"

"He tries," she answered sadly. "I see images, fragments. I see the Maya *brujo*, the priest, going up to a rock by the waterfall. I see a big stone carved with facial features. I see incense and candles, feathers from the wild birds, beautifully colored feathers and offerings of food."

"I understand," I responded.

She rocked a little in the chair, her eyes moving slowly from side to side. Then she took another drink of the rum in her glass. "Of course I remember things from the journey," she said in a slow voice.

"You were only ten years old," I said sympathetically. "And you mustn't think that because of these dreams you should go back now."

She ignored me. She drank her rum and she stared at the altar.

"There are so many ruins, so many highland basins," she said. "So many waterfalls, so many cloud forests. I need one more piece of information. Two pieces, really. The city to which we flew from Mexico City, and the name of the village where we camped. We took two planes to reach that city. I can't remember those names, if I ever knew them. I don't think I was paying attention. I was playing in the jungles. I was off by myself. I scarcely knew why we were there."

"Darling, listen to me—," I started.

"Don't. Forget it. I have to go back," she said sharply.

"Well, I assume you've combed all your books on the jungle terrain.

You've made lists of towns and villages?" I broke off. I had to remember I didn't want this dangerous trip to take place.

She didn't immediately respond to me, and then she stared at me very deliberately and her eyes appeared uncommonly hard and cold. The candlelight and the light of the lamps made them gorgeously green. I noticed that her fingernails were painted the same shade of shiny violet as her toes. Once again she seemed the incarnation of all I'd ever desired.

"Of course I've done that," she said to me gently. "But now I have to find the name of that village, the last real outpost, and the name of the city to which we flew on the plane. If I had that, I could go." She sighed. "Especially that village with the *brujo*, that's been there for centuries, inaccessible and waiting for us—if I had that, I'd know the way."

"How, precisely?" I asked her.

"Honey knows it," she answered. "Honey in the Sunshine was sixteen when we made that journey. Honey will remember. Honey will tell it to me."

"Merrick, you can't try to call up Honey!" I said. "You know that's far too dangerous, that's utterly reckless, you can't . . ."

"David, *you're* here."

"I can't protect you if you call up this spirit, good God."

"But you must protect me. You must protect me because Honey will be as dreadful as she ever was. She'll try to destroy me when she comes through."

"Then don't do it."

"I have to do it. I have to do it and I have to go back to that cave. I promised Matthew Kemp when he was dying I'd report those discoveries. He didn't know he was talking to me. He thought he was talking to Cold Sandra, or maybe even Honey, or maybe his mother, I couldn't tell. But I promised. I promised I would tell the world about that cave."

"The world does not care about one more Olmec ruin!" I said. "There are universities aplenty working all through the rain forests and jungles. There're ancient cities all over Central America! What does it matter now?"

"I promised Oncle Vervain," she said earnestly. "I promised him I'd get all the treasure. I promised I'd bring it back. 'When you grow up,' he said to me, and I promised."

"Sounds to me as if Cold Sandra promised," I said sharply. "And perhaps Honey in the Sunshine promised. You were what, seven years old when the old man died?"

"I have to do it," she said solemnly.

"Listen," I insisted, "we're going to stop this entire plan. It's too dangerous politically to go to those Central American jungles anyway," I declared. "I won't approve the trip. I'm the Superior General. You can't go over my head."

"I don't intend to," she said, her tone softening. "I need you with me. I need you now."

She stopped, and, leaning to one side, crushed out her cigarette, and refilled her glass from the bottle. She took a deep drink and settled back again in the chair.

"I have to call Honey," she whispered.

"Why not call Cold Sandra!" I demanded desperately.

"You don't understand," she said. "I've kept it locked in my soul all these years, but I have to call Honey. And Honey's near me. Honey's always near me! I've felt her near me. I've fended her off with my power. I've used my charms and my strength to protect myself. But she never really goes away." She took a deep drink of the rum. "David," she said, "Oncle Vervain loved Honey in the Sunshine. Honey's in these dreams too."

"I think it's your gruesome imagination!" I declared.

She gave a high sparkling laugh at this, full of true amusement. It startled me. "Listen to you, David, next you'll tell me there are no ghosts or vampires. And that the Talamasca is just a legend, such an Order doesn't exist."

"Why do you have to call Honey?"

She shook her head. She rested back in the chair, and her eyes filled with visible tears. I could see them in the flicker of the candles. I was becoming genuinely frantic.

I stood up, marched into the dining room, found the bottle of twenty-five-year-old Macallan Scotch and the lead crystal glasses on the sideboard, and poured myself a good drink. I returned to her. Then I went back and got the bottle. I brought it with me, settled in the chair, and put it on the nightstand to my left.

The Scotch tasted wonderful. I didn't drink on the plane at all, wanting to be alert for my reunion, and it took the edge off my nerves beautifully.

She was still crying.

"All right, you're going to call up Honey, and you think for some reason Honey knows the name of the town or the village."

"Honey liked those places," she said, unperturbed by my urgent voice. "Honey liked the name of the village from which we hiked to the cave." She turned to me. "Don't you see, these names are like jewels embedded in her conscious; she's there with all she ever knew! She doesn't have to remember like a living being. The knowledge is in her and I have to make her give it to me."

"All right, I see, I understand everything. I maintain that it's too dangerous, and besides, why hasn't the spirit of Honey gone on?"

"She can't until I tell her what she wants to know."

This baffled me completely. What could Honey want to know?

Suddenly Merrick rose from the chair, rather like a slumbering cat instantly propelled into predatory action, and she closed the door to the hall. I heard her turn the key.

I was on my feet. But I stood back, uncertain of what she meant to do. Certainly she wasn't drunk enough to be interfered with in any dramatic authoritarian fashion, and I wasn't surprised when she abandoned her glass for the bottle of rum and took it with her into the center of the room.

Only then did I realize there was no carpet. Her naked feet were soundless on the polished floor, and, with the bottle clutched in her right hand to her breast, she began to turn in a circle, humming and throwing back her head.

I pressed myself against the wall.

Round and round she spun, the violet cotton skirt flaring and the bottle sloshing rum into the air. She paid no attention to the spilt liquor, and, slowing her turns only for a moment, she took another deep drink and then turned so fast that her garments slapped against her legs.

Stopping dead as she faced the altar, she spit the rum between her teeth into a fine spray at the waiting saints.

A high-pitched wail came out of her clenched teeth as she continued to issue the rum from her mouth.

Once again she began to dance, almost deliberately slapping her feet and murmuring. I couldn't catch the language or the words. Her hair was tangled over her face. Again a swallow, again the rum flying, the candles sputtering and dancing as they caught the tiny droplets and ignited them.

Suddenly she hurled a stream of rum from the bottle all over the candles, and the flames went up before the saints in a dangerous flare. Mercifully the fire went out.

Head back, she screamed between her teeth in French:

"Honey, I did it! Honey, I did it. Honey, I did it!"

The room seemed to shake as she bent her knees and circled, pounding her feet in a loud dance.

"Honey, I put the curse on you and Cold Sandra!" she screamed. "Honey, I did it."

Suddenly she lunged at the altar, never letting go of her bottle, and, grabbing the green jade perforator in her left hand, she slashed a long cut into her right arm.

I gasped. What could I do to stop her, I thought, what could I do that wouldn't enrage her?

The blood streamed down her arm and she bowed her head, licked at it, drank the rum, and sprayed the offering on the patient saints once again.

I could see the blood flowing down her hand, over her knuckles. Her wound was superficial but the amount of blood was awful.

Again she lifted the knife.

"Honey, I did it to you and Cold Sandra. I killed you, I put the curse on you!" she screamed.

I resolved to grab hold of her as she went to cut herself again. But I couldn't move.

As God is my witness, I couldn't move. I was rooted to the spot. I tried with all my resources to overcome the paralysis, but it was useless. All I could do was cry to her,

"Stop it, Merrick!"

She slashed at her arm across the first cut, and again the blood flowed.

"Honey, come to me, Honey, give me your rage, give me your hatred, Honey, I killed you, Honey, I made the dolls of you and Cold Sandra, Honey, I drowned them in the ditch the night you left. Honey, I killed you. Honey, I sent you to the swamp water, Honey, I did it," she was screaming.

"For the love of Heaven, Merrick, let go!" I cried. Then suddenly, unable to watch her slash her arm again, I began to pray frantically to Oxalá:

"Give me the power to stop her, give me the power to divert her before she harms herself, give me the power, I beg you, Oxalá, I'm your loyal David, give me the power." I shut my eyes. The floor was trembling beneath me.

Suddenly the noise of her screams and her bare feet stopped.

I felt her against me. I opened my eyes. She stood in my embrace, both of us facing the doorway, which was indisputably open, and the shadowy figure who stood with her back to the light of the hall.

It was a graceful young girl with long tightly curling blond hair lathered all over her shoulders, her face veiled in shadow, her yellow eyes piercing in the candle glow.

"I did it!" Merrick whispered. "I killed you."

I felt Merrick's whole pliant body against me. I wrapped my arms tightly around her. Again, but silently, I prayed to Oxalá.

Protect us from this spirit if evil is the intent of this Spirit. Oxalá, you who made the world, you who rule in high places, you who are among the clouds, protect us, do not look at my faults as I call on you, but give me your mercy, protect us if this spirit would do us harm.

Merrick wasn't trembling, she was quaking, her body covered in sweat, as it had been during the possession so many years before.

"I put the dolls in the ditch, I drowned them in the ditch, I did it. I drowned them. I did it. I prayed, 'Let them die!' I knew from Cold Sandra that she was going to buy that car, I said, 'Let it go off a bridge, let them drown.' I said, 'When they drive across the lake, let them die.' Cold Sandra was so afraid of that lake, I said, 'Let them die.' "

The figure in the doorway appeared as solid as anything I'd ever beheld. The shadowy face showed no expression, but the yellow eyes remained fixed.

Then a voice issued from it, low, and full of hatred.

"Fool, you never caused it!" said the voice. "Fool, you think you caused that to happen to us? You never caused anything. Fool, you couldn't make a curse to save your soul!"

I thought Merrick would lose consciousness, but somehow she remained standing, though my arms were ready to hold her should she fail.

She nodded. "Forgive me that I wanted it," she said in a hoarse whisper that seemed entirely her own. "Forgive me, Honey, that I wanted it. I wanted to go with you, forgive me."

"Go to God to get your forgiveness," came the low voice from the darkened countenance. "Don't come to me."

Again Merrick nodded. I could feel the stickiness of her spilt blood coming down over my right fingers. Again I prayed to Oxalá! But my words were coming automatically. I was riveted heart and soul to the being in the doorway, who neither moved nor dissolved.

"Get down on your knees," said the voice. "Write in blood what I tell you."

"Don't do it!" I whispered.

Merrick sprang forward, falling on her knees on the floor that was wet and slippery with blood and spilt rum.

Once again, I tried to move, but I couldn't. It was as if my feet had been nailed to the boards.

Merrick's back was to me, but I knew she was pressing her left fingers to the wounds to make them bleed ever more deeply, and then I heard the creature in the doorway give two names.

I heard the first distinctly, "Guatemala City, there's where you land," said the spirit, "and Santa Cruz del Flores is as close as you can get to the cave."

Merrick sat back on her heels, her body heaving, her breaths coming rapid and hoarse as she squeezed the blood onto the floor and began to write with her right first finger the names now repeated from her own lips.

On and on I prayed for strength against the figure, but I cannot claim that it was my prayers which made the being begin to fade.

A horrid scream broke from Merrick:

"Honey, don't leave me!" she cried. "Honey, don't go. Honey, come back, please, please, come back," she sobbed. "Honey in the Sunshine, I love you. Don't leave me here alone."

But the spirit was gone.

13

ERRICK'S CUTS were not deep, though the flood of blood had been quite terrifying. I was able to bandage her up fairly decently, and then take her to the nearest hospital, where she was given the proper treatment for the wounds.

I don't remember what nonsense we told the attending physician, except that we convinced him that though the wounds had been self-inflicted, Merrick was in her right mind. Then I insisted we return to the Motherhouse, and Merrick, who was at that time in some sort of daze, agreed. I went back for the Scotch, I'm ashamed to say, but then one tends to remember the flavor of a twenty-five-year-old single-malt Highland Scotch like Macallan.

Besides, I'm not sure *I* was in my right mind. I remember drinking in the car, which I never do, and Merrick falling asleep against my shoulder, her right hand clamped to my wrist.

You can well imagine my state of mind.

The visible spirit of Honey in the Sunshine had been one of the more ominous ghosts I'd ever beheld. I was used to shadows, interior voices, and even possession; but to see the seemingly solid form of Honey in the Sunshine standing in the doorway was utterly shattering. The voice alone had been terrifying, but the shape, its apparent solidity and duration, the manner in which the light had played upon it, the eyes being so very reflective—all of this was a little more than I could easily bear.

Then there was the question of my own paralysis during this experience. How had Merrick accomplished this thing? In sum, I was badly shaken but very deeply impressed.

Of course Merrick was not going to say how she had done any part of it. In fact, Merrick didn't want to speak of it at all. At the mere mention of Honey's name, she began to cry. As a man, I found that maddening and unfair. But there was nothing I could do about it. Merrick would wipe her tears, and at once turned the subject to our jungle venture.

As for my opinion of the ritual she had used to summon Honey, I had found it simple, its chief component Merrick's own personal power, and the sudden dreadful connection with a spirit who apparently was not at rest.

Whatever, that night and on the following day, all Merrick wanted to talk about was the jungle trip. She had become a mono-maniac of sorts. She'd bought her khaki garments. She'd even ordered mine! We must go to Central America directly. We must have the finest camera equipment and all the support which the Talamasca could provide.

She wanted to return to the cave because there were other items there, and she wanted to see the land which had been important to her ancient Oncle Vervain. Oncle Vervain would not be haunting her if there were not substantial treasure there which he wanted for her to possess. Oncle Vervain was not going to let her alone.

For two days afterwards, while imbibing ridiculous quantities of the delicious full-bodied Macallan Scotch, of which she had laid in several bottles, I tried to control Merrick, to prevent the journey from taking place. But it was quite useless. I was getting drunk over and over again, and Merrick was determined. If I did not give Talamasca authority and support, she would take off on her own.

But the fact was, though I advised against everything, I felt young again on account of these experiences. I felt the curious excitement of one who has seen a ghost firsthand. And I also did not want to go to my grave without ever seeing a tropical jungle again. Even the arguments with Merrick had a wildly stimulating effect. That this beautiful and strong young woman wanted me to go with her, this went to my head.

"We're going," said Merrick, who was poring over a map in the Talamasca library. "Look, I know the way now. Honey's given me the only keys I required. I remember the landmarks and I know that part of the jungle's still unexplored. I've been through all the recent books on the territory."

"But you haven't found Santa Cruz del Flores in your books, have you?" I protested.

"Never mind. It's there. It's simply too small to be on the maps we purchase here. They'll know it when we reach northern Guatemala. Leave it to me. There simply isn't enough money for every ruin to be studied, and there are a nest of ruins in that part of the jungle, possibly a temple complex or even a city. You said this to me yourself.

"I remember seeing a spectacular temple. Don't you want to see it with your own eyes?" She was as cross and unpretentious as a child. "David, please do spring into life as Superior General, or whatever, and arrange everything for us both at once."

"But why do you think Honey in the Sunshine gave you the answers to your questions so easily?" I asked. "Has that not aroused your suspicion?"

"David, that's simple," said Merrick. "Honey wanted to say something of value, because Honey wants me to call her again."

The obvious truth of that statement shocked me somewhat.

"God knows, Merrick, you're strengthening this spirit. Certainly it should be encouraged to move towards the Light."

"Of course I urge her to go," Merrick answered, "but Honey's not leaving me. I told you that evening, I told you I've been feeling Honey's presence for years. All this time I've been pretending there was no Honey, there was no jungle, I didn't have to go back to these painful memories, I could bury myself in academic studies. You know that.

"But I've completed the basic academic portion of my life. And now I must go back. Now, stop mentioning Honey; for the love of Heaven, you think I want to think about what I did?" Then back she went to the maps again, sending for another bottle of Macallan for me, and telling me that we would need tent equipment on this trip, and I should be starting the arrangements now.

At last I pleaded that it was the rainy season in those jungles and we should wait until Christmas when the rains had stopped. She was ready for that objection; the rains were over; she had checked the reports daily. We could go now.

There was nothing to be done except to proceed with the journey. If I had condemned the plan as Superior General, Merrick would have taken off for Central America alone. As a full-fledged member of the Order, she had drawn a large allowance for several years and she had banked every penny of it. She could go off on her own and she told me as much.

"Look," she said, "it will break my heart to go against your wishes, but I will if I must."

And so it was that we arranged to have four Talamasca field assistants accompany us, both to handle all camp equipment and to carry firearms in case we encountered bandits where we meant to go.

Now let me explain briefly about these field assistants for anyone reading this story who might be curious on their account. The Talamasca has many such field assistants throughout the world. They are not full-fledged members of the Order, they have no access to the archives and certainly no access to or knowledge of the Talamasca's vaults. They do not take vows as do true members of the Order. They do not need or have psychic ability. They are not committed for any number of years or for life.

Indeed, they are employees of the Talamasca under its various corporate names, and their prime purpose is to accompany members on archaeological or exploratory expeditions, to assist us in foreign cities and countries, and in general to do what they are asked to do. They are expert in obtaining passports, visas, and the right to carry arms in other countries. Many have a background in law, as well as the armed services of different nations. They are reliable to a remarkable degree.

Were we to find this cave and its treasure, it was the field assistants who would arrange for the artifacts to be legally and securely transported out of the country with all appropriate permissions obtained and fees paid. Now, whether this latter type of activity would involve anything that wasn't legal, I honestly didn't know. It was the field assistants' department, so to speak.

These people do have some vague knowledge that the Talamasca is a tightly organized Order of psychic investigators, but in general they like what they do, enjoying enormous salaries, and they never seek to penetrate or fathom the Order at all. Many of them are seasoned soldiers of fortune. Their work for us almost never involves deliberate violence. And they cherish the opportunity to receive good pay from a relatively benign source.

At last the day came for us to leave. Aaron was past all patience with both of us, and, having never been a jungle traveler, he was greatly agitated, but he accompanied us agreeably to the plane.

We flew south, to Guatemala City, where we confirmed the existence and the location of the Maya village of Santa Cruz del Flores to the northeast. Merrick was wonderfully excited.

A small plane took us to a lovely northern city closer to our destination. And from there we set out with the field assistants in two well-stocked jeeps.

I loved the warmth, the sound of the soft rain, the lilt of Spanish and the native Amerindian voices; and the sight of so many Amerindians in their beautiful white clothes and with their gentle faces made me feel wonderfully drenched in the cultural riches of a foreign and still unspoiled place.

Actually there is plenty of trouble in that part of the world, but we were able to stay well away from it. And my eyes were for the pleasant detail.

No matter. I found myself extraordinarily happy. It was as if I were young again, and the sight of Merrick in her khaki safari jacket and short culottes was as marvelously stimulating as her air of command was soothing to my nerves.

Merrick drove our jeep rather like a maniac, but as long as the second car in our little caravan kept up with us, I didn't complain. I chose not to think about the gallons of petrol we were carrying, and how it might explode were we to crash into a chicle tree. I merely trusted that any woman who could evoke a ghost could drive a jeep on a dangerous road.

The jungle was breathtaking. Banana and citrus trees all but blocked our way on both sides of the winding uphill drive; here and there were giant mahogany trees soaring to a hundred and fifty feet; and out of the high canopy above came the frightening but unmistakable roar of the howler monkeys and the cry of countless species of exotic bird.

Our little world was drenched in green, but again and again we found ourselves on a high promontory from which we could view the canopy of the jungle as it spread out on the volcanic slopes below.

Very soon it became apparent that we had entered a cloud forest, and again and again we experienced that marvelous sensation when the clouds truly enveloped us and the sweet dampness penetrated the coverless windows of the jeep and settled on our skin.

Merrick knew I was loving it.

"I promise you," she said, "the last part won't be hard."

At last we reached Santa Cruz del Flores, a jungle village, so small and so out of the way that the recent political strife in the country had not touched it at all.

Merrick announced that it was very much as she remembered it— a small grouping of brightly painted thatched-roof buildings, and a small but remarkably beautiful old stone Spanish church. There were pigs, chickens, and turkeys roaming about everywhere. And I spied some cornfields cut from the jungle, but not very much. The town plaza was beaten dirt.

When our two jeeps pulled in, the gentle local inhabitants came out to greet us quite sympathetically, enforcing my opinion that the native Maya Indians are some of the most enchanting people in the world. They were for the most part women, dressed in pretty white garments with remarkable embroidery on them. I saw faces about me which reminded me immediately of the ancient countenances of Central America preserved in Maya, and possibly Olmec, art.

Most of the men of the village had gone off to work on the distant sugarcane plantations, or at the nearest chicle ranch, I was told. I wondered if it were forced labor, and decided it was best not to ask. As for the women, they often walked many miles in a day to offer their skillfully woven baskets and embroidered linens for sale at a big native market. They were thankful for a chance to display their wares at home.

There was no hotel of any sort whatsoever, indeed no post office, no phone, and no telegraph—but there were several old women who would eagerly give us lodgings in their houses. Our dollars were welcome. There were lovely local crafts for sale and we purchased freely. There was plenty of food to be had.

I at once wanted to see the church, and was informed by one of the locals in Spanish that I must not enter by the front door without first asking permission of the deity who governed that entrance. Of course, I could go in by the side, if I wished.

Not wishing to offend anyone, I took the side entrance and found myself in a simple white-walled building amid ancient Spanish wooden statues and the usual flickering candles, a very comforting place indeed.

I think I prayed the way I had in the old days, in Brazil. I prayed to all those benevolent deities unseen to be with us and protect us from any form of harm.

Merrick joined me a few moments later—making the Sign of the

Cross and kneeling at the Communion Rail for long moments of prayer. Eventually I went outside to wait.

There I spied a somewhat wrinkled old man, short of stature, and with shoulder-length black hair. He was dressed simply in a machine-made shirt and pants. I knew at once that he was the local shaman. I gave him a respectful bow, and though his eyes lingered on me with no hint of menace, I went my way.

I was hot but I was supremely happy. The village was fringed with coconut palms and there were even some pine trees due to the elevation, and for the first time in my life, as I walked about the bordering jungles I saw many exquisite butterflies in the dappled gloom.

There were moments when I was so purely happy that I could have given way to tears. I was secretly grateful to Merrick for this journey. And I concluded in my heart of hearts that no matter what happened from here on out, the experience had been well worth it for me.

When it came to our lodging, we chose a compromise.

Merrick sent the four field assistants to live in the village homes, after they had pitched and stocked a tent for us just behind the most far-flung village house. All of this seemed perfectly reasonable to me until I realized we were an unmarried man and woman residing in this tent, and it wasn't very proper at all.

Never mind. Merrick was powerfully stimulated by our adventure, as was I, and I was eager for her company alone. The Talamasca assistants outfitted the tent with cots, lanterns, camp desks, and chairs; made certain Merrick had ample batteries for her laptop computer; and, after a wonderful supper—tortillas, beans, and delicious wild turkey meat—we were left alone as night fell, in marvelous privacy, to discuss what we meant to do the following day.

"I don't intend taking the others with us," Merrick averred. "We're way beyond the danger of bandits, and, as I told you, it isn't far. I remember one small settlement along the way. It's tiny compared to this one. The people will leave us alone."

She was more excited than I'd ever known her to be.

"Of course we can cover some of the road with the jeep before we start walking, and you'll see Maya ruins around us just as soon as we set out. We're going to drive through those, and walk where the trails gives out."

She settled back on her cot, resting on one elbow, and drank her dark Flor de Caña rum, which she'd bought in the city before we set out.

"Wooh! This is good," she told me, and of course this struck predictable terror in me that she meant to go on a bender here in the jungle.

"Don't worry about it, David," she said. "Fact is, you ought to take a drink of this yourself."

I suspected her motives, but nevertheless succumbed. I was really in Heaven, I have to confess.

What I remember of that evening still produces in me a certain amount of guilt. I did drink far too much of the delicious aromatic rum. At some point, I remember lying back on my bed and looking up into the face of Merrick, who had come to sit beside me. Then Merrick leant down to kiss me and I pulled her very close, responding a little more rashly perhaps than she had expected. But she was not displeased.

Now, I was a person for whom sexuality had pretty much lost its appeal. When I had been occasionally aroused, during those last twenty years of my mortal life, it was almost always by a young man.

But the attraction of Merrick seemed somehow to have nothing to do with gender. I found myself overly excited and eager to consummate what had so haphazardly begun. Only as I shifted to let her lie beneath me, where I wanted her to be, did I gain some control over myself, and rise from the cot.

"David," she whispered. I heard my name echo: David, David. I couldn't move.

I saw her shadowy form there waiting for me. And for the first time I realized that the lanterns had been put out. A little light came from the nearest house, barely penetrating the fabric of the tent, and of course it was quite sufficient for me to see that she had taken off her clothes.

"Damn it, I can't do this," I said. But in truth I was afraid that I couldn't finish it. I was afraid that I was too old.

She rose with that same suddenness which had startled me when she began to summon Honey in her little séance, and she wrapped her naked arms around me and began to kiss me in earnest, her skilled hand going directly to the root of my desire.

I do believe I hesitated, but that I don't recall. What is vivid still is that we lay together and that, though I failed myself morally, I did not fail her at all. I did not fail the two of us as a man and a woman, and there was afterwards both a drowsiness and a sense of exultation that left no room for shame.

It seemed, as I drifted off to sleep with my arms around her, that this had been building all of the years during which I'd known her. I belonged to her now, quite completely. I was drenched with the scent of her perfume and her rum, of her skin and her hair. I wanted nothing but to be with her and to sleep beside her, and that the warmth of her would penetrate my inevitable dreams.

When I awoke in the morning, right at dawn, I was too shocked by everything that had taken place to know quite what to do. She was sleeping soundly, in a marvelously disheveled state, and I, humiliated that I had so dreadfully betrayed my position as Superior General, ripped my eyes off her, bathed, dressed, reached for my journal, and went out and into the little Spanish church so that I could write about my sins.

Once again I spied the shaman, who was standing to one side of the church building and watching me as though he knew everything that had taken place. His presence made me extremely uncomfortable. I no longer thought him to be innocent or quaint. And of course I despised myself utterly, but I had to admit I was invigorated, as is always the case with this kind of encounter, and, naturally, oh yes, naturally, I felt very young.

In the quiet and cool of the little church with its sloped roof and its uncritical saints, I wrote for perhaps an hour.

Then Merrick came in, said her prayers, and came to sit beside me, as if nothing at all had happened, and then whispered to me excitedly that we should go.

"I've betrayed your trust, young woman," I whispered immediately.

"Don't be so foolish," she fired back. "You did exactly what I wanted you to do. Do you think I wanted to be humiliated? Of course not!"

"You're putting the wrong meaning on everything," I argued.

She reached for the back of my neck, held my head as firmly as she could, and kissed me.

"Let's go," she said, as if speaking to a child. "We're wasting time. Come on."

14

IN THE JEEP, we managed an hour before the road gave out. Then, hefting our machetes, we proceeded to follow the trail on foot.

There was very little conversation between us, all of our energy being given over to the difficult and steady assent. But again that sense of bliss descended upon me, and the sight of Merrick's forceful slim body up ahead of me was a constant guilty delight.

The jungle now seemed impenetrable, regardless of the altitude, and again there came the clouds with their wondrous sweetness and damp.

I had my eye out all the time for ruins of any sort, and indeed we saw them, on both sides of us, but whether they were temples or pyramids or whatever, I was not meant to know. Merrick dismissed them out of hand, and insisted that we press doggedly on.

The heat ate through my clothing. My right arm ached from the weight of the machete. The insects became an unendurable nuisance, but I would not have been in any other place just then for anything in the world.

Quite suddenly Merrick stopped, and motioned for me to come to her side.

We had come upon a clearing of sorts, or the remains of one, I should say, and I saw decayed plaster hovels where there had once been houses, and one or two shelters which still maintained their old thatched roofs.

"The little village is gone," Merrick said as she surveyed the disaster.

I remembered Matthew Kemp's mention of Village One and Village Two on his map and in his letters of years ago.

She stood for a long moment staring into the remnants of the place and then she spoke in a secretive voice. "Do you feel anything?"

I had not felt anything until she asked me, but no sooner did I hear the question than I was aware of something spiritually turbulent in the air. I resolved to apply all my senses to it. It was quite strong. I cannot say I felt personalities or an attitude. I felt a commotion. For one moment I felt menace, and then nothing at all.

"What do you make of it?" I asked her.

Her very stillness made me uneasy.

"It's not the spirits of this village," she answered. "And I'll bet you anything that whatever we're feeling is precisely what caused the villagers to move on." She started off again, and I had no choice but to follow her. I was almost as obsessed as she.

Once we had circled the entangled village ruin, the trail appeared again.

However, the jungle soon became denser; we had to hack our way all the more fiercely, and at times I felt a dreadful pain in my chest.

Quite suddenly, as if it had appeared by magic, I saw the huge bulk of a pale stone pyramid looming before us, its steps covered by scrub growth and dense vine.

Someone at some time had cleared it, and much of its strange carving was visible, as well as its flight of steep steps. No, it wasn't Maya, at least not insofar as I could see.

"Ah, let me savor this," I said to Merrick.

She didn't answer me. She seemed to be listening for an important sound. I too listened and there came again that awareness that we were not alone. Something moved in the atmosphere, something pushed against us, something sought with great determination to move against gravity and affect my body as I stood there, machete in hand.

Merrick suddenly veered to the left, and began hacking her way around the side of the pyramid and onward in the same direction that we'd taken before.

There was no trail now. There was nothing but the jungle, and I soon realized that another pyramid loomed to our left, and that it was much higher than the building to our right. We were in a small alleyway before the two immense monuments, and we had to make our way through cumbersome rubble, as someone had done digging here at some time before.

"Thieves," she said, as if reading my thoughts. "They've plundered the pyramids many times."

That was hardly uncommon with regard to Maya ruins. So why should it not happen to these strange alien buildings as well?

"Ah, but look," I said, "at what they've left behind. I want to climb one of these. Let's tackle the smaller one. I want to see if I can make it to the platform on top."

She knew as well as I did that that is where a thatched-roof temple might have stood in ancient times.

As for the age of these monuments, I had no indication. They might have been built before the Birth of Christ or a thousand years after. Whatever, they seemed marvelous to me and they maddened my already boyish sense of adventure. I wanted to get out my camera.

Meantime, the spiritual tumult continued. It was wondrously intriguing. It was as if the air were whipped by the spirits. The sense of menace was strong.

"Good Lord, Merrick, how they're trying to stop us," I whispered. The jungle gave forth its chorus of cries, as if answering me. Something moved in the brush.

But Merrick, after stopping for only a few moments, pressed on.

"I have to find the cave," she said in a dull flat voice. "They didn't stop us last time and they're not going to stop you and me now." On she went, the jungle closing all too readily behind her.

"Yes," I cried out. "It's not one soul, it's many. They don't want us near these pyramids."

"It's not the pyramids," she insisted, chopping at the vines and pushing through the undergrowth. "It's the cave, they know we are going to the cave."

I did my best to keep up with her, and to aid her, but she was definitely the one clearing our path.

We had gone some yards when it seemed the jungle grew impossibly thick and that the light was suddenly altered, and I realized we had come to the blackened doorway of an immense edifice, which spread its sloping walls to our right and our left. It was a temple, surely, and I could see the impressive carvings on either side of the entrance, and also above as the wall rose to a great apron of stone with intricate carvings visible in the scarce high rays of the desperate sun.

"Lord, Merrick, wait," I called out. "Let me photograph this." I struggled to reach my small camera, but I would have to remove my backpack and my arms were simply too tired.

The airy turbulence grew extremely intense. I felt something similar to the light tap of fingers against my eyelids and my cheeks. It was altogether different from the constant barrage of the insect world. I felt something touch the back of my hands, and it seemed that I almost lost my grip on the machete, but I quickly recovered.

As for Merrick, she stood staring into the darkness of the hallway or passage in front of her.

"My God," she whispered. "They're much stronger than they were before. They don't want us to go inside."

"And why would we do that?" I asked quickly. "We're searching for a cave."

"They know that's what we're doing," she said. "The cave is on the other side of the temple. The simplest way is straight through."

"God in Heaven," I said. "This is the way you went before?"

"Yes," she answered. "The villagers wouldn't go with us. Some never made it as far. We went on, through there."

"And what if the ceiling of this passage collapses on us?" I asked.

"I'm going through it," she answered. "The temple's built of solid limestone. Nothing's changed, and nothing will."

She removed her small flashlight from her belt and sent the beam into the opening. I could see the stone floor in spite of the few pallid plants which had struggled to cover it. I could make out lavish paintings on the walls!

Her flashlight hit great rich figures of dark skin and golden clothes proceeding against a backdrop of vivid blue. Above, as the walls rose to a vaulted ceiling, I saw another procession against the deep shade of Roman red.

The entire chamber seemed some fifty feet in length and her feeble light struck a bit of greenery at the other end.

Again, there came those spirits, swarming around me, silent yet nevertheless intensely active, trying once more to strike my eyelids and my cheeks.

I saw Merrick flinch. "Get away from me!" she whispered. "You have no power over me!"

There was an immense response. The jungle around us appeared to tremble, as if an errant breeze had worked its way down to us, and a shower of leaves fell at our feet. Once again I heard the unearthly roar of the howler monkeys high in the trees. It seemed to give voice to the spirits.

"Come on, David," Merrick said; but as she meant to go forward something invisible appeared to stop her, because she stepped back off-balance and raised her left hand as if to shield herself. Another volley of leaves descended upon us.

"Not good enough!" she said aloud and plunged into the vaulted chamber, her light growing brighter and fuller so that we found ourselves surrounded by some of the most vivid murals which I've ever seen.

Everywhere around us there rose splendid processional figures, tall and thin, complete with ornate kilts, earrings, and lavish headdresses. I could not mark the style as Maya or Egyptian. It was like nothing I'd ever studied or seen. Matthew's old photographs had failed to capture one tenth of the vibrancy or detail. A lovely detailed black-and-white border ran along the floor on either sides.

On and on we went, our every footfall echoing off the walls as we proceeded, but the air had grown intolerably hot. Dust rose in my nostrils. I felt the touch of fingers all over me. Indeed there came the grip of hands on my upper arm, and a muffled blow against my face.

I reached out for Merrick's shoulder, both to hurry her and to stay with her.

We were in the very middle of the passage when she came to a standstill and flinched as if receiving a shock.

"Get away from me, you won't stop me!" she whispered. And then in a long stream of French she called on Honey in the Sunshine to make the way.

We hurried on. I wasn't at all sure that Honey would do anything of the sort. It seemed far more likely that Honey would bring the temple down on our heads.

At last we came out in the jungle once more, and I coughed to clear my throat. I looked back at the edifice. Less was visible on this side than on the front. I felt the spirits all around us. I felt threats without language. I felt myself pushed and shoved by weak creatures desperate to stop my advance.

I needed my handkerchief for the millionth time, to wipe the insects off my face.

Merrick immediately moved on.

The path went steeply upwards. And I beheld the sparkle of the waterfall before I heard its music. There came a narrow place where the water ran deep, and Merrick crossed over to the right bank as I followed, my machete working as hard as hers.

The climb up the waterfall was not difficult at all. But the activity of the spirits became increasingly stronger. Again and again Merrick cursed under her breath. I called on Oxalá to show the way.

"Honey, get me there," Merrick said.

Quite abruptly I perceived, just beneath an overhang, where the waterfall jetted forward, a monstrous open-mouthed face carved deep into the volcanic rock that surrounded an obvious cave. It was precisely as the doomed Matthew had described it. His camera had been ruined by moisture before he could photograph it, however, and its size was something of a shock.

Now, you can well imagine my satisfaction that we had reached this mythic place. For years I had heard tell of it, it was inextricably bound up in my mind with Merrick, and now we were there. Though the spirits kept up their assault, the gentle mist from the waterfall was cooling my hands and face.

I made my way up to stand beside Merrick, when suddenly the spirits exerted immense pressure against my body, and I felt my left foot go out from under me.

Though I never cried out, but merely reached for purchase, Merrick turned and grabbed hold of me by the loose shoulder of my jacket. That was all I needed to recover my footing and climb the remaining few feet to be at the flattened entrance of the cave.

"Look at the offerings," Merrick said, putting her left hand on my right.

The spirits redoubled their efforts, but I held firm and so did Merrick, though twice she swiped at something near to her face.

As for "the offerings," what I beheld was a giant basalt head. It struck me as similar to the Olmec, but that was all I could say. Did it resemble the murals in the temple? Impossible to judge. Whatever it was, I loved it. It was helmeted and tilted upwards so that the face with its open eyes and unique smiling mouth received the rain that inevitably fell here, and at its uneven base, amid piles of blackened stones, stood an amazing array of candles, feathers, and wilted flowers, as well as pottery. I could smell the incense where I stood.

The blackened rocks testified to many years of candles, but the last of these offerings could not have been more than two or three days old.

I felt something change in the air around us. But Merrick seemed as distressed by the spirits as before. She made another involuntary gesture, as though to drive something unseen away.

"So nothing stopped them from coming," I said quickly, looking at the offering. "Let me try something." I reached into my jacket pocket and took out a pack of Rothmans, which I was keeping for the inevitability that I would smoke.

I opened them hastily, lighted one with my butane lighter, in spite of the incessant spray of the waterfall, drew in the smoke, and then put the cigarette before the immense head. I put the entire pack with it. Silently I said the prayers to the spirits, asking them to allow us access to this place.

I felt no change in the assault of the spirits. I felt them pushing on me with renewed energy in a way that was beginning to unnerve me, certain though I might be that they would never gain very much strength.

"They know our motives," said Merrick, gazing at the giant upturned head and its withered flowers. "Let's go into the cave."

We used our large flashlights, and at once the silence from the waterfall descended upon us, along with the smell of dry earth and ash.

Immediately, I saw the paintings, or what I perceived to be paintings. They were well inside, and we walked upright and swiftly towards them, ignoring the spirits which had now produced a whistling sound near my ears.

To my utter shock, I saw that these splendidly colored wall coverings were in fact mosaics made with millions of tiny chips of semiprecious stones! The figures were far simpler than those of temple murals, which argued perhaps for a more ancient date.

The spirits had gone quiet.

"This is marvelous," I whispered, because I had to say something. And again I tried to reach for my camera, but the pain in my arm was simply too sharp. "Merrick, we must take photographs," I told her. "Look, darling, there's writing. We must photograph it. I'm sure those are glyphs."

She didn't answer. She stared at the walls as I did. She seemed entranced.

I could not quite make out a procession, or indeed attribute any activity to the tall slender figures, except to say that they appeared to be in profile, to wear long garments, and to be carrying important objects in their hands. I did not see bloody victims struggling. I did not see clear figures of priests.

But as I struggled to make out the intermittent and glittering splendor, my foot struck something hollow. I looked down at a wealth of richly colored pottery gleaming before us as far as we could see.

"This isn't a cave at all, is it?" Merrick said. "I remember Matthew saying it was a tunnel. It *is* a tunnel. It's been carved out entirely by man."

The stillness was shocking.

Stepping as carefully as she could, she went on, and I behind her, though I had to reach down several times to move some of the small vessels out of my way.

"This is a burial place, that's what it is, and all these are offerings," I said.

At that I felt a sharp blow to the back of my head. I spun around and shone my flashlight on nothing. The light from the cave entrance hurt my eyes.

Something pushed my left side and then my right shoulder. It was the spirits coming at me again. I saw that Merrick was jerking and moving to the side, as if something were striking her also.

I uttered a prayer to Oxalá again, and heard Merrick issuing her own refusals to back down.

"This is as far as we got last time," said Merrick, turning to look at me, her face dark above her flashlight, which she politely directed to the ground. "We took everything we found here. Now I'm going on."

I was right with her, but the assault of the spirits grew stronger. I saw her pushed to one side. But quickly she steadied herself. I heard the crunch of pottery beneath her feet.

"You've made us angry," I said to the spirits. "Maybe we don't have any right here. And maybe we do!"

At this I received a heavy silent blow to the stomach, but it was not sufficient to cause pain. I felt a sharp increase in my exhilaration suddenly.

"Go on, do your damndest," I said. "Oxalá, who is buried here? Would he or she have it remain secret forever? Why did Oncle Vervain send us to this place?"

Merrick, who was several yards ahead of me, let out a gasp.

I caught up with her at once. The tunnel had opened into a great hollow round chamber where the mosaics ascended the low dome. Much had fallen away from age or dampness, I knew not which, but it was a glorious room nevertheless. Round both walls the figures proceeded, until there stood one individual whose facial features had long ago been broken away.

On the floor of the room, in its very center, surrounded by clear circles of pottery offerings and fine jade statues, lay a beautiful arrangement of ornaments in a nest of dust.

"Look, the mask, the mask in which he was buried," Merrick said, her light falling upon the most glorious polished green jade image, which lay as it had been placed perhaps thousands of years before, the body of the wearer having long since melted away.

Neither of us dared take a step. The precious articles surrounding the burial were too beautifully arranged. We could see the ear ornaments now, glinting, as the soft moldering earth nearly swallowed them, and across the would-be chest of the being we saw a long richly carved scepter, which perhaps he had held in his hand.

"Look at all the debris," she said. "No doubt he was wrapped in fabric full of precious amulets and sacrifices. Now the fabric's gone and only the stone objects remain."

There was a loud noise behind us. I could hear pottery smashing. Merrick gave a short cry, as though something had struck her.

Then willfully, indeed, as if driven, she plunged forward, dropped to her knees, and picked up the brilliant green mask. She darted back with it, away from the remains of the corpse.

A flying stone struck me on the forehead. Something shoved at my back.

"Come on, let's leave the rest for the archaeologists," she said. "I have what I came for. It's what Oncle Vervain told me to get."

"The mask? You mean you knew all the time there was a mask in this tunnel, and that's what you wanted?"

She was already on her way to the outside air.

Scarcely had I caught up with her when she was pushed backwards.

"I'm taking it, I have to have it," she declared.

As we both tried to continue, something unseen blocked our path. I reached out. I could touch it. It was like a soft silent wall of energy.

Merrick suddenly gave over her flashlight to me and in both hands she held the mask.

At any other time of my life, I would have been admiring it, for it had an immense amount of expression and detail. Though there were holes for eyes and a gash for the mouth, all features were deeply contoured and the gloss of the thing was beautiful in itself.

As it was, I moved with all my strength against this force that sought to block me, lifting both flashlights as if they were clubs.

Merrick again startled me with a gasp. She held the mask to her face, and as she turned to look at me it appeared brilliant and faintly ghastly in the light. It seemed suspended in the darkness, for I could scarce make out her hands or her body at all.

She turned it away from me, still holding it to her face. And again there came a gasp from her.

The air in the cave fell silent and still.

All I could hear was her breathing and then my own. It seemed she began to whisper something in a foreign tongue, though I didn't know what tongue it was.

"Merrick?" I asked gently. In the abrupt and welcome stillness, the air of the cave felt moist and sweetly cool. "Merrick," I said again, but I could not rouse her. She stood with the mask over her face, peering ahead of us, and then, with a surprising gesture, she ripped the thing away and gave it over to me.

"Take it, look through it," she whispered.

I shoved my flashlight through my belt loop, gave hers back to her, and took the mask in both hands. I remember those little gestures because they were so ordinary, and I didn't know yet what I thought about the stillness around us or the dimness in which we stood.

Far, far away was the greenery of the jungle, and everywhere above us and around us the coarse but beautiful mosaics glittered with their tiny bits of stone.

I lifted the mask as she had directed me. A swimming sensation overcame me. I took several steps backwards, but whatever else I did, I don't know. The mask remained in place and my hands remained on it, and all else had subtly changed.

The cave was full of flaring torches, there was the sound of someone chanting in a low and repetitive manner, and before me in the dimness there stood a figure, wavering as if he were not entirely solid, but rather made of silk, and left to the mercy of the scant draught from the entrance of the cave.

I could see his expression clearly, though not define it entirely or

say what feature conspired in his young male face to evince what emotion or how. He was begging me in dumb eloquence to get out of the
cave and to leave the mask behind.

"We can't take it," I said. Or rather I heard myself say this. The
chanting grew louder. More shapes closed in around the one wavering but determined figure. It seemed he stretched out his arms to
beseech me.

"We can't take it," I said again. His arms were a golden brown and
covered with gorgeous stone bracelets. His face was oval and his eyes
dark and quick. I saw tears on his cheeks.

"We can't take it," I said, and then I felt myself falling. "We must
leave it. We must bring back the things that were taken before!"

An overwhelming sadness and grief swallowed me; I wanted to lie
on the ground; so great was this emotion and so right was it that I felt it
and expressed it with my entire form.

Yet no sooner had I hit the ground—at least I think I did—than I
was jerked upright, and the mask was ripped away. One moment I felt
it in my fingers and against my face, and the next I felt nothing and saw
nothing but the distant light flickering in the green leaves.

The figure was gone, the chanting had stopped, the grief was broken. Merrick was pulling me with all her strength:

"David, come on!" she said. "Come on!" She would not be denied.

And I myself felt an overwhelming desire to get out of the cave with
her, and to take the mask; to steal this magic, this indescribable magic
which had enabled me to see the spirits of the place with my own eyes.
Boldly, wretchedly, without any excuse whatsoever, I reached down,
without losing a pace, and caught up a handful of brilliant glinting
stone artifacts from the thick moldering floor, stuffing them into my
pockets as I went on.

We were in the open jungle in a matter of moments. We ignored
the unseen hands that assailed us, the volleys of leaves, and the urgent
cries of the howler monkeys, as though they'd joined in the assault. A
slender banana tree crashed down into our path, and we moved over it,
hacking the others that seemed to be bowing to strike us in the face.

We made remarkable time, moving through the hallway of the temple. We were almost running when we found the remnants of the trail.
The spirits sent more of the banana trees flapping towards us. There
was a rain of coconuts, which did not strike us. From time to time
small pebbles came in a little gale.

But as we continued, the assault gradually fell away. At last there was nothing but a soundless howling. I was crazed. I was a perfect devil. I didn't care. She had the mask. She had the mask which enabled a person to see spirits. She had it. Oncle Vervain hadn't been strong enough to get it, I knew it. And neither had been Cold Sandra nor Honey nor Matthew. The spirits had driven them out.

Silently, Merrick clutched the mask to her chest and kept going. Neither of us stopped, no matter how bad the ground under us, no matter how bad the heat, until we reached the jeep.

Only then did she open her backpack and put the mask inside of it. She threw the jeep into reverse, backed up into the jungles, turned the car around, and headed for Santa Cruz del Flores at a boisterous and furious speed.

I remained silent until we were alone together in our tent.

15

MERRICK FLOPPED DOWN on her cot and for a moment did and said nothing. Then she reached for the bottle of Flor de Caña rum and drank a deep gulp.

I preferred water for the moment, and though we'd been driving for a considerable time, my heart was still pounding, and I felt my age miserably as I sat there trying to catch my breath.

Finally, when I started to say something about what we'd done and how we'd done it, when I raised my voice in an attempt to put things in some sort of perspective, Merrick gestured for me to be quiet.

Her face was flushed. She sat as if her heart too were giving her the worst, though I knew better, and then she took another sizable drink of her rum.

Her cheeks were blazing as she looked across at me as I sat on my cot facing her. Her face was wet with sweat.

"What did you see?" she asked, "when you looked through it?"

"I saw them!" I said. "I saw a weeping man, a priest, perhaps, perhaps a king, perhaps a nobody, except that he was beautifully dressed. He wore fine bracelets. He wore long robes. He pleaded with me. He was grieving and miserable. He let me know it was a dreadful thing. He let me know the dead of the place weren't gone!"

She sat back, resting on both her arms, her breasts thrust forward, her eyes fixed on the top of the tent.

"And you?" I asked. "What did you see?"

She wanted to answer, but she seemed unable. She sat forward again and reached for her backpack, her eyes moving from side to side, her expression what is aptly called wild.

"Did you see the same thing?" I asked her.

She nodded. Then she opened the backpack and removed the mask so carefully one would have thought it was made of glass. It was now, in the dim daylight of the tent and the gold light of the one lantern, that I perceived how carefully and deeply the features were carved. The lips were thick and long and spread back as if in a scream. The eye ridges gave no surprise to the expression, only a sense of calm.

"Look," she said, putting her fingers through an opening at the top of the forehead, and then pointing out an opening over each ear. "It was strapped to his face with leather, most likely. It wasn't merely laid over his bones."

"And what do you think it means?"

"That it was his, for looking at spirits. That it was his, and he knew the magic wasn't intended for just anyone; that he knew it was magic that could give harm."

She turned over the mask and lifted it. She wanted clearly to put it over her face again but something stopped her. At last she stood up and went to the door of the tent. There was an open seam there through which she could peer out and along the mud street to the little plaza, and she seemed to be doing this, holding the mask below her face.

"Go on, do it," I said, "or give it to me and I will."

Hesitantly she pursued her course. She lifted the mask and held it firm over her face for a long moment, and then jerked it roughly away. She sat down exhausted on the cot, as though the entire little enterprise of only a few precious moments had tapped her strength at the core. Once again, her pupils danced wildly. Then she looked at me, and she grew a little calm.

"What did you see?" I asked. "Spirits of the village?"

"No," she answered. "I saw Honey in the Sunshine. I saw her watching me. I saw Honey. Oh, dear God, I saw Honey. Don't you see what's she done?"

I didn't immediately respond, but of course I saw. I let her speak the words.

"She's led me here, led me to a mask through which I can see her; she's brought me to a means by which she can come through!"

"Listen to me, darling," I said, and I reached out and took her wrist. "Fight this spirit. It has no claim on you any more than any other spirit. Life belongs to those who are alive, Merrick, and life is to be honored over death! You didn't drown Honey in the Sunshine, you have that from her own lips."

She didn't answer me. She put her elbow on her knee and rested her forehead in her right hand. The mask she held with her left. I think she was staring at it but I couldn't be sure. She began to tremble.

Gently, I took the mask from her. I laid it carefully on my cot. Then I remembered the objects I'd collected before leaving the cave. I reached inside my pocket to retrieve them. They were four perfectly carved little Olmecoid figures, two of bald, somewhat fat, creatures, the other two of lean scowling gods. A shiver passed through me as I looked at these small faces. I could have sworn I heard a chorus of voices for an instant, as though someone had turned up the dial on a piece of amplified music. Then the silence rushed at me as if it were palpable. I broke out in a sweat.

These little creatures, these little gods, had the same luster as the mask.

"We're taking this all back with us," I declared. "And as far as I'm concerned, I want to revisit the cave as soon as I've regained my strength."

She looked up at me.

"You can't be serious," she said. "You would challenge those spirits?"

"Yes, I'd challenge them. I don't say we take the mask back to the cave to look through. Dear God, I wouldn't dream of such a thing. But I can't leave behind such an unexplored mystery. I have to go back. What I want to do is examine what's there as carefully as I can. Then I think we must contact one of the universities active here and let them know of just what we found. I don't mean to speak of the mask, you understand. At least not until we've made certain that it's ours to keep beyond any dispute."

It was a tangled question, this matter of universities and digs and claims to antiquities, and I was in no mood for it just then. I felt hot all over. My stomach was heaving, which almost never happens to me. "I've got to see that cave again. God help me, I know why you came back here. I understand everything. I want to go back at least once, maybe twice, how do I know—." I broke off. The wave of sickness passed.

She was staring at me as if she were in grave and secret distress. She looked as sick as I felt. With both her hands, she clawed at her thick hair and drew it back from her lovely forehead. Her green eyes appeared hot.

"Now, you know," I said, "that we have four men with us that can get this mask out of the country and back to New Orleans with no difficulty. Shall I give it to them now?"

"No, don't do anything with it just yet," she said. She stood up. "I'm going to the church."

"What for?" I asked her.

"To pray, David!" she said impatiently, glowering down at me. "Don't you believe in anything really?" she demanded. "I'm going into the church to pray." And on her way she went.

She'd been gone for about twenty minutes when I finally poured myself a glass of the rum. I was so thirsty. It was strange to be thirsty and sick at the same time. Except for the sound of a few chickens or turkeys, I didn't honestly know which, the village was quiet, and no one came to disturb my solitude in the tent.

I stared at the mask, and I realized that my head was aching terribly, that indeed a throbbing had commenced behind my eyes. I didn't think too much about it, as headaches have never been a torment to me, until I realized that the mask was becoming a blur in my sight.

I tried to refocus. I couldn't. Indeed, I felt hot all over, and every tiny insect bite which I'd suffered began to make itself known.

"This is nonsense," I said aloud, "I've had every damned injection known to modern medicine, including several that weren't known when Matthew got his fever." Then I realized I was talking to myself. I poured another good shot of the rum and drank it down straight. It seemed to me, rather vaguely, that I would feel much better if the tent weren't so crowded, and I wished that all the people would leave.

Then I realized that there couldn't be people in the tent with me. No one had come in. I tried to regain a consistent memory of the last few moments, but something had been lost. I turned and looked at the mask again and then I drank some of the rum, which by now tasted marvelous, and I put down the glass and picked up the mask.

It seemed as light as it was precious, and I held it up so that the light shone through it, and it seemed for a moment to be quite definitely alive. A voice was whispering to me rather feverishly as to all manner of small things which I had to worry about, and someone said:

"Others will come when thousands of years have passed." Only the words I heard were not in a language which I understood. "But I do understand you," I said aloud, and then the whispering voice said something that seemed a curse and an ominous prediction. It had to do with the fact that certain things were best left unexplored.

The tent seemed to be moving. Rather, the place where I was seemed to be moving. I put the mask against my skin and I felt steadier. But the entire world had changed. I had changed.

I was standing on a high pavilion and I could see the beautiful mountains all around me, the lower portions of the slopes covered in deep green forest, and the sky itself was brightly blue.

I looked down and I saw a crowd of thousands surrounding the pavilion. Over on the tops of other pyramids there stood huge masses of people. The people were whispering and shouting and chanting. And there was a small group on my pavilion, all of them faithfully at my side.

"You will call down the rain," said the voice in my ear, "and it will come. But one day, the snow will come instead of the rain, and on that day, you will die."

"No, that will never happen!" I said. I realized I was growing dizzy. I was going to fall from the pavilion. I turned around and reached out for the hands of my fellows. "Are you priests, tell me, what you are." I asked. "I'm David and I demand that you tell me, I'm not the person you believe me to be!"

I realized that I was in the cave. I had all but fallen to the thick soft floor. Merrick was shouting at me to get up. Before me stood the weeping spirit.

"The Lonely Spirit, how many times have you called me?" said the tall being sadly. "How many times have you, the magician, reached out for the lonely soul? You have no right to call those between life and death. Leave the mask behind you. The mask is wrong, don't you understand what I'm telling you!"

Merrick cried my name. I felt the mask ripped from my face. I looked up. I was lying down on my cot, and she was standing over me.

"Good God, I'm sick," I told her. "I'm very sick. Get me the shaman. No, there's no time for the shaman. We must set out for the airport now."

"Quiet, be quiet, lie still," said Merrick. But her face was dark with fear. I heard her thoughts clearly. *It's happening all over again, just as it happened to Matthew. It's happening to David. I myself have some deep immunity, but it's happening to David.*

I grew very quiet within myself. I'll fight it, I resolved, and I let my head roll to one side on the pillow, hoping that the pillow would be cool against my cheek. Though I heard Merrick crying out for the men to come to the tent immediately, I saw another person sitting on her cot.

It was a tall lean man with brown skin and a narrow face, and arms covered with jade bracelets. He had a high forehead and shoulder-length black hair. He was looking at me in a quiet manner. I saw the dark red of his long gown, and the gleam of his toenail in the light.

"It's you again," I said. "You think you're going to kill me. You think you can reach out from your ancient grave to take my life?"

"I don't want to kill you," he whispered, with little or no change in his placid expression. "Give back the mask for your own sake and for hers."

"No," I said. "You must realize I can't do it. I can't leave such a mystery. I can't simply turn my back. You had your time and now is my time, and I'm taking the mask back with me. She's taking it with her, really. But even if she surrendered, I would do it on my own."

I went on pleading with him, in a low reasonable voice, that he should understand. I said, "Life belongs to those who are alive." But by then the tent was truly crowded with the men who had come with us. Someone had asked me to keep a thermometer under my tongue. And Merrick was saying, "I can't get a pulse."

Of the journey to Guatemala City, I remember nothing.

As for the hospital, it might have been a medical facility anywhere in the world.

Repeatedly I turned my head and I found myself alone with the bronze-skinned man with the oval face and the jade bracelets, though more often than not he did not speak. When I tried to speak, others answered, and the man simply melted as another world seemed to supplant that which I'd left behind.

When I was fully conscious, which wasn't often, I seemed convinced that people in Guatemala would know more of the tropical illness from which I suffered. I wasn't afraid. I knew from the expression of my bronze-skinned visitor that I wasn't dying. And I do not remember being transferred to a hospital in New Orleans at all.

The visitor never appeared after the return to New Orleans.

By that time I was on the mend, and when days did begin to connect with one another, I was running only a low grade temperature, and the "toxin" was completely gone. Soon I no longer required intravenous nourishment. My strength was coming back.

My case was nothing exceptional. It had to do with a species of amphibian which I must have encountered in the brush. Even touching this creature can be fatal. My contact must have been indirect.

Merrick and the others were not afflicted, that was soon made clear to me, and I was much relieved, though in my state of confusion, I had to confess I had not thought of them as I should.

Merrick spent a great deal of time with me, but Aaron was almost always there as well. As soon as I would start to address an important question to Merrick, a nurse or a doctor came into the room. At other times I was confused as to the order of events and didn't want to reveal that confusion. And occasionally, very occasionally, I would wake in the night, convinced I'd been back in the jungles in my dreams.

At last, though I was still technically sick, I was brought by ambulance to Oak Haven and moved into the upstairs left front room.

This is one of the more gracious and lovely bedrooms in the house, and, in my robe and slippers, I was walking out on the front porch by the evening of that day. It was winter, but wondrously green all around me, and the breeze off the river was welcome.

At last, after two days of "small talk," which was threatening to drive me out of my mind, Merrick came to my room alone. She wore a nightgown and robe and she appeared exhausted. Her rich brown hair was held back from her temples by two amber combs. I could see the relief in her face as she looked at me.

I was in bed, with pillows propped and a book on the Maya people open in my lap.

"I thought you were going to die," she said plainly. "I prayed for you in a way I've never prayed before."

"Do you think God heard your prayers?" I asked. Then I realized she hadn't mentioned praying to God at all. "Tell me," I asked, "was I ever in real danger?"

She seemed shocked by the question. Then she fell quiet, as though debating what she might say. I already had part of my answer, purely from her reaction to the question, so I waited patiently until she meant to speak.

"There were times in Guatemala," she said, "when they told me you were not likely to make it much longer. I sent them away, insofar as they'd listen, and I put the mask over my face. I could see your spirit just above your body; I could see it struggling to rise and free itself from your body. I could see it stretched over you, the double of you, rising, and I put out my hand and I pressed on it, and made it go back into its place."

I felt a dreadful overwhelming love for her.

"Thank God you did it," I said.

She repeated my words from the jungle village.

"Life belongs to those who are alive."

"You remember me saying it?" I asked her, or rather I expressed to her my gratitude.

"You said it often," she replied. "You thought you were talking to someone, the someone we'd both seen in the mouth of the cave before we'd made our escape. You thought you were engaged in a debate with him. And then one morning, very early, when I woke up in the chair and found you conscious, you told me you'd won."

"What are we going to do with the mask?" I asked. "I see myself becoming enthralled with it. I see myself testing it on others, but in secret. I see myself becoming its unwholesome slave."

"We won't let that happen," she said. "Besides, others aren't affected in the same way."

"How do you know?" I asked.

"The men in the tent, when you were getting sicker and sicker, they picked it up, they thought it was a curio, of course. One of them thought we'd bought it from the village people. He was the first to look through it. He saw nothing. Then another one of the men did the same thing. So forth and so on."

"What about here in New Orleans?"

"Aaron saw nothing through it," she said. And then in something of a sad voice she added: "I didn't tell him all that happened. That's for you to do, if you wish."

"And you?" I pressed. "What do you see when you look through the mask now?"

She shook her head. She looked off a bit, desperately biting into her lip, and then she looked at me.

"I see Honey when I look through it. Almost always. I see Honey in the Sunshine, and that's all. I see her in the oaks outside of the Mother-house. I see her in the garden. I see her whenever I look through the mask. The world is as it is around her. But she's always there." There was a passage of time and then she confessed:

"I believe it was all Honey's doing. Honey goaded me with nightmares. Oncle Vervain was never really there. It was always Honey in the Sunshine, greedy for life, and how can I blame her? She sent us back there to get the mask so that she could come through. I've vowed I won't let her do it. I mean, I won't let her grow stronger and stronger through me. I won't be used and destroyed by her. It's like you said. Life belongs to those who are alive."

"Would it do no good to speak to her? Would it do no good to tell her that she's dead?"

"She knows," said Merrick sadly. "She's a powerful and crafty spirit. If you tell me as Superior General that you want to attempt an exorcism, and that you want me to communicate with her, I'll do it—but on my own, never, never will I give in to her. She's too clever. She's too strong."

"I'll never ask you to do such a thing," I said quickly. "Come, sit beside me here. Let me hold you. I'm too weak to do you any harm."

Now that I look back on these things, I'm not sure why I didn't tell Merrick all about the spirit with the oval face and how he had continued to appear to me throughout my illness, and especially when I was close to death. Perhaps we had exchanged confidences about my visions when I was feverish. I only know that we did not discuss them in detail when we took stock of the whole event.

As for my personal reaction to the spirit, I was afraid of him. I had robbed a place that was precious to him. I had done it fiercely and selfishly, and though the illness had burnt away much of my desire to explore the mystery of the cave, I feared the spirit's return.

As a matter of fact, I did see this spirit again.

It was many years later. It was on the night in Barbados when Lestat came to see me, and decided to make me a vampire against my will.

As you well know, I was no longer the elder David. It was after our dreadful ordeal with the Body Thief. I felt invincible in my new young body and I had no thought to ask Lestat for eternal life. When it was clear that he meant to force me, I fought him with all I had.

At some point in this vain attempt to save myself from the vampiric blood, I called on God, the angels, anyone who might help me. I called on my orisha, Oxalá, in the old Portuguese Candomble tongue.

I don't know if my prayers were heard by my orisha, but the room was suddenly assailed by small spirits, none of whom could frighten or hinder Lestat in any way. And as he drained my blood to the very point of death, it was the bronze-skinned spirit of the cave whom I glimpsed as my eyes closed.

It seemed to me, as I was losing the battle to live, let alone the battle to be mortal, that I saw the cave spirit standing near me with his arms out, and I saw pain in his face.

The figure was wavering, yet fully realized. I saw the bracelets on his arms. I saw his long red robe. I saw the tears on his cheeks.

It was only an instant. The world of solid things and spiritual things flickered and went out.

I fell into a stupor. I remember nothing until the moment when Lestat's supernatural blood flooded my mouth. By then, I saw only Lestat and I knew my soul was entering on yet another adventure, one which would carry me forward beyond my most appalling dreams.

I never saw the cave spirit again.

But let me finish my tale of Merrick. There is not a great deal more to be said.

After a week of convalescence in the New Orleans Motherhouse, I dressed in my usual tweed suit and came downstairs for breakfast, with the other members assembled there.

Later, Merrick and I walked in the garden, which was filled with lush beautiful dark-leafed camillias, which thrive in the winter, even through light frost. I saw blossoms of pink and red and white which I never forgot. Giant green elephant ear and purple flowering orchid plants were growing everywhere. How beautiful Louisiana can be in winter. How verdant and vigorous and remote.

"I've put the mask into the vault, in a sealed box, under my name," Merrick told me. "I suggest we leave it there."

"Absolutely," I said. "But you must promise me, that if you ever change your mind about the mask, you'll call me before you take even the simplest steps."

"I don't want to see Honey anymore!" she said under her breath. "I told you. She wants to use me, and that I won't allow. I was ten years old when she was murdered. I'm tired, oh so tired of grieving for Honey. You'll never have to worry. I won't touch the mask again if I can help it, believe me."

Insofar as I ever knew, Merrick was faithful to her vow.

After we completed a detailed letter regarding our expedition, for a university of our choice, we sealed the records and the mask permanently, along with the idols, the perforator that Merrick had used in her magic, all of Michael's original papers, and the remnants of Oncle

Vervain's map. All was kept in storage at Oak Haven, with access only allowed to Merrick or to me.

In the spring, I got a call from America, from Aaron, telling me that investigators in the area of Lafayette, Louisiana, had found the wreck of Cold Sandra's car.

Apparently Merrick had led them to a portion of the swamp where the vehicle had been submerged years before. Enough remained of the corpses to ascertain that two women had been in the vehicle at the time that it sank. The skull bones of both showed severe and potentially life-threatening fractures. But no one could determine whether or not either victim had survived the blows long enough to be drowned.

Cold Sandra was identified by the remnants of a plastic purse and the random objects inside of it, most particularly a gold pocket watch in a small leather pouch. Merrick had recognized the pocket watch immediately, and the inscription had born her out.

"To my beloved son, Vervain, from your Father, Alexias André Mayfair, 1910."

As for Honey in the Sunshine, the remaining bones supported the identification of a sixteen-year-old girl. No more could be known.

Immediately I packed a bag. On the telephone, I told Merrick I was on my way.

"Don't come, David," she said calmly. "It's all over. They've both been buried in the family grave in the St. Louis Cemetery. There's no more to be done. I'm going back to Cairo to work, just as soon as you give me leave."

"My darling, you can go immediately. But surely you must stop in London."

"Wouldn't think of going on without seeing you," she said. She was about to ring off when I stopped her.

"Merrick, the gold pocket watch is yours now. Clean it. Repair it. Keep it. No one can deny it to you now."

There was a disturbing silence on the other end.

"I told you, David, Oncle Vervain always said I didn't need it," she replied. "He said it ticked for Cold Sandra and Honey. Not for me."

I found those words a little frightening.

"Honor their memories, Merrick, and honor your wishes," I insisted. "But life, and its treasures, belong to those who are alive."

A week later, we had lunch together. She looked as fresh and inviting as ever, her brown hair drawn back in the leather barrette that I'd come to love.

"I didn't use the mask to find those bodies," she explained at once. "I want you to know that." She continued on. "I went out to Lafayette and I went on instinct and prayers. We dredged in several areas before we got lucky. Or you might say Great Nananne helped me find the bodies. Great Nananne knew how much I wanted to find them. As for Honey, I can still feel her near me. Sometimes I feel so sad for her, sometimes I get weak—."

"No, you're talking about a spirit," I interjected, "and a spirit is not necessarily the person you knew or loved."

After that, she spoke of nothing but her work in Egypt. She was happy to be headed back there. There had been some new discoveries in the desert, due to aerial photography, and she had a meeting scheduled which might lead to her seeing a new, previously undocumented tomb.

It was marvelous to see her in such fine form. As I paid the check, she brought out Oncle Vervain's gold pocket watch.

"I almost forgot about this," she said. It was quite well polished and it opened at the touch of her finger with an audible snap. "It can't really be repaired, of course," she explained as she held it lovingly. "But I like having it. See? Its hands are fixed at ten minutes before eight."

"Do you think it has some connection," I asked gingerly, "I mean, to the time that they met their deaths?"

"I don't think so," she said with a light shrug. "I don't think Cold Sandra ever remembered to wind it. I think she carried it in her purse for sentimental reasons. It's a wonder she didn't pawn it. She pawned other things." She put it back into her purse and gave me a reassuring smile.

I took the long drive with her out to the airport and walked her to the plane.

Everything was calm until the final moments. We were two civilized human beings, saying goodbye, who meant to see each other soon again.

Then something broke inside me. It was sweet and terrible and too immense for me. I took her in my arms.

"My darling, my love," I said to her, feeling the fool dreadfully, and wanting her youth and her devotion with my whole soul. She was utterly unresisting, giving way to kisses that broke my heart.

"There never will be anyone else," she whispered in my ear.

I remember pushing her aside and holding her by her shoulders, and then I turned, without so much as a backwards glance, and I walked swiftly away.

What was I doing to this young woman? I had just passed my seventieth birthday. And she had not yet reached her twenty-fifth.

But on the long drive back to the Motherhouse, I realized that, try as I might I could not plunge myself into the requisite state of guilt.

I had loved Merrick the way I had once loved Joshua, the young boy who had thought me the most marvelous lover in the world. I had loved her through temptation and through giving in to that temptation, and nothing would ever make me deny that love to myself, to her, or to God.

For all the remaining years that I knew her, Merrick remained in Egypt, going home via London to New Orleans perhaps twice a year.

Once I dared to ask her boldly why she was not interested in Maya lore.

I think the question irritated her. She didn't like to think of those jungles, let alone speak of them. She thought I ought to know that, but she answered me in a civil manner nevertheless.

She explained clearly that she met with too many obstacles in studying Mesoamerica, in particular the question of the dialects, of which she knew nothing, and of archaeological experience in the field, of which she had none. Her learning had led her to Egypt, where she knew the writing, knew the story, knew the history. It was where she meant to stay.

"Magic is the same everywhere," she said more than often. But that didn't deter her from making it her life's work.

There is one more piece to the puzzle of Merrick which I possess.

While Merrick was working in Egypt that year after our trip to the jungles, Aaron wrote me a strange missive which I'll never forget.

He told me that the license plates of the car found in the swamp had led the authorities to the used-car salesman who had murdered his young customers Cold Sandra and Honey. Indeed, the man was a drifter with a long criminal record, and it had not been difficult to trace him at all. Belligerent and somewhat cruel by nature, the miscreant had gone back several times over the years to work at the very car lot where he'd met his victims, and his identity was well known to any number of people who could connect him to the car found in the swamps.

A confession to the crimes was not long in coming, though the man was judged to be insane.

"The authorities have advised me that the fellow is terrified," wrote Aaron. "He insists that he is being hounded by a spirit, and that he would do anything to expiate his guilt. He begs for drugs to render him unconscious. I do believe he will be placed in a mental hospital, in spite of the clear viciousness of the crimes."

Naturally, Merrick was advised of the whole affair. Aaron sent her a pack of newspaper clippings, as well as what court records he could obtain.

But much to my great relief, Merrick did not wish to go back to Louisiana at that time.

"There is no need for me to confront this person," she wrote to me. "I'm sure, from all that Aaron's told me, that justice has been done."

Less than two weeks later, Aaron advised me by letter that the murderer of Cold Sandra and Honey had died by his own hand.

I called Aaron at once:

"Have you told Merrick?" I asked.

After a long pause, Aaron said, quite calmly:

"I suspect that Merrick knows."

"Why on earth do you say that?" I asked immediately. I was always too impatient with Aaron's reticence. However, this time he was not to keep me in the dark.

"The spirit who haunted this fellow," said Aaron, "was a tall woman with brown hair and green eyes. Now that does not square with our pictures of Cold Sandra or Honey in the Sunshine, does it?"

I answered no, that it did not.

"Well, he's dead now, poor fool," said Aaron. "And maybe Merrick can continue her work in peace."

That is exactly what Merrick did: continue her work in peace.

And now:

Now, after all these years, I have come back to her, asking her to raise the soul of the Dead Child Claudia for Louis, and for me.

I have asked her in so many words to use her magic, which might surely mean using the mask, which I know to be in her possession at Oak Haven, as it had always been, the mask which could let her see spirits between life and death.

I have done that, I who know what she has suffered, and what a good and happy person she could be, and is.

16

IT WAS AN HOUR before dawn when I finished the story.

Louis had listened all of this time in silence, never bringing a question, never making a distraction, but merely absorbing my words.

Out of respect for me, he remained silent, but I could see a flood of emotion in his face. His dark-green eyes made me think of Merrick's, and for one moment I felt such a desire for her, such a horror of what I'd done, that I couldn't speak.

Finally Louis explained the very perceptions and sensations that were overwhelming me as I thought about all I'd said.

"I never realized how much you loved this woman," he said. "I never realized how very different you are from me."

"I love her, yes, and perhaps I myself didn't realize how much until I told you the history. I made myself see it. I made myself remember. I made myself experience my union with her again. But when you speak of you and me being different, you must tell me what you mean."

"You're wise," he said, "wise in ways that only an elderly human being can be. You experienced old age in a way that none of the rest of us has ever known. Not even the great mother, Maharet, knew infirmity before she was made a vampire centuries ago. Certainly, Lestat has never grasped it, in spite of all his injuries. And I? I've been too young for too long."

"Don't condemn yourself for it. Do you think human beings are meant to know the bitterness and loneliness I knew in my last mortal years? I don't think so. Like all creatures, we're made to live until our prime. All the rest is spiritual and physical disaster. Of that I'm convinced."

"I can't agree with you," he said modestly. "What tribe on earth has not had elders? How much of our art and our knowledge comes from those who've lived into old age? You sound like Lestat when you say such things, speaking of his Savage Garden. The world has never seemed a hopelessly savage place to me."

I smiled.

"You believe so many things," I said. "One has only to press you to discover them, yet you deny the value of everything you've learned, in your constant melancholy. You do, you know."

He nodded. "I can't make sense of things, David," he said.

"Maybe we're not meant to, any of us, whether we're old or very young."

"Possibly so," he said. "But what's very important now is that we both make a solemn vow. We will not injure this vital and unique woman. Her strength won't blind us. We will feed her curiosity and be just to her, and protective of her, but we will not bring her any harm."

I nodded. I knew his meaning quite plainly. Oh, how I knew it.

"Would that I could say," he whispered, "that we would withdraw our request. Would that I could endure without Merrick's magic. Would that I could leave this world without ever seeing Claudia's ghost."

"Don't talk of ending it, please, I can't listen to it," I hastened to say.

"Oh, but I must talk of it. It's all I think about."

"Then think of those words I spoke to the spirit in the cave. Life belongs to those who are alive. You are alive."

"At such a price," he said.

"Louis, we are both of us desperate to live," I said. "We look to Merrick's magic for consolation. We dream of looking through the mask ourselves, don't we? We want to see something that does make it all come together, is that not so?"

"I don't know that I'm so deliberate, David," he responded. His face was dark with worry, heavy with fine lines at the corners of his eyes and mouth, lines that vanished whenever his face was still. "I don't know what I want," he confessed. "Oh, but to see spirits as Merrick has seen them, as you've seen them. Oh, if only I could hear the ghostly harpsichord that others hear in this place. Oh, if I could talk to a spirit with the strength of Honey in the Sunshine, what that would mean to me."

"Louis, what can make you want to continue?" I asked. "What

could make you see that we are privileged witnesses of what the world has to offer on all sides?"

He laughed, a short polite but contemptuous laugh.

"A clear conscience, David," he replied. "What else?"

"Then take the blood I have to give," I said to him. "Take the blood Lestat has offered you more than once. Take the blood that you've refused so many times, and be strong enough to live by the 'little drink' and push death out of your way."

I was a bit surprised at the vehemence with which I recommended this, because before this conversation—before this long night of storytelling—I had thought his decision to refuse the powerful blood to be very wise.

As I've stated in this narrative, he was weak enough that the sun might easily destroy him, and in that lay an immense consolation which Lestat and I did not share.

Now, he studied me with a look of interest. I saw no condemnation in his eyes.

I rose and walked slowly about the room. Once again, I looked at the bright and confident painting by Monet. All my life seemed close to me suddenly; all my determination was to live.

"No, I can't die by my own will," I murmured, "not even if it's as simple as going into the sunlight. That I cannot do. I want to know what happens! I want to know when and if Lestat wakes from his dreamy sleep. I want to know what will become of Merrick! I want to know what will become of Armand. That I can live forever? Oh, how I cherish it! I cannot pretend to be the mortal who once refused Lestat. I cannot reach back and claim that being's unimaginative heart."

I turned and it seemed the room was pulsing violently around me, all its color coalescing, as though Monet's spirit had infected the very fabric of the solid matter and the air. All the objects of the room seemed arbitrary and symbolic. And beyond lay the savage night— Lestat's Savage Garden—and random unanswerable stars.

As for Louis, he was captivated as only he can become, yielding as men almost never yield, no matter in what shape or form the male spirit may be clothed.

"You're all so very strong," he said in a low, reverent, and sad voice. "All so very strong."

"But we'll make that vow, old friend," I said, "with regard to Merrick. There will come a time when Merrick will want this magic and reproach us with our selfishness, that we have begged for hers while refusing her our own."

Louis seemed almost on the edge of tears.

"Don't underestimate her, David," he said in a raw voice. "Perhaps she's quite as invincible as you were, in her own way. Perhaps she has shocks in store for us, of which we're unaware."

"Have I lead you to believe so?" I asked. "With all I've said?"

"You've given me her picture in deep and enduring detail," he answered. "Don't you think she knows my misery? Don't you think she will feel it when we meet?" He hesitated, then continued, "She won't want to share our existence. Why should she when she can make herself appear to others, when she can look through a jade mask and see her sister's ghost. From all you've said, I've drawn the conclusion that she won't be at all eager to give up forever the sight of the Egyptian sand in the noonday sun."

I smiled. I couldn't stop myself. I thought he was completely wrong.

"I don't know, old friend," I said, straining for courtesy. "I simply don't know. I know only I'm committed to our wretched purpose. And all that I've deliberately recalled has not taught me to be wary or kind."

He rose from his chair slowly, silently, and walked to the door of the room. I realized it was time for him to go now and find his coffin, and that shortly I should do the same thing.

I followed him, and we went out of the town house together, down the back iron steps and through the wet garden and to the front gate.

I did see the black cat for one instant on the top of the rear wall, but I made no mention of it, determined that cats were simply common in New Orleans and I was being just a bit of a fool.

At last it came time for us to part.

"I'll spend the next few evenings with Lestat," Louis said quietly. "I want to read to him. He doesn't respond but he doesn't stop me. You'll know where to find me when Merrick returns."

"Does he never say anything to you?" I asked, regarding Lestat.

"Sometimes he speaks, just a little. He'll ask for Mozart perhaps, or that I read him some old poetry. But in the main, he's as you see him yourself, unchanged." He paused, then looked directly at the sky. "I want to be alone with him for a few nights, I suppose, before Merrick comes back."

His tone had a finality to it, and a sadness that touched me to the quick. He was saying farewell to Lestat, that's what he was doing, and I knew that Lestat's slumber was so deep and so troubled, that even such a dreadful message from Louis might not rouse him at all.

I watched Louis walk away as the sky grew ever more lighter. I could hear the morning birds singing. I thought of Merrick, and I wanted her. I wanted her purely as a man might want her. And as a vampire I wanted to drain her soul and have her eternally there for my visits, always safe. I was alone with her again for one precious instant in the tent in Santa Cruz del Flores, and I felt that mercurial pleasure connect my orgasmic body and brain.

It was a curse to bring too many mortal memories into vampiric existence. To have been old did mean sublime experience and knowledge. And the curse had richness to it, and a splendor I could not deny.

And it occurred to me, if Louis does end his life, if he does bring his supernatural journey to a conclusion, how will I ever answer for it to Lestat or Armand, or myself?

IT WAS A WEEK before I received a handwritten letter from Merrick. She was back in Louisiana.

> Beloved David,
>   Come to my old house tomorrow evening as soon as you can. The caretaker will be safely off the property. And I will be alone in the front room.
>   It's my desire to meet Louis and hear from his own lips what he wants for me to do.
>   As to those items which once belonged to Claudia, I have the rosary, the diary, and the doll.
>   All the rest can be arranged.

I could scarce contain my exhilaration. Waiting till tomorrow would be a torment. I went at once to St. Elizabeth's, the building where Lestat spent his lonely hours sleeping on the old chapel floor.

Louis was there, seated on the marble beside Lestat, reading in a hushed voice from an old book of English poetry when I came in.

I read the letter to Louis.

There was no change whatsoever in Lestat's demeanor.

"I know where the house is," said Louis. He was extremely excited, though I think he struggled to conceal it. "I'll be there. I suppose I should have asked your permission. But I went to find it last night."

"Perfect," I responded. "I'll meet you there tomorrow evening. But listen, you must—."

"Go on, say it," he coaxed me gently.

"You must remember, she's a powerful woman. We've vowed to protect her, but don't for a moment think of her as weak."

"And so we go back and forth about her," he said patiently. "I understand you. I know your meaning. When I vowed to take this path, I braced myself for disaster. And tomorrow night, I shall brace myself as completely as I can."

Lestat showed not the slightest sign of having heard our discourse. He lay as before, his red velvet coat creased and dusty, his yellow hair a tangled mass.

I knelt down and laid a reverent kiss on Lestat's cheek. He continued to gaze into the gloom before him. Once again, I had the distinct impression that his soul was not in his body, not in the way that we believed it to be. I wanted so to tell him of our enterprise, but then again, I wasn't sure that I wanted him to know.

It struck me quite completely that if he knew what we meant to do he would stop us. How far from us his thoughts must have been.

As I left, I heard Louis continue to read in a low, melodious, and faintly passionate voice.

17

ON THE EVENING of the appointed meeting, the sky was very clear except for a few distinct and brightly white clouds. The stars were small but I could see them, faint comfort that they were. The air itself was not so terribly humid, yet it was delightfully warm.

Louis came to meet me at the carriageway gate in the Rue Royale, and in my excitement, I noticed very little about his appearance except that he was uncommonly well dressed.

As I've mentioned before, his clothes are not usually very well chosen, but he had of late been enjoying a certain improvement, and on this evening he had clearly gone out of his way.

To repeat, I was too interested in our meeting with Merrick to pay it much attention. Having observed that he was not thirsting, indeed that he seemed quite flushed and human—a confirmation that he had already fed—I set out with him at once for Merrick's house.

As we made our way through the desolate and godforsaken old neighborhood, neither of us spoke a word.

Many thoughts tumbled through my mind. My telling of the tale of Merrick had brought me much closer to her than I had been on the night of our meeting in the café in the Rue St. Anne, and my desire to see Merrick again, under any and all circumstances, was more powerful than I cared to admit.

But the subject of Merrick's recent spell tormented me. Why had she sent visions of herself to dazzle me? I wanted to ask her directly, and felt that it must be settled before we could go on.

When we reached the restored house, with its high black picket fence, I insisted that Louis wait patiently for a moment until I walked around the place.

At once I surmised that the little houses on either side of Merrick's large property were in utter ruin. And the property itself, as I've mentioned, was bounded on three sides and in part of the front by very high brick walls.

I could see a thick forest of trees in Merrick's yard, of which two were immense oaks and another a high sprawling pecan tree, trying to free itself of the rampant yew trees which crowded against the walls. There was a shuddering light emanating upwards against the foliage and its entanglement of branches. I could smell incense and the wax of candles. Indeed, I caught many scents but not the scent of an intruder, and that is what mattered just now.

As for the rear upstairs apartment of the caretaker, it was empty and locked up. This pleased me mightily, as I did not want to deal with this mortal at all.

With regard to Merrick, I could easily sense her presence, walls or no walls, so I quickly made my way back to Louis, who stood before the iron gate which separated the front garden from the street.

Merrick's oleanders were not in bloom yet, but they created a mighty evergreen shrubbery, and many other flowers were growing wild, especially the bright-red African hibiscus and the purple Althea with its stiff branches, and thick rampant white calla lilies with waxy spear-shaped leaves.

The magnolia trees which I scarcely remembered had grown hugely in the past decade, and they now composed a group of impressive sentinels for the front porch.

Louis stood patiently, staring at the leaded glass of the front doors as though he was madly excited. The house was entirely dark except for the front parlor, the room in which Great Nananne's coffin had been set so long ago. I could detect the flicker of candles in the front bedroom, but I doubt a mortal eye could have seen it through the drawn drapes.

Quickly we went in the gate, rattling the ominous shrubbery, and up the steps and rang the bell. I heard Merrick's soft voice from the interior:

"David, come in."

We found ourselves in the shadowy front hall. A great shiny Chinese rug covered the polished floor in flashy modern splendor, and the large new crystal chandelier above was dark, and looked as if it were made of so much intricate ice.

I escorted Louis into the parlor, and there sat Merrick clothed in a shirtwaist dress of white silk, quite relaxed, in one of Great Nananne's old mahogany chairs.

The dim light of a stand-up lamp fell wonderfully upon her. At once we locked eyes, and I felt a rush of love for her. I wanted her to know somehow that I'd revisited all our memories, that I'd chosen the prerogative of confiding them in one whom I trusted completely, and that I loved her as much as I did.

I also wanted her to know that I disliked intensely the visions she'd so recently sent after me, and if she had had any doings with the pesty black cat, that I was not amused!

I think she knew it. I saw her smile faintly at me as we moved further into the room.

I was about to take up the subject of her evil magic. But something stopped me.

It was, very simply, the expression on her face when her eyes fell upon Louis as he stepped into the light.

Though she was as poised and clever as always, there came about a complete change in her face.

She rose to her feet to meet him, which surprised me, and her countenance was smooth and open with utter shock.

It was then that I realized how skillfully Louis had attired himself in a finely tailored suit of thin black wool. He wore a shirt of a cream-colored silk with a small gold pin beneath his rose-colored tie. Even his shoes were deliberately perfect, buffed to a high luster, and his rich black curly hair was combed neatly and entirely. But the glory of his appearance was, of course, his keen features and his lustrous eyes.

I need not repeat that they are a dark-green color, because it was not the color of his eyes which mattered so much. Rather, it was the expression with which he gazed at Merrick, the seeming awe that settled over him, and the way that his well-shaped mouth slowly relaxed.

He had seen her before, yes, but he was not prepared to find her so very interesting and comely at the same time.

And she, with her long hair brushed straight back to the leather barrette, looked utterly inviting in her sharp-shouldered white silk dress, with its small fabric belt and its loose shimmering skirt.

Around her neck, over the fabric of the dress, she wore pearls, in fact, the triple strand of pearls that I myself had long ago given her, and in her ears were pearls, and on the ring finger of her right hand she wore a stunning pearl as well.

I recite these details because I sought to find some sanity in them, but what I was experiencing, what humbled me and made me livid was that the two of them were so impressed with each other, that, for the moment, I was not there.

It was undeniable, the fascination with which she stared at Louis. And there was not the slightest question about the overwhelming awe in which he held her.

"Merrick, my darling," I said softly, "let me present Louis." But I might as well have been babbling. She never heard a single syllable I uttered. She was silently transported, and I could see in her face a provocative expression which up until this time I had never beheld in her except when she was looking at me.

Quickly, obviously struggling to disguise her immense response, she reached out for his hand.

With a vampire's reluctance, he met her gesture, and then, to my complete consternation, he bent down and kissed her—not on the hand which he gripped so tenaciously—but on both her lovely cheeks.

Why in the world hadn't I foreseen this? Why had I thought that she would not see him except as an unapproachable wonder? Why hadn't I realized that I was bringing into her presence one of the most alluring beings I've ever known?

I felt the fool for having not foreseen it, and I also felt the fool for caring so very much.

As he settled in the chair closest to hers, as she sat down and turned her attention to him, I found a place on the sofa across the room. Her eyes never left him, not for a second, and then I heard his voice come low and rich, with his French accent as well as the feeling with which he always spoke.

"You know why I've come to you, Merrick," he said as tenderly as if he was telling her that he loved her. "I live in torment thinking of one creature, one creature I once betrayed and then nurtured, and then lost. I come because I believe you can bring that creature's spirit to speak with me. I come to you because I believe I can determine through you whether that spirit is at rest."

Immediately she answered.

"But what is unrest for spirits, Louis," she said familiarly. "Do you believe in a purgatory, or is it merely a darkness in which spirits languish, unable to seek a light that would lead them on?"

"I'm not convinced of anything," Louis said in answer. His face was full of vehement eloquence. "If ever a creature was earthbound, it's the vampire. We're wed, soul and body, hopelessly. Only the most painful death by fire can rip that bond. Claudia was my child. Claudia was my love. Claudia died by fire, the fire of the sun. But Claudia has appeared to others. Claudia may come if you call her. That's what I want. That's my extravagant dream."

Merrick was lost to him, utterly lost to him. I knew it. Her mind, insofar as I could read it, was ravaged. She was deeply affected by his seeming pain. Nothing of her sympathies was reserved.

"Spirits exist, Louis," she said, her voice slightly tremulous, "they exist, but they tell lies. One spirit can come in the guise of another. Spirits are sometimes greedy and depraved."

It was quite exquisite, the way that he frowned and put the back of his finger to his lip before he answered. As for her, well, I was furious with her, and saw not the slightest physical or mental fault in her. She was the woman to whom I'd surrendered passion, pride, and honor a long time before.

"I'll know her, Merrick," said Louis. "I can't be deceived. If you can call her, and if she comes, I'll know her. I have no doubt."

"But what if I doubt, Louis?" she responded. "What if I tell you that we've failed? Will you at least try to believe what I say?"

"It's all settled, isn't it?" I blurted out. "We mean to do it, then, don't we?"

"Yes, oh, yes," Louis answered, looking across the room at me considerately enough, though his large inquisitive eyes shot right back to Merrick. "Let me beg your forgiveness, Merrick, that we've troubled you for your power. I tell myself in my most awful moments that you'll take away from us some valuable knowledge and experience, that perhaps we'll confirm your faith—in God. I tell myself these things because I can't believe we've merely ruptured your life with our very presence. I hope it's so. I beg you to understand."

He was using the very words that had come to my mind in my many feverish ruminations. I was furious with him as well as her, suddenly. Detestable that he should say these things, and the hell he couldn't read minds. I had to get myself in hand.

She smiled, suddenly, one of the most magnificent smiles I'd ever seen. Her creamy cheeks, her dramatic green eyes, her long hair—all her charms conspired to make her irresistible, and I could see the effect of her smile upon Louis, as if she'd rushed into his arms.

"I have no doubts or regrets, Louis," she told me. "Mine is a great and unusual power. You've given me a reason to use it. You speak of a soul that may be in torment; indeed, you speak of long, long suffering, and you suggest that we might somehow bring that soul's torment to a close."

At this point, his cheeks colored deeply and he leant over and clasped her hand again tightly.

"Merrick, what can I give you in exchange for what you mean to do?"

This alarmed me. He should not have said it! It led too directly to the most powerful and unique gift that we had to give. No, he shouldn't have said it, but I remained silent, watching these two creatures become ever more enthralled with each other, watching them quite definitely fall in love.

"Wait until it's done, and let us talk then of such things," she said, "if we ever talk of them at all. I need nothing in return, really. As I've said, you are giving me a way to use my power and that in itself is quite enough. But again, you must assure me, you will listen to my estimation of what happens. If I think we have raised something which is not from God I will say so, and you must at least try to believe what I say."

She rose and went directly past me, with only a faint smile for me as she did so, into the open dining room behind me to fetch something, it seemed, from the sideboard along the distant wall.

Of course, Louis, the consummate gentleman, was on his feet. Again I noticed the splendid clothing, and how lean and feline were his simplest gestures, and how stunningly beautiful his immaculate hands.

She reentered the light before me as if reentering a stage.

"Here, this is what I have from your darling," she said. She held a small bundle, wrapped in velvet. "Sit down, Louis, please," she resumed. "And let me put these items into your hands." She took her chair again, beneath the lamp facing him, the precious goods in her lap.

He obeyed her with the open radiance of a schoolboy before a miraculous and brilliant teacher. He sat back as though he would yield to her slightest command.

I watched her in profile and nothing filled my mind so much as pure, utter, base jealousy! But loving her as I did, I was wise enough to acknowledge some genuine concern as well.

As for him, there was little doubt that he was completely as interested in her as he was in the things which had belonged to Claudia.

"This rosary, why did she have it?" asked Merrick, extracting the sparkling beads from her little bundle. "Surely she didn't pray."

"No, she liked it for the look of it," he said, his eyes full of a dignified plea that Merrick should understand. "I think I bought it for her. I don't think I ever even told her what it was. Learning with her was strange, you see. We thought of her as a child, when we should have realized, and then the outward form of a person has such a mysterious connection with the disposition."

"How so?" Merrick asked.

"Oh, you understand," he said shyly, almost modestly. "The beautiful know they have power, and she had, in her diminutive charm, a certain power of which she was always casually aware." He hesitated. It seemed he was painfully shy. "We fussed over her; we gloried in her. She looked no more than six or seven at most." The light in his face went out for a moment, as if an interior switch had shut it off.

Merrick reached forward again and took his hand. He let her have it. He bowed his head just a little, and he lifted the hand she held, as if saying, Give me a moment. Then he resumed.

"She liked the rosary," he said. "Maybe I did tell her the prayers. I don't remember. She liked sometimes to go with me to the Cathedral. She liked to hear the music of the evening ceremonies. She liked all things that were sensual and which involved beauty. She was girlish in her enthusiasms for a long time."

Merrick let his hand go but very reluctantly.

"And this?" she asked. She lifted the small white leather-bound diary. "A long time ago, this was found in the flat in the Rue Royale, in a hiding place. You never knew that she kept it."

"No," he said. "I gave it to her as a gift, that I well recall. But I never saw her write in it. That she kept it came as something of a surprise. She was quite the reader of books, that I can tell you. She knew so much poetry. She was always quoting this or that verse in an offhanded manner. I try to remember the things she quoted, the poets she loved."

He gazed at the diary now as if he were reticent to open it, or even to touch it. As if it still belonged to her.

Merrick withdrew it, and lifted the doll.

"No," Louis said adamantly, "she never liked them. They were always a mistake. No, that doesn't matter, that doll. Although if recollection serves me right, it was found with the diary and the rosary. I don't know why she saved it. I don't know why she put it away. Maybe she wanted someone in the far distant future to find it and mourn for her, to know that she herself had been locked in a doll's body; wanted some one lone individual to shed tears for her. Yes, I think that's how it must have been."

"Rosary, doll, diary," said Merrick delicately. "And the diary entries, do you know what they say?"

"Only one, the one Jesse Reeves read and related to me. Lestat had given her the doll on her birthday and she'd hated it. She'd tried to wound him; she'd mocked him; and he'd answered her with those lines from an old play which I can't forget."

He bowed his head, but he wouldn't give in to his sadness, not entirely. His eyes were dry for all the pain in them as he recited the words:

Cover her face;
mine eyes dazzle;
she died young.

I winced at the recollection. Lestat had been condemning himself when he'd spoken those words to her, he'd been offering himself up to her rage. She'd known it. That's why she'd recorded the entire incident—his unwelcome gift, her weariness of playthings, her anger at her limitations, and then his carefully chosen verse.

Merrick allowed for a small interval, and then, letting the doll rest in her lap, she offered Louis the diary once more.

"There are several entries," she said. "Two are of no importance, and for one of these I'll ask you to work my magic. But there is another telling one, and that you must read before we go on."

Still Louis did not reach for the diary. He looked at her respectfully, as before, but he didn't reach for the little white book.

"Why must I read it?" he asked Merrick.

"Louis, think of what you've asked me to do. And yet you can't read the words she herself wrote here?"

"That was long ago, Merrick," he said. "It was years before she died that she concealed that diary. Isn't what we do of much greater importance? Yes, take a page if you need it. Take any page of the diary, it doesn't matter, use it as you will, only don't ask that I read a word."

"No, you must read it," Merrick said with exquisite gentleness. "Read it to me and to David. I know what is written there, and you must know, and David is here to help both of us. Please, the last entry: read it aloud."

He stared hard at her, and now there came the faint film of red tears to his eyes, but he gave a tiny, near imperceptible, shake of his head, and then he took the diary from her outstretched hand.

He opened it, gazing down at it, having no need as a mortal might to move the page into the light.

"Yes," said Merrick coaxingly. "See, that one is unimportant. She says only that you went to the theater together. She says that she saw *Macbeth*, which was Lestat's favorite play."

He nodded, turning the small pages.

"And that one, that one is not significant," she went on, as though leading him through the fire with her words. "She says that she loves white chrysanthemums, she says she purchased some from an old woman, she says they are the flowers for the dead."

Again he seemed on the very brink of losing his composure utterly, but he kept his tears to himself. Again he turned the pages.

"There, that one. You must read it," said Merrick, and she laid her hand on his knee. I could see her fingers stretched out and embracing him in that age-old gesture. "Please, Louis, read it to me."

He looked at her for a long moment, and then down at the page. His voice came tenderly in a whisper, but I knew that she could hear it as well as I.

"September 21, 1859

It has been so many decades since Louis presented me with this little book in which I might record my private thoughts. I have not been successful, having made only a few entries, and whether these have been written for my benefit I am unsure.

Tonight, I confide with pen and paper because I know which direction my hatred will take me. And I fear for those who have aroused my wrath.

By those I mean, of course, my evil parents, my splendid fathers, those who have led me from a long forgotten mortality into this questionable state of timeless 'bliss.'

To do away with Louis would be foolish, as he is without question the more malleable of the pair."

Louis paused as though he couldn't continue.

I saw Merrick's fingers tighten on his knee.

"Read it, please, I beg you," she said gently. "You must go on."

Louis began again, his voice soft as before, and quite deliberately smooth.

"Louis will do as I wish, even unto the very destruction of Lestat, which I plan in every detail. Whereas Lestat would never cooperate with my designs upon Louis. So there my loyalty lies, under the guise of love even in my own heart.

"What mysteries we are, human, vampire, monster, mortal, that we can love and hate simultaneously, and that emotions of all sorts might not parade for what they are not. I look at Louis and I despise him totally for the making of me, and yet I do love him. But then I love Lestat every bit as well.

"Perhaps in the court of my heart, I hold Louis far more accountable for my present state than ever I could blame my impulsive and simple Lestat. The fact is, one must die for this or the pain in me will never be sealed off, and immortality is but a monstrous measurement of what I shall suffer till the world revolves to its ultimate end. One must die so that the other will become ever more dependent upon me, ever more completely my slave. I would travel the world afterwards; I would have my way; I cannot endure either one of them unless that one becomes my servant in thought, word, and deed.

"Such a fate is simply unthinkable with Lestat's ungovernable and irascible character. Such a fate seems made for my melancholy Louis, though the destroying of Lestat will open new passages for Louis into the labyrinthian Hell in which I already wander with every new thought that comes in my mind.

"When I shall strike and how, I know not, only that it gives me supreme delight to watch Lestat in his unguarded gaiety, knowing that I shall humiliate him utterly in destroying him, and in so doing bring down the lofty useless conscience of my Louis, so that his soul, if not his body, is the same size at last as my own."

It was finished.

I could tell this merely by the blank expression of pain on his face, the way that his eyebrows quivered for one moment, and then the way he drew back in the chair, and closed the little book, and held it idly as if he'd forgotten it altogether, in his left hand. He looked neither to me nor to Merrick.

"Do you still want to communicate with this spirit?" Merrick asked reverently. She reached for the small diary, and he gave it over without objection.

"Oh, yes," he said in a long sigh. "I want it above anything else."

I wanted so to comfort him, but there were no words to touch such a private pain.

"I can't blame her for what she expressed," he resumed in a frail voice. "It always goes so tragically wrong with us." His eyes moved feverishly to Merrick. "The Dark Gift, imagine calling it that, when it goes so very wrong in the end." He drew back as if struggling against his emotions.

"Merrick," he said, "where do they come from, the spirits? I know the conventional wisdom and how foolish it can be. Tell me your thoughts."

"I know less now than I ever did," answered Merrick. "I think when I was a girl I was very sure of such things. We prayed to the untimely dead because we believed they hovered close to earth, vengeful or confused, and thereby could be reached. From time immemorial, witches have frequented cemeteries looking for those angry, muddled spirits, calling upon them to find the way to greater powers whose secrets might be revealed. I believed in those lonely souls, those suffering lost ones. Perhaps in my own way, I believe in them still.

"As David can tell you, they seem to hunger for the warmth and the light of life; they seem to hunger even for blood. But who knows the true intentions of any spirit? From what depth did the prophet Samuel rise in the Bible? Are we to believe Scripture, that the magic of the Witch of Endor was strong?"

Louis was fastened to her every word.

He reached out suddenly and took her hand again, letting her curl her fingers around his thumb.

"And what do you see, Merrick, when you look at David and at me? Do you see the spirit that inhabits us, the hungry spirit that makes us vampires?"

"Yes, I see it, but it's mute and mindless, utterly subordinate to your brains and hearts. It knows nothing now, if it ever did, except that it wants the blood. And for the blood it slowly works its spell on your tissues, it slowly commands your every cell to obey. The longer you live, the more it thrives, and it is angry now, angry insofar as it can choose any emotion, because you blood drinkers are so few."

Louis appeared mystified, but surely it wasn't so difficult to understand.

"The massacres, Louis, the last here in New Orleans. They clear away the rogues and baseborn. And the spirit shrinks back into those who remain."

"Yes," said Merrick, with a passing glance at me. "That's precisely why your thirst now is doubly terrible, and why you are so far from being satisfied with the 'little drink.' You asked a moment ago: what do I want from you? Let me say what I want *of* you. Let me be so bold as to answer you now."

He said nothing. He merely gazed at her as if he could refuse her nothing. She went on.

"Take the strong blood David can give you," she said. "Take it so you can exist without killing, take it so you can cease your heated search for the evildoer. Yes, I know, I use your language, perhaps too freely and too proudly. Pride is always a sin with those of us who persevere in the Talamasca. We believe we have seen miracles; we believe we have worked miracles. We forget that we know nothing; we forget that there may be nothing to find out."

"No, there is something, there's more than something," he insisted, gently moving her hand with his emphasis. "You and David have convinced me, even though it was never your intention, either of you. There are things to know. Tell me, when can we move to speak to Claudia's spirit? What more do you require of me before you'll make the spell?"

"Make the spell?" she asked gently. "Yes, it will be a spell. Here, take this diary," she gave it over to him, "rip a page from it, whatever page you feel is strongest or whatever part you are most willing to give up."

He took it with his left hand, unwilling to let her go.

"What page do you want me to tear out?" he insisted.

"You make the choice. I'll burn it when I'm ready. You'll never see those particular words again."

She released him, and urged him on with a small gesture. He opened the book with both hands. He sighed again, as if he couldn't endure this, but then he commenced to read in a low unhurried voice:

" 'And tonight, as I passed the cemetery, a lost child wandering dangerously alone for all the world to pity me, I bought these chrysanthemums, and lingered for some time within the scent of the fresh graves and their decaying dead, wondering what death life would have had for me had I been let to live it. Wondering if I could have hated as a mere human as much as I hate now? Wondering if I could have loved as much as I love now?' "

Carefully, pressing the book to his leg with his left hand, he tore the page with his right hand, held it under the light for a moment, then gave it over to Merrick, his eyes following it as though he were committing a terrible theft.

She received it respectfully and placed it carefully beside the doll in her lap.

"Think well now," she said, "before you answer. Did you ever know the name of her mother?"

"No," he said at once, and then hesitated, but then shook his head and said softly that he did not.

"She never spoke the name?"

"She spoke of Mother; she was a little girl."

"Think again," she said. "Go back, go back to those earliest nights with her; go back to when she babbled as children babble, before her womanly voice replaced those memories in your heart. Go back. What is the name of her mother? I need it."

"I don't know it," he confessed. "I don't think she ever—. But I didn't listen, you see, the woman was dead. That's how I found her, alive, clinging to the corpse of her mother." I could see that he was defeated. Rather helplessly he looked at Merrick.

Merrick nodded. She looked down and then she looked to him again, and her voice was especially kind as she spoke.

"There is something else," she said. "You're holding something back."

Again, he seemed exceedingly distressed.

"How so?" he asked abjectly. "What can you mean?"

"I have her written page," said Merrick. "I have the doll she kept when she might have destroyed it. But you hold on to something else."

"Oh, but I can't," he said, his dark brows knotting. He reached into his coat and brought out the small daguerreotype in its gutter perche case. "I can't give it over to be destroyed, I can't," he whispered.

"You think you'll cherish it afterwards?" asked Merrick in a consoling voice. "Or you think our magic fire will fail?"

"I don't know," he confessed. "I know only that I want it." He moved the tiny clasp and opened the small case and looked down until he seemed unable to bear what he saw, and then he closed his eyes.

"Give it to me for my altar," said Merrick. "I promise it will not be destroyed."

He didn't move or answer. He simply allowed her to take the picture from his hands. I watched her. She was amazed by it, the ancient image of a vampire, captured forever so dimly in the fragile silver and glass.

"Ah, but she was lovely, wasn't she?" asked Louis.

"She was many things," said Merrick. She shut the little gutter perche case, but she did not move the small gold clasp. She laid the daguerreotype in her lap with the doll and the page from the diary, and with both hands reached for Louis's right hand again.

She opened his palm beneath the lamplight.

She drew up as if she was shocked.

"Never have I seen a life line such as this," she whispered. "It's deeply graven, look at it, there is no end to it really," she turned his hand this way and that, "and all the small lines have long ago melted away."

"I can die," he answered with a polite defiance. "I know I can," he said sadly. "I shall when I've got the courage. My eyes will close forever, like those of every mortal of my time who ever lived."

She didn't answer. She looked down into his open palm again. She felt of the hand, and I could see her loving its silky skin.

"I see three great loves," she whispered, as if she needed his permission to say it aloud. "Three deep loves in all this time. Lestat? Yes. Claudia. Most assuredly. And who is the other? Can you tell me that?"

He was in a state of complete confusion as he looked at her, but he hadn't the strength to answer. The color flared in his cheeks and his eyes seemed to flash as if a light inside them had increased its incandescence.

She let his hand go, and she blushed.

Quite suddenly, he looked to me, exactly as if he'd suddenly remembered me again and he needed me desperately. I had never seen him so agitated or seemingly vital. No one entering the room would have known him to be anything but a compelling young man.

"Are you for it, old friend?" he asked. "Are you ready for it to begin?"

She looked up, her own eyes watering faintly, and she seemed to pick me out of the shadows and then to give the smallest, most trusting smile.

"What's your counsel, Superior General?" she asked in a muted voice, filled with conviction.

"Don't mock me," I said, because it made me feel good to say it. I was not surprised to see the quick flash of pain in her eyes.

"I don't mock you, David. I ask if you're ready."

"I'm ready, Merrick," I said, "as ready as I ever was in all my life to call a spirit in whom I scarcely believe, in whom I have no trust."

She held the page in both hands and studied it, perhaps reading the words herself, for her lips moved.

Then she looked at me again, and then at Louis.

"One hour. Come back to me. I'll be ready by that time. We'll meet in the rear of the house. The old altar's been restored for our purpose. The candles are already lighted. The coals will soon be ready. It's there that we will execute this plan."

I started to rise.

"But you must go now," she said, "and bring a sacrifice, because we cannot proceed without that."

"A sacrifice?" I asked. "Good Lord, what manner of sacrifice?" I was on my feet.

"A human sacrifice," she answered, her eyes sharpening as she glanced up at me, and then back to Louis, who remained in his chair. "This spirit won't come for anything less than human blood."

"You don't mean it, Merrick," I said furiously, my voice rising. "Good Lord, woman, would you make yourself a party to murder?"

"Am I not that already?" she answered, her eyes full of honesty and fierce will. "David, how many human beings have you killed since

Lestat brought you over? And you, Louis, they're beyond count. I sit with you and plot with you to attempt this thing. I'm a party to your crimes, am I not? And for this spell, I tell you I need blood. I need to brew a far greater magic than anything I've ever attempted before. I need a burnt offering; I need the smoke to rise from heated blood."

"I won't do it," I said. "I won't bring some mortal here to be slaughtered. You're being foolish and naive if you think you could tolerate such a spectacle. You'll be changed forever. What, do you think because we're pretty to look at that this murder will be fancy and clean?"

"David, do as I say," she replied, "or I won't do this thing."

"I will not," I responded. "You've overreached yourself. A murder there will not be."

"Let me be the sacrifice," said Louis suddenly. He rose to his feet and looked down upon her. "I don't mean that I shall die to do it," he said compassionately. "I mean, let the blood that flows be mine." He took her hand again, locking his fingers around her wrist. He bent and kissed her hand, then stood erect, his eyes lovingly fastened to her own.

"Years ago," he said, "you used your own blood, did you not, in this very house, to call your sister, Honey in the Sunshine. Let us use my blood to call Claudia tonight. I have blood enough for a burnt offering; I have blood enough for a cauldron or a fire."

Her face was quite tranquil again as she looked at him.

"A cauldron it shall be," she said. "One hour. The rear yard is filled with its old saints, as I've told you. The stones on which my ancestors danced are swept clean for our purpose. The old pot sits on the coals. The trees have witnessed many such a spectacle. There's only a little more that I need do to prepare now. Go and return to me, as I've said."

18

I WAS BESIDE MYSELF with anxiety. As soon as we reached the pavement, I grabbed Louis by the shoulders and spun him round to face me.

"We're not going on with this," I said. "I'm going back there to tell her it will not happen."

"No, David, it will happen," he said without raising his voice. "You will not stop it!"

I realized that for the first time since I'd ever set eyes on him, he was passionate and angry, though the anger was not purely for me.

"It will happen," he repeated, clenching his teeth, his face hardening in his quiet fury. "And we will leave her unharmed as we promised! But this will go on."

"Louis, don't you understand what she's feeling?" I asked. "She's falling in love with you! She'll never be the same after this. I can't let this deepen. I can't let it become any worse than it already is."

"She's not in love with me, that's wrong," he declared in an emphatic whisper. "She thinks what mortals always think. We're beautiful to them. We're exotic. We have such exquisite sensitivity! I've seen it before. All I need do is to take a victim in her presence to cure her romantic dreams. And it won't come to that, I promise you. Now, David, listen, this hour of waiting will be the longest of the night. I'm thirsting. I mean to hunt. Let go of me, David. Get out of my way."

Of course I didn't leave him.

"And what about your emotions, Louis?" I walked beside him, determined he wouldn't leave me behind. "Can you tell me you're not completely taken by her?"

"And what if I am, David?" he responded, never slacking in his pace. "David, you didn't describe her truly. You told me how strong she was, how wily, and how clever. But you didn't do justice to her." He gave me a shy passing glance. "You never talked about her simplicity or her sweetness. You didn't tell me she was so inherently kind."

"That's how you see her?"

"That's how she is, my friend." Now he wouldn't look at me. "Some school, the Talamasca, that it produced both of you. She has a patient soul and a knowing heart."

"I want this broken off now," I insisted. "I don't trust either of you. Louis, listen to me."

"David, do you really believe I would hurt her?" he asked sharply. He continued walking. "Do I seek out for my victims those whom I believe to be gentle by nature, humans I believe to be both good and uncommonly strong? She'll be safe with me forever, David, don't you understand that? Only once in my wretched life did I make a fledging and that was over a century ago. Merrick couldn't be safer from any of us than she is from me. Bind me to protect her till the day she dies and I'll probably do it! I'll slip away from her after this is done, I promise you." On he walked. He continued to speak: "I'll find a way to thank her, to satisfy her, to leave her at peace. We'll do that together, David, you and I. Don't harry me now in this matter. I can't be stopped. It's gone too far."

I believed him. I believed him completely. "What am I to do?" I asked dejectedly. "I don't even know my own heart in the matter. I'm afraid for hers."

"You're to do nothing," he said, his voice a little more calm than before. "Let it happen as planned."

We walked on through the ruined neighborhood together.

At last the bent red neon sign of a barroom appeared, blinkering under the rangy branches of an ancient and dying tree. There were hand-painted words of advertisement all over the boarded-up facade, and the light inside was so feeble that scarcely anything could be seen through the dirty glass of the door.

Louis went inside and I followed him, quite amazed at the large crowd of Anglo-Saxon males that chattered and drank at the long mahogany bar, and the myriad dirty little tables. Here and there were denim-clad women, young and old, as were their gentlemen companions. A garish red light shone from covered bulbs near the ceiling.

Everywhere I saw naked arms and dirty sleeveless shirts, secretive faces, and cynicism beneath a veil of smiles and flashing teeth.

Louis made his way to the corner of the room, and took the wooden chair beside a large unshaven and bushy-haired man who sat at a table alone and morosely over his stagnant bottle of beer.

I followed, my nostrils assailed by the stench of sweat and the thick cigarette smoke. The volume of the voices was harsh, and the beat of music beneath it ugly, ugly in words and rhythm, ugly in its hostile chant.

I sat down opposite the same poor degenerate mortal who cast his pale failing eyes on Louis and then on me, as though he were about to have some sport.

"So what do you want, gentlemen," he said in a deep voice. His huge chest heaved under the worn shirt that covered it. He lifted his brown bottle and let the golden beer slide down his throat.

"Come on, gentlemen, tell me," he said thickly, drunkenly. "When men dressed like you come downtown, you want something. Now what is it? Am I saying that you came to the wrong place? Hell no, gentlemen. Somebody else might say so. Somebody else might say you've made a bad mistake. But I'm not saying it, gentlemen. I understand everything. I'm all ears for the both of you. Is it broads you want, or is it a little ticket to fly?" He smiled at both of us. "I've got all kinds of goodies, gentlemen. Let's pretend it's Christmas. Just tell me what's your hearts' desire."

He laughed at himself proudly, then drank from his greasy brown bottle. His lips were pink, and his chin covered in a grizzled beard.

Louis stared at him without answering. I watched in fascination. Louis's face gradually lost all expression, all semblance of feeling. It might have belonged to a dead man as he sat there, as he stared at the victim, as he marked the victim, as he let the victim lose his poor desperate humanity, as the kill passed from possible to probable and finally, to a foregone conclusion.

"I want to kill you," Louis said softly. He leant forward and peered very close into the man's pale and red-rimmed gray eyes.

"To kill me?" said the man, raising one eyebrow. "You think you can do that?" he asked.

"I can do it," said Louis gently. "Just like this." He bent and sank his teeth into the man's thick unshaven neck. I saw the man's eyes brighten for one instant as he stared over Louis's shoulder, then the eyes became fixed, and very gradually they went dull.

The man's cumbersome and bulky body rested against Louis, his thick-fingered right hand quivering before it went limp beside the bottle of beer.

After a long moment, Louis drew back and helped the man to lay his head and shoulders down on the table. Lovingly, he touched the man's thick grayish hair.

On the street, Louis breathed deep of the fresh night air. His face was full of the blood of his victim, and richly colored with the tints of a human. He smiled a sad, bitter smile as he looked up, his eyes seeking the faintest stars.

"Agatha," he said softly, as if it were a prayer.

"Agatha?" I repeated. How I feared for him.

"Claudia's mother," he replied, looking at me. "She said the name once in those first few nights, exactly as Merrick put it. She recited both their names, father and mother, in the manner in which she'd been taught to tell strangers. Agatha was her mother's name."

"I see," I replied. "Merrick will be very pleased with that. It's the style of the old charms, you understand, when calling a spirit, to include its mother's name."

"Pity about that man drinking only beer," he said as we commenced our walk back to Merrick. "I could have used just a little heat in the blood, you know, but then perhaps it's better. Better to have a strong clear mind for what happens. I believe Merrick can do what I want."

19

A s we made our way along the side of the house, I saw the candles burning, and when we emerged into the rear yard, I saw the great altar under the shed, with all its tall blessed saints and virgins, and indeed, the Three Magi, and the angels Michael and Gabriel with their spectacular white wings and in their colorful garb.

The scent of incense was strong and delicious to my nostrils. And the trees hung low over the broad clean flagstone terrace with its uneven purple stones.

Far back from the shed, indeed, very near the closest edge of the terrace, there stood the old iron pot atop the brazier tripod, the coals beneath it already glowing. And on either side were long iron tables, rectangular in shape, on which many different objects had been laid out with obvious care.

The complexity of the whole display amazed me faintly, but then I saw, standing on the back steps of the house, only a couple of yards from the tables and the cauldron, the figure of Merrick, her face covered in the green jade mask.

A shock went through my system. The eye holes and mouth opening of the mask appeared empty; only the brilliant green jade was filled with reflected light. Merrick's shadowy hair and body were scarcely visible, though I saw her hand when she lifted it and beckoned for us to come close.

"Here," she said, her voice slightly muffled by the mask as she spoke, "you will stand with me behind the cauldron and the tables. You on my right, Louis, and you on my left, David, and you must promise me now before we commence that you will make no interruption, that you will try no interference in what I mean to do."

She reached out for my arm and guided me into position.

Even at this closeness, the mask was inherently frightening and appeared to float before her lost countenance, perhaps her lost soul. With an anxious and meddlesome hand I confirmed that the mask was firmly affixed to her head by strong leather thongs.

Louis had stepped behind her, and now stood over the iron table to the right of the cauldron, at her right hand, peering ahead at the glowing altar with its banks of glass-contained candles, and at the eerie but lovely faces of the saints.

I took my place by her left.

"What do you mean, we're not to interrupt?" I asked, though it seemed a terrible irreverence, in the midst of this spectacle which had taken on a high beauty, what with the plaster saints, and tall dark yew trees crowding in upon us, and the low twisted black limbs of the oaks shutting out the stars above.

"Just what I told you," she said in a low voice. "You're not to stop me, whatever happens. You're to stay behind this table, both of you; you're never to move in front of it, no matter what you see or think you may see."

"I understand you," said Louis. "The name you wanted. Claudia's mother. It's Agatha. Of that I'm almost certain."

"Thank you," Merrick replied. She gestured before her. "There, on the stones," she said, "the spirits will come if they're meant to come, but you must not go to them, you must not engage in any struggle with them, you must do only as I say."

"I understand you," Louis repeated.

"David, do I have your word?" she asked calmly.

"Very well, Merrick," I said crossly.

"David, stop your interference!" she declared.

"What can I say, Merrick?" I demanded. "How can I give my inner feelings to this thing? Isn't it enough that I stand here? Isn't it enough that I do as you say?"

"David, trust in me," she said. "You came to me with the request for this magic. Now I give you what you asked for. Trust that it will be for the good of Louis. Trust that I can control what I do."

"To speak of magic," I said softly, "to read of it, and study it—all that is one matter, but to participate, to be in the presence of one who believes in it and knows it—that is quite another thing."

"Govern your heart, please, David," said Louis. "I want this more than anything I have ever wanted. Merrick, please, proceed."

"Give me your word with honesty, David," said Merrick. "You will not try to interfere with the things I will say and the things I will do."

"Very well, Merrick," I said, defeated.

Only then did I have the freedom to inspect the objects covering the two tables. There lay the poor pitiful old doll which had belonged to Claudia, limp as a tiny dead body. And the page of the diary, weighted down by the doll's round porcelain head. There was the rosary heaped beside it, and the small daguerreotype in its dark case. There was an iron knife.

I also saw a gold chalice, beautifully ornamented and rimmed with inset jewels. There was a tall crystal bottle filled with what appeared to be clear yellow oil. I saw the jade perforator, a wicked and awful thing in my sight, sharp and dangerous, lying close to the cauldron. And then quite suddenly I saw what appeared to be a human skull.

I was furious at this last discovery. Quickly, I considered the contents of the other table, the one before Louis, and saw there a rib bone covered with markings, and that loathsome old shriveled black hand. There were three bottles of rum. There were other items—a fine golden pitcher of honey, which I could smell in its sweetness, another silver pitcher of pure white milk, and a bronze bowl of shining salt.

As for the incense, I realized it had all been distributed and was already burning before the distant unsuspecting saints.

Indeed, a great deal more of the incense, very black and only faintly aglow as its smoke rose in the darkness, had been poured out to make a great circle on the purple flagstone before us, a circle which my eyes only now observed.

I wanted to demand: where did the skull come from? Had Merrick robbed some anonymous grave? A dreadful thought occurred to me and I tried to banish it. I looked at the skull again and saw it was covered with incised writing. It was lurid and awful, and the beauty embracing all of this was seductive, potent, and obscene.

Instead I spoke only of the circle.

"They will appear in it," I murmured, "and you think the incense will contain them."

"If I must, I will tell them that the incense contains them," she said coldly. "Now, you must govern your tongue if you can't govern your heart. Offer no prayers as you watch this. I am ready for this to begin."

"What if there isn't enough incense!" I demanded in a whisper.

"There is plenty of it to burn for hours. Look at the small cones with your clever vampire eyes, and don't ask me such a foolish question again."

I resigned myself: I couldn't stop this. And only now did I feel in my resignation a certain attraction to the entire process as she made to begin.

From beneath the table, she lifted a small bundle of twigs and fed these quickly to the coals in the brazier beneath the iron pot.

"Make this fire hot for our purposes," she whispered. "May all the saints and angels witness, may the glorious Virgin Mary witness, make this fire burn for us."

"Such names, such words," I murmured before I could stop myself. "Merrick, you play with the strongest powers known to us."

But on she went, poking at the fire until its flames licked the sides of the cauldron. Then she lifted the first bottle of rum, uncapped it, and emptied its acrid contents into the pot. Quickly, she took up the crystal bottle and poured out the pure, fragrant oil.

"Papa Legba!" she called out as the smoke rose before her. "I can begin nothing without your intercession. Look here at your servant Merrick, listen to her voice as she calls you, unlock the doors to the world of the mysteries, that Merrick may have what she desires."

The dark perfume of the heated concoction overcame me as it rose from the iron pot. I felt as if I ought to be drunk, when I wasn't, and it seemed my balance had been affected, though why I couldn't know.

"Papa Legba," she cried. "Open the way."

My eyes shot to the distant statue of St. Peter, and only then did I realize he stood in the center of the altar, a fine effigy of wood, his glass eyes glaring back at her, his dark hand wrapped about its golden keys.

It seemed to me that the air changed suddenly about us, but I told myself it was only my raw nerves. Vampire or human, I was susceptible to the tiniest suggestion. Yet the yews began ever so slightly to sway on the outskirts of the garden, and there came through the trees above a soft wind that sent the leaves down all around us, tiny and light, without a sound.

"Open the gates, Papa Legba," she called out, as her deft hands emptied the second bottle of rum into the cauldron. "Let the saints in Heaven hear me, let the Virgin Mary hear me, let the angels be unable to turn away their ears."

Her voice was low yet full of certainty.

"Hear me, St. Peter," she declared, "or I shall pray to Him who gave His Only Divine Son for our Salvation that He turns His back on you in Heaven. I am Merrick. I cannot be denied!"

I heard Louis give out a faint gasp.

"Now, you angels, Michael and Gabriel," she said, her voice rising with increasing authority, "I command you, open the way to the eternal darkness, to the very souls whom you yourself may have driven out of Heaven; put your flaming swords to my purpose. I am Merrick. I command you. I cannot be denied. I will call upon all the Celestial hosts to turn their backs on you should you hesitate. I will call upon God The Father to condemn you, I will condemn you, I will loathe you, should you not listen; I am Merrick, I cannot be denied."

There was a low rumbling from the statues in the shed, a sound very like the earth makes when it's shifting—a sound which no one can imitate, but which anyone can hear.

Again came the sound of the rum pouring, from the third bottle.

"Drink from my cauldron, all you angels and saints," said Merrick, "and allow that my words and my sacrifice rise to Heaven. Hear my voice."

I strained in my focus upon the statues. Was I losing my mind? They appeared animate and the smoke rising from the incense and candles seemed thicker. Indeed the whole spectacle intensified, colors becoming richer, and the distance between the saints and us smaller, though we had not moved.

Merrick lifted the perforator with her left hand. Instantly, she cut the inside of her right arm. The blood poured down into the cauldron. Her voice rose above it:

"You Watcher Angels, the first to teach mankind magic, I call upon you now for my purpose, or those spirits that answer to your name.

"Ham, you son of Noah and pupil of the Watchers, I call upon you now for my purpose, or that powerful spirit which answers to your name.

"Mestran, son of Ham, who passed on the secrets of magic to his children and others, I call upon you now for my purpose, or that powerful spirit which answers to your name."

Again she slashed herself with the knife, the blood sliding down her bare arm and into the cauldron. Again there came that sound, as if from the earth beneath us, a low rumbling that mortal ears perhaps would disregard. I looked helplessly to my feet and to the statues. I saw the faint shiver of the entire altar.

"I give you my own blood as I call you," Merrick said. "Listen to my words, I am Merrick, daughter of Cold Sandra, I cannot be denied.

"Nebrod, son of Mestran, and powerful teacher of magic to those who came after him, bearer of the wisdom of the Watchers, I call upon you for my purpose, or upon that powerful spirit which answers to your name.

"Zoroaster, great teacher and magician, who passed on the mighty secrets of the Watchers, who brought down to himself from the very stars the fire which destroyed his earthly body, I call on you, or that spirit which answers to your name.

"Listen to me, all you who have gone before me, I am Merrick, daughter of Cold Sandra, I cannot be denied.

"I shall cause the Host of Heaven to declare you anathema should you attempt to resist my powers. I shall withdraw my faith and withdraw my blandishments should you not grant the wish that comes from my tongue. I am Merrick, daughter of Cold Sandra; you will bring to me those spirits whom I call."

Again the perforator was lifted. She cut her own flesh. A long gleaming seam of blood flowed into the aromatic brew. The scent of it inflamed me. The smoke from the mixture stung my eyes.

"Yes, I command you," she said, "all of you, most powerful and illustrious ones, I command you that I may achieve what I say, that I may bring forth out of the whirlwind those lost souls who will find Claudia, daughter of Agatha, yield up to me those Purgatorial souls who will, in exchange for my prayers, bring forth the spirit of Claudia. Do as I command!"

The iron altar before me was shivering. I could see the skull moving with the altar. I could not discount what I saw. I could not challenge what I heard, the low rumbling of the ground beneath me. Tiny leaves came down in a swirl, like ashes before us. The giant yew trees had begun to sway as if in the early breezes of an approaching storm.

I tried to see Louis, but Merrick stood between us. Her voice came unceasingly:

"All you powerful ones, command Honey in the Sunshine, restless spirit of my sister, daughter of Cold Sandra, that she bring Claudia, daughter of Agatha, out of the whirlwind. Honey in the Sunshine, I command you. I will turn all Heaven against you if you do not obey me. I will heap infamy upon your name. I am Merrick. I will not be denied."

Even as the blood flowed down over her right hand, she reached with it for the skull beside the smoking cauldron and lifted it up.

"Honey in the Sunshine, I have here your very skull from the grave in which you were buried, and all your names are written upon it in my hand. Honey Isabella, daughter of Cold Sandra, you cannot deny me. I call you and command you to bring Claudia, daughter of Agatha, here now, to answer to me."

It was exactly as I'd suspected. She had done the awful deed of violating Honey's poor pathetic remains. How vicious and how dreadful, and for how long had she kept this secret, that she possessed the skull of her own sister, her own blood kin.

I was revolted yet magnetized. The smoke from the candles grew dense before the statues. It seemed their faces were full of movement, their eyes sweeping the scene before them. Even their drapery appeared alive. The incense burnt bright in the circle on the flagstones, fanned by the breeze that steadily increased.

Merrick laid aside the cursed skull and the perforator.

From the table she lifted the gold pitcher of honey, and poured it into the jeweled chalice. This she lifted with her bloody right hand as she went on:

"Ah, yes, all you lonely spirits, and you, Honey, and you, Claudia, smell this sweet offering—Honey, the very substance after which you in your beauty were named." Into the cauldron she poured the thick sparkling liquid.

Then she lifted the pitcher of milk. Into the chalice it went, and then she lifted the chalice, gathering up the deadly perforator again in her left hand.

"And this, too, I offer you, so delicious to your desperate senses, come here and breathe this sacrifice, drink of this milk and honey, drink it from the smoke that rises from my cauldron. Here, it comes to you through this chalice which once contained The Blood of Our Lord. Here, partake of it. Do not refuse me. I am Merrick, daughter of

Cold Sandra. Come, Honey, I command you, and bring Claudia to me. I will not be denied."

A loud breath came from Louis.

In the circle before the statues, something amorphous and dark had taken shape. I felt my heart skipping as my eyes strained to make it out. It was the form of Honey, it was the very figure which I had seen many years before. It flickered and wavered in the heat as Merrick chanted:

"Come, Honey, come closer, come in answer to me. Where is Claudia, daughter of Agatha? Bring her here to Louis de Pointe du Lac, I command you. I cannot be denied."

The figure was almost solid! I saw the familiar yellow hair, the candlelight behind it rendering it transparent, the white dress more spectral than the solid outline of the body itself. I was too stunned to utter the prayers that Merrick had forbidden. The words never formed on my lips.

Suddenly Merrick laid down the skull. She turned and caught Louis's left arm with her bloodstained hand.

I saw his white wrist above the cauldron. With a swift movement, she slashed at his wrist. I heard him gasp again, and I saw the glittering vampiric blood gushing from the veins into the rising smoke. Again she gashed the white flesh and again the blood flowed, thickly, freely, and more abundantly than her own blood before.

In no way did Louis resist her. Mute, he stared at the figure of Honey.

"Honey, my beloved sister," said Merrick, "bring Claudia. Bring Claudia to Louis de Pointe du Lac. I am Merrick, your sister. I command you. Honey, show your power!" Her voice became low, crooning. "Honey, show your immense strength! Bring Claudia here now."

Again, she cut the wrist, for the preternatural flesh was healing just as soon as she opened it, and she again made the blood flow.

"Savor this blood which is shed for you, Claudia. I call your name and your name only now, Claudia. I would have you here!" Once more the wound was opened.

But now she gave over the perforator to Louis, and she lifted the doll in both her hands.

I glanced from Merrick to the solid image of Honey, so dark, so distant, so seemingly without human movement.

"Your possessions, my sweet Claudia," Merrick called out, snatching up a twig from the fire and lighting the clothes of the unfortunate doll, which all but exploded in a draught of flames. The little face turned black in the blaze. Still Merrick held it with both hands.

The figure of Honey suddenly began to dissolve.

Into the cauldron Merrick dropped the burning object, and then lifted the page of the diary, as she continued to speak.

"Your words, my sweet Claudia, accept this offering, accept this acknowledgment, accept this devotion." She dipped the page into the fire of the brazier, then held it aloft as it was consumed.

The ashes fell into the cauldron. She took up the perforator once again.

The form of Honey lingered only in shape and then appeared to be blown away by the natural breeze. Again the candles blazed violently before the statues.

"Claudia, daughter of Agatha," said Merrick, "I command you, come forward, become material, answer me from the whirlwind, answer your servant Merrick—all you angels and saints, and Blessed Mother Ever Virgin compel Claudia, compel her to answer my command."

I couldn't take my eyes off the smoky darkness. Honey was gone but something else had taken her place. The very gloom seemed to shape itself into a smaller figure, indistinct but gathering strength as it appeared to extend its small arms and move towards the table behind which we stood. It was above the ground, this small being, the sudden glint of its eye on our level and its feet walking on nothing as it proceeded towards us, its hands becoming clearly visible, as well as its shining golden hair.

It was Claudia, it was the child of the daguerreotype, it was white-faced and delicate, its eyes wide and brilliant, its skin luminous, its loose and flowing white garments soft and ruffled by the wind.

I stepped backwards. I couldn't stop myself, but the figure had stopped; it remained suspended above the ground and its pale arms relaxed and fell naturally at its sides. It was as solid in the dim light as Honey had been so many years before.

Its small stunning features were filled with a look of love and quickening sensibility. It was a child, a living child. It was undeniable. It was there.

A voice came out of it, fresh and sweet, a girl's natural treble:

"Why have you called me, Louis?" it asked with heartbreaking sincerity. "Why have you roused me from my wandering sleep for your own consolation? Why wasn't memory enough?"

I was weak almost to fainting.

The child's eyes flashed suddenly on Merrick. The voice came again with its tender clarity:

"Stop now with your chants and commands. I do not answer to you, Merrick Mayfair. I come for the one who stands to the right of you. I come demanding why you've called me, Louis; what is it that you would have me give you now? In life did I not give you all my love?"

"Claudia," Louis murmured in a tortured voice. "Where is your spirit? Is it at rest or does it wander? Would you have me come to you? Claudia, I'm ready to do it. Claudia I'm ready to be at your side."

"You? Come to me?" the child asked. The little voice had taken on a dark deliberate coloration. "You, after all those many years of evil tutelage, you think that I in death would be united with you?" The voice went on, its timbre sweet as if saying words of love. "I loathe you, evil Father," it confided. A dark laughter came from the small lips.

"Father, understand me," she whispered, her face infected with the tenderest expression. "I never could find words to tell you truths when I was living." There was the sound of breath, and a visible despair seemed to wrap itself about the creature. "In this measureless place I have no use for such curses," said the voice, with touching simplicity. "What is it to me, the love you lavished on me once in a vibrant and feverish world?"

On she went as if consoling him.

"You want vows from me," she said with seeming wonder, her whisper growing softer. "And from the coldest heart imaginable I condemn you—condemn you that you took my life—" the voice was fatigued, defeated "—condemn you that you had no charity for the mortal I once was, condemn you that you saw in me only what filled your eyes and insatiable veins . . . condemn you that you brought me over into the lively Hell which you and Lestat so richly shared."

The small solid figure moved closer, the luminous face of plump cheeks and lustrous eyes now directly before the cauldron, the tiny hands curled but not raised. I lifted my hand. I wanted to touch this shape, so vivid was it. Yet I wanted to back away from it, shield myself somehow from it, shield Louis, as if such a thing could be done.

"Take your life, yes," she said with her relentless tenderness, her eyes large and wondering—"give it up in memory of me, yes, I would have you do it, I would have you give over to me your last breath. Do it with pain for me, Louis, do it with pain that I may see your spirit through the whirlwind, struggling to free itself from your tormented flesh."

Louis reached out for her, but Merrick caught his wrist and pushed him back.

The child continued, her words unhurried, her tone solicitous as she went on:

"Oh, how it will warm my soul to see you suffer, oh, how it will speed me on my endless wanderings. Never would I linger to be with you here. Never would I wish for it. Never would I seek you out in the abyss."

Her face was stamped with the purest curiosity as she looked at him. There was nothing of visible hatred in her expression at all.

"Such pride," she whispered, smiling, "that you would call me out of your habitual misery. Such pride that you would bring me here to answer your common prayers." There came a small chilling laughter.

"How immense is your self-pity," she said, "that you don't fear me, when I—had I the power from this witch or any other—would take your life with my own hands." She lifted her little hands to her face as if she would weep in them, and then let them drop to her sides again.

"Die for me, my doting one," she said tremulously. "I think I shall like it. I shall like it as much as I liked the sufferings of Lestat, which I can scarce remember. I think, yes, that I might know pleasure once again, briefly, in your pain. Now, if you are done with me, done with my toys and your memories, release me that I may return to forgetfulness. I cannot recall the terms of my perdition. I fear I understand eternity. Let me go."

All at once, she moved forward, her small right hand snatching up the jade perforator from the iron table, and with a great lunge, she flew at Louis, thrusting the perforator into his chest.

He fell forward over the makeshift altar, his right hand clutching at the wound in which she ground the jade pick, the cauldron spilling over onto the stones beneath her, Merrick backing up in seeming horror, and I unable to move.

The blood gushed out of Louis's heart. His face was knotted, his mouth open, his eyes shut.

"Forgive me," he whispered. He gave a soft groan of pure and terrible pain.

"Go back to Hell!" cried Merrick, suddenly. She ran at the floating image, arms out to reach over the cauldron, but the child withdrew with the ease of vapor, and, still clutching the jade pick, she lifted her right hand and knocked Merrick back with it, the frigid little face all the while quite still.

Merrick stumbled on the back steps of the house. I caught her arm and lifted her back on her feet.

Again, the child turned to Louis as she held the dangerous pick in both her small hands. Down the front of her sheer white dress was the dark stain from the boiling fluids of the cauldron. It meant nothing to her.

The cauldron, on its side, poured forth its contents onto the stones.

"Did you think I wasn't suffering, Father?" she asked softly in the same small girlish voice. "Did you think that death had freed me from all my pain?" Her small finger touched the point of the jade instrument. "That's what you thought, wasn't it, Father," she spoke slowly, "and that, if this woman did your will, you'd take away some precious consolation from my very lips. You believed that God would give you that, didn't you? It seemed so very right for you after all your penitential years."

Louis still held his wound, though his flesh was healing and the blood oozed more slowly out of his splayed hand.

"The gates can't be locked to you, Claudia," he said, the tears rising in his eyes. His voice was strong and sure. "That would be too monstrous a cruelty—."

"To whom, Father?" she answered, cutting off his words. "Too monstrous a cruelty to you? I suffer, Father, I suffer and I wander; I know nothing, and all I once knew seems illusory! I have nothing, Father. My senses are not even a memory. I have nothing here at all."

The voice grew weaker, yet it was clearly audible. Her exquisite face was infused with a look of discovery.

"Did you think I'd tell you nursery stories about Lestat's angels?" she asked with a low kindly tone. "Did you think I'd paint a picture of the glassy heavens with palaces and mansions? Did you think I'd sing to you some song learnt from the Morning Stars? No, Father, you will not draw such ethereal comfort from me."

On went her subdued voice:

"And when you come following me I shall be lost again, Father. How can I promise that I shall be there to witness your cries or tears?"

The image had begun to waver. Her large dark eyes fixed upon

Merrick, and then on me. Back to Louis she looked. She was fading. The perforator fell from her white hand and struck the stones, breaking in two.

"Come, Louis," she said faintly, the sound of her invitation mingling with the softly stirring trees, "come into this dreary place with me, and leave behind your comforts—leave behind your wealth, your dreams, your blood-soaked pleasures. Leave behind your ever hungry eyes. Leave it all, my beloved, leave it for this dim and insubstantial realm."

The figure was rigid and flat, the light barely shining upon its uncertain contours. I could scarcely see the small mouth as it smiled.

"Claudia, please, I beg you," said Louis. "Merrick, don't let her go into uncertain darkness. Merrick, guide her!"

But Merrick did not move.

Louis turned frantically from Merrick to the fading image.

"Claudia!" he cried out. With all his soul he wanted to say more, but there was no conviction in him. All was despair. I could feel it. I could read it on his stricken face.

Merrick stood back, staring through the gleaming jade mask, her left hand poised in the air as if to fend off the ghost if it should strike again.

"Come to me, Father," said the child, the voice toneless now, devoid of feeling. The image was transparent, dim.

The outline of the small face slowly evaporated. Only the eyes held their luster.

"Come to me," she whispered, her voice dry and thin. "Come, do it with deep pain, as your offering. You'll never find me. Come."

Only a dark shape remained for a few moments, and then the space was empty, and the yard with its shrine and with its tall forbidding trees was still.

I could see no more of her. The candles, what had happened to them? They had all gone out. The burning incense was so much soot on the flagstones. The breeze had scattered it. A great shower of tiny leaves came down languidly from the branches, and the air was full of a subtle yet biting cold.

Only the distant gleam of the heavens gave us illumination. The dreadful chill lingered around us. It penetrated my clothes and settled on my skin.

Louis peered into the darkness with a look of inexpressible grief. He began to shiver. The tears didn't flow; they merely stood in his uncomprehending eyes.

Suddenly Merrick ripped off the jade mask and overturned both tables, and the brazier, the contents smashing onto the flags. The mask she cast into the shrubbery by the rear steps.

I stared in horror at the skull of Honey lying in the heap of cast-off instruments. Bitter smoke rose from the wet coals. The burnt remnants of the doll were visible in the flowing liquid. The jeweled chalice rolled on its golden rim.

Merrick took hold of Louis by both arms.

"Come inside," she said, "come out of this awful place now. Come inside with me, where we can light the lamps. Come inside where we'll be safe and warm."

"No, not now, my dear," he answered. "I must leave you. Oh, I promise, I'll see you again. Let me alone for now. Take whatever promises I must give you, to quiet you. Take whatever thanks I can express from my heart. But let me go."

He bent down and retrieved the little picture of Claudia from the wreckage of the altar. Then off he went down the shadowy alley, pushing the young banana leaves out of his path, his steps growing ever faster, until he was gone altogether, vanished on his own path in the familiar and unchanging night.

20

I LEFT HER CURLED UP on Great Nananne's bed in the front room.

I went back into the garden, picked up the broken pieces of the jade perforator, and found the mask broken in half. How brittle was this strong jade. How bad had been my intentions, how evil the result.

These things I brought with me into the house. I could not bring myself to lay my superstitious hands upon the skull of Honey in the Sunshine.

I put the collection of jade remnants on the bedroom altar, amid the glass-covered candles, and then I settled next to her, sitting beside her, and I put my arm around her.

She turned and laid her head on my shoulder. Her skin felt feverish and sweet. I wanted to cover her in kisses, but I couldn't give in to this impulse, anymore than I could give in to the darker impulse to bring through the blood the rhythm of her heart in time with my own.

There was dried blood all over her white silk dress, and on the inside of her right arm.

"I should never have done it, never," she said in a hushed and anxious voice, her breasts yielding softly against me. "It was madness. I knew what would happen. I knew his brain would be fodder for disaster. I knew it. And now he's lost; he's wounded and lost to us both."

I lifted her so that I could look into her eyes. As always their brilliant green color startled me, and enthralled me, but I couldn't concern myself with her charms now.

"But you do believe that it was Claudia?" I asked.

"Oh, yes," she said. Her eyes were still red around the edges from her crying. I saw the tears standing there. "It was Claudia," she declared.

"Or that thing which now calls itself Claudia, but the words it spoke? They were lies."

"How can you know that?"

"The same way I know when a human being is lying to me. The same way I know when someone's read another one's mind and is preying upon that other's weakness. The spirit was hostile, once called into our realm. The spirit was confused. The spirit told lies."

"I didn't feel it was lying," I argued.

"Don't you see," she said, "it took Louis's very, very worst fears and morbid thoughts for its matter. His mind was full of the verbal instruments by which he could bring about his own despair. He's found his conviction. And whatever he is—wonder, horror, damnable monster—he's lost now. Lost to us both."

"Why couldn't it have been speaking pure truth?" I asked.

"No spirit speaks pure truth," she insisted. She wiped at her reddened eyes with the back of her hand. I gave her my linen handkerchief. She pressed it to her eyes. Then she looked up at me again. "Not when it's called, it doesn't. It speaks truth only when it comes on its own."

I took this idea into my thoughts. I had heard it before. Every member of the Talamasca had heard it. Spirits who are called are treacherous. Spirits who come on their own possess some guiding will. But no spirit can in fact be trusted. It was old knowledge. It gave neither comfort nor clarity to me just now.

"Then the picture of eternity," I said, "it was false, that's what you're saying."

"Yes," she said, "that's exactly what I'm saying." She wiped her nose with the handkerchief. She began to shiver. "But he will never accept it." She shook her head. "The lies are too near to what he absolutely believes."

I didn't speak. The words of the spirit were too nearly to what I actually believed as well.

She rested her head on my chest again, her arm about me loosely. I held her, staring before me at the smaller altar between the front windows, staring at the patient faces of the different saints.

A quiet and dangerous mood fell over me, in which I saw rather plainly all the long years of my life. One thing remained constant during this journey, whether I was the young man in the Candomble temples of Brazil, or the vampire prowling the streets of New York in the company of Lestat. That constant thing was that, no matter what I'd said to the contrary, I suspected there was nothing beyond this earthly life.

Of course now and then I gladly "believed" otherwise. I made my case to myself with seeming miracles—spirit winds and vampiric blood flowing. But in the final analysis, I feared there was nothing, nothing perhaps but the "measureless darkness" which this phantom, this vicious and angry phantom, had described.

Yes, I'm saying that I believe we might linger. Of course. Lingering after death for some while is not beyond the realm of science to explain someday—a soul of definable substance detached from the flesh and caught in some energy field that wreaths the planet. It is not beyond imagining, no, not at all. But it doesn't mean immortality. It doesn't mean Paradise or an Inferno. It doesn't mean justice or recognition. It doesn't mean ecstasy or unending pain.

As for the vampires, they were a flashy miracle, but consider how relentlessly materialistic and how very small that miracle is.

Picture the night when one of us is captured and carefully fastened to the table in the laboratory, housed perhaps in a tank of aerospace plastic, safe from the sun, day and night beneath a flickering gush of fluorescent light.

There he would lie, this helpless specimen of the Nosferatu, bleeding into syringes and test tubes, as doctors gave to our longevity, our changelessness, our connection to some binding and ageless spirit—a long Latin scientific name.

Amel, that ancient spirit said by the eldest of us to organize our bodies and connect them—it would one day be classified as some force quite similar to that which organizes the tiny ant in its vast and intricate colony, or the marvelous bees in their exquisite and impossibly sophisticated hive.

If I died, there might be nothing. If I died, there might be lingering. If I died, I might never even know what became of my soul. The lights around me—the warmth of which the child phantom had spoken so tauntingly—the warmth would simply go away.

I bowed my head. I pressed my left fingers hard to my temples, my right arm tightening against Merrick who seemed so precious, so frail.

My mind shot back to the dark spell and the luminous child phantom in the middle of it. It shot back to the moment when her arm was lifted, when Merrick cried out and was thrown back. It shot back to the child's wonderfully realized eyes and lips, and the low musical voice issuing from her. It shot back to the seeming validity of the vision itself.

Of course, it *could have been* Louis's despair which fueled her fount of misery. It might well have been my own. How much did I, myself, want to believe in Lestat's articulate angels or Armand's glimpse of crystalline celestial splendor? How much did I myself project upon the seeming void my own late and grossly lamented conscience, straining again and again to voice love for the maker of the wind, the tides, the moon, the stars?

I could not end my own earthly existence. I was as fearful as any mortal that I might be resigning forever the only magical experience that I'd been privileged to know. And that Louis might perish seemed a simple horror, rather like seeing an exotic and poisonous flower, fallen from its secretive jungle perch and crushed underfoot.

Did I fear for him? I wasn't certain. I loved him, I wanted him with us now in this room. I did. But I wasn't certain that I had the moral stamina to coax him to remain in this world another twenty-four hours. I wasn't certain of anything at all. I wanted him for my companion, mirror of my emotions, witness of my aesthetic progress, yes, all those things. I wanted him to be quiet and gentle Louis, that I knew. And if he did not choose to go on with us, if he did in fact take his own life by walking into the sunlight, then it would be all the harder for me to continue, even with my fear.

Merrick had begun to shake all over. Her tears were not stopping. I gave in to my desire to kiss her, to breathe in the fragrance of her warm flesh.

"There, there, my darling," I whispered.

The handkerchief clutched in her right hand was small and wet.

I lifted her as I stood up. I pulled down the heavy white chenille spread and laid her on the clean sheets. Never mind her soiled dress. She was cold and frightened. Her hair was tangled beneath her. I lifted her head and brought her hair up and over the linen. I saw her sink into the down pillows, and I kissed her eyelids to bid them to close.

"Rest now, precious darling," I said. "You only did what he asked."

"Don't leave me just now," she said in a raw voice, "except if you think you can find him. If you know where he is, then find him. Otherwise stay here with me, just for this little while."

I went down the hall in search of a bathroom and found it to the very rear of the house, a spacious and somewhat lavish arrangement with a little coal fireplace as well as a great claw-foot tub. There was the usual pile of clean white terry cloth towels one expects amid such luxury. I moistened the end of one of these and brought it back to the front room.

Merrick was on her side, knees curled up, her hands clasped together. I could hear a low whispering coming from her lips.

"Here, let me wipe your face," I said. I did it without any further concessions, and then I wiped the caked blood from her inner arm. The scratches went clear from her palm to the inside of her elbow. But they were very shallow. One began to bleed a little as I cleaned it, but I pressed on it for a moment and the blood ceased to flow.

I found the dry clean end of the towel, and patted Merrick's face with it, and then the wounds, which were now completely clean and healed.

"I can't remain here like this," Merrick said. Her head went from side to side. "I have to get the bones from the rear yard. It was a terrible thing to overturn the altars."

"Be quiet now," I said. "I'll bring them in."

It filled me with revulsion to do this. But I was as good as my word.

I went back to the scene of the crime. The dark rear yard seemed uncommonly still. The dead candles before the saints seemed negligent and evidence of grave sins.

Out of the detritus fallen from the iron tables, I picked up the skull of Honey in the Sunshine. I felt a sudden chill run through my hands, but I put it off to my imagination. I gathered up the rib bone, and I saw again that both of these bore all kinds of deeply incised writing. I refused to read the writing. I brought them back with me into the house and into the front room.

"Put them on the altar," she said. She sat up, pushing the heavy covers off her.

I saw that she had taken off her bloodsoaked dress of white silk, and that it lay in a heap on the floor.

She wore only her silk petticoat, and I could see her large pink nipples through it. There was blood on the petticoat too. Her shoulders were very straight and her breasts high set, and her arms were just rounded enough to be delicious to my sight.

I went to pick up the dress. I wanted to clean her up completely. I wanted her to be all right.

"It's monstrously unfair that you're so frightened," I said.

"No, leave the dress," she answered, reaching out for my wrist. "Let it go, and sit here, beside me. Take my hand and talk to me. The spirit's a liar, I swear it. You must believe what I say."

Once again, I sat down on the bed. I wanted to be close to her. I leant over and kissed her bowed head. I wished I couldn't see so much of her breasts, and I wondered if the younger vampires knew—those brought over early in their manhood—how such carnal details still distracted me. Of course the blood lust rose with this distraction. It was not an easy thing to love her so terribly and not taste of her soul through her blood.

"Why do I have to believe you?" I asked gently.

She dug her fingers into her hair and swept it back behind her shoulders.

"Because you must," she said urgently yet quietly. "You must see that I knew what I was doing, you must believe that I can tell a truth-telling spirit from one who lies. That was something, yes, that being which pretended to be Claudia—something very powerful that it could lift the pick and sink it into Louis's flesh. I'll wager anything that it was a spirit who hated him due to his very nature, that he can be dead and still walk the earth. It was something deeply offended by his very existence. But it was taking its verses from his own thoughts."

"How can you be so sure?" I asked. I shrugged my shoulders. "God knows, I wish you were right. But you yourself called on Honey; is not Honey lost in the same realm that this spirit of Claudia described? Doesn't Honey's presence prove there's nothing better for either one of them? You saw the shape of Honey out there before the altar—."

She nodded.

"—and you went on to call Claudia from the same realm."

"Honey wants to be called," she declared, looking up at me, her fingers driven into her hair, tugging it cruelly back, away from her tormented face. "Honey's always there. Honey's waiting for me. That's how I knew for certain that I could call on Honey. But what about Cold Sandra? What about Great Nananne? What about Aaron Lightner? When I opened the door none of those spirits came through. They've long since gone on into the Light, David. If they hadn't they would have long ago let me know. I would have felt them the way I feel Honey. I would have hints of them, as Jesse Reeves had of Claudia when she heard the music in the Rue Royale."

I was puzzled by this last statement. Very puzzled. I shook my head in an emphatic no.

"Merrick, you're holding back from me," I said, deciding I must address it directly. "You have called Great Nananne. You think I don't remember what happened only a few nights ago, the night we met in the café in the Rue St. Anne?"

"Yes? What about that night?" she asked. "What are you trying to say?"

"Maybe you don't know what happened," I said. "Is that possible? You called down a spell and didn't know how strong it was yourself?"

"David, talk straight to me," she responded. Her eyes were clearing and she had stopped trembling. Of this I was glad.

"That night," I said, "after we met and spoke together, you put a spell on me, Merrick. On my way back to the Rue Royale, I kept seeing you everywhere; to the right of me, and to the left of me, Merrick. And then I saw Great Nananne."

"Great Nananne?" she asked in a subdued voice, but one which couldn't conceal her disbelief. "What do you mean, you saw Great Nananne?"

"When I reached the carriageway of my town house," I said, "I saw two spirits behind the iron bars—one in the image of you, a girl of ten, the way you were when I first met you, and the other, Great Nananne in her nightgown, as she was on the only day I was ever to know her, the day of her death. These two spirits stood in the carriageway and spoke together, intimately, tête à tête, their eyes fixed on me. And when I approached them, they disappeared."

For a moment, she said nothing. Her eyes were narrow and her lips slightly parted, as if she was pondering this with extreme concentration.

"Great Nananne," she said again.

"Just as I've told you, Merrick," I said. "Am I to understand now that you yourself didn't call her? You know what happened next, don't you? I went back to the Windsor Court, to the suite where I'd left you. I found you dead drunk on the bed."

"Don't use such a charming expression for it," she whispered crossly. "You came back, yes, and you wrote me a note."

"But after I wrote that note, Merrick, I saw Great Nananne there in the hotel, standing in the door of your bedroom. She was challenging me, Merrick. She was challenging me by her very presence and posture. It was a dense and undeniable apparition. It endured for moments—chilling moments, Merrick. Am I to understand this wasn't part of your spell?"

Merrick sat silent for a long moment, her hands still splayed in her hair. She lifted her knees and drew them close to her breasts. Her sharp gaze never left me.

"Great Nananne," she whispered. "You're telling me the truth. Of course you are. And you thought that I called my godmother? You thought I could call her and make her appear like that?"

"Merrick, I saw the statue of St. Peter. I saw my own handkerchief beneath it with the drops of blood on it. I saw the candle you'd lighted. I saw the offerings. You had cast a spell."

"Yes, my darling," she said quickly, her right hand clutching mine to quiet me. "I fixed you, yes, I put a little fixing spell on you to make you want me, to make you quite unable to think of anything else but me, to make you come back if by the slightest chance you had decided never to come to me again. Just a fixing spell, David, you know what I'm saying. I wanted to see if I could do it now that you were a vampire. And you see what happened? You didn't feel love or obsession, David, you saw images of me instead. Your strength came to the fore, David, that's all that happened. And you wrote your sharp little note to me, and when I read it, I think I might have even laughed."

She broke off, deeply troubled, her eyes large as she stared in front her, perhaps into her own thoughts.

"And Great Nananne?" I pressed. "You didn't call her?"

"I can't call my godmother," she said, her tone serious, her eyes narrow as she looked at me again. "I pray to my godmother, David, don't you realize that, as I pray to Cold Sandra, as I pray to Oncle Vervain. They're no longer near us, any of them, my ancestors. I pray to them in Heaven as I would to the angels and the saints."

"I'm telling you I saw her spirit."

"And I'm telling you I've never seen it," she whispered. "I'm telling you I'd give anything I possess if only I could."

She looked at my hand, the one which she held in her own, and then she pressed it warmly and she let it go. Her hands went up to her temples again and her fingers found their way again into her hair.

"Great Nananne's in the Light," she said, as though she were arguing with me, and perhaps she was. But her gaze was lost to me. "Great Nananne's in the Light, David," she said again. "I tell you I know she is." She looked up into the airy semi-darkness, and then her eyes drifted to the altar and the candles in their long flickering rows.

"I don't believe she came," she whispered. "I don't believe they're all in some 'insubstantial realm!' No, I tell you, I don't believe it," she said. She put her hands on her knees. "I don't believe anything so absolutely awful—that all the souls of the 'faithful departed' are lost in darkness. No, I can't believe such a thing."

"Very well, then," I said, wanting for the moment only to comfort her, and remembering too keenly the spirits at the gate once more, old woman and young girl. "Great Nananne came of her own accord. It's as you indicated earlier—you said that spirits only tell the truth if they come of their own accord. Great Nananne didn't want me near you, Merrick. Great Nananne has told me that. And maybe she'll come again if I don't somewhat repair the damage I've done to you, and leave you alone."

She appeared to be thinking this over.

A long interval ensued during which I watched her intently, and she gave me no clue of her feelings or her intentions, and then finally, she took my hand again. She drew it up to her lips and she kissed it. It was painfully sweet.

"David, my beloved David," she said, but her eyes were secretive. "Leave me now."

"No, I won't even think of it, until I have to do it."

"No, I want you to go," she said. "I'll be quite all right on my own."

"Call the caretaker," I said. "I want him here before I leave the property at dawn."

She reached over to the night table and produced one of those small modern cellular phones that is no bigger than a man's wallet. She punched in a series of numbers. I heard the appropriate voice on the other end, "Yes, Ma'am, coming directly."

I was satisfied.

I stood up. I took several steps towards the center of the room, and then the most desolate feeling descended upon me.

I turned around and looked at her as she sat there, her knees up close to her breasts, her head resting on her knees, her arms locked around her legs.

"Am I fixed now with a spell, Merrick?" I asked her, my voice even more gentle than I meant for it to be. "I don't want to leave you, my precious darling," I said. "I can't bear the thought of it, but I know that

we have to part from one another, you and I. One more meeting, perhaps two. No more than two."

She looked up, startled, and her face was touched with fear.

"Bring him back to me, David," she said imploringly. "In the name
of God, you have to do that. I must see Louis and talk to him again."
She waited a moment, during which time I didn't answer her. "As for
you and me, don't talk as if we can simply say goodbye to one another.
David, I can't bear that just now. You must assure me—."

"It won't be abrupt," I said, cutting her off, "and it won't be without
your knowledge. But we can't go on, Merrick. If we try to go on, you'll
lose faith in yourself and everything that matters to you. Believe me, I
know."

"But it never happened to you, dearest," she said, with strong confidence, as though she'd thought through this very matter. "You were
happy and independent when the Vampire Lestat brought you over.
You told me so. Don't you give me credit for that much, David? Each
of us is different."

"Know that I love you, Merrick," I said softly.

"Don't try to say farewell, David. Come here and kiss me and come
back to me tomorrow night."

I went to the bed, and I took her in my arms. I kissed her on both
cheeks. And then in a sinful, wretchedly strong-willed manner, I kissed
her unresisting breasts, kissed both her nipples, and I drew back, full of
her scent and furious with myself.

"For now, darling," I said.

And I went out and home to the Rue Royale.

21

LOUIS WAS HOME when I reached the flat. I could sense his presence even as I came up the stairs. Only a few hours remained of the night for both of us, but I was so glad to see him that I went directly into the front parlor where he stood at the window, looking out over the Rue Royale below.

The room was full of lighted lamps, and the paintings of Matisse and Monet seemed to be singing on the walls.

He had taken off his bloodsoiled clothes, and wore now a simple turtleneck shirt of black cotton, and black pants. His shoes were old and tattered, but had once been very fine.

He turned as I entered the room, and I took him in my arms. With him, I could give vent to the affection I'd held so severely in check with Merrick. I held him to myself and kissed him as men might do with other men when they are alone. I kissed his dark black hair and kissed his eyes, and then I kissed his lips.

For the first time in our existence together, I felt a great outpouring of affection from him, a deep affinity, yet something else made him stiffen suddenly, against his will.

It was the pain in his chest from the wound.

"I should have come with you," I confessed. "I should never have let you go off, but I felt she needed me. And I remained with her. It was what I had to do."

"Of course, you did," he said, "and I wouldn't have allowed you to leave her. She needed you much more than I did. Never mind this wound; it's already healing. I've decades enough behind me on the Devil's Road that it will heal in a few nights."

"Not so, and you know it," I said. "Let me give you my blood, my blood's infinitely stronger. Don't turn away from me, man, listen to me. If you won't drink from me, then let me put my blood to the wound."

He was deeply distressed. He sat down in a chair and put his elbows on his knees. I couldn't see his face. I took the chair nearby and I waited.

"It will heal, I told you," he said softly.

I let the matter drop. What else could I do? Yet I could see that the wound was hurting him powerfully. I could tell it by his slightest gestures—how they began in utter fluidity, and were suddenly cut short.

"And the spirit, what did you make of it, yourself?" I asked. "Let me hear it from your lips before I tell you what Merrick felt, and what I saw."

"I know what you both think," he said. He looked up finally and sat back gingerly in the chair. For the first time I saw the darkness of the blood on his shirt. The wound was wretched. I didn't like it. I didn't like seeing blood on him any more than I liked seeing it on Merrick. It struck me hard how much I loved them both.

"You both think the spirit preyed upon my fears," he said calmly. "I knew it was what you'd say even before we ever began. But you see, I remember her too vividly. I know her French, I know her cadences, I know the very rhythm of her speech. And it was Claudia, and she had come out of darkness just as she confided, she had come from a terrible place where she's not at rest."

"You know my arguments," I said, shaking my head. "What will you do now? Whatever your plan, you can't go forward without telling me what it is."

"I know, *mon ami*, I'm aware of that," he answered. "And you must know now I won't be with you for very long."

"Louis, I beg you—."

"David, I'm weary," he said, "and I would swap one pain for another. There was something she said, you see, which I can't forget. She asked if I would give up my comforts for her? Do you remember?"

"No, old man, you've got it wrong. She asked if you'd give up your comforts for death, but she never promised that she would be there! That's just the point. She won't be. Good Lord, how many years in the Talamasca did I study the history of apparitions and their messages, how many years did I pore over first person accounts of those who'd trafficked with ghosts and recorded their wisdom. You can choose what you will believe about the hereafter. It doesn't matter. But once you choose death, Louis, you can't choose life again. Belief ends. Don't make that choice, I implore you. Stay for me, if you won't for any other reason. Stay for me, because I need you, and stay for Lestat, because he needs you as well."

Of course my words didn't surprise him. He put his left hand to his chest and pressed on the wound lightly, and a grimace, for one moment, disfigured his face.

He shook his head.

"For you and Lestat, yes, I've thought of that. And what of her? What of our lovely Merrick? What does she need from me too?"

It seemed he had a great deal more to say, but suddenly he fell silent, and his brows were knitted, and he looked young and impossibly innocent as his head quickly turned to the side.

"David, do you hear it?" he asked with mounting excitement. "David, listen!"

I heard nothing but the noises of the city.

"What is it, man?" I asked.

"David, listen to it. It's all around us." He rose to his feet, his left hand still pressed to the pain he felt. "David, it's Claudia, it's the music, it's the harpsichord. I hear it all around us. David, she wants me to come. I know it."

I was on my feet in a second. I took hold of him.

"You're not going to do it, friend, you can't do it without a farewell to Merrick, without a farewell to Lestat, and there are not enough hours left in this night for that."

He was gazing off, mesmerized and comforted, and his eyes were glazed and his face was softened and unchallenging. "I know that sonata. I remember it. And yes, she loved it, she loved it because Mozart had written it when he was only a child. You can't hear, can you? But you did once, think back on it. It's so very lovely, and how fast she plays, my Claudia."

He made a dazed laugh. The tears thickened; his eyes were veiled in blood.

"I hear the birds singing. Listen. I hear them in their cage. The others—all our kind who know of her—they think of her as heartless, but she wasn't heartless. She was only aware of things which I didn't learn till so many decades had passed. She knew secrets that only suffering can teach. . . ."

His voice trailed off. He pulled back gracefully from my grasp and he walked to the center of the room. He turned about as though the music were truly surrounding him.

"Don't you see what a kindness she's done?" he whispered. "It's going on and on, David, it's getting all the more rapid. Claudia, I'm listening to you." He broke off, and turned again, his eyes moving over everything yet seeing nothing. "Claudia, I'll be with you very soon."

"Louis," I said, "it's almost morning. Come with me now."

He stood still with his head bowed. His hands had dropped to his sides. He seemed infinitely sad and infinitely defeated.

"Has it stopped?" I asked.

"Yes," he whispered. Slowly he looked up, lost for the moment, then getting his bearings. He looked at me. "Two nights won't matter, will it? And then I can thank Merrick. I can give her the picture. The Talamasca may want it." He gestured to the nearby table, the low oval table which stood before the couch.

I saw the daguerreotype open on the table. Claudia's image jarred me as I met its gaze. I wanted to close the little case, but never mind. I knew that I could never allow the picture to fall into the hands of the Talamasca. I could never allow such a contact, let alone the possession of such a potent object by seers as powerful as Merrick. I could never allow such evidence to remain for the Talamasca to investigate whatever we had all seen this night.

But I didn't say this thing.

As for him, he stood as before, elegant in his faded black, a man dreaming, the blood dried in his eyes and giving him a dreadful look, as he stared off again, distant from my heated compassion, cutting himself off from any solace I could bring.

"You'll meet me tomorrow," I said.

He nodded. "The birds are gone now," he whispered. "I can't even hum the music inside my head." He seemed unbearably distressed.

"All is stillness in the place she described," I said rather desperately. "Think on that, Louis. And meet me tomorrow night."

"Yes, my friend, I've already promised," he said in a dazed manner.

He frowned as if trying to remember something in particular. "I have to thank Merrick, and you of course, you, old friend, who did everything that I asked."

We went out of the town house together.

He went off to the place where he lies by day, the location of which I didn't know.

I had more time than he had. Like Lestat, my powerful maker, I was not hounded by the first hint of dawn to the grave. The sun would have to come over the horizon for me to feel the paralytic vampire sleep.

Indeed, I had an hour or more perhaps, though the morning birds were singing in the few trees of the Quarter, and when I reached uptown the sky had turned from a deep dark blue to a faint purple twilight color, which I lingered to enjoy before I went inside the dusty building and up the stairs.

Nothing stirred in the old convent. Even the rats were gone from it. Its thick brick walls were chilly, though it was spring. My footfalls echoed as always. I allowed that. It was respectful to Lestat to allow it, to mark my coming before I entered his vast and simple domain.

The great yawning courtyard was empty. The birds sang loudly in the lush trees of Napoléon Avenue. I stopped to glance out from one of the upstairs windows. I wished I could sleep by day high in the branches of the nearby oak. What a mad thought, but perhaps somewhere, far away from all the pain we'd experienced here, there was some deep uninhabited forest where I could build a dark and thick cocoon for hiding among the branches, like an evil insect, dormant before it rises to bring death to its prey.

I thought of Merrick. I couldn't know what the coming day would be like for her. I feared for her. I despised myself. And I wanted Merrick terribly. I wanted Louis. I wanted them as my companions, and it was utterly selfish, and yet it seemed a creature could not live without the simple companionship which I had in mind.

At last I went in the great white-walled chapel. All the stained-glass windows were still draped in black serge, as was required now, for Lestat could no longer easily be moved to shelter with the rising sun.

No candles burnt before these random and stately saints.

I found Lestat as he always was, on his left side, a man resting, his violet eyes open, the lovely piano music pouring out of the black machine which had been set to play the small disc recording over and over without end.

The usual dust had settled on Lestat's hair and shoulders. It horrified me to see the dust, even on his face. But would I disturb him if I sought to clean it away? I didn't know, and my sorrow was leaden and terrible.

I sat down beside him.

I sat where he might see me. And then boldly I turned off the music. And in a hurried voice, a voice more full of agitation than ever I imagined it would be, I poured out the tale.

I told him all of it—of my love for Merrick and of her powers. I told him of Louis's request. I told him of the phantom that had come to us. I told him of Louis, listening to Claudia's music. I told him of Louis's resolve to leave us in a matter of nights.

"What can stop him now I don't know," I said. "He won't wait for you to wake, my dearest friend. He's going. And there's nothing I can do really to change his mind. I can plead that he must wait until you've recovered, but I don't think he wants to lose his nerve again. That's what it's all about, you see, his nerve. He has the nerve to end it. And that is what's been lacking for so long."

I went back over the details. I described Louis as he listened to the music that I couldn't hear. I described the séance once more. Perhaps I told things now which I'd left out before.

"Was it really Claudia?" I asked. "Who can tell us whether or not it was?"

And then I leant over and I kissed Lestat and I said to him:

"I need you so much now. I need you if only to say farewell to him."

I drew back and inspected the sleeping body. There was no change in awareness or posture that I could detect.

"You woke once," I declared. "You woke when Sybelle played her music for you, but then, taking the music back with you, you returned to your selfish sleep. That's what it is, Lestat, selfish, because you've left behind those you made—Louis and me. You've left us, and it's not fair of you to do it. You must come out of it, my beloved Master, you must rouse yourself for Louis and for me."

No change in the expression on his smooth face. His large violet eyes were too open for those of a dead man. But the body gave no other sign of life.

I leant down. I pressed my ear to his cold cheek. Though I couldn't read his thoughts as a fledging, surely I could divine something of what went on in his soul.

But nothing came to me. I turned on the music once more.

I kissed him and left him there, and went to my lair, more ready for oblivion perhaps than I had ever been before.

22

THE FOLLOWING NIGHT, I went in search of Merrick.

Her home in the derelict neighborhood was dark and unin-habited. Only the caretaker remained on the property. And it was no problem for me to climb up to the second story window over the shed to see that the old fellow was contentedly inside, drinking his beer and watching his monstrous color TV.

I was dreadfully disconcerted. I felt that Merrick had all but prom-ised to meet me, and where else if not in the old house?

I had to find her. I searched the city for her tirelessly, using every ounce of telepathic ability which I possessed.

As for Louis, he was also absent. I returned to the flat in the Rue Royale more than four times during my search for Merrick. And at no time did I find Louis or the simplest evidence that he'd been there.

At last, very much against my better judgment, but desperate, I approached Oak Haven, the Motherhouse, to see if I could spy Mer-rick within.

The discovery took only a matter of minutes. As I stood in the thick oak forest to the far north of the building, I could see her tiny figure in the library.

Indeed Merrick sat in the very oxblood leather chair which she'd claimed for her own as a child when we first met. Nestled in the cracked old leather, she appeared to be sleeping, but as I drew closer my fine vampiric senses confirmed that she was drunk. I could make out the bottle of Flor de Caña rum beside her, and the glass. Both were empty.

As for the other members, one was busy in the very same room, going over the shelves for some seemingly routine matter, and several others were at home upstairs.

I couldn't conceivably approach Merrick where she was. And I was keenly aware that Merrick might have planned this. And if she had planned it, it might have been for her own mental safety, a cause of which I highly approved.

Once released from that tidy little spectacle—Merrick out cold with no regard for what the other members thought of her—I resumed my search for Louis from one end of the town to the next with no luck.

The hours before dawn found me striding back and forth before the slumbering figure of Lestat in the darkened chapel, explaining to him that Merrick had delivered herself into hiding and that Louis appeared to be gone.

At last I sat down on the cold marble floor, as I had done the night before.

"I'd know it, wouldn't I?" I demanded of my sleeping master. "If Louis has put an end to himself, isn't that so? I'd feel it somehow, wouldn't I? If it happened at dawn yesterday, I would have felt it before I ever closed my eyes."

Lestat gave no answer and there was no promise in his posture or facial expression that he ever would.

I felt as if I were speaking fervently to one of the statues of the saints.

When the second night went in exactly the same fashion, I was thoroughly unnerved.

Whatever Merrick had done by day, I couldn't imagine, but once again she was drunk in the library, a slouched figure, quite alone now, in one of her splendid silk shirtwaist dresses, this one a vivid red. While I watched from a safe distance, one of the members, an old man whom I once knew and loved dearly, came into the library and covered up Merrick with a white wool blanket that looked quite soft.

I sped off lest I be detected.

As for Louis, as I prowled those portions of the city which were always his favorites, I cursed myself that I'd been so respectful of his mind that I'd never learnt to read it, so respectful of his privacy that I'd never learnt to scan for his presence; cursed myself that I'd not bound him to a strong promise to meet me in the flat in the Rue Royale at a certain time.

At last the third night came.

Having given up on Merrick to do anything but intoxicate herself thoroughly with rum in her typical fashion, I went directly to the flat in the Rue Royale with the purpose of writing a note for Louis, should it be that he was stopping in when I was not there.

I was filled with misery. It now seemed entirely possible to me that Louis no longer existed in his earthly form. It seemed entirely reasonable that he had let the morning sun cremate him precisely as he wanted, and that I was writing words in this note that would never be read.

Nevertheless, I sat down at Lestat's fancy desk in the back parlor, the desk which faces the room, and I wrote hastily.

" 'You must talk with me. You must let me talk with you. It's unfair for you not to do this. I am so anxious on your behalf. Remember, L., that I did what you asked of me. I cooperated with you completely. Of course I had my motives. I'm willing to admit them candidly. I missed her. My heart was breaking for her. But you must let me know how things go with you.' "

I had scarcely finished writing the initial "D," when I looked up and saw Louis standing in the hallway door.

Quite unharmed, his black curly hair combed, he stood looking at me searchingly, and I, pleasantly shocked, sat back and gave a deep sigh.

"Look at you, and here I've been racing around like a madman," I said. I surveyed his handsome gray velvet suit, and the dark-violet tie he wore with it. In amazement I noted the jeweled rings on his hands.

"Why all this unusual attention to your person?" I asked. "Talk to me, man. I'm quite ready to go out of my mind."

He shook his head, and gestured quickly with his longer slender hand for me to be quiet. He sat down on the couch across the room and stared at me.

"I've never seen you so fancily dressed," I said. "You're positively dapper. What's happened?"

"I don't know what's happened," he said almost sharply. "You have to tell me." He gestured urgently. "Come here, David, take your old chair here, sit close to me."

I did as I was asked.

He wasn't only handsomely turned out, he wore a faint masculine perfume.

His eyes flashed on me with a nervous energy.

"I can't think of anything but her, David. I tell you, it's as if I never loved Claudia," he confessed, his voice breaking. "I mean it, it's as if I never knew love or grief before I met Merrick. It's as if I'm Merrick's slave. No matter where I go, no matter what I do, I think of Merrick," he declared. "When I feed, the victim turns to Merrick in my very arms. Hush, don't say anything till I'm finished. I think of Merrick when I lie in my coffin before the coming sunlight. I think of Merrick when I wake up. I must go to Merrick, and as soon as I've fed, I go to where I can see her, David, yes, near the Motherhouse, the place you long ago forbade us ever to trouble. I go there. I was there last night when you came to spy on her. I saw you. The night before, I was there as well. I live for her, and the sight of her through those long windows only inflames me, David. I want her. If she doesn't come out of that place soon, I tell you, whether I mean to or not, I'm going in after her, though what I want of her, except to be with her, I swear to you, I can't say."

"Stop it, Louis, let me explain what's happened—."

"How the hell can you explain such a thing? Let me pour it out, man," he said. "Let me confess that it all began when I laid eyes on her. You knew it. You saw it. You tried to warn me. But I had no idea that the feelings would become so very intense. I was certain I could control them. Good Lord, how many mortals have I resisted over these two centuries, how many times have I turned my back on some random soul who drew me so painfully that I had to weep?"

"Stop it, Louis, listen to me."

"I won't hurt her, David," he said, "I swear it. I don't want to hurt her. I can't bear the thought of feeding from her as I once did from Claudia, oh, that awful awful mistake, the making of Claudia. I won't hurt her, I swear it, but I must see her, I must be with her, I must hear her voice. David, can you get her out of Oak Haven? Can you make her meet with me? Can you make her stop her love affair with her rum and come to her old house? You must be able to do it. I tell you, I'm losing my mind."

He had scarcely paused when I broke in and would not be silenced.

"She's fixed you, Louis!" I declared. "It's a spell. Now, you must be quiet and listen to me. I know her tricks. And I know magic. And hers is a magic as old as Egypt, as old as Rome and Greece. She's fixed you, man, made you fall in love with her through witchcraft. Damn, I should have never let her keep that bloodstained dress. No wonder she wouldn't let me touch it. It had your blood on it. Oh, what a fool I was not to see what she was doing. We even talked of such charms together. Oh, she is beyond all patience. I let her keep that blood-stained silk dress, and she's used it to make an age-old charm."

"No, that's not possible," he said caustically. "I simply won't accept it. I love her, David. You force me to use the words that will hurt you most of all. I love her, and I want her; I want her company, I want the wisdom and the kindness that I saw in her. It's no spell."

"It is, man, believe me," I said. "I know her and I know magic. She used your blood to do it. Don't you see, this woman not only believes in magic, she understands it. Perhaps a million mortal magicians have lived and died during the past millennia, but how many of them were the genuine article? She knows what she's doing! Your blood was in the weave of her own garment. She's cast a spell on you that I don't know how to break!"

He was silent but not for very long.

"I don't believe you," he said. "No, it can't be true. I feel this too completely."

"Think back, Louis, on what I told you of her, of the visions of her I had after our first contact only a few nights ago. You remember, I told you I saw her everywhere—."

"This is not the same. I'm speaking of my heart, David—."

"It is the same, man," I insisted. "I saw her everywhere, and after we saw the vision of Claudia, Merrick admitted to me that those visions of her were part of a spell. I told you all this, Louis. I told you about her little altar in the hotel room, the way she'd gotten my handkerchief with my blood on it from the sweat of my brow. Louis, pay attention."

"You're vilifying her," he said as gently as he could, "and I won't have it. I don't see her in that manner. I think of her and want her. I want the woman I saw in that room. What will you tell me next? That Merrick wasn't beautiful? That Merrick wasn't filled with innate sweetness? That Merrick wasn't the one mortal in thousands whom I might come to love?"

"Louis, do you trust yourself in her presence?" I demanded.

"Yes, I trust myself," he answered righteously. "You think I would harm her?"

"I think you have learnt the meaning of the word 'desire.'"

"The desire is to be in her company, David. It's to be close to her.

It's to talk with her about what I saw. It's . . ." His voice trailed off. He shut his eyes tight for a moment. "It's unbearable, this need of her, this longing for her. And she hides in that huge house in the country, and I can't be near to her without hurting the Talamasca, without rupturing the delicate privacy on which our very existence depends."

"Thank God you have that much sense," I said forcefully. "I tell you it is a spell, and if you trust yourself with her, then as soon as she leaves that house, we'll go together and ask her! We'll demand the truth from her. Demand from her whether or not this is nothing but a spell."

"Nothing," he repeated the word contemptuously, "nothing, you say, *nothing but a spell?*" He peered into my eyes accusingly. Never had I seen him so hostile. In fact, never had I seen him hostile at all. "You don't want me to love her, do you? It's just as simple as all that."

"No, it isn't, truly it isn't. But say for instance that you're right, that there is no spell, and only your heart's speaking to you; do I want this love of her to increase in you? No, definitely not. We made a vow, you and I, that this woman wouldn't be hurt by us, that we wouldn't destroy her fragile mortal world with our desires! Keep to that vow if you love her so damned much, Louis. That's what loving her means, you realize. It means leaving her completely alone."

"I can't do it," he whispered. He shook his head. "She deserves to know what my heart is telling me. She deserves that truth. Nothing will ever come of it, nothing can, but she ought to know it. She ought to know that I'm devoted to her, that she's supplanted a grief in me which could have destroyed me, which may destroy me still."

"This is intolerable," I said. I was so angry with Merrick. "I propose we approach Oak Haven. But you must allow me to direct what we do there. If I can, I'll draw close to the window, and I'll try to wake her. It's possible, in the small hours, that she'll be alone on the main floor. I might possibly be able to go inside. Nights ago I would have considered such an act unconscionable. But remember, you must leave such a gesture to me."

He nodded. "I want to be near her. But I must feed first. I can't be thirsting when I see her. That would be foolish. Come with me to hunt. And then, after midnight, well after midnight, we'll approach."

It didn't take us long to find our victims.

It was the hour of two a.m. when we drew close to Oak Haven, and, as I'd hoped, the house was darkened throughout. No one remained awake. It took me only a few moments to survey the library.

Merrick wasn't there. Her rum and her glass weren't there, either. And when I went along the upper galleries, as quietly as I could, I did not find her in her room.

I came back to Louis in the thick of the oaks, as he waited.

"She's not at Oak Haven. I feel we've miscalculated. She must be at her home in New Orleans. She's probably there waiting, waiting for her little spell to do its work."

"You can't go on despising her for all this," Louis said angrily. "David, for the love of Heaven, allow me to go to her alone."

"Not a chance of it," I answered.

We proceeded towards the city.

"You can't approach her with this contempt for her," said Louis. "Let me talk to her. You can't prevent it. You have no right."

"I will be there when you talk to her," I said coldly. And I meant to keep my word.

When we reached the old house in New Orleans, I knew immediately that Merrick was at home.

Bidding Louis to wait, I went around the property, as I had several nights ago, made certain the caretaker had been sent off, and indeed, he had been, and then I returned to Louis, and I said we could approach the door.

As for Merrick, I knew she was in the front bedroom. The parlor didn't mean much to her. It was Great Nananne's room that she loved.

"I want to go alone," said Louis. "You can wait here, if you wish."

He was on the porch before I'd moved, but I quickly caught up with him. He opened the unlocked front door, its leaded glass glinting in the light.

Once inside he went into the large front bedroom. I was just behind him.

I saw Merrick, as lovely as ever in a dress of red silk, rise from her rocking chair and fly into his arms.

Every particle of my being was on alert for danger, and my heart was breaking in two. The room was dreamy and sweet with its vigilant candles.

And they loved each other, this pair of beings, Louis and Merrick, there was no denying it. I watched silently as Louis kissed Merrick repeatedly, as he ran his long white fingers through her hair. I watched as he kissed her long throat.

He drew back and he let out a long sigh.

"A spell, is it?" he asked her, but the question was really meant for me. "That I can think of nothing but you, no matter where I go, or what I do? That in each victim I take, I find you? Oh, yes, think on it, Merrick, think on what I do to survive, don't please live in dreams. Think of the awful price of this power. Think of the Purgatory in which I live."

"Am I with you in that Purgatory?" asked Merrick. "Do I give you some consolation in the very midst of the fire? My days and nights without you have been Purgatory. I understand your suffering. I did before we ever looked into each other's eyes."

"Tell him the truth, Merrick," I said. I stood apart from them, near the door. "Speak true words, Merrick. He'll know if you're lying. Is this a spell you've put over him? Don't lie to me, either, Merrick."

She broke away from him for the moment. She looked at me.

"What did I give *you* with my spell, David?" she said. "What was it but random visions? Did you feel desire?" She looked again at Louis. "What do you want from me, Louis? To hear that my soul is your slave as surely as your soul is mine? If that's a spell, we've fixed each other with it, Louis. David knows I speak the truth."

Try as I might, I could find no lie in her. What I found were secrets, and I couldn't crack them open. Her thoughts were too well guarded.

"You play a game," I said. "What is it you want?"

"No, David, you mustn't speak to her in that manner," said Louis, "I won't tolerate it. Go now and let me talk to her. She's safer with me than Claudia ever was or any mortal I've ever touched. Go now, David. Let me alone with her. Or I swear, man, it will be a battle between you and me."

"David, please," said Merrick. "Let me have these few hours with him; then the rest will be as you wish. I want him here with me. I want to talk to him. I want to tell him that the spirit was a liar. I need to do that slowly, I need an atmosphere of intimacy and trust."

She came towards me, the red silk rustling as she walked. I caught her perfume. She put her arms around me and I felt the warmth of her naked breasts beneath the thin cloth.

"Go now, David, please," she said, her voice full of gentle emotion, her face compassionate as she looked into my eyes.

Never in all my years of knowing her, wanting her, missing her—
had anything hurt so much as this simple request.

"Go." I repeated the word in a small voice. "Leave you both
together? Go?"

I looked into her eyes for a long moment. How she seemed to suffer, how she seemed to implore me. And then I turned to Louis, who
watched with an innocent anxious expression, as if his fate was in my
hands.

"Harm her and I swear to you," I said, "your wish for death will be
granted." My voice was low and too full of malice. "I tell you I'm
strong enough to destroy you in precisely the way you fear."

I saw the terrible dismay in his expression.

"It will be by fire," I said, "and it will be slowly, if you harm her." I
paused. Then: "I give you my word."

I saw him swallow hard and then he nodded. It seemed there was
much he wanted to say to me, and his eyes were sad and eloquent of a
deeper pain. At last he murmured in answer:

"Trust me, my brother. You needn't make such terrible threats to
one you cherish, and I needn't hear them, not when both of us love this
mortal woman so very much."

I turned to her. Her eyes were on Louis. She was as distant from me
in these moments as she had ever been. I kissed her tenderly. She
scarcely looked at me, returning my kisses as if she must remind herself
to do it, as smitten with Louis as he was with her.

"Goodbye for now, my precious," I whispered, and I went out of
the house.

For one moment, I considered remaining, concealed in the shrubbery, spying upon both of them as they talked to each other inside the
front room. It seemed the wise thing to do, to remain nearby, for her
protection; and it seemed the very thing she would hate.

She would know I was there more surely than Louis could ever
know it—know as she had known that night when I came to her window at Oak Haven, know with a witch's sensibility that was stronger
than his vampiric powers, know and condemn me utterly for what I
tried to do.

When I thought of the possibility of her coming out to accuse me,
when I thought of the humiliation I might risk with such a choice, I left
the house behind me and walked fast, and alone, uptown.

Once again, in the desolate chapel of St. Elizabeth's Orphanage, Lestat was my confidant.

And once again, I was certain that no spirit occupied his body. To my woes he gave no ear.

I only prayed that Merrick would be safe, that Louis would not risk my rage, and that some night Lestat's soul would return to his body, because I needed him. I needed him desperately. I felt alone with all my years and all my lessons, with all my experiences and all my pain.

The sky was growing dangerously light when I left Lestat and made my way to the secret place, below an abandoned building where I kept the iron coffin in which I lie.

This is no unusual configuration among our kind—the sad old building, my title to it, or the cellar room cut off from the world above by iron doors no mortal could independently seek to lift.

I had lain down in the frigid darkness, the cover of the casket in its place, when I was suddenly overcome with the strangest panic. It was as if someone were speaking to me, demanding that I listen, seeking to tell me that I had made a dreadful error, and that I would pay for it with my conscience; that I had done a foolish and vain thing.

It was too late for me to respond to this lively mixture of emotion. The morning crept over me, stealing all warmth and life from me. And the last thought I remember was that I had left the two of them alone out of vanity, because they had excluded me. I had behaved like a schoolboy out of vanity, and I would pay as the result.

Inevitably the sunset followed on the sunrise, and, after some unmeasured sleep, I woke to the new evening, my eyes open, my hands reaching at once for the lid of the coffin and then withdrawing and falling to my sides.

Something kept me from opening the coffin just yet. Even though I hated its stifling atmosphere, I remained in this, the only true blackness ever bequeathed to my powerful vampire eyes.

I remained, because last night's panic had come back to me—that keen awareness that I'd been a proud fool to leave Merrick and Louis alone. It seemed some turbulence in the very air surrounded me, indeed, penetrated the iron of the coffin so that I might breathe it into my lungs.

Something has gone horridly wrong, yet it was inevitable, I thought dismally, and I lay motionless, as if fixed by one of Merrick's ruthless spells. But it was not a spell of her doing. It was grief and regret—terrible, harrowing regret.

I had lost her to Louis. Of course I'd find her unharmed, for nothing on earth could make Louis give her the Dark Blood, I reasoned, nothing, not even Merrick's own pleas. And as for her, she would never request it, never be fool enough to relinquish her brilliant and unique soul. No, it was grief because they loved each other, those two, and I'd brought them together, and now they would have whatever might have belonged to Merrick and me.

Well, I could not mourn for it. It was done, and I must go and find them now, I reasoned. I must go and find them together, and see the manner in which they looked at each other, and I must wring more promises from them, which was nothing more than a means of interposing myself between them, and then I must accept that Louis had become the brilliant star for Merrick, and by that light I shone no more.

Only after a long while did I open the coffin, the lid creaking loudly, and step out of it, and begin my assent, up through the steps of the damp old cellar, towards the dreary rooms above.

At last I came to a stop in a great unused brick-walled room which had once many years ago served as a department store. Nothing remained now of its former glory except a few very dirty display cases and broken shelves, and a thick layer of soil on its old uneven wooden floor.

I stood in the spring heat and in the soft dust, breathing in the scent of the mold and the red bricks around me, and peering towards the unwashed show windows, beyond which the street, now much neglected, gave forth its few persistent and sorrowful lights.

Why was I standing here?

Why had I not gone directly out to meet Louis and Merrick? Why had I not gone to feed, if it was blood I wanted, and indeed, I did thirst, I knew that much. Why did I stand alone in the shadows, waiting, as if for my grief to be redoubled, as if for my loneliness to be sharpened, so that I would hunt with the fine-tuned senses of a beast?

Then, gradually, the awareness stole over me, separating me totally from the melancholy surroundings, so I tingled in every portion of my being as my eyes saw what my mind wanted desperately to deny.

Merrick stood before me in the very red silk of last night's brief meeting, and all her physiognomy was changed by the Dark Gift.

Her creamy skin was almost luminous with vampiric powers; her green eyes had taken on the iridescence so common to Lestat, Armand, Marius, yes, yes, and yes again, yes, all of the rest. Her long brown hair had its unholy luster, and her beautiful lips their inevitable, eternal, and perfect unnatural sheen.

"David," she cried out, even her distinctive voice colored by the blood inside her, and she flew into my arms.

"Oh, dear God in Heaven, how could I have let it happen!" I was unable to touch her, my hands hovering above her shoulders, and suddenly I gave in to the embrace with all my heart. "God forgive me. God forgive me!" I cried out even as I held her tight enough to harm her, held her close to me as if no one could ever pry her loose. I didn't care if mortals heard me. I didn't care if all the world knew.

"No, David, wait," she begged as I went to speak again. "You don't understand what's happened. He's done it, David, he's gone into the sun. He did it at dawn, after he'd taken me and hidden me away, and showed me everything he could, and promised me that he would meet me tonight. He's done it, David. He's gone, and there's nothing left of him now that isn't burnt black."

The terrible tears flooding down her cheeks were glittering with unwholesome blood.

"David, can't you do anything to rescue him? Can't you do anything to bring him back? It's all my fault that it happened. David, I knew what I was doing, I led him into it, I worked him so skillfully. I did use his blood and I used the silk of my dress. I used every power natural and unnatural. I'll confess to more when there's time for it. I'll pour it all out to you. It's my fault that he's gone, I swear it, but can't you bring him back?"

H E HAD DONE a most careful thing.

He had brought his coffin, a relic of venerable age and luster, to the rear courtyard of the town house in the Rue Royale, a most secluded and high-walled place.

He had left his last letter on the desk upstairs, a desk which all of us—I, Lestat, and Louis—had at one time used for important writings of our own. Then he had gone down into the courtyard, and he had removed the lid from the coffin, and he had laid down in it to receive the morning sun.

He had addressed to me his candid farewell.

If I am correct I will be cremated by the sunlight. I am not old enough to remain as one severely burned, or young enough to bequeath bloody flesh to those who come to carry off what is left. I shall be ashes as Claudia once was ashes, and you, my beloved David, must scatter those ashes for me.

That you will oversee my final release is quite beyond doubt, for by the time you come upon what is left of me, you will have seen Merrick and you will know the measure of my treachery and the measure of my love.

Yes, I plead love in the matter of what I've done in creating Merrick a vampire. I cannot lie to you on this score. But if it matters at all, let me assure you that I imagined I meant only to frighten her, to bring her close to death so as to deter her, to force her to beg to be saved.

But once begun, the process was brought by me to a speedy conclusion, with the purest ambition and the purest yearning

I've ever known. And now—being the romantic fool I have always been, being the champion of questionable actions and little endurance, being quite unable as always to live with the price of my will and my desires, I bequeath to you this exquisite fledgling, Merrick, whom I know you will love with an educated heart.

Whatever your hatred of me, I ask that you give to Merrick the few jewels and relics I possess. I ask that you give over to her also all those paintings which I have collected so haphazardly over the centuries, paintings which have become masterpieces in my eyes and in the eyes of the world. Anything of worth should be hers if only you concur.

As for my sweet Master, Lestat, when he wakes, tell him that I went into the darkness without hoping for his terrifying angels, that I went into the darkness expecting only the whirlwind, or the nothingness, both of which he has in his own words so often described. Ask him to forgive me that I could not wait to take my leave of him.

Which brings me now to you, my friend. I do not hope for your forgiveness. Indeed, I do not even ask.

I don't believe you can bring me back from the ashes to torment me, but if you think you can, and you succeed with it, your will be done. That I have betrayed your trust is beyond doubt. No talk from Merrick of her potent spells can excuse my actions, though in fact, she does indeed claim to have brought me to her with magic I cannot understand.

What I understand is that I love her, and cannot think of existence without her. Yet existence is no longer something which I can contemplate at all.

I go now to what I regard as a certainty; the form of death which took my Claudia—relentless, inescapable, absolute.

That was the letter, written in his archaic hand on new parchment paper, the letters tall yet deeply impressed.

And the body?

Had he guessed correctly, and had he become ashes like the child he'd lost to bitter fortune so long ago?

Quite simply, no.

In the lidless coffin, open to the night air, there lay a burnt black replica of the being I had known as Louis, as seemingly solid as any ancient mummy stripped of its wrappings, flesh closed securely over all visible bone. The clothes were severely scorched yet intact. The coffin was blackened around the gruesome figure. The face and hands—indeed, the entire form—was untouched by the wind and included the most minute detail.

And there beside it, on her knees on the cold paving stones, was Merrick, gazing down at the coal-black body, her hands clasped in grief.

Slowly, ever so slowly, she reached forward, and with her tender first finger touched the back of Louis's burnt hand. At once, she drew back in horror. I saw no impression made in the blackened flesh.

"It's hard as coal, David," she cried. "How can the wind scatter these remains unless you take them from the coffin and trample them underfoot? You can't do it, David. Tell me you cannot."

"No, I can't do it!" I declared. I began to pace frantically. "Oh, what a thankless and miserable legacy," I whispered. "Louis, I would I could bury you as you were."

"That could be the most dreadful cruelty," she said imploringly. "David, can he still be living in this form? David, you know the stories of the vampires better than I do. David, can he still be alive in this form?"

Back and forth I went past her, without answering her, past the lifeless effigy in its charred clothing, and I looked up listlessly, miserably, to the distant stars.

Behind me, I heard her crying softly, giving full vent to emotions which now raged inside her with a new vigor, passions that would sweep over her so totally no human could gauge what she felt.

"David," she called out to me. I could hear her weeping.

Slowly I turned to look down on her as she knelt beside him, appealing to me as if I were one of her saints.

"David, if you cut your wrist, if you let the blood flow down onto him, what will happen, will he come back?"

"That's just it, my darling, I don't know. I know only he's done as he wished and he's told me what he would have me do."

"But you can't let him go so easily," she protested. "David, please . . ." Helplessly, her voice died away.

A faint stirring of the air caught the banana trees. I turned and looked at the body in terror. All the garden around us whispered and sighed against the brick walls. But the body remained intact, immobile, safe in its burnt sanctuary.

But another breeze would come, something stronger. Maybe even the rain would come, as it did so often on these warm spring nights, and it would wash away the face, with its closed eyes, which was so visible still.

I couldn't find words to stop her crying. I couldn't find words to confess my heart. Was he gone, or was he lingering? And what would he have me do now—not last night when in the safety of the morning twilight he'd written his brave letter, but now, now, if he were locked in the form in the burnt wooden box.

What had been his thoughts when the sun had risen, when he'd felt the fatal weakness and then the inevitable fire? He hadn't the strength of the great ones to climb from his coffin and bury himself deep under fresh earth. Had he regretted his actions? Did he feel intolerable pain? Could I not learn something merely from studying his still burnt face or his hands?

I came back to the side of the coffin. I saw that his head was laid there as properly as that of any body to be formally interred. I saw that his hands were clasped loosely over his chest, as an undertaker might have placed them. He had not reached to shield his eyes. He had not tried to turn his back on death.

But what did these aspects of the matter really mean?

Perhaps he hadn't had the strength to do those things in the final moments. He had been numb with the coming of the light until it filled his eyes and made him shut them. Did I dare to touch the fragile blackened flesh? Did I dare to see if the eyes were still there?

I was lost in these hideous thoughts, lost and wanting only some other sound except that of Merrick's soft tears.

I went to the iron steps, which came down in a curve from the upstairs balcony. And I sat down on the step which provided for me the most comfortable rest. I put my face in my hands.

"Scatter the remains," I whispered. "If only the others were here."

At once, as if in answer to my pathetic prayer, I heard the creak of the carriageway gate. I heard the low shriek of its old hinges as it was thrown open, and then the click as it was closed once more, iron upon iron.

No scent of a mortal signaled an intruder. In fact, I knew the step that was approaching. I had heard it so many times in my life both mortal and preternatural. Yet I didn't dare to believe in such a rescue from my misery, until the unheralded figure appeared in the courtyard, his velvet coat dusty, his yellow hair tangled, his violet eyes looking at once to the grim and appalling visage of Louis:

It was Lestat.

With an awkward step, as though his body, so long unused, revolted against him, he made his way closer to Merrick, who turned her tear-stained face to him as if she too were seeing a Savior come in answer to her directionless prayers.

She sat back, a low sigh escaping her lips.

"So it's come to this, has it?" Lestat asked. His voice was hoarse, as it had been when he was waked by Sybelle's music, the very last time he'd abandoned his endless sleep.

He turned and looked to me, his smooth face devoid of warmth or expression, the thin light from the distant street illuminating his fierce eyes as he looked away and back to the body in the coffin on the stones. I think his eyes quivered. I think his whole body shivered ever so slightly as though the simplest movements were exhausting him, as if he longed to rub the backs of his own arms and beat a hasty retreat.

But he was not about to abandon us.

"Come here, David," he said, appealing to me kindly in the same hoarse whisper. "Come, and listen. I can't hear him. I made him. Listen, and tell me if he's there."

I obeyed him. I stood beside him.

"He's like coal, Lestat," I answered quickly. "I haven't dared to touch him. Should we do it?"

Slowly, languidly, Lestat turned to look down again at the painful sight.

"His skin feels firm, I tell you," Merrick said quickly. She rose to her feet and backed away from the coffin, inviting Lestat to take her place. "Test it yourself, Lestat," she said. "Come, touch him." Her voice was full of suppressed pain.

"And you?" Lestat asked reaching out for her, clasping her shoulder with his right hand. "What do you hear, *chérie*?" he asked in his raw whisper.

She shook her head. "Silence," she said, her lips trembling, the blood tears having left their streaks on her pale cheeks. "But then he brought me over. I charmed him, I seduced him. He had no chance against my plan. And now this, this for my interference, this, and I can hear the mortals whispering in the houses near to us, but I hear nothing from him."

"Merrick," he pressed. "Listen as you've always been able to listen. Be the witch now, still, if you can't be the vampire. Yes, I know, he made you. But a witch you were before that." He looked from one to the other of us, some little visible emotion quickening in him. "Tell me if he wants to come back."

The tears came to her eyes again. Grieving, miserable, she looked down at the seeming corpse.

"He could be crying for life," she said, "but I can't hear it. The witch in me hears nothing but silence. And the human being in me knows only remorse. Lestat, give your blood to him. Bring him back."

Lestat turned from her to me.

She reached out for his arm, and forced him to look again at her.

"Work your magic," she said in a low heated and insistent tone. "Work your magic and believe in it as I worked mine."

He nodded, covering her hand gently as if to soothe her, most certainly to soothe her.

"Speak to me, David," he said in his roughened voice. "What does *he want*, David? Did he do this thing because he made Merrick, and he thought for that he should pay with his life?"

How could I answer? How could I be faithful now to all my companion had confided over so many nights?

"I hear nothing," I said. "But then it is an old habit, not spying on his thoughts, not ravaging his soul. It is an old habit letting him do what he wishes, only now and then offering him the strong blood, never challenging his weaknesses. I hear nothing. I hear nothing, but what does it mean that I hear nothing? I walk in the cemeteries of this city at night and I hear nothing. I walk among mortals and sometimes I hear nothing. I walk alone and I hear nothing, as if I myself had no inner voice."

I looked down at his blackened face again. I could see the perfect image of his mouth there. And now I realized that even the hairs of his head remained intact.

"I hear nothing," I said, "and yet I see spirits. Many a time I have seen spirits. Many a time they've come to me. Is there a spirit lurking there in those remains? I don't know."

Lestat appeared to stagger, as if from a constitutional weakness, then he forced himself to remain upright. I felt ashamed when I saw the gray dust coating the velvet of his long sleeves. I felt ashamed when I saw the knots and dirt in his thick flowing hair. But these things didn't matter to him.

Nothing mattered to him but the figure in the coffin, and, as Merrick wept, he reached out almost absently and put his right arm around her, gathering her against his powerful body, and saying in a hoarse whisper,

"There, there, *chérie*. He did what he wanted."

"But it's gone wrong!" she answered. The words spilled out of her. "He's too old for one day's fire to end it. And he may be locked inside these charred remains in fear of what's to come. He might, like a dying man, hear us in his fatal trance and be unable to respond." She moaned plaintively as she continued: "He may be crying for us to help him, and we stand here and we argue and we pray."

"And if I spill my blood down into this coffin now," Lestat asked her, "what do you think will come back? Do you think it will be our Louis that will rise in these burnt rags? What if it's not, *chérie*, what if it's some wounded revenant that we must destroy?"

"Choose life, Lestat," she said. She turned to him, pulled loose of him, and appealed to him. "Choose life, no matter in what form. Choose life and bring him back. If he would die, it can be finished afterwards."

"My blood's too strong now, *chérie*," said Lestat. He cleared his throat and wiped at the dust on his own eyelids. He ran his hand into his hair and pulled it roughly out of his face. "My blood will make a monster of what's there."

"Do it!" she said. "And if he wants to die, if he asks again, then I will be his servant in his extremity, I promise you." How seductive were her eyes, her voice. "I'll make a brew that he can swallow, of poisons in the blood of animals, the blood of wild things. I'll feed him such a potion that he'll sleep as the sun rises." Her voice became more impassioned. "He'll sleep, and should he live again to sunset, I'll be his guardian through the night until the sun rises again."

For a long time, Lestat's brilliant violet eyes were fastened to her, as though he were considering her will, her plan, her very commitment, and then slowly he turned his eyes to me.

"And you, beloved one? What would you have me do?" he asked. His face had now a livelier aspect to it, for all his sorrow.

"I can't tell you," I said, shaking my head. "You've come and it's your decision, yours by right, because you are the eldest and I'm thankful that you're here." Then I found myself prey to the most awful and grim considerations, and I looked down at the dark figure again, and up once more to Lestat.

"If I had tried and failed," I said, "I would want to come back."

What was it that made me give voice to such a sentiment? Was it fear? I couldn't say. But it was true, and I knew it, as if my lips had sought to instruct my heart.

"Yes, if I had seen the sun rise," I said, "and I had lived past it, I might well have lost my courage, and courage he very much required."

Lestat seemed to be considering these things. How could he not? Once, he himself had gone into the sunlight in a distant desert place, and, having been burnt again and again, without release, he came back. His skin was still golden from this hurtful and terrible disaster. He would carry that imprint of the sun's power for many years to come.

Straightaway, he stepped in front of Merrick, and as both of us watched, he knelt down beside the coffin, and he moved very close to the figure, and then he drew back. With his fingers, quite as delicately as she had done it, he touched the blackened hands, and he left no mark. Slowly, lightly, he touched the forehead, and once more, he left no mark.

He drew back, kneeling up, and, lifting his right hand to his mouth, he gashed his wrist with his own teeth before either Merrick or I knew what he meant to do.

At once a thick stream of blood poured down onto the perfectly molded face of the figure in the coffin, and as the vein sought to heal itself, again Lestat gashed it and let the blood flow.

"Help me, Merrick. Help me, David!" he called out. "What I've begun I'll pay for, but do not let it fail. I need you now."

At once, I went to join him, pushing back my awkward cotton cuff and tearing the flesh of my wrist with my eye teeth. Merrick knelt at the very foot of the coffin, and from her tender fledgling wrist the blood had begun to flow.

A pungent smoke rose from the remains in front of us. The blood appeared to seep into every pore of the figure. It drenched the burnt clothing. And, tearing aside this fabric, Lestat gave yet another gush of blood to his frantic work.

The smoke was a thick layer above the bloody remains before us. I couldn't see through it. But I could hear a faint murmuring, a terrible agonized groan. On and on I let the blood flow, my preternatural skin seeking to heal and halt the operation, and my teeth coming to my rescue again and again.

Suddenly a cry came from Merrick. I saw before me in the haze the figure of Louis sitting up from the coffin, his face a mass of tiny lines and wrinkles. I saw Lestat reach out for him and take hold of his head and press it to his throat.

"Drink now, Louis," he commanded.

"Don't stop, David," said Merrick. "The blood, he needs it, every part of his body is drinking it."

I obeyed, only then realizing that I was growing weaker and weaker, that I could not remain steady, and that she herself was tumbling forward yet still determined to go on.

I saw below me a naked foot, and then the outline of a man's leg, and then, quite visible in the semi-darkness, the hard muscles of a man's chest.

"Harder, yes, take it from me," came Lestat's low insistent command. He spoke in French now. "Harder, more of it, take it, take all that I have to give."

My vision was hopeless. It seemed the entire courtyard was full of a pungent vapor, and the two forms—Louis and Lestat—shimmered for a moment before I felt myself lie down on the cool soothing stones, before I felt Merrick's soft body snuggled beside me, before I smelled the sweet lovely perfume of Merrick's hair. My head rolled on the stones as I tried to raise my hands, but could not.

I closed my eyes. I saw nothing, and then when I opened them, Louis stood there, naked and restored and gazing down at me, his figure covered in a thin film of blood, as though he were a newborn, and I saw the green of his eyes, and the white of his teeth.

I heard Lestat's sore voice again. "More, Louis," he said. "More, take it."

"But David and Merrick—," said Louis.

And Lestat answered, "David and Merrick will be all right."

24

WE BATHED HIM and dressed him, all of us together, in the upstairs rooms.

His skin had a white sheen to it, due to the near omnipotent blood of Lestat which had so restored him, and it was plain as we helped him with the smallest articles of clothing that he was not the same Louis whom we had so often dared to pity in the strength of our love.

At last, when he was comfortably covered in a loose black turtleneck shirt and cotton pants, his shoes tied, and his thick black hair combed, he sat down with us in the back parlor—that gathering place which had been witness to so many agreeable discussions in my brief preternatural life.

His eyes would now have to be masked with sunglasses, for they'd taken on the iridescence which had always burdened Lestat. But what of the inner being? What had he to say to us as we all looked at him, as we all waited for him to share his thoughts?

He settled more deeply into the dark velvet chair and looked about himself as if he were a monstrous newborn, dropped whole and entire into life, by myth or legend. And only gradually did his sharp green eyes move to us.

Lestat had by this time brushed off the cumbersome covering of dust he wore, and taken from his own closet a new coat of dark-brown velvet, and fresh linen, so that he wore his usual thick and faintly discolored old lace. He had shaken out his hair and combed it, and put on new boots.

In sum, we made a fine picture, the four of us, though Merrick, in her customary shirtwaist of silk, bore some few stains of blood. The dress was red, however, and showed little or nothing to the eye, and about her neck she wore—and had worn all evening, of course—my gift to her of years ago, the triple-strand necklace of pearls.

I suppose I found some solace in these details, and so I record them. But that detail which had the most salubrious effect upon me was the calm, wondering expression on Louis's face.

Let me add that Merrick had been greatly weakened by the blood she'd given to our communal effort, and I could see that shortly she must go out to be the vampire in the most dark and dangerous streets of the city, and it was my vow that I would go at her side.

I had too well rehearsed in my imagination what it might mean to have her with us for me to claim now some rigid moral shock. As for her beauty, Louis's gentle blood of nights past had greatly enhanced it, and her green eyes were all the more vivid, though she could still pass for human with comparative ease.

The resurrection of Louis had taken all of her heart's reserve, it seemed, and she settled on the settee beside the comely figure of Lestat, as though she might like nothing better than to fall asleep.

How well she concealed the thirst she must be feeling, I thought to myself, only to see her raise her head and glance at me. She had read my thoughts.

"Only a glimmer," she said. "I don't want to know more than that."

I made a concerted effort to conceal whatever I was feeling, thinking it best for all of us to follow such a rule, as Louis and Lestat and I had followed it in the past.

At last it was Lestat who broke the silence.

"It's not complete," he said, staring sharply at Louis. "It requires more blood." His voice was strong now and wonderfully familiar to my ears. He was speaking his usual American English. "It requires," he said, "that you drink from me, Louis, and that I give the blood back. It requires no less than that to give you all the strength that's mine to give and not lose. I want you to take it now without argument, as much for my sake, perhaps, as your own."

Just for a moment Lestat's face became haggard again, as if he were the sleepwalker he'd been when last he rose. But within a split second his vitality returned, and he went on to the purpose, addressing me:

"And you, David, take Merrick with you, and go out now and feed to replenish what you've lost. Teach her, David, what she needs to know, though I think she is well versed in everything already. I think that Louis, in the little time he had last night, has instructed her rather well."

I was certain that Louis would rouse himself from his solemn silence and protest against Lestat's domination, but he did nothing of the sort. In fact, I detected in him a visible self-confidence which he had not possessed in the past.

"Yes, do it, give me all you can," he said in a low vigorous tone. "And what of Merrick? Will you give your potent blood to her as well?"

Lestat was even surprised at such an easy victory. He rose to his feet. I took Merrick by the hand and made to go.

"Yes," Lestat answered, pushing back his blond hair from his face. "I'll give my blood to Merrick if Merrick wants it. Merrick, it's what I want above anything else, I assure you. But it is your choice whether or not you take the Dark Gift from me again. Once you drink from me, you'll be quite as strong as David and Louis. Once you drink from me, we will all be fit companions for each other. And that's precisely my desire."

"Yes, I want it," she answered. "But I need to hunt first, do I not?"

He nodded, and made a small eloquent gesture for us to leave him with Louis alone.

I took her with me quickly down the iron steps and out and away from the Quarter.

We walked in silence except for the tantalizing click of her heels on the pavement. At once we came to the blighted and shabby neighborhood where her old house stood.

We did not go to her house, however. We pushed on.

Finally a sweet laugh escaped her lips, and she stopped me long enough for her to deposit a kiss on my cheek. She had things to say but she was cut off.

A large American automobile came crawling close to us, and we could hear from behind its thick windows the deep bass of the radio, and the nasty words of a hateful song. It seemed like so much of modern music, a din to drive human beings mad.

The car stopped only a few feet ahead of us, and we continued on. I knew the two mortals in the car meant to hurt us; I sang their requiem. Perhaps I smiled. It is a sinister thing, but I believe I smiled.

What I did not expect was the quick snap of a gun, and the shining streak of a bullet before my eyes. Merrick's laugh came again, for she too had seen its brilliant arc before us.

The door of the car opened, and a dark shape moved towards Merrick, and she turned, extending her slender arms in welcome, and caught her victim in midstep. I saw the man freeze as she sank her teeth; I saw him go limp; I saw her arms easily hold his bulk. I smelled the blood, and I was nothing if not the vampire.

Out of the car came the driver, abandoning his running engine and outraged by the little scheme of rape or robbery gone wrong. Once again the gun gave its loud crack, but the bullet was lost in the blackness.

I rushed the assailant and caught him as simply as she had caught her prey. My teeth were swift and the taste of the blood magnificent. Never have I drunk so greedily, so urgently. Never have I played it out, swimming for elastic moments in the desperate memories and dreams of this sad individual before I quietly flung his remains away from me and out of sight in the high grass of an abandoned lot.

Swiftly, Merrick deposited her dying victim in the same overgrown patch of earth.

"You healed the puncture wounds?" I questioned her. "You did it so as not to leave any trace of how he died?"

"Of course I did," she answered.

"Why didn't you kill him?" I asked. "You should have killed him."

"Once I drink from Lestat, I can kill them," she answered. "Besides, he can't live. He'll be dead by the time we return to the flat."

We turned for home.

She walked on beside me. I wondered if she knew what I felt. I felt that I had betrayed her and destroyed her. I felt that I had done every conceivable evil to her that I had sworn to avoid. When I looked back on our plan, that she should raise a ghost for me and for Louis, I saw there the seeds of all that had come to pass. I was broken, a man humiliated by his own failure and enduring it with a vampire's cold passivity, which can coexist so dreadfully with human pain.

I wanted to tell her how sorry I was that her full measure of mortal life had not been enjoyed. I wanted to tell her that destiny had marked her for great things, perhaps, and I had broken that destiny with my careless selfishness, with an ego that couldn't be restrained.

But why spoil these precious moments for her? Why place a shroud over all the splendor she saw around her, her vampire eyes feasting as surely as she herself had feasted, on all that we saw? Why take from her the few virgin nights in which force and menace would seem sacred and righteous? Why try to turn it with grief and pain? They would come soon enough.

Perhaps she read my thoughts. I certainly didn't try to prevent it. But when she spoke, there was no evidence in her words:

"All my life," she said in a sweet confidential voice, "I've been afraid of things, as a child and a woman must be. I lied about it naturally. I fancied myself a witch and walked in dark streets to punish myself for my doubts. But I knew what it meant to be afraid.

"And now, in this darkness, I fear nothing. If you were to leave me here, I would feel nothing. I would walk as I am walking now. As a man, you can't know what I mean by what I say. You can't know a woman's vulnerability. You can't know the sense of power that belongs to me now."

"I think I know something of it," I answered in a conciliatory tone. "I was old, you must remember, and when I was old, I knew a fear I'd never experienced when I was young."

"Yes, then you do understand perhaps the wariness a woman carries always in her heart. Then you do know the force which is so glorious to me now."

I put my arm around her. I gently turned her to kiss me and I felt her cool preternatural skin beneath my lips. Her perfume now seemed something alien to her, not belonging to her deeply, though it was sweet still, and abundantly caught in the long dark tresses which I felt so lovingly with both hands.

"Know I love you," I said, and I could hear the terrible remorse, the terrible plea for penance in my own voice.

"Don't you understand, I'm with you now forever?" she asked. "Why should any one of us break away from the others?"

"It happens. In time, it happens," I answered. "Don't ask me why."

Gradually our wanderings led us to Merrick's house.

She went inside alone, bidding me wait patiently for her, and came out carrying her old familiar canvas purse. My keen senses detected a strange scent from it, something acrid and chemical, something utterly alien to all I knew.

It did not really matter to me, this scent, and so as we walked on together, I forgot about it, or grew accustomed to it, or stopped noticing it at all. I had no taste for lesser mysteries. My misery and my happiness were too immense.

When we returned to the flat, we found Louis once more dramatically changed.

Sitting quietly again in the rear parlor with Lestat beside him, he was now so bleached and sculpted by the increased blood that he seemed, like his maker, a thing of marble rather than flesh and bone. He would have to crush ashes between his palms and spread them over his skin if he wanted to walk in places of light.

His eyes had an even greater luster than I'd observed before.

But what of his soul? What had he to say to us? Was he the same being in his heart?

I took a chair, as did Merrick, dropping her canvas bag near her feet. And I think we both agreed to wait until Louis would speak.

A long interval found us still together, still waiting, Lestat's eyes returning again and again to Merrick out of an understandable fascination, and then Louis finally began to talk:

"My heartfelt thanks go to all of you that you brought me back." It was the old cadence, the old sincerity. Maybe there was something of the old timidity as well. "All my long life among the Undead, I searched for something which I had come to believe I would never possess. Over a century ago, I went to the Old World in search of this. And after a decade, found myself in Paris, searching for this thing."

He continued, his tone rich with the old feeling.

"What I searched for was a place, a place somewhere in which I would be a part of something greater than myself. It was to be other than a perfect outcast. It was to be with those who would enclose me in a group to which I truly belonged. But nowhere did I find this, until now."

He looked at me pointedly and then to Merrick, and I saw the love come up warmly into his face.

"I'm as strong as you are now, David. And soon Merrick will be the same." He turned his steady eyes on Lestat. "I'm almost as strong as you are now, my blessed Maker. For better or for worse I feel that I am one of you all."

There came from his glistening white face a long drawn-out sigh then, which was all too characteristic of him and had always been.

"Thoughts," he said, "I hear them. Music from faraway, I hear it. Those who come and go in the streets outside, I hear them. I catch their scent and it's sweet and welcoming. I look out at the night and I see far."

A great wondering relief came over me. I did my best to express it by my gestures and the warmth of the expression on my face.

I felt Merrick shared it. Her love for Louis was palpable. It was infinitely more aggressive and demanding than the love she felt for me.

Lestat, somewhat weakened perhaps from all he'd endured, and his long fast of the past months, merely nodded at these words.

He looked to Merrick as if he had a task before him, and I was eager myself for that task to be done. It would be difficult for me to see Lestat take Merrick in his arms. Perhaps it would be private, as the blood exchange had been with Louis. I was ready enough to be sent away again to walk, with only the comfort of my thoughts, in the night.

But I sensed that our small company was by no means ready to disband.

Merrick sat forward in her chair. She made it quite evident that she meant to address all of us.

"I have something which must be said," she began, her eyes hesitating respectfully on me for a long moment before she looked at the other two. "There is much guilt here on the part of Louis and David that I'm now one of you. And perhaps there are questions in your mind, Lestat, as well.

"Hear me out, then, for all your sakes, and decide what your feelings should be when you know the key parts of the tale. I am here because I chose to be here a long time ago.

"It has been years since David Talbot, our revered Superior General, disappeared out of the warm protective arms of the Talamasca, and I was by no means mollified by lies about how he had come to the end of his mortal life.

"As David knows, I learnt the secrets of the body switch that had removed David from the elderly body in which I'd always loved him with all my heart. But I didn't need a secret narrative written by my friend Aaron Lightner to tell me what had become of David's soul.

"I learnt the truth when I flew to London, after the death of that elderly body, that body which we called David Talbot, to pay my respects, alone with the body in the coffin before it was forever sealed. I knew when I touched the body that David had not suffered death in it, and at that unique moment my ambitions began.

"Only a short time later, I found Aaron Lightner's papers, which made it clear that David had indeed been the happy victim of a Faustian Switch, and that something unforgivable in Aaron's mind had taken David, within the young body, out of our world.

"Of course I knew it was the vampires. I didn't need popular fictions masking facts to figure how Lestat had had his way with David at last.

"But by the time I read those curious pages, with all their euphemism and initials, I had already made a potent and age-old spell. I had made it to bring David Talbot, whatever he was—young man, vampire, even ghost—back to me, back to the warmth of my affection, back to his old sense of responsibility for me, back to the love we'd once shared."

She stopped speaking, and reached down and drew up a small cloth-wrapped parcel from her bag. There came the acrid smell again, which I could not classify, and then she opened the cloth to reveal what appeared to be a yellowish and somewhat molded human hand.

It was not that old blackened hand I had more than once seen on her altar. It was something altogether more recently alive, and I realized what my nostrils had failed to tell me. Before it had been severed, it had been embalmed. It was the fluid that caused the faint noxious odor. But the fluid had long since dried up and left the hand as it was, fleshly, shrunken, and curled.

"Do you recognize it, David?" she asked me gravely.

I was chilled as I stared at her.

"I took it from your body, David," she said. "I took it because I wouldn't let you go."

Lestat gave a small laugh that was tender and full of easy pleasure. I think that Louis was too stunned to speak.

As for me, I could say nothing. I only stared at the hand.

In the palm was engraved a whole series of small words. I knew the tongue to be Coptic, which I could not read.

"It's an old spell, David; it binds you to come to me, it binds the spirits who listen to me to drive you towards me. It binds them to fill your dreams and your waking hours with thoughts of me. As the spell builds in power it presses out all other considerations, and finally there is one obsession, that you come to me, and nothing else will do."

Now it was Louis's turn for a small smile of recognition.

Lestat sat back, merely regarding the remarkable object with a raised eyebrow and a rueful smile.

I shook my head.

"I don't accept it!" I whispered.

"You had no chance against it, David," she insisted. "You're blameless, blameless, as Louis was blameless for what ultimately happened to me."

"No, Merrick," said Louis gently. "I've known too much genuine love in my years to doubt what I feel for you."

"What does it say, this scribble!" I demanded angrily.

"What it says," she answered, "is a particle of what I have recited countless times as I called my spirits, the very spirits I called for you and Louis the other night. What it says is:

" 'I command you to drench his soul, his mind, his heart with a heat for me, to inflict upon his nights and days a relentless and torturous longing for me; to invade his dreams with the images of me; to let there be nothing that he eats or drinks that will solace him as he thinks of me, until he returns to me, until he stands in my presence, until I can use every power at my command on him as we speak together. Do not for a moment let him be quiet; do not for a moment let him turn away.' "

"It wasn't like that," I insisted.

She went on, her voice lower, kinder:

" 'May he be a slave to me, may he be the faithful servant of my designs, may he have no power to refuse what I have confided to you, my great and faithful spirits. May he fulfill that destiny which I choose of my own accord.' "

She let the silence fill the room again. I heard nothing for the moment, except a low secretive laughter from Lestat.

But it was not mocking, this laughter. It was simply eloquent of astonishment, and then Lestat spoke:

"And so you are absolved, gentlemen," he said. "Why don't you accept it, accept it as an absolutely priceless gift which Merrick has the right to give?"

"Nothing can ever absolve me," said Louis.

"Let it be your choice, then, both of you," answered Merrick, "if you wish to believe you are responsible. And this, this remnant of your corpse I'll return to the earth. But let me say, before I put a seal on the subject for both of your hearts, that the future was foretold."

"By whom? How?" I demanded.

"An old man," she said, addressing me most particularly, "who used to sit in the dining room of my house listening to Sunday Mass on the radio, an old man with a gold pocket watch which I coveted, a watch which he told me, simply, was not ticking for me."

I winced. "Oncle Vervain," I whispered.

"Those were his only words on the matter," she said with soft humility. "But he sent me to the jungles of Central America to find the mask I would use to raise Claudia. He had sent me earlier, with my mother and my sister, to find the perforator with which I would slash Louis's wrist to get the blood from him, not only for my raising of a spirit, but for the spell with which I brought Louis to me."

The others said nothing. But Louis and Lestat understood her. And it was the pattern, the intricate pattern which won me over to accept her utterly, rather than keep her at a remove, the evidence of my awful guilt.

It was now close to morning. We had only a couple of hours left. Lestat wanted to use this time to give Merrick his power.

But before we disbanded, Lestat turned to Louis and asked a question which mattered to us all.

"When the sun rose," he said, "when you saw it, when it burnt you before you were unconscious, what did you see?"

Louis stared at Lestat for some few minutes, his face blank, as it always becomes when he is in a state of high emotion, and then his features softened, his brows knitted, and there came the dreaded tears to his eyes.

"Nothing," he said. He bowed his head, but then he looked up helplessly. "Nothing. I saw nothing and I felt that there was nothing. I felt it—empty, colorless, timeless. Nothing. That I had ever lived in any shape seemed unreal." His eyes were shut tight, and he brought up his hand to hide his face from us. He was weeping. "Nothing," he said. "Nothing at all."

25

NO AMOUNT of blood from Lestat could make Merrick his equal. No amount could make any of us his equal. But by the relentless blood exchange, Merrick was immensely enhanced.

And so we formed a new coven, lively, and delighted in each other's company, and excusing each other all past sins. With every passing hour, Lestat became more the old creature of action and impulse which I had loved for so long.

Do I believe that Merrick brought me to herself with a spell? I do not. I do not believe that my reason is so susceptible, but what am I to make of Oncle Vervain's designs?

Quite deliberately, I put the matter away from my thoughts, and I embraced Merrick as truly as I ever had, even though I had to endure the sight of her fascination for Louis, and the fascination which he held for her.

I had Lestat again, did I not?

It was two nights later—nights of no remarkable events or achievements, except for Merrick's ever increasing experience—that I put the question to him that had so troubled me about his long sleep.

He was in the beautifully appointed front parlor in the Rue Royale, looking quite wonderful in his sleekly cut black velvet, what with cameo buttons, no less, and his handsome yellow hair shimmering as it ought to do in the familiar light of his numerous lamps.

"Your long slumber frightened me," I confessed. "There were times when I could have sworn you were no longer in the body. Of course I talk again of a form of hearing denied to me as your pupil. But I speak of a human instinct in me which is quite strong."

I went on telling him how it had so completely unnerved me to see him thus, to be unable to rouse him, and to fear that his soul had taken to wandering and might not return.

He was silent for some moments, and I thought for a split second that I saw a shadow fall over his face. Then he gave me a warm smile and gestured for me to worry no more.

"Maybe some night I'll tell you about it," he said. "For now let me say that there was some truth in your conjecture. I wasn't always there." He broke off, thinking, even whispering something which I couldn't hear. Then he went on. "As for where I was, I can't now explain it. But again, maybe some night, to you, above all others, I will try."

My curiosity was dreadfully aroused and for a moment I was maddened by him, but when he began to laugh at me, I remained silent.

"I won't go back to my slumber," he said finally. He became quite sober and convincing. "I want you all to be assured of it. Years have passed since Memnoch came to me. You might say it took all my reserve to weather that terrible ordeal. As for the time when I was waked before by Sybelle's music, I was more nearly close to all of you than I came to be some time later on."

"You tease me with hints that something happened to you," I said.

"Perhaps it did," he answered, his vacillations and his playful tone infuriating me. "Perhaps it did not. David, how am I to know? Be patient. We have each other now again, and Louis has ceased to be the emblem of our discontent. Believe me, I'm happy for that."

I smiled and I nodded, but the mere thought of Louis brought to mind the gruesome sight of his burnt remains in the casket. It had been the living proof that the quiet omnipotent glory of the daily sun would never shine upon me again. It had been the living proof that we can perish so very easily, that all the mortal world is a lethal enemy during those hours between dawn and dusk.

"I've lost so much time," Lestat remarked in his habitual energetic fashion, eyes moving about the room. "There are so many books I mean to read, and things I mean to see. The world's around me again. I'm where I belong."

I suppose we might have spent a quiet evening after that, both of us reading, both of us enjoying the comfort of those lushly domestic Impressionist paintings, if Merrick and Louis had not come so suddenly up the iron stairs and down the corridor to the front room.

Merrick had not given up her penchant for shirtwaisted dresses and she looked splendid in her dark-green silk. She led the way, the more reticent Louis coming behind her. They both sat upon the brocade sofa opposite, and straightaway Lestat asked:

"What's wrong?"

"The Talamasca," said Merrick. "I think it's wise to leave New Orleans. I think we should do it at once."

"That's sheer nonsense," said Lestat immediately. "I won't hear of it." At once his face was flushed with expression. "I've never been afraid of mortals in my life. I have no fear of the Talamasca."

"Perhaps you should have," said Louis. "You must listen to the letter which Merrick has received."

"What do you mean, 'received?' " asked Lestat crossly. "Merrick, you didn't go back to the Motherhouse! Surely you knew such a thing couldn't be done."

"Of course I didn't, and my loyalty to the rest of you is total, don't question it," she fired back. "But this letter was left at my old house here in New Orleans. I found it this evening, and I don't like it, and I think it's time that we reconsider everything, though you may lay it down as my fault."

"I won't reconsider anything," said Lestat. "Read it."

As soon as she drew it out of her canvas bag, I saw it was a hand-delivered missive from the Elders. It was written on a true parchment meant to stand the test of centuries, though a machine had no doubt printed it for when did the Elders ever put their own hands to what they wrote?

"Merrick,

We have learnt with great dismay about your recent experiments in the old house in which you were born. We order you to leave New Orleans as soon as you possibly can. Have no further discourse with your fellow members in the Talamasca, or with that select and dangerous company which has so obviously seduced you, and come to us in Amsterdam directly.

Your room is already prepared for you in the Motherhouse, and we expect these instructions to be obeyed.

Please understand that we want, as always, to learn with you from your recent and ill-advised experiences, but there can be no miscalculation as to our admonitions. You are to break off your relations with those who can never have our sanction and you are to come to us at once."

She laid it down in her lap.

"It bears the seal of the Elders," she said.

I could see this wax stamp plainly.

"Why are we to care that it bears their seal," demanded Lestat, "or the seal of anyone else? They can't force you to come to Amsterdam. Why do you even entertain such an idea?"

"Be patient with me," she spoke up immediately. "I'm not entertaining any such idea. What I'm saying is that we've been carefully watched."

Lestat shook his head. "We've always been carefully watched. I've masqueraded as one of my own fictions for over a decade. What do I care if I'm carefully watched? I defy anyone to harm me. I always have in my fashion. I've rarely . . . rarely . . . been wrong."

"But Lestat," said Louis, leaning forward and looking him directly in the eyes. "This means the Talamasca has made what they believe to be a sighting of us—David and me—on Merrick's premises. And that's dangerous, dangerous because it can make enemies for us among those who truly believe in what we are."

"They don't believe it," declared Lestat. "No one believes it. That's what always protects us. No one believes in what we are but us."

"You're wrong," said Merrick before I could speak up. "They do believe in you—."

"And so 'they watch and they are always here,' " said Lestat, mocking the old motto of the Order, the very motto printed on the calling cards I once carried when I walked the earth as a regular man.

"Nevertheless," I said quickly, "we should leave for now. We cannot go back to Merrick's house, any of us. As for here in the Rue Royale, we cannot remain."

"I won't give in to them," said Lestat. "They won't order me about in this city which belongs to me. By day we sleep in hiding—at least the three of you choose to sleep in hiding—but the night and the city belong to us."

"How so does the city belong to us?" asked Louis with near touching innocence.

Lestat cut him off with a contemptuous gesture. "For two hundred years I've lived here," he said in a passionate low voice. "I won't leave because of an Order of scholars. How many years ago was it, David, that I came to visit you in the Motherhouse in London? I was never afraid of you. I challenged you with my questions. I demanded you make a separate file for me among your voluminous records."

"Yes, Lestat, but I think now things might be different." I was looking intently at Merrick. "Have you told us everything, darling?" I asked.

"Yes," she said, staring before her as if at the workings of the very problem. "I've told you everything, but you see, this was written some days ago. And now everything's changed." She looked up at me, finally. "If we're being watched, as I suspect we are, then they know just how much everything has changed."

Lestat rose to his feet.

"I don't fear the Talamasca," he declared with heavy emphasis. "I don't fear anyone. If the Talamasca had wanted me it might have come for me during all the years I've slept in the dust at St. Elizabeth's."

"But you see, that's just it," said Merrick. "They didn't want you. They wanted to watch you. They wanted to be close, as always, privy to knowledge which no one else possessed, but they didn't want to touch you. They didn't want to turn your considerable power against themselves."

"Ah, that's well put," he said. "I like that. My considerable power. They'd do well to think on that."

"Please, I beg you," I said, "don't threaten the Talamasca."

"And why not threaten them?" he asked of me.

"You can't think of actually doing harm to members of the Talamasca," I said, speaking a bit too sharply, in my concern. "You can't do this out of respect for Merrick and for me."

"You're being threatened, aren't you?" asked Lestat. "We're all being threatened."

"But you don't understand," said Merrick. "It's too dangerous for you to do anything to the Talamasca. They are a large organization, an ancient organization—."

"I don't care," Lestat said.

"—and they do know what you are," she replied.

"Lestat, sit down again, please," said Louis. "Don't you see the point? It isn't merely their considerable age and power. It isn't merely their resources. It's who they truly are. They know of us, they can resolve to interfere with us. They can resolve to cause us great harm wherever we might go, anywhere in this world."

"You're dreaming, handsome friend," Lestat said. "Think on the blood I've shared with you. Think on it, Merrick. And think on the Talamasca and its stodgy ways. What did it do when Jesse Reeves was lost to the Order? There were no threats then."

"I do think of their ways, Lestat," Merrick said forcefully. "I think we should leave here. We should take with us all evidence that would feed their investigation. We should go."

Lestat glared at each and every one of us, and then stormed out of the flat.

All that long night, we didn't know where he was. We knew his feelings, yes, and we understood them and we respected them, and in some unspoken fashion we resolved that we would do what he said. If we had a leader, it was Lestat. As dawn approached we took great care in going to our hiding places. We shared the common sentiment that we were no longer concealed by the human crowd.

After sunset the following evening, Lestat returned to the flat in the Rue Royale.

Merrick had gone down to receive another letter from a special courier, a letter of which I was in dread, and Lestat appeared in the front parlor of the flat just before her return.

Lestat was windblown and flushed and angry, and he walked about with noisy strides, a bit like an archangel looking for a lost sword.

"Please get yourself in hand," I said to him adamantly. He glared at me, but then took a chair, and, looking furiously from me to Louis, he waited for Merrick to come into the room.

At last Merrick appeared with the opened envelope and the parchment paper in her hand. I can only describe the expression on her face as one of astonishment, and she looked to me before she glanced at the others, and then she looked to me again.

Patiently, gesturing to Lestat to be still, I watched her take her place on the damask sofa, at Louis's side. I couldn't help but notice that he made no attempt to read the letter over her shoulder. He merely waited, but he was as anxious as I.

"It's so very extraordinary," she said in a halting manner. "I've never known the Elders to take such a stand. I've never known anyone in our Order to be so very explicit. I've known scholarship, I've known observation, I've known endless reports of ghosts, witchcraft, vampires, yes, even vampires. But I've never seen anything quite like this."

She opened the single page and with a dazed expression read it aloud:

"We know what you have done to Merrick Mayfair. We advise you now that Merrick Mayfair must return to us. We will accept no explanations, no excuses, no apologies. We do not mean to traffic in words with regard to this matter. Merrick Mayfair must return and we will settle for nothing else."

Lestat laughed softly. "What do they think you are, *chérie*," he said, "that they tell us to give you over to them? Do they think you're a precious jewel? My, but these mossbacked scholars are misogynist. I've never been such a perfect brute myself."

"What more does it say?" I asked quickly. "You haven't read it all."

She seemed to wake from her daze, and then to look down again at the paper.

"We are prepared to abandon our passive posture of centuries with regard to your existence. We are prepared to declare you an enemy which must be exterminated at all costs. We are prepared to use our considerable power and resources to see that you are destroyed.

Comply with our request and we will tolerate your presence in New Orleans and its environs. We will return to our harmless observations. But if Merrick Mayfair does not return at once to the Motherhouse called Oak Haven, we will take steps to make of you a quarry in any part of the world to which you might go."

Only now did Lestat's face lose its stamp of anger and contempt. Only now did he become quiet and thoughtful, which I did not interpret altogether as a good sign.

"It's quite interesting actually," he said, raising his eyebrows. "Quite interesting indeed."

A long silence gripped Merrick, during which time I think Louis asked some question about the age of the Elders, their identity, hitting upon things of which I knew nothing, and about which I had grave doubts. I think I managed to convey to him that no one within the

Order knew who the Elders were. There were times when their very communications had been corrupted, but in the main they ruled the Order. It was authoritarian and always had been since its cloudy origins, of which we knew so little, even those of us who had spent our lives within the Order's walls.

Finally Merrick spoke.

"Don't you see what's happened?" she said. "In all my selfish plotting, I've thrown down a gauntlet to the Elders."

"Not you alone, darling," I was quick to add.

"No, of course not," she said, her expression still one of shock, "but only insomuch as I was responsible for the spells. But we've gone so far in these last few nights that they can no longer ignore us. Long ago it was Jesse. Then it was David, and now it's Merrick. Don't you see? Their long scholarly flirtation with the vampires has led to disaster, and now they're challenged to do something that—as far as we know— they've never done before."

"Nothing will come of this," said Lestat. "You mark my words."

"And what of the other vampires?" said Merrick softly, looking at him as she spoke. "What will *your* own elders say when they learn of what's been done here? Novels with fancy covers, vampire films, eerie music—these things don't rouse a human enemy. In fact, they make a comforting and flexible disguise. But what we've done has now roused the Talamasca, and it doesn't declare war on us alone, it declares war on our species, and that means others, don't you see?"

Lestat looked both stymied and infuriated. I could all but see the little wheels turning in his brain. There crept into his expression something utterly hostile and mischievous which I had certainly seen in years past.

"Of course, if I go to them," said Merrick, "if I give myself over to them—."

"That's unthinkable," said Louis. "Even they must know that themselves."

"That's the worst thing you could do," I interjected.

"Put yourself in their hands?" asked Lestat sarcastically, "in this era of a technology that could probably reproduce your cells within your own blood in a laboratory? No. Unthinkable. Good word."

"I don't want to be in their hands," said Merrick. "I don't want to be surrounded by those who share a life I've lost completely. That was never, never my plan."

"And you won't be," said Louis. "You'll be with us, and we're leaving here. We should be making preparations, destroying any evidence with which they can back their designs for the rank and file."

"Will the old ones understand why I didn't go to them," she asked, "when they find their peace and solitude invaded by a new type of scholar? Don't you see what's involved?"

"You underestimate us all," I said calmly. "But I think we are spending our last night in this flat; and to all these various objects which have been such a solace, I'm saying my farewell, as should we all."

We looked to Lestat, each of us, studying his knotted angry face. Finally, he spoke.

"You do realize, don't you?" he asked me directly, "that I can easily wipe out the very members who made the observations that are threatening us now."

At once Merrick protested, and so did I. It was all a matter of desperate gestures, and then I gave in to a rapid plea.

"Don't do this thing, Lestat," I said. "Let's leave here. Let's kill their faith, not them. Like a small retreating army, we'll burn all evidence which might have become their trophies. I cannot endure the thought of turning against the Talamasca. I cannot. What more can I say?"

Merrick nodded, though she remained quiet.

Finally, Lestat spoke up.

"All right then," he said with vengeful finality. "I give in to you all because I love you. We'll go. We'll leave this house which has been my home for so many years; we'll leave this city which we all love; we'll leave all this, and we'll find someplace where no one can pick us out of the multitudes. We'll do it, but I tell you, I don't like it, and for me the members of the Order have lost by these very communications any special protective shield they might have once possessed."

It was settled.

We went to work, swiftly, silently, making certain that nothing remained which contained the potent blood which the Talamasca would seek to examine as soon as it could.

The flat was soon clean of all that might have been claimed as evidence, and then the four of us went over to Merrick's house and carried out the same thorough cleansing, burning the white silk dress of the terrible séance, and destroying her altars as well.

I had then to visit my erstwhile study at St. Elizabeth's and burn the contents of my many journals and essays, a task for which I had no taste at all.

It was tiresome, it was defeating, it was demoralizing. But it was done.

And so, on the very next night, we came to leave New Orleans. And well before morning, the three—Louis and Merrick and Lestat—went ahead.

I remained behind in the Rue Royale, at the desk in the back parlor, to write a letter to those whom I had once trusted so very much, those I had once so dearly loved.

In my own hand I wrote it, so that they might recognize that the writing was of special significance to me, if to no one else.

To my beloved Elders, whoever you might truly be,

It was unwise of you to send to us such caustic and combative letters, and I fear that some night you might—some of you— have to pay dearly for what you've done.

Please understand, this is no challenge. I am leaving, and by the time you claim this letter by means of your questionable procedures, I will be well beyond your reach.

But know this. Your threats have greatly roused the tender pride of the strongest among us, one who had for some time now regarded you as quite beyond his eager reach.

By your ill-chosen words and threats you have forfeited the formidable sanctuary which enshrined you. You are now as exquisitely vulnerable to those whom you thought to frighten as any other mortal woman or man.

Indeed, you have made another rather grievous error, and I advise you to think on it long and well before plotting any further action in regard to the secrets we both share.

You have made yourselves an interesting adversary to one who loves challenges, and it will require all of my considerable influence to protect you individually and collectively from the avid lust which you have so foolishly aroused.

I had read this over carefully, and was in the act of affixing my signature when I felt Lestat's cold hand on my shoulder, pressing firmly on my flesh.

He repeated the words "an interesting adversary," and there came from him a sly laugh.

"Don't hurt them, please," I whispered.

"Come on, David," he said confidently, "it's time for us to leave here. Come. Prompt me to tell you about my ethereal wanderings, or perhaps give you some other tale."

I bent over the paper, completing my signature carefully, and it occurred to me that I had no count of the many documents I had written for, and in, the Talamasca, and that once more, to one such document, a document which would go into their files, I had put my name.

"All right, old friend, I'm ready," I said. "But give me your word."

We walked down the long corridor to the back of the flat together, his hand heavy but welcome on my shoulder, his clothes and hair smelling of the wind.

"There are tales to be written, David," he said. "You won't keep us all from that, will you? Surely we can go on with our confessions and maintain our new hiding place as well."

"Oh, yes," I answered. "That we can do. The written word belongs to us, Lestat. Isn't that enough?"

"I'll tell you what, old boy," he said, stopping on the rear balcony and throwing a passing glance over the flat which he had so loved. "Let's leave it up to the Talamasca, shall we? I'll become the very saint of patience for you, I promise, unless they raise the stakes. Is that not fair enough?"

"Fair enough," I answered.

And so I close this account of how Merrick Mayfair came to be one of us. So I close the account of how we left New Orleans and went to lose ourselves in the great world.

And for you, my brothers and sisters in the Talamasca, as well as for a multitude of others, I have penned this tale.

4:30 p.m.
Sunday
July 25, 1999